AFTER HIM

ALL FOR YOU DUET, 1

KELLY FINLEY

*In cherished memory of J
I remember your angels, not your demons.*

PREFACE

Content warning: Please be aware this story deals with characters with a traumatic past of possible sexual violence. There are no on-the-page graphic descriptions of said violence, abuse or harm to minors.

This is a story about surviving and a love that wins above all.

AFTER HIM

BY KELLY FINLEY

AFTER HIM PLAYLIST

Running Up That Hill by Meg Myers
Chasing Cars by Snow Patrol
Looking Too Closely by Fink
Fire For You by Cannons
deja vu by Costanza
Make Me Feel by Olivia Rodrigo
17 by MK
Keep Running by Geographer
MIDDLE OF THE NIGHT by Elly Duhé
Her Touch by SŸDE
Bad Together by Dua Lipa
Hot Blooded by New Constellations
Savages by Kerli
Sink In by Amy Shark
Bad Love by RY X
Wild Horses by The Sundays
Gravedigger by MXMS
LOVE ME HARD by Elly Duhé
Fine Line by Harry Styles

Available on SPOTIFY

THE WRONG ONE

I'LL MAKE THIS FAST.

I'm dead. I got all the time in the world.

You don't.

So let me tell you... she did it. I'm here at the bottom of the ocean. It's where I belong. It's what I deserve.

I was an evil man, and it all started with her. I was always after her—then after him—and she knew it.

I couldn't help it. The way she looks, she makes you crazy. Like, dude, you gotta have her.

No matter what. No matter how many distractions I

toyed with. No matter how much she loved that pretty boy. Deep down, I knew she wanted me too.

But I was the fucking fool. I didn't know when it came to her—"looks that could kill"—it wasn't a joke.

I can't hate her though. It's a relief. To be free of my evil life; it was exhausting. I could never be satisfied. I could never hurt enough.

The irony is... she got the wrong one.

Yeah, I deserved to die for all that I did. But I'm not the guiltiest one.

He's still alive.

CHAPTER ONE

CADE

Running Up That Hill by Meg Myers

Two years before...

Tonight I'll make a deal with you, God.

I'm watching three men in this ballroom.

If I promise to kill one and ruin the other, can I finally be free of the third one? The beautiful man I hate so much that I'll love him forever?

After all... you know it too.

They deserve it after what they did.

That deal tastes sweet. Sweet like the candied almond

sliding over my glossed lips. The crunch—the sugary shards pulverized by my hard bite—I love it. Candy calms me.

Sitting at this table while a magnolia centerpiece blocks the view of one of my targets across the room; *that annoys me.*

My other target stands at nine o'clock, slamming SoCo and lime shots down his throat. I can feel his glower sliding down my body. He deserves the heel of my stiletto stabbed in his neck. But that'd be bad manners.

I won't make the hard-working staff at this golf resort scrub blood from the cream carpet.

The third man?

Redix Dean, Hollywood's Romeo.

Of course, he fucking smolders over my right shoulder, sitting beside his sexy date.

My hand shakes to the syrup of his voice. Fighting back every emotion, every pain and memory, I don't think I can do this.

Ten years is a long time to go without seeing the love of your life.

The stunning sight of him walking into the ballroom an hour ago slammed my heart into a brick wall when I didn't think it could break anymore. I was wrong.

Redix makes calm breath and logic impossible. He destroys me all over again.

But it doesn't hurt me anymore.

That's what I tell myself so I can breathe.

"Don't you dare let him get to you." A silky hand grabs mine trembling under the table. "You hear me, Cade Bryant? Keep your chin up and your cheeks dry. You can cry about him later."

My mama can see past my stone facade. Her command fills my heart, steeling my spine.

"I know, Mama." I force a smile her way. "I won't give him the satisfaction. None of them."

"That's my girl. You can live with a broken heart. But like hell if you won't die with your pride too."

She lifts a crystal glass of sweet tea to her lips. It rattles against her teeth. Mama hides it well, what the second round of chemo's doing to her. But I see it, hiding my concern. Mama refuses pity.

"You should be drinking water," I warn, "not sugar and caffeine."

"Take my sweet tea from my grasp"—she winks—"and I'll give you a fight you won't win."

Damn, I love her.

If people think *I'm* headstrong, Mama wears hardheaded like a well-coifed hairdo hiding hairpins that can take your eyes out. No one fucks with her. Sheriff Gloria Bryant is a force.

And as her daughter, Sergeant Cade Bryant, I'd be wiser stealing a steak from a starving Rottweiler before fighting with Mama.

"I'm fine." She takes another ornery sip. "Quit fussin' over me and focus on this shindig."

"This shindig is bullshit."

No, it's hell.

A hell I won't back down from. No way I'd miss this confrontation with Redix, no matter how he left me in pieces.

"No, it's part of this island's game and you know how to win it." Mama raises her chin, considering the swanky ballroom full of Hilton Head Island's biggest players. "Smile pretty for these bow tie-wearing, golf-club swinging, rich men in God-awful madras pants and you can get away with murder... like *they* try to do."

Redix didn't wear madras tonight.

No, he's proudly freeballing in tuxedo pants, making my mouth water. I mutter, "Madras pants shrivel my dick."

Mama cackles, patting my hand again. "Not as much as bow ties shrivel mine."

Our inside jokes. Our crass mouths. I can't live without her.

Please God, give me more time with her.

Okay, fine, I've been making lots of deals with heaven, and hell, so why break a bad habit?

But after six years on the police force, I know Mama's right. Madras pants or khakis—not all these men are as innocent as their attire.

I resisted it at first. Fighting like mad, I went in the opposite direction of my mama. All the boys who bullied me, calling me "giraffe". All the adults who cooed, "You're so pretty you should be a model." Well, far be it from me to ever listen, but I did.

I spent a decade in that hellacious industry. What else can you do when you're thirteen and soaring to five feet ten? Because like hell if I was playing basketball.

But after what happened. To me? To Redix? I became just like my mama—the law. Because I want justice.

And apparently, I still want Redix Dean.

Because my pulse is racing. My cheeks are flushed. My thighs are weak. My pussy wants to put on these Christian Louboutin heels herself and walk the runway to him and jump his dumbass, sexy bones.

But my heart won't budge. It's barely holding back the tears stinging to fall. What's even worse? I can feel Redix feet away, laughing.

Is it at me?

"Are you gonna work the room?" Mama tries scratching,

unseen, at the brunette wig itching her scalp. "You got seven pairs of eyes on you; three sets I know you're watching too."

"No." Facing straight ahead, I raise an eyebrow. "I'll make them come to me."

Finally, my target steps into view from behind that damn centerpiece. That smirk on his face? It's for me. His grasp is controlling his wife's body, but his eyes are fucking mine.

That evil man deserves to choke blood on a magnolia flower.

That stain? I'd scrub it myself with my toothbrush from this carpet.

Uncrossing my long legs, I pour one back over the other. The attention it draws. The heat of his stare sliding up my bare calves. It's been a long time since I wore this dress with these heels.

So fuck Redix Dean.

If he thinks he can come back after ten years, strolling barefoot in his tux across this ballroom, smiling while every asshole on Hilton Head Island toasts to his charitable contributions... he can *suck it.*

Laugh all he wants; he's watching me.

This outfit is driving him wild with tender memories. The Hervé Léger vintage purple bandage dress wraps my curves so tight; men can vacation in my cleavage. And these black heels let me tower over most in the room.

Not Redix.

His beauty reigns supreme—I grin—but he dropped to one knee for me in this dress.

We were eighteen then, officially adults, hating the glamorous job, but loving each other always. We were supposed to get married that summer. No one could stop us —young love on a rampage. With the money from our modeling exploits, Redix wanted to buy a house for us somewhere high over an ocean cliff, together as we were destined to be.

Turns out—destiny is a motherfucker.

It ruins everything, including us.

Now marriage isn't on my mind; murder is. It's either that or release this sob choking my throat. Pain swirling with passion and revenge, I can't stop the memory of that soul-destroying night.

The one when Redix left ten years ago and never spoke to me again.

Why's he back?

Is it to make me pay for the fault that's mine?

That pain threatens to fall over my lashes... but I won't do it. I'll take this damn salad fork on the table and stab my smoky-lined eyes out before I let him see a tear fall for his celebrity ass.

"Well, I'll be,"—Mama elbows me—"here comes one now."

I didn't need the alert. The approach of his body tingles my flesh. His aroma—vanilla and leather—it arrives next.

Goddamnit. I'm still attracted to him. And it's on a he-better-fuck-me-now-before-I-kill-him level making a black widow blush. But the shell of my skin hides it.

"Mama G,"—Redix purrs the childhood name he gave my mama—"I just had to come over and sit down next to the prettiest lady in the room."

"I'm no lady." Mama's not amused. "I'm the law."

That bad-boy grin on his face? Curling his lush lips back to his square jaw? That's the look that drops panties and shatters hearts, including mine.

His big hand turns a small gold chair around. His strapping thighs straddle it like he's riding a horse across the ballroom, lassoing every pussy in sight. He takes the empty spot on the other side of my mama while my teeth clench, fighting it all back.

"You're looking beautiful as always, Mama G." His sky blue eyes won't meet mine. "I've missed you." The genuine concern in his voice? Fuck him. He has no right after all this time. "How you been feelin'?"

"I feel right as rain anytime a handsome man sits down beside me."

Typical. Mama's playing back. No man gets the upper hand on her, not even one she's known since he was nine years old. Redix was a beautiful boy back then. By his teens, he left beauty behind for hot-as-fucking-hell.

Secretly, I've watched him on the flatscreen since. Sometimes it hurts too much. Remembering the kiss of his lips, his tongue teasing my mouth, how he used to dance with my heart.

But sitting this close now in the flesh at twenty-eight?

Redix Dean's allure travels across a room like a sexy slug leaving a trail of slick lust behind. A trail that everyone wants to slip in and break their necks, because his sex is worth the fall.

"My mama told me about this last diagnosis." Redix props his chin on his forearms folded in front of him, obvious he actually cares. "But if anyone can kick cancer's ass, it's you."

"I feel like kicking more than cancer's ass," Mama answers. "I feel like kickin' yours. You just up and left. You got a lot of nerve coming back now."

God, if I could reach out and hug Mama. Every furious thought I have... it's firing from her mouth.

"Ah, come on *now*. You can't stay mad at me." No matter how many years Redix spent in Hollywood, he still deploys his Southern drawl with a sly grin. It disarms nukes. "I'm too cute. Besides, I'm a good boy now, here for a good cause and all."

"You can sponsor all the Teen Crisis centers you want across this state, that don't excuse it." Nope, Mama's locked and loaded. "It's pretty damn rude coming home without a peep prior. Who do you think you are? A boy raised with manners, that's who. But it seems you've sold 'em and your soul to Hollywood."

"No, ma'am." Redix doesn't flinch. He's smiling at her smack down. "I could never forget you, my manners... or my home."

That butter knife on the table? It just stabbed my heart.

Redix didn't forget Mama. Or his home. But he forgot me and the manners it takes to even look at me.

It's willful. Past ignoring me—it kills me. He's blaming me for what destroyed us.

In perfect, bullshit timing, his date approaches our table. Resting her hand on his shoulder, offering a smile to the table, "Are you going to introduce me?" *she* has the manners he forgot.

He cups his hand gently over hers. Their intimate touch backslaps my jaw. "Angie Conrad, meet Sheriff Gloria Bryant. 'Mama G' as I called her because she kicked my ass to Sunday and back with all my trouble."

"Ms. Conrad"—Mama's smile is sincere—"it's a pleasure."

My ribs heave two inches higher. Redix didn't even introduce me.

"Ms. Conrad, this is my daughter, Sergeant Cade Bryant." Mama flicks her eyes at me with a don't-lose-your-shit look. "She and Redix were quite close growing up. 'Friends' doesn't even describe it."

"Oh?" Angie barely grins my way. "Redix has never mentioned you." Was that innocent or bitchy? "Still, nice to meet you."

"Likewise." I smile, emptying the gun of my glare, firing back at her, and then aiming five shots into Redix who refuses to turn his face my way.

It's embarrassing me, hurting me... and he knows it. My God, he really hates me.

Fine. The feeling *is* mutual.

And *I'm* full of shit.

Tension takes a seat at our table. The urge to run hits me but *hell no*, I won't move.

"I'm off to the Ladies Room." Angie can't handle it. "And then"—she's cooing into Redix's ear—"I want that sexy dance you promised."

Redix smiles, shamelessly eyeing her ass while she sashays away.

Is it possible to want to cry, kill, and fuck someone all at the same time? Yes, right here on this table. I want to rip Redix Dean into sex-stained shreds.

"To what do we owe the honor then?" Mama's raising questions and her iced tea. "What finally brought the King of Coligny Beach home?"

That beach? That night? That pain? It surges through me, remembering Redix there. Along with the other man stalking me on my left and the third one looming across the ballroom.

These three men haven't stopped haunting my world like a nightmare that won't end until God makes good on her deal.

I see it; how the same memory washes over Redix too, making his asshole act waver. He rakes his left hand through his long strands before tucking one side behind his ear. That gesture? It's the last one Redix made before he turned his back on me and walked away.

And I never stopped loving him since.

"I came home for amends." He answers Mama... before slowly... and finally... aiming his penetrating eyes into my soul. "Ain't that right, Candy Cade?"

Murder or mad sex?

I'm gonna commit both.

CHAPTER TWO

CADE

Chasing Cars by Snow Patrol

"Isn't the Man of the Hour your ex-boyfriend?"

Jameson, my colleague, is never subtle. Neither is his hard body pressed against mine on the dance floor and…

This night is torture.

I glance up and he's grinning, squeezing my waist even tighter like I'm his.

But I'm not annoyed. Jameson saved me. I didn't answer Redix's ominous question. Right after it, Jameson came over and asked me for a dance. Hell, I'd do one buck-naked on a pole just to piss off Redix and ignore him back.

"He's not my ex-boyfriend." Damn, Jameson's shoulders are broad. "He's my ex-fiancé."

"When?"

"Ten years and a lifetime ago."

"Well, he's staring now like he wants to beat the shit out of me."

"Don't worry. I'll beat the shit out of him first."

Really, Jameson can defend himself. So can I.

In the three years since Jameson joined the Sheriff's office, we've had a love-hate-respect-annoy the fuck out of each other relationship. But I've got his back. Even though he wants to bend me over and take me hard that way too. That's not a guess. He told me one night over too many beers.

Jameson keeps my back to Redix and his date and I can feel it; Redix's glare searing into Jameson's hands pressed above my swaying ass.

I don't like teasing Jameson. But I do like the jealousy he stirs in Redix. Because he can...

Jameson is one of the few men as tall as Redix. His frat-boy face has aged into handsome—making him so fuckable as long as he shuts up. And I've seen him on the beach with his girlfriend of the season. His body won't stop with a brunette happy trail that travels over shredded abs... to a place I've wondered about.

But I'd become a nun before I fuck on the job.

As one of the few women in the office, and the retired Sheriff's daughter to boot? No sex is worth losing the respect I had to earn. Even though I can feel Jameson's dick against my hip.

It's a giant distraction.

"I'm touched, Bryant." He sways into me. "You'll get my

back but you'll be a bitch, busting into my crime scenes whenever the hell you want."

"Those victims deserve me being a bitch for them."

"Do you even have a life? Or do you sleep with your radio, waiting for a call to come through?"

"What I sleep with is none of your business." My eye catches Redix. He's glaring at us. Good. "Besides, they're not *your* investigations. They're mine too."

"Why can't you be like most detectives?" Jameson's question lifts my eyes to his green ones. Fuck, they sparkle. "Why can't you just wait for the case to land on your desk a day later?"

I smile. God, Jameson *is* hot. "Because I have no patience."

"It's a virtue you know."

"I'm not a virtuous woman."

His erection firms and when it comes to sex, I have no shame. I'm an angel in many ways, but not when I need a fuck. But at work, I'm going for sainthood, the patron saint of *Revenge Against Evil Men*.

Does this saint exist?

Yep. I made her up. I burn candles for her every night. Penis candles.

But my body reacts. Redix's body feet away awakens it. It makes me brush against Jameson's hard dick, wishing for what I really miss.

"Damn, Bryant," Jameson sighs, his hands teasing the crest of my ass cheek, responding to my slight tease. "You and your banging body are gonna get me in trouble with HR."

Normally, I'd knee a handsy guy. But this is my fault. On paper, Jameson and I are a perfect match. But he's not *him*—the man whose soul is intertwined with mine.

No man can replace Redix Dean, though I wish one could.

I've built a life for myself in his void. It's full of hard work, grueling training, and a lethal deal and that deal doesn't involve me using Jameson. I can't hurt him like that.

I pull back, letting his hands remain on my body because I feel the audience we have—the man doing the same to his date.

Redix is practically fucking Angie on the dance floor. Everyone in the ballroom knows he has the moves to do it. Those blockbuster male stripper movies he made tortured me for five years. The billboards and ads with Redix's shredded torso all oiled up? They stuck pins in my aching eyes.

"You're a big boy." Jameson rubs against me. "Control yourself or I will."

"We're just dancing, Bryant." Jameson smiles at my subtle rebuke. "Every man and a few women in the office want you, but we all know... you're off limits."

"Like your investigations?"

He chuckles, turning us more. Redix and Angie are right there. My heart tightens. My ankles wobble. The sight silences me but I can't look away. Redix is caressing Angie with his nose buried in her long brown hair and it's wrong. My body's in Jameson's arms, knowing where it truly belongs. It's not right.

Redix and I belong together.

We always have.

All whip-smart comebacks leave me. Only the pain of missing him for so many years remains. It's left me not knowing what love is anymore. I haven't felt it since him. I can't. Redix left and took my soul with him.

"It's been a while, you know?" Jameson's tone is grave.

Oblivious to my pain; he's talking shop instead. "It's been six months since the last case. Another one's coming along with the spring break tourists."

That snaps me into focus; the job. The one I give everything to. The twists of bitter fate that find me here—I was called to do it. "I know." The certainty unnerves me too.

The string of sexual assault victims who remember nothing about their attack has plagued this island and me for years. Someone's targeting the tourists—a fact that the powers that be on this island move heaven and earth to hide.

"That's why I sleep with my radio by my bed."

"Yeah,"—Jameson's shoulders tense under my touch—"me too."

See, that's why I like Jameson. He can whine all he wants; we're a good team.

But the unsolved cases are piling up. Five last year. Two the year before. One the year before that. They're escalating.

Jameson is chasing the forensic evidence, or lack thereof. I focus on the human side—the survivors who remember nothing but going out, hitting a string of bars, and then waking up in a parking lot or on a park bench. It makes me clutch Jameson. I'm desperate. I need to stop the person targeting young women.

The young women who look like me when I was eighteen.

The song changes.

I need to check on Mama, to make sure she's not ready to leave. But the notes of the next tune drop along with my heart to the floor. My eyes flick up, catching Redix's. They're glued to mine while his hands hold another woman. No way the DJ randomly picked this song.

Redix did. He's looking right at me.

No...

His look is plunging straight into my heart, plowing through every memory we made to this song, leaving behind broken pieces of me; the debris of my life.

A sob, it constricts my throat, burning like hot ash through what we shared to the intensity of these lyrics.

"Chasing Cars" by Snow Patrol.

Why is he killing me? Didn't we suffer enough? Didn't we share every first to this song, only to have it all stolen, leaving us smashed like shells on the beach? That beach? Where we were both left in pieces that no one can glue back together.

The lyrics sing across the dance floor; across a decade. There's no space between the look in Redix's eyes and my soul, knowing exactly what he's thinking, despite who he's touching. It doesn't matter. I have his heart. And he has mine. It's a curse killing us both.

So many secrets we created together to this song, to us sharing a depth of love we couldn't explain. And I can't explain it now. Why it's wrecking me again.

"I gotta go."

I pull away from Jameson. Away from any man who's not Redix. Since I can't have him, at least I'll have this...

The tears that are coming, no matter how hard I fight them back. My steps take me fast, kissing Mama's cheek goodbye. She whispers she'll be fine. There's a room full of her friends who'll dote on her. And if anyone understands, it's my mama, witnessing my pain and raising me to leave with my dignity.

Running, my heels click fast across the parquet floors, my grip searching desperately for my keys at the bottom of my clutch. But the song chases me; the driving beat and heart-breaking lyrics follow as the sweetest memories slam the heavy front door open.

Tears blur my vision. *I need to get out of here.* My red Cruiser beckons me from the shadows under the Spanish moss dripping from the trees above. My car? Redix was there when I bought it.

Fuck, I can't escape him.

In a blur, I'm in my front seat, hands trembling, fumbling to start the engine.

A bang hits my window. "Open the fucking door, Cade!"

The shout startles my frayed nerves, dropping my keys on the floorboard. I turn and look up at the last person I want to see through crying eyes.

CHAPTER THREE

CADE

Redix looms like an alluring nightmare.

"Fuck you!" I shout.

"You already have. Many times. Now open the fucking door!"

Goddamnit, where are my keys?

My shaking hand searches, trying to pick them and my heart up from the floorboard.

"You're many things but not a coward, Cade. Get out here and talk to me now." The thunder of my pulse, it only pisses me off more. "Talk to me before I break this fucking window."

"Break my fucking window and I'll break your fucking face."

"I wish you would." He's laughing. "That would save me a lotta trouble." That grin? I want to punch it off his sexy lips. "Are you afraid of me, Candy Cade, after all this time?"

The taunt works. I'm a sucker for it.

Dare me not to die and I will just out of spite.

This asshole knows me too well.

I yank the door handle, kicking the door open to make him jump back from its swinging punch.

"Call me 'Candy Cade' one more time and I'll choke you to death on a piece of it."

Amusement smears across his face as he mocks, "*Wellll helloooo, darlinn'.*"

"Fuck you and the horse you rode in on."

"Didn't know you were into threesomes." I want to kill him. "But okay." But that hair? I want to fuck him first. "Ride me and my big horse, Candy Cade, just like our first time."

"Whip it out and *I'll rein it in.*" I sneer. "I dare you."

"Damn woman." His grin cocks up so high, even I can't smack it away. "How's it possible you're even finer after ten years? You're givin' me a boner just watchin' you fuss n' fight."

"Is that what you want to talk about, Redix? You wanna talk about hard dicks after ten years?" I stand as tall as I can, my lips still inches below his but close enough to fight back. "You're such a coward. Jerk your dick around, but not me. I'm not playing your fucking game."

"Oh, Candy Cade..."

He leans closer, his heat steaming inches from my flesh.

"I do jerk around, every morning, remembering you and every fucking game we played."

He isn't lying. I see it in his eyes.

The vision of him stroking his gorgeous cock rushes my body so damn fast, imagining his hips jerking, coming with my name on his moaning lips.

Shit, I'm in trouble.

"What's your motive, Redix? This is the first time you've dared to speak to me after what happened. Even you aren't pathetic enough to only talk about your dick."

He licks his lips. "My, my, Detective. You'd be surprised." He braces his arm against the car, leaning into me. "With you in front of me, my dick demands *all* my focus."

I glance around. We're alone in a parking lot and Redix towers over me like he wants to lift his favorite dress up and fuck me til I'm sore for days.

And I'm terrified...

Because I want it too.

"You're such an asshole."

Nope, not happening, no matter how my pussy screams for him. My heart refuses. My mind rebels. No way in hell, even if he is the most beautiful devil.

"You followed me out here to flirt about fucking while you left your date in the ballroom."

"I don't date." His breath tickles my ear. "I dabble."

If my eyes could roll any farther, they'd see the back of my skull.

"Drop your Romeo bullshit. I knew you before you had pubes. What are you after, Redix? They've named three of these teen centers after you using your money without you coming home.

"But tonight you waltz back in, hosting a party for *this*

one, the one down the street from my house? Then you send me an embossed invitation like you have no memory, no heart. And now you're holding court with those men? They're here too? Fuck, you've changed. You're pure evil now."

How much can a night of hell and a decade of depravity alter someone into a soul you don't recognize? Because that's all I see. A man who left me in hell while he spent years earning millions and cashing in on California sin.

"You've changed too, Candy Cade."

Redix Dean is the one asshole I can't intimidate. His arrogance fires back.

"You went from walking runways to running line-ups. You've got small guns for arms now, and you cut all your long brown hair off. I used to love wrapping it around my fist while I fucked you so hard. Did you do it to spite me?"

Yes, I did.

"Don't flatter yourself."

"It only backfired." He unbuttons his shirt twice, revealing his weapon, his body underneath. No one can resist it. Not even me. "Bless my wicked soul, I walked into that ballroom and saw you with that short hair. *Fuck me*, you're even hotter now. Only you, a model woman with a cock-teasing body and a heart-stopping face can make that look drop-dead sexy."

The long bangs I kept cloak my left eye. Strands tickle my lips while the spring air brushes the nape of my neck. My one-eyed glare refuses his admiration.

Fuck his flirt; I fire the big guns.

"I cut my hair off after that night. You man enough to talk about *that*?"

The flirt disappears from his face. "Stop it, Cade." His

body moves, pushing mine against the car. "We're never talking about that night again."

"Again? You left, but I never did. I'm still here and planning to do something about it. But what did you do? Get famous and fucked for the past ten years."

"No, I became a drunk, an addict for nine years, so *fuck you.*" His vulnerable reveal grabs my heart. I didn't know that. "This is my first sober year since. *That's* why I'm back. I'm not here for you. I'm here to make amends. To move the hell on. Maybe you should too."

If anyone knows why I can't move on, why I'll get revenge, no matter what it costs me... it's Redix. He's my reason why.

Years can pass but this fact remains—I have a deal to keep.

"But when I saw you tonight, Cade." Truth and seduction drip from his lips nearing mine. "Fuck, I may be sober but I gotta taste you again; my first drug. We could play games for old times' sake."

"You've got a date and I've got pride."

I try moving but find no space with his body pressing mine against the car. A white-hot grin takes his face. "Damn darlin', I forgot how hot you are when your panties are all up in a twist." He braces both arms beside me, trapping me with a grind into my core. "I bet they're wet for me too." Yes, they are. "Face it, Candy Cade. We do this to each other, don't we?"

Oh God, I can feel him again.

His hard cock hits my body at the exact aching spot. The alignment of our lust is perfect alchemy. Ten years of abandon; it washes away in the hurricane that is Redix Dean surging over my shore. He floods me. Memories of him, of how he took me from a shy virgin to a shameless vixen; only for him.

How I did the same to him; from shaking and nervous, to confident and commanding, able to make me come with his fingers, his tongue, his cock.

Even the mere sight of him pulls my body taut to snap with an urge for his sex.

But I *have* changed. Three things dominate more than his allure: my pride, my pain, and my plan.

"This is my motive, Cade." His hips roll into mine. Breath leaves my lungs while heat storms in, dizzying my brain. "Give me a taste of your sweet candy, just a few good licks."

Did he just say that?

"Like those three women who gave you head while you sucked a watermelon Blow Pop, asking if they wanted to lick that too?"

His eyes shock back.

"Yeah, I saw the video, Redix. Me and millions. The only thing that shocked me was that it was watermelon. You used to be a cherry guy."

He sneers. "You don't know the whole story."

"There's a lot I don't know, and I begged you to tell me, but you walked away, and left me ruined."

"Make peace with it, Cade. Ten years is plenty of time."

My God, what's wrong with him?

This isn't the boy who was my best friend riding bikes. This isn't the sweet teen who'd be a clown to make me smile. Who always held my hand and gave me the last piece of his candy.

Where is the man who tried protecting me and swore he'd never leave?

Until he did. For ten years.

"Okay then." I grab his tuxedo lapels, pulling his lips close to mine. The surge is sudden. It's so fast through me with his cock pressing between my thighs, gasps escape our mouths at the reunion, at the power of it. We're underestimating this; every part of us wails for the other. "You wanna taste me again? You wanna play games, Redix?" Something's different in his eyes, glimpses I don't recognize. Touching his lips to mine, a tide of memories washes in.

No.

This tender dance; he used to be so sweet, I used to be so soft, we used to be in love.

For years I've waited for him to come back and swear it, saying he was sorry, making my pain go away. He was my best friend. My first and only love and that hope washes away while the horror rushes in...

He only wants to fuck me again—that's it—just like everyone else.

I shove him away.

"Go to hell, Redix Dean"—my force stumbles his steps back—"and taste the Devil's sweet pussy instead."

I escape, jumping into my car, slamming the door, and finding my keys with a quick swipe.

Yes, you can have the love of your life, the one who will hold your heart forever. And he can smash it in his grasp before you leave him standing in a parking lot alone.

And don't you dare look back, no matter how hard you're crying about it.

CHAPTER FOUR

REDIX

Looking Too Closely by Fink

DEAR CANDY CADE,

My sponsor told me a year ago to keep a journal. I never listen.

I mean, I don't even write fucking grocery lists.

The only things I write are notes on my pages that help my buzzing brain remember my lines.

But when I saw you tonight dancing with another man... either I start writing or I start drinking.

And I'm not drinking again.

I don't know what to do around you now, so I'm an asshole—I <u>know</u> how to do that.

And YOU know how to leave me standing in a parking lot like the asshole I am.

So here I sit, like an idiot, on my childhood bed in my mama's old house and this pen in my hand feels weird.

I'd rather it be a bottle. Or a glass. Or a shot.

That I know too.

I don't know where to start, but my sponsor said to start at the beginning.

Okay.

Here I go...

YOU ARE MY BEGINNING, Cade.

I'm writing this to you because my life started with you.

And trust me, I almost died trying to change that. I couldn't empty enough bottles to free my heart of you.

A boy doesn't remember when he started loving his mom, or his sister. You're just born with that love in your heart, I guess.

But I remember the moment I first felt love.

It was with you. It was the day we met.

Do you remember it?

I do. I think about it all the time.

It was August at a shoot for a Christmas ad. Jesus, remember the outfits they made us wear? Santa's little elves?

But it paid the bills for my mom. I was only nine years old but the man of the house. I had to take care of her and my baby sister. So I smiled for every camera she sat me in front of.

It was so hot that day, I was hating life. No kid should wear red velvet in August in South Carolina.

Then you plopped down beside me on the park bench with bouncy curls in your long, brown hair, swinging your legs, and handing me a candy cane.

I took one look at you, at your dollface and those lips I'll die for, and my insides were a marshmallow. I went all squishy inside for you.

Suddenly, I didn't feel hot. You made me feel warm.

"What's your name?"

"Cade."

Your voice makes me smile, even when you're pissed off. Sorry. Not sorry.

"Like 'Candy Cade'?"

I was pretty damn clever with that joke. Back then, you liked it too.

"Yep." You licked those red stripes and I was fascinated by your tongue. "What's your name?"

"Redix."

"What kind of name is that?"

"Don't know. It was my granddaddy's name." I crunched the cane, not able to take my eyes off you. "What kind of name is Cade?"

"My first name is stupid, so I make my mama use my middle name—Cade."

"Your name is 'Stupid Cade'?"

"Funny." You hit my arm. I liked it. "No, it's 'Magnolia' and I hate that name."

"I like magnolias." I hit your arm back. You smiled. "They're fun to climb."

We sat beside each other and didn't need to talk.

That's when you became my best friend.

"Thanks for the candy."

"You're welcome." That's when your smile became my sunshine. "I got plenty to share."

You opened your Hello Kitty purse and showed me your constant stash.

I swear, Candy Cade.

How you don't have cavities and how you still have that sinful body, I don't know. I never met someone so addicted to candy, or someone who tasted as sweet as it either.

But I get it.

Because you became my addiction that day and I tried replacing you with everything else.

That failed.

And now I'm back.

I'm trying to fight that demon that makes me find a bottle in my hand or a pill in my mouth without even thinking about it.

I'm doing my steps. Every damn day, sometimes hour by hour, I fight to stay sober. And I can do it.

But I lied to you tonight.

I do have a motive.

It's you.

I came home to find us again.

The first thing I did when I got out of rehab was get an ice cream cone.

By myself, I sat on the patio outside the shop, licking lemon sherbet and watching an old couple. They were married I assumed, but I could tell they were best friends too. Like we were. They were sharing a spoon over a cup of chocolate ice cream.

Then, the sweet old woman got a drop on her chin. The man smiled and wiped it off with a napkin before pecking her cheek.

And all I could think in that moment was...

<u>I want that life. That love.</u>
And I knew with who.

You're the only woman I'll carry a napkin for.

The only one who can share my spoon.

The only one who I share my heart with.

So I made myself wait a year. To get stronger. To stay sober. To come back for you.

But then those guys were there tonight.

I didn't know they'd be, I swear. I'd never do that to you. But there you were too, and I thought I'd be strong enough to take it.

I'm not.

We were all in that room and I did the one thing I've perfected. I acted like I was the cock of the walk.

That's the only way I can see them, and see your face, and not want to kill them or a bottle of Absolut.

I'm a fucking shitstorm. I know.

Angie being there didn't help. She's been warm enough to remind me that I'm human, but she's cold enough not to see I'm in pain.

So I came over to talk to Mama G.

You know I love her like my own. I'm scared that she has cancer. I know it's scaring you too. And I thought she'd help me talk to you.

(Ha! She's pissed at me too. I love her.)

I need people to give me the lines, Cade. To tell me what to say to you because I can't find my own.

I just feel so much now that I can't handle it.

It makes me want to drink. I fucking love it. Drinking numbs those feelings while the pills take away my memories and I'm free.

Without them?

I'm sitting here wanting to rip my hair out, or make love to you, or kill those assholes.

What the fuck do I do, Cade?

So I had the DJ play our song.

I thought you'd hear my heart.

The one I've been hiding for ten years.

Do you know how many times I've played that song?

Every time I do, I see you on top of me with me inside you. God, your tits are my undoing.

Sorry, but I could fill this journal with every raunchy thought I have of you.

Shit, you'll never see this, so I'll confess right here—I've never been fucked better. And God, you have the prettiest pussy.

Even though we didn't know what we were doing, goddamn if we didn't figure it out together until our sex became poetry.

How you would go so slow for us, making it last for as long as you could. Every time I watched you come, it made me do it, so damn hard.

No one makes me feel like you do, Cade.

That's the genius of staying drunk or high.

You don't have to suffer how no one else can fill the void. How there's only one person in this world for you but you can't have them. So if you stay fucked up that reality won't kill you.

But even sober, I keep fucking up.

I told the DJ to play our song and it only made you cry. So I ran after you.

Then I fucked up <u>again</u> because I got so overwhelmed standing that close to you. I just lost it. I played the asshole and earned the Oscar.

What can I say to you after all this time?

Because I'm not talking about it.

You want answers I won't give because the truth <u>will</u> hurt you.

And like always, I'll protect you. No matter what.

So I guess we're both fucked.

Because I still love you, Cade.

But love already killed us once.

CHAPTER FIVE

CADE

It happened again.

Poor Ms. Ryan used two cups of salt, not sugar, for her lemon pound cake. While I chew a piece, smiling, my lips are sucking back into my face, never to be seen again.

Ms. Ryan pats my hand. "Want some more coffee, dear?"

Coffee? I'll need to drink Lake Marion if I ever want to pucker up again. "Yes, please."

Never would I offend Ms. Ryan.

"I found another loose deck board." She gets up from the table. "Have I sweetened you up enough to help me?"

Everyone knows my addiction to anything sweet and lemon. For Ms. Ryan, that includes salty too.

"Yes, ma'am." My tongue is two feet thick. "I'd be happy to help."

Every weekend I stop by Ms. Ryan's house.

For her, it gives her plans, a reason to bake for a guest.

For me, it reminds me why I sacrifice everything for this job. Why I've been fixing up her old dock and doing yard maintenance too.

It never ends... and I don't want it to.

"Did I hear right?" She fills my cup. "That Redix Dean is home again? He's staying over at his mama's place?"

"I guess." Ah, Ms. Ryan's serving gossip too. Usually, I love it. Not this time. "I don't really know."

"You don't know? You and Redix Dean were thick as thieves. And your mamas are best friends. I know all my spark plugs aren't firing, but even I remember as much."

Shit, playing dumb won't work.

Funny how memory serves at the worst time.

"We haven't spoken since he left," I explain. "We had a falling out of sorts."

A falling out? No.

More like we plummeted to our deaths off the rim of the Grand Canyon of love.

"Well, you, him, and my Pamela, y'all used to tear through here on your bikes and eat me out of house and home and all the candy on this island."

That last part was me.

Pamela had loved Oreos. I remember that about her. And that her favorite color was yellow. She wore it all the time.

"Yes ma'am, we sure did." The mention of Pamela urges me to stand. "And you were so kind to put up with us."

"You make her proud, you know." She cups my cheek. "My Pamela may be an angel now but she's smiling down, as proud of you as I am."

The sudden lump in my throat burns; the tablespoon of salt I swallowed down doesn't help.

Pamela Ryan has been missing for eight years. Presumed dead is the only peace we've found.

When I went to Clemson University, Pamela went to the College of Charleston. Our sophomore year she came home for spring break, took her roommates out on the town one night, and then she disappeared.

She was last seen at a bar, and poof! She was gone.

I came home for the search parties, combing through every pond and pile of pine needles on this island.

Finding Pamela would've been easier.

Forgetting Pamela, I never could.

My friend's disappearance is the second reason why I became a cop. I can't replace Ms. Ryan's daughter, but I'll be here as much as I can, keeping Pamela's spirit alive.

And eating salted, lemon pound cake with a puckered smile on my face.

The boards on Ms. Ryan's dock are almost all new. I've been replacing them over the years.

She stays inside, avoiding the mosquitoes that never bother me. Guess my blood isn't sweet enough for their bite.

Being here brings it all back.

How I lost my best friends in the span of two years—Redix and Pamela.

I wasn't the same after that.

But if I think my grief is bad, it's nothing compared to what Ms. Ryan has survived.

It's not that her spark plugs aren't firing, as she jokes. The woman is losing her mind to the hell of not knowing what happened to her daughter. She hasn't moved since, hoping that Pamela will show up one day at her front door.

I'm guilty of the same.

And I can drill new screws into a board or whatever else she needs to give her small relief.

Setting the power drill down, I suddenly hear dispatch crack over my police radio by my backpack on the porch steps.

The number calls out across the humid morning shooting shivers down my spine.

"Ten-ninety-five."

A sex crime.

My boots take off across the dock, up the backyard hearing the rest of the call.

Suddenly, a rut in the ground traps my left foot, twisting my ankle and slamming me to the ground.

The pain is instant, but I ignore it, crawling toward my radio.

Jameson's voice cracks back, taking the call.

I hear the location—the parking lot by the vacation club hotel on the beach. Grabbing my radio, I accept as the second response vehicle.

"Oh! Bless your heart!" Ms. Ryan rushes out, shocked by my sprawl over the stairs. "What did you do?"

"Just rolled my ankle a bit. No biggie." I hop up on my right foot; my left foot screaming "hell no!" to any weight I threaten it with.

"We need to get you to the emergency room."

"No, ma'am. I'm fine." I smile through the pain. "I gotta get to work." Cringing through a hop and a shuffle, I grab my bag. "I'll finish up later. I promise."

Hobbling to my car, thank God I didn't fuck up my right foot. I need it to press the gas pedal down and race across the island. Killing my blue response lights three blocks before the resort, I never draw attention to the victim.

By the time I'm on the scene, my ankle is swollen like a stuffed pork loin and I don't care.

Jameson has the victim in the passenger seat of his patrol car, trying to protect her from the onlookers craning their necks.

"Her name is Natalie." He fills me in. "Twenty-one and from Ohio. Here with her family. She's not remembering much and doesn't want to go inside to let her parents know." His eyebrow raises to my lop-sided stance. "Jesus, Bryant. What did you do?"

"Nothing. I just twisted my ankle." I focus on Natalie in the car. "Lemme talk to her."

I slide into the driver's seat. "Hi, Natalie. I'm Sergeant Cade Bryant." She glances at me, wary. "I'm here to help. You're safe now. Would you like for me to take you to the hospital? I'll stay with you. You're in control. Just tell me what you need."

"Can we just sit for a minute?" Natalie's hands are shaking. "I need to think."

There's an empty lot down the street. The gathering crowd in this one pisses me off. Natalie deserves privacy so I aim the car that way.

"I don't remember anything." She shakes her head while I drive. "I went out with my cousin. We were having drinks at The Pelican and got separated in the crowd. I tried to find her. I remember walking to the restroom, looking for her, and then... nothing. I woke up in the parking lot to some nice lady walking her dog and she let me use her phone to call 911."

I know that bar—The Pelican.

It's the same as many on this island, pouring drink specials along and dollar drafts with people packed to the rafters. Normal vacation revelry.

But what happened to Natalie?

That's never okay.

"I shouldn't have been drinking like that." She stares out the window, her face stunned. "I know better. It's all my fault."

I draw a deep breath, parking the car before turning to her.

"Natalie, you're not the criminal here. You have every right to drink. You can get drunk as hell just as long as you don't drive. It's not your fault."

"But look at me." She gestures to her jean shorts and pretty, yellow peasant top.

"You look cute."

I know where this is going.

"Dressed like this? Everyone's going to blame me."

"So if you called the police this morning because someone broke into your new BMW, would you feel like you were to blame because you had a nice car?"

That turns her startled eyes to mine. "No. I guess not."

"Exactly." Natalie looks like all the victims so far: young, brunette, pretty. "Because it's a crime to take someone's property."

Natalie looks like me at eighteen.

"And above all, Natalie, your body is your property and yours alone. No one has the right to it because it's pretty, dressed cute, or even drunk. If a businessman has drinks with his colleagues, wearing a nice suit, and then he gets robbed, do others blame him for dressing like that? Like he has money?"

"No."

"Damn, right. You have the right to dress however you like. That doesn't give anyone a reason to touch you or hurt you."

My blood is boiling.

It happens every damn time I respond to one of these calls, or hear people blame the victim.

Like there's some outfit that keeps women safe.

Bullshit. If there were, we'd all be wearing it.

The tragic thing is when I take these calls and hear the victim blame themselves.

"You sound mad, Sergeant."

I sigh. "I'm sorry. I'm not mad at *you*, Natalie."

I inhale, taking my rage down a notch to only "I'm gonna kill *the fucker* who did this" instead of "*all fuckers*" level.

"Natalie, it's my job to be mad *for you* until you get mad for yourself." I barely touch her trembling hand. There may be evidence on it. "Because mad gets you justice, blame won't."

"I remember some guys at the bar. One was in a striped shirt, talking to my cousin. Another one had a parrot on his T-shirt. He was older..."

Now... we're talking.

I listen while anger starts dripping through Natalie's veins, firing up whatever memory she has.

I jot down notes on my steno pad, as many details as I can get without re-traumatizing Natalie.

When we're done, I pull the patrol car back into the resort parking lot. Jameson is standing there with Natalie's parents. The crowd gathered got their attention. After we park, they open the door and pull Natalie into a hug so fast it softens my angry heart.

But then I see it.

Some guy standing in the crowd has his phone aimed at Natalie.

I don't remember getting to him so fast, but I do. Grabbing his wrist, I twist it behind his back and slam him against the trunk of a pine tree.

"Show me right now," I snarl, "how you're gonna delete those pictures."

"What?" He's stunned by my swift attack.

"It's a federal offense taking those pictures. Deal with me now or deal with the guys down at the jail who love preppy boys in palm tree shorts."

I watch him thumb over his phone, deleting the photos of Natalie from the device. "*And* from the cloud," I insist as he finishes. "Show me your ID."

Reaching into his pocket, he hands me his wallet. I toss it to Jameson who's got my back. Jameson takes a photo of the voyeur's ID before handing it over.

"Now, if I see pictures of this crime scene online." I cram the wallet back into his pocket. "I'll find you. Do you believe me?"

"Yes, ma'am."

I smash his lips against the bark, whispering in his ear, "And you're gonna respect women and their privacy from now on, aren't you?"

"Yes, ma'am." His smushed mouth can barely reply.

"Because if you don't"—I can taste the salt on his ear— "I'll end you and no one will ever know. It'll be the secret highlight of my week." I twist his wrist, harder. "Am I bluffing?"

"No, ma'am."

"Now leave."

I shove him away.

Jameson lowers his voice. "It's not a crime to take those pictures."

"It's not my fault he's a dumbass." I watch, making sure the guy leaves. "It's only my job to protect the victims from him."

"One day, Bryant"—Jameson shakes his head—"you're gonna snap."

I wink at him. "Yep. I'll save you a front-row seat for it."

The rest of the day I spend at the hospital with Natalie. There's no other place I belong.

She consents to the rape kit. Tragically, there's evidence of an assault. I grind my teeth because yet again, there's no evidence left of who did it.

I stay with her until she's back safe with her family. They have to pack to leave, and after what happened to their daughter, they want off this island fast. I share my contact information and promise Natalie... I will get her justice.

That promise I'll keep above all others.

"Wanna grab a beer?" Jameson hovers over my desk later. "You need one after today and a bag of ice on that ankle. It looks like shit."

"You sure know how to charm a lady." I've ignored the throbbing all day. Now, while I'm staring at reports on my computer screen, I can feel the pulse in my foot.

"Did you ever notice this?" Fuck it, I'm on to something, pointing at the screen and then my notes. "Natalie was targeted the night before her family was scheduled to check out. And look"—I point to three open files on my desk—"so were these victims. All targeted the night before they left."

"This island is a revolving door," Jameson replies. "That's four out of nine victims. Not really a trend."

"Are they combing the surveillance videos from The Pelican?"

"Yep. Standard protocol. There isn't much."

"That fucker." I tap my pen. "Mr. Davis. He owns that fucking bar and won't post cameras where we need them. All he cares about are the bartenders at the registers, not the customers in the crowd. That makes two victims who last remember that bar."

Jameson sits on the edge of my desk. "Yeah, but that place is iconic. I swear every tourist goes in. Good fucking luck finding a lead there."

But it fries my nerves.

I know who owns a third of that bar.

My target number two. The man I'll ruin.

"Maybe I'm wrong about that bar and these checkout patterns." I save Natalie's file. "And when I'm wrong... it feels so right. It makes me do crazy shit."

"Don't tease, Bryant." Jameson's grin rises. "Doing crazy shit with you is my love language."

"Excuse me." I reach for the phone on my desk. "Gotta call HR."

"Have a good night." He laughs, throwing his hands up and walking away. "Put some ice on that ankle before you come back in here Monday."

By the time I drive home to my condo, the pain is so bad it sours my stomach as I take the elevator to my third-level unit.

It's a simple one-bedroom place, but all I care about is the ocean view. That's why I used my modeling money years before to buy it, and the one for my mama down the row.

I hobble there first.

"Mama!" I open the door without knocking. "Do you have a bandage? I messed up my ankle."

The blind foyer I hop down opens into a living room with an adjoining dining area.

I look... and stifle a gasp.

Redix Dean is sitting right there at Mama's dining table.

The grin on his face? Pure delight at my shock.

"What's he doing here?"

CHAPTER SIX

CADE

Fire for You by Cannons

Dammit, is he gonna ruin my every day now?

Doesn't he have a gazillion horny fans to feed his ego instead of my ailing mama?

"They're visiting," Mama answers, sitting between Redix and his mom.

His "not a date" Angie sits across from him and won't look at me.

Mama taps Redix's arm. "Go in my bathroom and get her an ACE bandage out of my medicine cabinet."

"Yes, ma'am." He sounds way too happy.

"I'm fine." I start limping that way. I want help from Redix like I want a migraine. "I'll get it."

"Sit down, young lady." Mama's command wins. I plop down in the chair by the table.

"Hey, Elise." I greet Redix's mom, ignoring Angie like she's ignoring me. "Y'all been here long?"

Elise visiting my mama is normal.

Redix visiting is bullshit.

And his not-a-girlfriend joining him is a big pile of it with buzzing flies stinking up the room.

Elise answers with a pained smile, "We just came by to deliver some dinner and to let Redix visit a spell."

Like the Devil, he returns to the room, scorching the temperature up.

I roll my eyes.

Smoking hot in jeans and a thin white T-shirt, his steps bring him inches from me. The throb in my ankle, like a traitor it climbs up my thighs, morphing pain into pleasure.

The sinister smile on his face is a mile wide and making it worse.

"Need me?" he asks.

I try snatching the bandage from his grasp with a, "Hell no," but he yanks it back, chuckling.

"Quit being so damn proud and let the man help you." Mama already sounds exasperated by our silent drama.

Great.

The asshole's been home forty-eight hours and already won her over.

Now I'm the only hold-out with spite.

I want to roll my eyes again while Redix kneels before me, but they rebel too. They want to watch him.

The tan on his skin. The silver rings on his fingers. The

hairs on his sinewed forearms. The gloss of his sun-kissed strands.

I'm so fucked.

The way muscles curve across his shoulders, I remember grabbing them while he did things to my body it can't forget. It's vibrating on a higher level with his proximity, the sultry smell of him filling my senses.

As he lifts the cuff of my jeans, his fingertips brush my flesh and a shock travels my depths, pulsing my heart and tingling my sex.

Every time he touched me that happened.

And despite how I fight it, it's happening again...

"So, like, we're flying back to LA tonight." Angie tries burning away the tension in the air with her vocal fry of a voice. "Redix is coming to my premiere next week. My dress is a Prada and..."

I'm not listening.

I'm watching while Redix unlaces my boot with his back to Angie.

He's going so slow... and only I can see it. It warms my heart before it bursts into flames when he suddenly lifts his gaze from my ankle to find my stare.

His hands are shaking.

The sky of his eyes holds mine, speaking memories of all the times he touched me, thrilling me with sensations I'd never felt. I can't stop them.

How he'd unbutton my pants, tug my zipper down, and ease his way into every part of me.

He's there now, surging through my every aching nerve.

Good god, I'd forgotten how he steals human breath when he gets this close.

He murmurs, "We need to get you in bed with this ankle, Candy Cade."

The naughty innuendo makes him smirk.

No, he needs to swallow a box of rat poison, or pick me up and fuck me hard on that table. Either one would be fine, but not a soft bed with him, not his soothing touch having this much control over me again.

"Lord, I haven't heard that nickname in years—'Candy Cade'," Elise says, adding to my unease. "You two have such history."

I can't talk.

Angie doesn't stop, skipping past that comment, she rambles on, proud of how TMZ stalks her and Redix.

I wince at him gently tugging off my boot. The warmth of his fingertips pulling my sock off next slowly exposes my bare flesh begging for his touch.

He doesn't speak either. He's caressing my skin, heat oozing between my thighs and *his eyes won't leave mine.*

Why?

He's here with her, not me. That hurts. Much more than my ankle.

But he's binding my injury, my pain, careful with my flesh like a relic he's cherishing.

Who is he now?

A cocky celebrity heartthrob or the love who used to rub my feet?

He's gently wrapping around me time and again like he does my mind, at least every hour, of every day, for ten years. I never stopped thinking about him.

Guess he did though. Drunk or high, he forgot about me.

For four years, he soared to success with his series "Romeo Returns" landing him in every horny heart and then on the big screen with one blockbuster after another.

My favorite's the movie he made about a homeless teen

who surfs his way to success, and love. It reminds me of us, but I'll never admit that to him.

No, we don't say a word. We just spin, swirling together in pain and lust. And maybe our love is still inside him, *somewhere?*

"They even followed us on our first date," Angie drones on. "He took me to an ice cream shop in Malibu."

Redix winces, closing his eyes before they flick back to mine. Because he sees it. He feels it across my flesh. My shock of pain at what Angie just said.

That was *our* thing... and that *hurt.*

So. Damn. Much.

My ankle. My heart. My god, I can't take it.

"I'm fine." Kicking away his finished touch, anger surges me to my feet.

Mama's voice fills the raw air between us. "Are you staying for barbecue?"

Usually, I would. On nights I don't go out, scoring a one-night distraction from the ego Redix battered, I visit with Mama, especially lately given how sick she's been.

"No, thank you." I glare at Redix. "I'd only throw it back up."

Pride hides my pain as every part of me feels bruised in his presence.

It's not fair. How many times can someone break your heart?

Redix stands up, scolding me. "Don't be rude to your mother."

It's on. It's war. Words fire like canons from my mouth.

"*Rude?*" Six foot four and he doesn't intimidate me. "You won Best Actor in Rude, Redix Dean. Coming back here like you're morally superior. Where were your morals when you made *your* mom lie to me, making up stories as to why you weren't calling me back, or even texting me? Not once."

He's glaring, seething. "Stop it, Cade."

"No, I won't stop, and I didn't then. I kept asking her, begging her to have you call me until it broke her heart." I glance to his mom at the table. Tears are in her eyes. They're in mine too. "Until she had to tell me the truth. That you didn't wanna speak to me again and that hurt us both, so much. It should've been you, man enough to tell me, but no, you made your mom do it, and your sister too."

"You need to chill out."

Angie finally speaks to me.

That was a mistake.

Three excruciating steps her way, I don't feel them as I'm about to clothesline her neck. "You need to mind your fucking business." I sneer closer. "Do you even know what happened between me and Redix?"

"That's enough!" Redix's shout shakes the room, his frantic eyes staring me down.

"Did you tell her about our *ice cream date*?" My voice thunders too, turning to confront him. "Or how you followed me into the parking lot last night? How you said you wanted me again? Shall I tell her how *hard* you did?"

Angie gasps.

Mama starts drumming her fingernails on the glass table. "Alright, you two," she says. "If I want a soap opera, I'll turn on my TV."

Breath huffs from Redix's chest. I see it along with his flared nostrils.

They match mine.

"Sorry, Mama." I glance at her. I mean it. "And I'm sorry, Elise." I catch her eyes next. "I'm sorry that y'all have been caught between us for so long. But don't worry"—I pick up my boot, sock, and backpack from the floor—"there's no 'us' anymore."

I have to say it. I have to look him in the eye.

"And I wish like hell there never was." To make him hurt like I do.

I limp across my mama's foyer, my wounded ego following me out the door.

Destroyed hearts don't say goodbye.

CHAPTER SEVEN

CADE

April is my favorite month.

Its warming breeze eases through my wet hair, calming me down. That and the Lemonheads I crunch while sitting on my balcony, letting the night ocean soothe my rage. The shower I took helped too; anything to wash this horrible day away.

I shouldn't have lost it like that at Mama.

It's been hard on her, on Redix's mom too. They know how much we loved each other.

Redix's mom, Elise, was the sweetest about it. She never mocked us.

"Love is real at any age," she said. "So are broken hearts.

You two just need to be careful. I don't want to see you get hurt."

We got more than hurt.

The worst part is that our moms don't know just how bad. I stare at the inky waves, hoping they never find out.

That wish traps my gaze until a sudden knock on my door startles me.

Mama should be asleep. But nope. She's here to give me an earful for my rude outburst and I deserve it.

I shuffle to the front door in my smiley-face hipster panties and tank. An ironic purchase, I know.

"Alright"—I flip the lock and turn the doorknob—"lemme have it." I swing the door open without checking the peephole...

And huff at the sight.

"Why do shitty days turn into diarrhea with you around?"

Redix stands there, glaring down at me, ready to wage another war.

But his eyes dart down to my panties and start fondling up my body, tickling over my happy breasts before they land on my pissed-off face.

"At least part of you's happy seeing me." His eyes fall back to my breasts. They're well aware he's feet away. "I bet I know what else is smiling for me too."

That sexy hair knot he's wearing makes me wanna yank it and use it like a steering wheel, traveling his mouth down to where, yes, I'm smiling.

"What do you want?" I ask instead.

He steps into my foyer, uninvited. "For that to never happen again."

I'm too proud to make another scene, so I step back and shut the door behind him.

"No one can ever know, Cade." The look on his face is fierce, with no flirt in sight. "I know you have a helluva temper but control it."

"Quit pissing me off and I will."

"I'm serious."

"I am too. As a heart attack."

I lean against the wall. My ankle throbs. Other parts of my body join in.

His white T-shirt is cling wrap revealing the abs I'm counting down his torso. Reminds me I have panties to wash.

"And tell that girlfriend of yours to mind her own business or I'll feed her her teeth for breakfast."

"I told you..."

He mimics me, leaning against the opposite wall. The jut of his hips features his generous package. I force my eyes not to glance down at it... remembering.

"She's not my girlfriend."

"Seems she didn't get that memo. Guess she's too focused on her premiere and Prada dress." I nod toward the door. "Does she know you're over here talking to me? *Again?*"

"She just flew back to LA. *Alone.* I think someone pissed her off."

"You should've known better than to bring her here. You might as well have dropped a lit match in a fireworks store."

He laughs. "You jealous?"

"Nope. But I own a mirror and I see my reflection looking at her, minus the long brown hair." His eyes can't deny it. "Am I your type now?"

"All of LA is gorgeous."

"So I'm gorgeous to you?"

"You know you are. To everyone. You also know you got a goddamn temper like a viper. I want you to control it. And your mouth."

"Yeah, I wanted things too and didn't get them either. So go fuck Angie's mouth and control it instead."

He's quiet, raising his chin. Like he's trying to read between my lines and my panties.

His stare drops between my thighs, starting the tingle, the delicious hunger only he can fill.

"You're such a jealous hellcat over Angie." Finally, his eyes rise to mine. They're a prison, holding me captive. "What about that dude you were dancing with?"

"I work with him. That's all."

"Seems he didn't get that memo. He was too focused on your ass and wanting to fuck it. Him and every man in that room."

Why did that suddenly hurt? So deep? Hitting so hard it forces every drop of pain in me to escape.

Redix knows why.

And that hurts worse.

Because it's painfully true... and proven.

I turn my chin, trying to hide the wound. I start hobbling away. I'll jump off that balcony before Redix sees my tears.

"Cade, wait." He gently grabs my arm. "I'm sorry. I didn't mean it like that."

I won't turn around. They're falling down my cheeks, drops of the vulnerability only he can draw from me.

"Please just leave."

For days, for months, years I've spent building muscles on my body, strength in my heart and skills in my hands to fight this off.

But he comes in my door and in minutes... it's all gone.

"Look at me, Candy Cade."

That gentle voice?

That's from ten years ago.

Redix didn't say words back then. He poured them like warm oil over my heart, healing my every ache.

Tonight, it only causes me more.

"I've never told anyone." I can't look at him while I keep our promise.

I know what I'll see; a face I can't stop loving; a body I can't stop wanting; a soul I'm bound to.

The man I can't have.

"It's our secret, Redix. And I'll die with it. I've been dying since it happened and you left."

He barely says it. "It breaks my heart when you cry."

I close my eyes. "Then you should have nothing left of it by now."

His hand won't let go of my arm. "Did you really mean it?" Tenderly, he's holding on. "That you wished we *never* happened?"

"I don't know." It's true. It's streaming tears down my cheeks. "I loved you so much." Saline spills over my lips. "But I hate how much this hurts now."

The heat of his touch, it's turning back pages to tender moments we shared, not brutal ones like this.

"We've always been too close, Cade." The wisdom in his words injures me more. "That's why I left. And why I didn't come back. I knew if I came home too soon, we'd get too close again. And that can't happen. I hurt you before and I'm not doing it again."

With three steps away and a soft whoosh, I hear him leave.

He does it every time.

I bite my lip so hard because the tears won't stop. They fall because I hate him.

Because he's right.

Because even a broken heart can love someone so much that it wishes for another chance with him, to fill its hopeless cracks.

CHAPTER EIGHT

REDIX

Dear Candy Cade,

This journaling shit works.

I'm not drinking.

Usually, with those tears I made you cry, I'd be throwing shots back until empty glasses fill the bar in front of me.

And when you said you wish we never happened?

Fuck, that hurt.

Because all that I am is <u>us</u>.

You've been my every thought, my every next breath, Cade, for so long.

So, yeah, the old me wouldn't need to hear more. He'd

be numbing that spit on my grave halfway through a bottle with his favorite buddy Johnny Walker by now.

But nope. I've changed.

Or at least, I'm trying to.

It ain't easy though. Not when I see you in pain. Even your swollen ankle melts my heart.

But touching you again.

God, I was losing my mind.

I know you saw my hands shaking while I took off your boot. The only thing that stopped them was the touch of your soft skin.

Damn, I just wanted to keep touching up your legs, feeling inside you, for every part of you I've missed.

I know we're still in pain, we're still in love... and we felt it.

Then Angie made that comment. The one about ice cream.

Fuck, I saw it on your face, and I might as well have slapped it because I know that hurt you.

I'm sorry.

It's not what you think. There's so much you don't know. About Angie. About that night. About the shit that's been my life since.

One day, I want the courage to tell you that one of the things I've lived for, through the hell of it all...

It's for that memory of us.

Of our first kiss over an ice cream cone.

I cherish it. I've shared it with no one but you, Cade, I swear.

Remember us before we kissed?

We'd hold hands on the bus. You'd fall asleep with me on the sofa watching TV. We couldn't stop holding each other. You were like water and I needed every drop of you.

It wasn't sexual at first.

I mean, it was with me after a while.

I can't tell you how many times I jerked off thinking about you from the age of thirteen. But I didn't know if you liked me that way. We were best friends.

Then you went away one summer with your dad when we were sixteen. He took you on long trips after your parents divorced and my heart hurt with you gone.

But you'd send me postcards with five things you liked about me on each. I still have them.

Some of my favorites I still remember...

1. You're a clown for me.
2. Boys call me "giraffe" and you said you love giraffes.
3. You let me put your long hair in pigtails.
4. Your smile is my candy.
5. I let you win at Uno.
5+++. You hold my hand and I'm safe.*

*That one's my favorite.

I waited on your mom's front steps the afternoon you said you'd be back. I didn't care how desperate I looked.

I was. I missed you.

You got out of your Dad's RV and said goodbye to him. He waved to me; he always liked me for some reason.

After he left, my jaw hit the ground.

It's like in two months you grew the best pair of tits I've ever seen. You had them before but not like that. In that green halter top, you didn't wear a bra and my mouth suddenly watered.

(Embarrassing confession number whatever: They fill my hands perfectly. Like they're made just for me. They are.)

You had a look in your eyes when you saw me again too.

Something had changed between us.

I couldn't stand up and hug you. You thought I was being a dick but I wasn't. Mine was hard as hell while you sat down beside me, and we talked for hours until your mom came home.

My world started spinning after that.

I started sweating around you because I wanted you. And I worried if I told you, I'd fuck up our friendship.

Because I lived for our friendship.

<u>I still do.</u>

Finally, you suggested we skip school. I was game as long as I was with you.

It was almost my 17th birthday and we both kept looking at each other for too long. And we kept smiling but weren't touching like we used to.

It's like we were scared of the new feeling between us.

I was.

We spent all day on Coligny Beach talking shit until my stomach growled, then you said, "Let's get some ice cream."

It was a blur. Holding your hand. Ordering a cone. You found us a private corner behind the store. My heart raced because I hoped what you were planning. But then we just stood there, licking cones with our eyes on each other.

I couldn't take it anymore.

I should've asked but your eyes told me to. Like they dared and begged me at the same time. I don't know what got into me. I just coated my lips until they dripped with lemon sherbet and leaned toward you.

"Wanna taste?" I asked.

I know. I'm sorry. I'm an arrogant asshole but you know the truth. It's an act.

"No," you said, smiling, "I want a kiss."

I don't know who kissed who first, but I lost it. Like there was no time, there was no one else. Not one thing in my world but your lips on mine.

Yes, I waited for my first kiss because I was waiting for you.

Sorry it took me so long.

But when we finally did, your kiss became the one thing that made sense to me. That made my life worth it.

It still is.

Our lips touched and you've had my heart since. Our cones melted while our bodies became like fucking fire for each other. And when I tongued you, trying my best like I'd seen in movies and porn, you moaned back.

I thought I was gonna come in my boardshorts.

Not to be a perv, but that's what you do to me.

It's more than sex with you, Cade. It's more than wanting every square inch of you. Of my body in pain craving yours. Of me knowing I <u>will</u> lose my mind if I touch you again.

It's you.

It's your lemon sherbet kiss. It's your dick-teasing, smiley-face panties tonight. It's your hot temper and smart mouth.

And it's your tender heart. I know it's there. It's my world.

And I'm so sorry because I can't stop breaking it.

CHAPTER NINE

CADE

Coating my thighs, I reapply sunscreen after two hours of sitting by the pool. At least the smell of it makes me happy.

"I can't stay much longer." Penny sighs, staring down at her full boobs. "These girls are gonna explode."

"They look amazing." I'm half jealous. "Nursing and maternity leave are doing you wonders. Maybe I'll get knocked up and take a few months off too."

Penny is my closest friend and colleague.

Really, it's been rough for her. She's not ready to come back and I don't blame her.

But we always joke like this.

"The hottest man alive is across this pool," she says. "He's looking happy to help you in that department." Her nod toward Redix is as subtle as a bomb. He's lounging beside his sister and his nephew. "I can see his huge package from here. It looks *very* ready to deliver."

"Fuck my life, why is he here?"

"Because this island isn't big enough for the two of you. And his sister lives in this complex too. You're destined to collide."

Penny adjusts her bikini top, staring at him. "I don't care who I'm married to... Mother of God, look at that body. I'd let Redix Dean fuck me *and* my life up. Don't you just wanna go over there and climb on top of him?"

Yes, I do.

Hell, once word gets out that Redix is lying out by this pool, the line of women who want to ride him like Space Mountain will wrap around the block three times.

"I just want him to leave." I drop my voice as low as I feel after last night. "That man won't stop breaking my heart."

With Penny, I drop my guard. Secrets don't exist between us. Neither does pride.

"I know." She nudges my knee. "Ignore me. I'm just a mess of horny hormones right now. I didn't mean to make fun. I know this is tough on you."

"You're entitled to your horny hormones." I nudge her back. "I bet your husband would love it if you climbed on top of him. I'm happy to babysit my goddaughter, any time."

"I wish. I'm still a human drive-thru, open twenty-four-seven for breast milk." She starts packing her beach bag. "Speaking of, I gotta bail. I need to feed her and maybe fuck my husband if we're lucky and don't fall asleep first."

Standing up, she puts her back to Redix. "You sure you're okay?"

"I'm fine. Thanks for coming by to listen to me bitch."

"Honey, that ain't bitching. That's called 'heartbreak' but you can take it. You've suffered it this long."

"I know and I promise—no matter what—he's not fucking up my life again."

Because after what happened to Natalie and eight other victims, I'm keeping my deal.

"Well, call me if you need me." Penny bends over, pecking my cheek. "Or if you decide to revenge fuck him."

"Never." I peck her back. "Love you."

"Love you too."

While I watch her leave, latching the pool gate behind her, I scope Redix.

He's hiding his famous hair tucked into a bucket hat and his impossibly blue eyes behind sunglasses, but there's no mistaking the sensation across my body.

He's watching me.

His gaze is a breeze across my sweaty flesh—perfect and opening me up for more.

I shift on my chair.

This I'll allow; spreading my thighs open for his stare. Even with my ankle wrapped, that's not the part of me trapping his attention.

My black bikini bottoms have it right where I can feel his heat.

I close my eyes and arch my back, lowering the lounger another notch.

The certainty of his eye fuck pools arousal between my slick thighs.

Damn, all the times we stole my dad's boat and fucked

in the sun. Our bodies had no tan lines because we spent hours nude.

The first time Redix went down on me, he burnt his back to a crisp and didn't care. He laughed, kissing me, swearing it was worth the time he took to make me come like that.

The feeling of his tongue opening me with that indulgence, I was so shy. Then he used his fingers too, taking me to my highest edge so far. I couldn't keep still until he grabbed my thigh and held me there under his moaning mouth, catching my first fall over his tongue.

We hadn't fucked yet, but we did everything else.

Redix drove me wild, making me wait, saying, "I'm not fucking the Sheriff's daughter until she's legal, I don't care how blue my balls get."

"Like my mama would arrest you."

"Like your dad ain't a former rogue cop who owns a shotgun. I swear if we get busted skipping school with me fucking his daughter on his boat, that man will shoot my balls off. No matter how much he likes me."

"You're like a son to him. He'd never hurt you and he never uses this boat. He's got his other one that he lives on. No wonder my parents are divorced. My dad's never around and my mama never leaves. They're complete opposites."

"But we're not." Redix had smiled down at me, twirling his fingertip around my nipple. "We're perfectly matched."

Yes, we were.

One month later when I turned eighteen, we shared even more.

And it hits me now.

A tear falls behind my sunglasses at what it felt like to be so in love... and how I feel now... so abandoned.

"Your hot body with that tattoo is gonna get some fucked up tan lines with an ankle wrap on."

That voice slithers into my ear. I recognize its hiss before I even open my eyes.

It's Sunday after all.

And if the weather allows, I'm always by this pool knowing this man always comes after me.

And the tattoo on my hip bone? He's been obsessed with it since the first time he saw it on my eighteen-year-old body at the beach.

Because he's target number one.

I open my eyes and his shadow hovers like a tombstone. But I can't let on.

Harnessing all my hate, I smile. "Funny. My ankle doesn't hurt when you're around."

He likes that, when I flatter him.

"Did you get my gift this week?" He makes me sick. How he knows where I live, leaving things at my door.

"Yes. I love your cologne."

It makes me sick. How he sprayed it on me at school. "So you'll smell me all day," he used to say.

"Good," he says with a sneer while I gag. "I smell better than him, don't I?" He's delighted Redix is across the pool. Like I finally belong to him and Redix has to watch just how much. "Better than that perfume ad y'all did together."

God, he's been obsessed with that too. The ad Redix and I shot ten years ago. The one of us for BOUND perfume that made Redix famous and me a target.

I flick my guilty eyes towards Redix across the pool deck, dread surging through my heart.

Because Redix is sitting straight up, hatred twisting his beautiful face.

This is killing him.

Me too... but it's part of my deal.

"TJ, why do you give a shit about Redix Dean?" I sit up strong, trying to stay in control of my target. "I don't."

It's taken me years to get TJ to trust me, to believe that I want him, and not Redix. Not anymore.

"That pretty boy doesn't belong back here." The sweat stains on TJ's white visor disgust me. "He never fucking did."

The air hangs heavy with more than humidity.

This game I'm playing with TJ usually has no witnesses. I make sure of it.

My biggest nightmare is having Redix across the pool, watching my betrayal.

It's the worst kind.

"Just ignore him." Chess pieces move in my mind. "That's what I do."

Redix, please don't do it. I send up the desperate prayer. *Don't start another fight over me. The last one destroyed us.*

"I saw you the other day." TJ won't look at Redix. His mirrored shades are focused on my generous cleavage as usual. "I liked the yellow one."

This sick fuck follows me around this island.

I knew he was watching me through the window of the surf shop, trying on bikinis. No shock he likes yellow. It's his M.O.

"Wear it," he insists, "and come out with me tonight. I'll buy you a few shots."

That's also TJ's M.O.—buying women *more* than a few shots.

I can prove that, but it's not a crime. Still, I know how guilty he is and one day, I'll dish out my own sentence.

No matter what.

"Not with this ankle." Right now, I need this monster to

leave. Redix's rage is palpable. I make myself flirt. "I'll let you know when I'm *ready* for you."

Never before have I taken it this far with TJ.

He's been after me since I was fifteen, like he marked me as his and tormented all who challenged his claim, especially Redix. TJ's family moved here when we were teens and he's been obsessed with me ever since.

One day on the school bus, he and Gentry Evans came after me, insulting my mama and mocking Redix who wasn't there that day to protect me. No, he was on some modeling job, and I was alone.

I had no one to save me.

And I felt it.

The threat of those two boys. Of just how much they wanted to have me, to hurt me. I'd never felt fear that great. It surged tears over my eyes.

But then that girl—Charlie Ravenel—she stood up on the bus.

She was a senior and such a badass. No one messed with her. She told them to leave me alone and punched TJ in the dick. Then she gave me a kind of look while I cowered in my seat, like "always fight back."

My life changed after that.

Thanks to Charlie, those boys left me alone for a while and I swore... *never would I feel that helpless again.*

My dad enrolled me in Krav Maga for self-defense and I was obsessed to the point of earning a black belt.

But belts can't protect me from TJ's obsession.

Not then. Not now. He's still after me.

To be fair, I'm equally obsessed with him but for another reason.

That reason has my mouth flirting with TJ while my heart twists with Redix watching me do it.

Because I'm not defenseless anymore.

No, I'm *lethal*.

This is my fight now... to the bitter end.

Satisfaction at his victory has TJ smiling like he can't believe his change of luck.

"That's a deal I'll make you keep, Sergeant."

No, he makes me cringe while he aims for his usual prowl toward the beach.

Once he disappears on the other side of the dunes, I slow my glance back to Redix. If I thought I saw hatred on him before, wrong. It's oozing from him and burning my way.

God, please. Do another woman a solid. Please make this deal worth it.

CHAPTER TEN

CADE

deja vu by Olivia Rodrigo

IT TAKES AN HOUR.

I thought he'd never talk to me again, but Redix dives into the pool and in one breath swims the length and jumps out on my side, dripping with pool water and rage.

"Is that what you've been doing for ten years?" He charges toward my chair. Thank God, no one's on my side of the pool, no witnesses for our drama. "While I've been gone have you been *fucking* him?"

Redix has every right to be mad.

So do I.

"Who I've been fucking for ten years is none of your goddamn business."

"You can fuck the US Marine Corps for all I care, but not him, Cade." With his hat and glasses off and his hair slicked back, every crease of pain across his face glares at me. "NOT. HIM."

I deflect. "Where's your girlfriend?"

There's too much passion, too much pain for reason to fit between us.

"Why don't you go dabble her and I'm *sure* you'll get over me. You have for ten years."

"I can fuck all of LA if I want. Nothing would be worse than you fucking TJ and you fucking know why."

"No, I don't know why, Redix, because you won't tell me what happened."

"Leave it alone, Detective." His lips snarl. "What you know is enough."

"What I know is Angie Conrad told TMZ that when you take her on those dates for ice cream, your favorite flavor is lemon sherbet, and you like to kiss her with it on your lips." Yes, I know. I never fight unarmed. "Sounds familiar. Does she know why?"

His face freezes.

I can't read him.

But I can see the tattoo on his hipbone. And I can read the outline of his package under his white Billabong shorts hanging low from beneath his Adonis belt. It flusters me, knocking me off my game for a second.

The silence between us has its own zip code.

I let it sit long enough; my thighs wanting to spread for his hard fuck while my fist wants to uppercut his perfect balls two feet from my face.

"Or what about that woman?" Nope, I'm not done.

"What was her name? Jenna? The one who told E! Online that y'all have matching tattoos. Does she know the story about your other one?"

That news had knifed my heart.

I almost dropped my phone on the floor of the drugstore when I read it, ready to vomit with the pain. Instead, I stood in the candy aisle, quietly wiping away tears.

He still won't answer me, so I keep firing.

"I don't know which was my favorite. Your post announcing that you were dating Heather Moore—your Juliet and co-star—and she was wearing *my* fucking jean jacket from high school. How low can you go? Because five million people loved that post. And millions more loved that video of you fucking another woman in a parking lot a week later.

"Seems America loves their Romeo with his pants unzipped and his cock balls deep in random pussy.

"Or is it the security footage of you in a hotel elevator? Yep, that one's my favorite. How you're looking at your phone with your big cock out of your zipper while some woman is on her knees, sucking you off. The whole world thought it was hot. It only *helped* your career.

"You don't need to fuck *all* of LA, Redix. The half of the city you've already fucked has you doing *just* fine."

Something dances in his eyes.

"I don't remember any of that." It's pain. It's remorse. "I was fucked up the whole time."

"Yeah, well I remember it. Every soul-killing second of it." Goddamnit, I hate the tears falling down my cheeks. "To answer your question, *that's* what I've been doing for ten years; dying on the sidelines of your celebrity sex life."

He drops down on the lounger beside me.

"Please don't cry." His tenderness suddenly soars my

heart rate to near-dizzy levels. "Not over me. I'm not worth it."

He reaches for my hand, but I jerk it away.

"Despite how you hate me, Redix, I would never do that to you, not with TJ."

"I don't hate you."

"You sure act like it. You can't stop blaming me or hurting me or insulting me."

His face softens.

"That's because I'm an addict and an asshole and after all this time, I don't know what to say to you, Cade."

His candor shocks me. He's being so honest, so vulnerable. The tender look in his eyes is like we're suddenly eighteen again and it rushes in so fast because I've missed him so much.

I can't stop it...

"Insult me one more time, Redix Louis Dean"—I know how to make him smile—"and I'll drown your pretty ass in that pool."

There it is.

It lifts his cheeks, softening me too, and glimpses of who we used to be together quickly reappear.

Did they ever leave?

"Drowning in your arms, Magnolia Cade Bryant, it would be the best death I could wish for."

"Don't say that." More tears suddenly fall, washing away my fury. "I'm so proud of you for getting sober."

The fact that Redix has a problem with alcohol and drugs, that he almost died because of it, it doesn't surprise me.

I have my own unhealthy addictions.

One's sitting right in front of me.

I'll die for him too.

He looks to the distance. "It ain't easy staying sober when TJ comes around." In that memory, he disappears for a moment before looking back at me. "And FYI. Angie is *not* my girlfriend. I told you; I don't do them or dates. That's just bullshit my manager makes up."

Warmth flushes my heart. The hope in it scares me.

"Tell that to Angie. That's not the look in her eyes when she's around you."

"I was right." The grin on his face is a dangerous curve. It makes me wanna wrap my arms around his neck. "She makes you jealous."

"I have no right to be."

"Since when does my Candy Cade care about being right?"

"Please stop calling me that. I'm serious."

"Why? You used to love that name."

Shaking his wet hair, his strands sprinkle drops across my belly, teasing my flesh.

"Because it brings back memories of us that hurt too much." I'm not afraid to confess it. "Like the one with lemon sherbet."

He flinches again, regret and the ocean reflecting in his eyes.

"I never did that with Angie. With anyone but you. I just told my publicist those stories to feed to the press, to hide the real truth. That I'm an addict."

"You sold *our* stories to the press to protect your career?"

His chin drops in shame.

What do I feel?

Sudden relief those stories aren't true. Dismay that he exploited our love for fame. Hurt that even though the stories aren't true, the videos are.

Every emotion storms through me as his eyes finally meet mine.

"I'm so sorry, Cade"—they cloud his too—"I'm so sorry for so much."

He reaches for my hand. I let him hold it.

"I don't have any matching tattoos but ours. And I never gave away your jacket. Heather found it in my closet, but I made her give it back. And all that other stuff? I wanna fucking die when I see those videos. I'm not proud of them. All I remember from these past ten years is my job and missing you."

It snaps.

The lock over my heart, it breaks open with those words from his lips. My soul's been crying to hear them.

He's sorry. He missed me.

Redix guards his emotions so when he shares them, they're gifts.

So I give too. "We need to talk."

He looks away. A crowd has gathered outside the pool fence with phones raised, recording us from a distance.

"Shit"—he winces—"that fucking TJ asshole leaked this, I know it. Dammit, I should know better."

We both know what's happening.

Our pain, our past... it's going viral.

"I don't care." I tell him, "They don't matter. We do." I step to the ledge one more time for him. "I've missed you, I've missed us, and we need to talk about that night."

He drops my hand, tension twitching across his face. Like I just put a knife to his throat.

He won't look at me. "I gotta get out of here."

It's like I'm not here.

Jumping up, he rushes to the other side of the pool. Not acknowledging his sister or nephew for their own good, he grabs his stuff and storms silently through the small crowd, pushing past smiling fans. They follow him like beggars while he rushes toward the parking lot and jumps in his mom's Volvo parked there.

And just like that...

Redix Dean leaves me again. Asking for his love. And watching him run away instead.

Yes, he breaks my heart.

Every—damn—time.

CHAPTER ELEVEN

REDIX

DEAR CANDY CADE,

How am I supposed to do this?

I'm parked outside the liquor store. Only this island would have one that looks like a five-star restaurant.

I want to go in and drink myself into oblivion, but I grabbed my journal from my backpack instead.

Because I feel like I'm sailing into a storm with you.

I can see its danger on the horizon and part of me wants the wrecking.

So bad.

I watched you with your friend at the pool today and I had to bend my knees up on the chair to hide my hard-on.

My nephew wanted to play.

I had to refuse because my fucking dick wouldn't stand down at the sight of you in a bikini.

So many times I pulled your bikini bottoms aside and slid inside you and I wanted that so bad today.

You spread your legs for me. You arched your back like you wanted me to pull your top up and take your gorgeous tits in my mouth.

Shit. I'm getting hard just thinking about you again.

I always do.

What I found inside you, Cade, years ago. It's better than what I found inside any bottle.

And trust me, from an alcoholic, that's the highest compliment.

I was going to come over and talk with you today. I felt happy just planning it, shooting the shit like we always used to.

Do you remember that? How we'd stay up until dawn on the beach over the weekends. I told you everything back then. And I was your only secret.

You were my best friend, Cade. Like my job was to make you happy, and yours was to take care of us. We could've lived to infinity like that together.

But TJ appeared—then and today—and I fucking saw red.

Truly, I almost lost my mind.

The only thing that kept me sane was my nephew worshipping every move I make. He means so much to me, so I fought it.

I felt sick, Cade.

What TJ and Gentry Evans did to us, how can you smile back at him? The sight of you letting him look at you like that?

The Candy Cade I love would have gouged his eyes out. I know you can. Mama G told me about all the training you've done, all the belts you have now.

Like you're preparing for war or something.

Fine by me. Kill him. Not me.

And I know you know that it kills me. You with TJ.

God, are you that hurt by me?

You must be with all the things you said about every drunken fuck up I've made along the way.

It's not all true what I said.

I do remember some of it.

The woman I fucked in the club parking lot?

She was wearing your perfume. Our perfume. BOUND. I was drunk but I remember smelling her and closing my eyes and only fucking you.

The woman in the elevator?

She got on with me and without a word went down on her knees. I took out my phone and in my half-drunk haze, I looked at pictures of you I've saved on it while she gave me head.

What that video doesn't show is that I didn't come. I rarely can. I start thinking about you too much.

How I miss you too much. How I'm so lonely and lost without you.

Because those women aren't <u>you</u>.

It's bullshit. How some think a kiss, a blowjob or a fuck is a betrayal. Maybe for some.

Not for me.

Those people have only given their bodies to a few while everyone's taken from mine. People have been using my body since I can remember. For the camera. For their profits. For their pleasure.

My body means nothing to me.

I sold what's left of it to the world long ago.

But my heart means everything to me.

And it only belongs to you.

I kept it protected behind a haze of drinks and drugs so no one could take it from you.

I never gave it to anyone else.

That's cheating. That's betrayal. Who we promise to love. That's what matters.

And I've kept my promise to you.

Every piece of me has been bought and sold, Cade, but not us.

Women in LA, Miami, hell Atlanta, Paris, and even Beijing. Honestly? Many have tried but no one is <u>you</u>.

No one can replace what you mean to me.

No one knows what this feels like except you. You've always understood me. Because we've shared so many happy years until we shared the same hell.

And now you want to talk about that night?

And I can't.

And I can't stay away from you either.

Because I want my best friend. I want her body and her love. I want to feel my heart again, Cade.

It's you... and I want you back.

CHAPTER TWELVE

CADE

1 7 by MK

ICE CUBES MELT in a bag over my numb ankle.

My heart feels the same.

Whatever's streaming on the screen in front of me, I'm not watching it.

One shot of tequila and three beers in and I don't give a shit. This is my pathetic life, my mind toying with revenge.

Natalie and eight other victims. The lack of clues, of my guilt that they look like me, the disconnected drops of evidence; they taunt me. It mocks my logic—*can you solve these cases?*

The next taunt?

Redix.

Goddamnit. When isn't he on my mind?

With a final swig of beer, I scroll for a show. Something please, distract me. And it better not be anything starring Redix Dean.

No, give me something happy.

A strange knock hits the air. It raps again on my front door.

"Don't shoot." A voice pours into my space. "Mama G gave me your key. She said I had to check on your ankle."

"I'm fine. You can leave."

Redix Dean better not enter my home.

He better not find me sitting on my sofa in pajama shorts and a sports bra with my wrapped foot propped on the ottoman beside my pathetic plate of pizza crusts, crushed candy boxes, and empty beer bottles.

I'm a Grade A pathetic sight and it's about to make his day.

Fuck me.

He appears in my living room looking like masculine perfection while I slouch on the sofa like a feminine cautionary tale.

"Take a break from the ice," Redix instructs like he's Dr. PleaseFuckMe entering the room. "Let's give it twenty minutes and then we'll ice it again."

"Let's give it a go fuck yourself for ten more years before you can kiss my sweet ass again."

And fuck him for leaving me hanging today.

The smile on his lips? A convent would be seduced.

"Pull those sexy shorts down," he says, "and I'll pucker up right now for that hot ass."

I cut my eyes back to the flatscreen, clicking over to

YouTube to find a song about women who murder their exes.

They exist.

Redix waltzes into my galley kitchen like he owns it.

I watch him through the pass-through, how he pulls open drawers until he finds the one with dishtowels. Without a word, he comes over and plucks the dripping bag of ice off my ankle. Wiping the puddle away before he wraps the bag in the towel, he tosses it across the room into the sink. Of course, he makes the shot with a grin.

"Satisfied?" Damn, those jeans look good on him. "You can leave now."

"I'm not leaving." He plops down in the side chair. "You said we need to talk."

"About that night?"

"Nope."

"Then don't let the door hit ya where my bullet can split ya."

He laughs, nudging his bare foot against the beer bottles. "Are you drunk?"

"I'm not drunk." I reach for my real vice—a fresh box of Lemonheads. "I don't have a drinking problem. I have an ex-fiancé who's a famous horny asshole problem."

"No, you have a messy condo problem."

He jumps back up and in one sweep has all my trash from the ottoman in his hands before promptly dropping it into the garbage can under the sink.

I crunch the sweet lemon candy I love.

"What are you doing?"

"Famous ex-fiancé horny assholes can clean too," he says and in five minutes, he has my kitchen tidy.

He noses around.

My bathroom is spotless. I'm a stickler for clean in

there. And my bedroom? The door is closed. He'll have to step over my dead body to get in there.

"Where's your vacuum?"

He's standing over me, blocking the light from the ceiling fan.

And my heart stops.

I love it when he wears his hair down like that. It's six inches past his shoulders and my weakness. I used to get off grabbing fists full of it when his face was buried in my pussy.

Okay, maybe I'm buzzing.

"If you're gonna keep being my maid"—I crunch more candies—"you have to put on a sexy outfit first."

"If you insist."

His T-shirt is off faster than I can protest. And holy hell, I'd sell my soul. Today at the pool and now tonight standing before me?

Redix Dean is sexual oxygen.

I need to fuck him right now to stay alive.

And he's giving it, looking down at me the same way.

"If you're gonna boss me around, Candy Cade"—he flops his hair over—"sit back and enjoy it with a smile."

I lean back, spreading my thighs.

"Men telling me to smile become my next target practice. The ones who call me 'Candy Cade', I hit them first."

That makes him laugh again, his abs flexing in front of me like a dozen hard glazed donuts I'm gonna lick.

God, he's beautiful like this. Happy. Flirting. Being sweet.

This is the one I fell in love with.

He doesn't wait for my answer. Nosing more around my place, he opens two closets until he finds my vacuum.

Just to egg him on, I lift my phone and record the sight.

How much will TMZ pay for Redix Dean vacuuming shirtless with his faded jeans barely hanging from his perfect ass? Thousands because he won't stop smiling at me like he loves the attention.

My pussy loves it too.

Talking over the vacuum, he asks what music I'm into now. I share my favorites. He shares his and the books he's been reading. He asks about my dad. The two of them have a powerful bond, part of the past he won't talk about.

He lifts the ottoman like it's dollhouse furniture, vacuuming under it. "How often do you get to see him?"

"We fish when we can. Other than that, he's running dolphin tours off Tybee and Daufuskie." I shout over the vacuum. "What about your mom? Who's she dating now?"

The drama of Redix's mom and her boyfriends is not his favorite topic, but he used to open up to me about it.

"She's got a new one. Renie likes him. She said he's not such an asshole to her."

I always liked Redix's little sister, Renie. But like his mom, she runs every time she sees me. Renie hates being stuck in the middle of whatever the hell this is, and that breaks my heart.

How I never met his nephew, Renie's son. I see him around the pool. I'd love to meet him but I'm not picking that scab tonight.

This is too much fun, too easy just catching up with him.

"I can't believe you still have your car," he says. "Need me to get it tuned up for you?"

"Nah. I've taken good care of it." Like the care he's showing me now. "Thanks though."

"Those bruises on your shins, on your wrists." He notices my marks? "They from all the fighting you do now?"

"Yeah."

I don't notice them anymore.

But I do notice him and the small patterns he's making in the carpet.

"Do you have competitions?" he asks. "I'd love to cheer you on." That makes him grin my way. "I'm proud of you. My sister tells me about the work you do. She'll text me articles if you make the news. I bet your parents are proud too."

He's kept up with my career? And he's proud of me? "Thanks." I don't know what to think, but it makes me feel… a lot. "We don't have competitions in Krav Maga. It's too brutal. It's fighting to stay alive, not for sport."

"That's my Candy Cade." He turns off the vacuum. "I loved how you fight."

Loved?

So we're past tense now?

Not for me.

Talking to him, watching him so close, all feeling returns. To my ankle. To my heart. To the part of me only Redix brings to life.

He sets the vacuum aside and grabs my watering can and starts wetting my hurricane plant and I can't help it. The swirling leaves. The attention he gives. Dirty thoughts fill my head. "She wants every drop."

He's pure porn looking like that.

That cocks his half-grin. "Does she now?"

He pours the last stream down his torso, water flowing over the rocks of his abs and soaking the top of his jeans.

Oh shit, fuck straws.

My tongue wants to lap those drops up.

This is more than how we flirted as teens.

This is desire in adult bodies at salacious levels. It's shallowing my breath.

He stares at me for too long before swaggering back into my kitchen. Setting the can down, he starts nosing in my fridge while I map the shredded muscles down his back, ones I crave to scratch again. *I'd rather he nose between my thighs.*

"Got anything to drink around here that's *not* alcohol?"

"The ocean."

"Funny."

He pours himself a cup of pineapple juice. Sipping on it as he returns to the living room, a lucky stream dribbles down his naked chest.

It's not fair.

In ten years he's gained twenty pounds of muscle along with another ton of sex appeal oozing from his pores.

"Whoops." His fingertip lifts the nectar off his pecs. He sucks it off his finger and I'm busted. "Enjoying the show?"

My clit bought tickets.

"You always did like my juice."

"Hell yes, I did." His grin slays me. "I'll make you laugh and give you a real show."

"What are you? A circus clown?"

"No." He grabs his package with a spark in his eyes. "But I do have an elephant you can ride."

"Shut up!" *Why did I just giggle?* "I remember how big it is. But Dumbo, you're not."

I'm lying.

It's huge.

And fuck yes, I want it.

"You sure?" He picks up my remote and starts entering something on the search bar of YouTube. "I'll jog your memory."

"What are you doing?"

"I'm giving you a private show."

"The hell you are." I sit up straight. "I don't want one."

He stands with his back to me, clicking the remote. "Tell that to your hard nipples." I glance down. *Fucking bitches.* They tattle on me every time. "I bet you're wet for me too, aren't you, Cade?"

Hell yes, I am.

"Watching a hot, shirtless man clean your house will wet any woman's pussy."

"So will this."

He presses play on a music video and turns around.

I glance at the screen and laugh. "'Pony' by Ginuwine?" I can't, but he does, and I'm giggling again like I'm fucking twelve. "Please, don't."

"You mean don't do this?" His hips start rolling as hard as my laughter. "Is this bringing anything back?"

As kids, he clowned around, dancing to get me to laugh.

As an adult, he's a clit-tease toying with my lust.

"Yes, I remember." But he never danced like *this* and I'm crying happy tears. "This is so bad."

Half embarrassed. Half aroused. Damn, he's hot, making my cheeks blush at the liquid flex of his obliques.

"You look painfully cliché."

I love cliché.

"Damn right, darlin'." He grins, rolling a wave down from his wide shoulders to his narrow waist, to right where he wants my stare. "I danced twenty-one million cliché dollars into my bank account"—he pops his hips—"twice with this blockbuster show."

I'm howling back on the sofa, surrendering to the spectacle. The way he makes me laugh, how it was his favorite thing to do, it always made me feel special.

And I feel it again... and more.

He grabs the vacuum cleaner like it's his dance pole.

"Are you fucking my Hoover?"

I'm jealous of a cleaning appliance.

"Uh-huh." Fuck, he can dance. "She's a good hard suck." He always could.

He can move like there's no gravity. Like he has no bones. Like he's one strong snaking muscle seeking its deep, wet home.

Me.

Heat flames through my body when he pops his hips like a jackhammer and then scoops them like a slow spoon through the lust he's piled up.

This is the sight that broke the box office and hearts.

"Okay, that's enough!" My abs hurt from laughing but what else can I do? *Fucking is my other choice.*

"Stop." I toss a throw pillow at him. "This is getting crazy." I throw another. "For both of us."

"Damn, Cade."

He smacks the pillows down before he starts slapping the air like he's slapping my ass bent over for him.

"You look so God." *Slap.* "Damn." *Slap.* "Beautiful." *Slap.* "When you laugh with me." He coils his hips in ways most men can't. "Or when you *come* with me."

The sudden cinch of my sex; it's lightning through my body responding to his words, to that image with him.

"Yeah," I sigh, "and you know how hot you look like that so you can just stop."

I hug the next pillow to my chest while laughter leaves my body. Only lust remains. Because he's fucking the air like the thrust of his hips can find new spots inside me, naming each one after him.

I lean back. I have no strength to fight this, watching him lick his lips while he steps closer... so close.

"Do I, Cade?"

He grinds inches from my face. The contours of his hardening dick make it obvious he's freeballing like usual.

"Do you think I look hot like this?"

I gaze up at him. "You know you do." With his cock pumping inches from my lips, he's getting harder, making my *everything* water.

"Want me to stop?" He unbuttons the top of his jeans. "Because if I'm making you laugh, or making you come, I don't wanna."

"Is that so?" His button-fly jeans press his erection down to his thigh and I feel the sudden slick in my shorts. "Am I who you want now, Redix?"

"You're all I want." He releases another button. "Everything I fucked for the camera; it was you. It was us."

The top of his sexy, trimmed patch appears.

I chew my lip remembering what's just below it.

"Imagine if we did it again, Cade." His hands travel the path down his perfect arching torso like it's flexing into the caress of my hands instead. "Can you? Can you imagine me fucking you again?"

Why do I suddenly feel shy?

And why does that turn me on even more?

Because our love was so pure, so innocent... but I'm *not* anymore.

No. I'm ready. I'll show him how shameless we can be together now.

"Yes, Redix. I can imagine you fucking my pussy again." Sliding my hand under my pajama shorts, I start giving him my own show. "Just like this."

"*Fuucck.*" His mouth drops open, watching my hand play under the silk of my peach shorts. He releases another button on his jeans. "Let me see your wet pussy again."

"Let me see your cock."

He's looped the video. It starts again and that means we can torture each other all night because that's what the past ten years have been for me.

It was torture without him making me confess, "So many times I did this. I fingered myself to you dancing in those movies."

With my ankle propped on the tufted ottoman, I let him see flashes of my fingers sliding slick into my pussy.

He kneels on the ottoman in front of me and his hips start matching the rhythm of my hand.

"Show me how you do it." He stares. I never held back with him, not ten years ago and not now. His body is my everything, my awakening, and my death. "Show me how you missed me, Cade."

I can't believe it.

The sight of him so close again. The smell of him so near.

God, how I've ached for him, for so long.

It makes the smack of my hand relentless, my palm striking against my clit to the tempo of his hammering hips.

It makes me demand, "Let me see you, Redix. Show me how you missed me too."

He rips the last button of his jeans open to his thick base and I moan at the sight while he insists, "Give me another taste." Leaning across the narrow divide between the ottoman and the sofa, he braces his ripped arms beside me on the sofa, trapping me between them.

I lie back like he's over me, fucking me with those expert hips.

Licking his lips, he's inches over mine and the heat of his flesh is so close it torches my skin without a touch.

He knows the rules of this strip. No touching, only teasing, "Come on. Remind me how sweet your pussy tastes on my tongue."

I offer him my two glistening fingers to suck. The feel of his soft lips, of his warm tongue across any part of my flesh, even on my fingers, damn, I'm close.

His eyes close, sucking them with a groan before I return them to my ache for him.

"Let me taste you too." I can see the drops of pre-cum. The dark spots on his light denim parch my mouth for his cream. I'm desperate for any part of him, touch, or taste. "Redix, please."

"You're so beautiful when you're gonna come." He pulls back and watches. "I know that look in your eyes; I put it there."

Yes, he did.

I'm in sweet pain for him. It has me writhing on the sofa, opening wide so he can see me plunge into my wet need. I'm rising so high for this fall from his sky eyes. *Let it destroy me.*

"Who made you come first, Cade?" His massive hand strokes over his length barely hidden by his jeans. "Who, Cade? Who touched your tight pussy and fingered you so slow at first. Who found your clit and taught you how to come?"

My body knows, my thighs trembling at the truth, at the sound of his voice, at that look in his eyes, "*You.*" I'm lost in them and don't want to be found, ever again.

The grip of his hand tightens over his shaft, along with a grind of his teeth.

"Say it. Say the name of the only man who makes you come. The one your pussy was made for. The one it begs for. The one it comes so fucking hard for."

It rips right through me. "Redix!"

His name bucks my hips, arching my spine, rolling my eyes back to the light, to the explosion at the sight of him, the thought of him; it snaps right through me. It steals my breath with the biggest orgasm I've had in ten years.

Huffing for air, I need to see him.

He's watching me like he can read every line of pleasure written across my body because he can.

He wrote them.

His lips are trembling. His whole body is. He's going to come. I know him too. I'm so ready for it. Ready to come again at the sight of it, even in his jeans, I don't care. Everything about him is seduction.

But the look in his eyes cracks and I don't recognize him.

"Fuck, Cade." He jumps up and storms down the hall.

"Redix?" My bathroom door slams shut. "Redix? What's wrong?"

I struggle to stand after coming so hard and with a twisted ankle.

What the hell?

I hobble down the hall to the white door of my guest bathroom.

"Redix? Are you okay?"

"Put your hand on the door." His voice sounds staggered, like his forehead is pressed against it and begging for me. "Cade, touch the door. My hand is too."

"Redix?" I hear the brush of his hand against the wood. I match my touch over his on the other side. "I'm touching the door, okay." I'd do anything for him. I'll always protect him too. "You're scaring me. What's wrong?"

"Nothing's wrong." His voice is dark but so clear, like it's pressed against my lips and not the door. "Fuck, you're perfect. You're so fucking perfect for me and so beautiful."

The staccato of his breath, I can hear it, he's about to come. "Every time, Cade, every time I do this, I think of you."

"Then let me touch you. I want you too, Redix." Why am I crying? Because as odd as this is, it's beautiful. It's us. "I always have."

It doesn't matter how many years apart, or how much pain separates us, or even a damn door—we belong together.

"Stay with me, Cade. Don't leave... oh fuck... I need to hear your voice."

"I love you, Redix." My lips salty with tears brush the door. "I never stopped loving you." With a painful groan of my name, his fist hits the other side. "No matter what, Redix." His deep gasps fill the air, flushing my body, recognizing the sound of him coming for me. "I love you."

I don't want to admit it, any of it, to him or me... but it's true.

We can't be within feet of each other and not feel it. We were bound together from the moment we met.

Silence fills the air.

"Redix?" I jiggle the door handle. It's locked. "You can open the door now." The water is running. Is he washing his hands? "Redix? Please. It's okay. Open the door."

Minutes I stand there, vulnerable with my love, alone and bewildered, scared in the hallway while his silence terrifies me.

Finally, the door opens.

"I gotta go."

He won't look at me.

I block his way. "Tell me what's going on."

"Let me by."

"No."

He grabs my arms, "Let me go, Cade," and shakes me. "Now!"

He has my heart.

"No!"

But I'm not afraid of him. Not his physical pain. I can defend myself from that.

But not this. My heart's in his grasp and it's defenseless against him.

Please don't break it again.

"Talk to me. You used to tell me everything, all your problems."

"No, I can't. I can't tell you." His massive arms press me back against the wall, pinning me there. "Because *you* are my fucking problem."

The craze in his eyes, there's an agony there.

I see a man I don't know. A past I can't remember. A secret he's hiding from me. It fills him with so much pain... I can see it.

Then it happens again.

The act that hurts me most. That rips my soul and breath away. The most excruciating turn of his body, of his heart leaving mine.

I slide down the wall at the sound of his slamming exit.

No more tears fall from my eyes.

They've left me too.

CHAPTER THIRTEEN

REDIX

Keep Running by Geographer

DEAR CANDY CADE,

There's not a bone in a body I wouldn't break for you. There's not a last breath I wouldn't give for you. There's not a day I wake up and you're not my first thought.

And I'm sorry.

I'm an asshole.

Because I'm embarrassed.

I didn't mean it. You're not my problem. You're my answer.

<u>I'm the problem.</u>

I'm the broken one and you're still perfect. Actually, you're more amazing now.

You didn't let them break you. You're even stronger.

But they broke me.

Yes, I put my pieces back together but it's ugly, all my scars and I don't want you to see them.

I want you to remember me like we were.

Like how we used to be on the beach at night. Lying on a blanket, we'd search the sky for shooting stars, and then we'd search each other. The way your touch and eyes used to adore every inch of me like nothing was wrong with me.

You more than made me come. You made me believe in myself.

That's not true anymore and that's why I run.

Because if I stay.

If I stop and let you look too closely, you'll see.

How half of me, the part you see, the part that danced for you tonight, it looks perfect. I make sure of it. It's my job.

The other half, the side I have to hide, it's fucked up. It's my secret.

And I'm scared that if you see that side of me, it'll break you too.

I want to tell the pilot to turn this plane around.

I want to go back to your place and pick you up and kiss away your tears and run away with you.

But you don't run. You're the brave one. You stay. You fight.

I know you don't understand but this is how I fight for you. This is how much I love you. And protect you.

And I'm so sorry I hurt you again, but if you ever find out.

You'd run too...

CHAPTER FOURTEEN

CADE

IT'S BEEN A MONTH.

My ankle is healed.

I'm not. Like the skin under a blister, I'm raw. Hurt. Exposed.

I try hiding it. Combing through files, trying to solve these cases; it helps. The only ones who notice my heart stunned by pain are Jameson and Penny.

Letting Redix back into my life, if only for a few days, I should've known better.

He's back in LA. Probably fucking Angie. Probably holding her.

Does he think of me when he does?

He doesn't call. Doesn't text. It's the usual.

And like hell if I'll reach out for him. I'll starve on my last piece of pride before I make the same mistake twice.

I'm used to this. It doesn't hurt me anymore.

Yeah... I'm full of shit.

Penny gives me the perfect dose of compassion and best friend "I told you so." The new mom in her adds a "I'm gonna fucking kill him if I see him" warning for good measure.

I half believe her.

But I might beat her to the killing.

Our history, the secret of what happened. It plagues my soul.

Someone needs to pay for it.

It works that way, right?

If I sacrifice myself to get rid of the evil, will I have revenge? Will Redix have peace? Will those victims have justice?

What'll happen to me when I do it? The afterward.

I don't care.

But with every year that's passed. Every crime that's been committed. Every victim that looks like me.

I will end it.

"Bryant." Jameson's voice sounds annoyed, pulling me back from hell. "If you don't answer me, I'm turning on the dubstep."

He reaches from the driver's seat of his patrol car. His phone is inches from his fingertip.

"You play that shit and you're buying lunch today."

We're on our way to Shelter Cove. I gotta deliver this package for my dad that came to my house. I'm meeting him at the marina. I talked Jameson into coming with me and splitting some oysters for lunch, killing two birds with one fun stone.

"Well then answer me." Jameson grins. It's cute. "What did you find on your wild goose chase?"

"It's not a wild goose chase. It's a score. Four of the victims so far were renting condos from Sunset Rentals."

"That means five *weren't* renting from them, remember?"

He parks his patrol car under the shade of a crepe myrtle.

"Yeah," I answer, "but guess who's the owner of Sunset Rentals and a partial silent investor in The Pelican?"

Jameson looks my way, intrigued by the new intel. "Who?"

"Our very own South Carolina's youngest State Senator, Gentry Evans."

He's target number two.

"Why do you hate him so much?" he asks as we aim toward the marina slip where I'm meeting my dad.

"Besides his sexist, racist, homophobic politics?" I slide on my shades. "Everything. Gentry Evans is loaded with power, money, and pure malice. Trust me."

"That's your hate, not proof. We need evidence."

"You and your evidence." I know he's right as I wave, spotting Dad standing on a yacht I don't recognize. "When are you gonna learn to trust your instinct too?"

"When instinct wins us cases."

Walking single-file, we make our way down the narrow dock.

If Dad's height doesn't make him stand out, his sun-bleached brown hair and handsome face do.

Yep, my dad, Jeff Bryant—he's a catch.

"My Magnolia," he calls out.

And I roll my eyes. That damn name is his fault. I hate it, but I love him.

Jameson and I jump aboard the Grady White. Dad already knows my sidekick. But I don't know the man who emerges from the boat's cabin, punching my breath away at the sight of him.

"Silas," my dad says, "this is my daughter, Sergeant Cade Bryant, and the man who puts up with her on the daily, Deputy Grant Jameson."

"Hey, y'all."

This Silas guy smiles, and my nerves go haywire. *God, he looks so much like Redix.*

"Nice to finally meet you, Cade. Your dad won't shut up about you."

I clear my throat. "How do y'all know each other?"

Because fuck me sideways, who knew Dad had such hot friends?

"Silas owns Marshside Marine on Daufuskie," Dad answers. "He's helping me on my busted engine. This is his boat."

I hand Dad the package, the new water pump he's been waiting for.

"He's taking me over to my old boat. I gotta use it for now," Dad informs me. "So don't go sneaking out with it like you have for the past fifteen years."

Dad winks and I blush. I don't know why.

Like he didn't figure out all the times Redix and I took his boat out for days of sex on the water.

But in the past few years, I've been using it for other reasons, mapping secluded rivers at night, ones where only gators are my company.

Does he know about that too?

"I hear Redix came home." Dad sets the box down on

the captain's chair. "All of Tybee lost their shit over it. Every damn bar I go to, someone's going on about him."

"And on Daufuskie," Silas adds, taking out a pocketknife to open the box. "Everyone always asks me if I'm his brother."

It's eerie. He looks like it.

But I don't miss it, how Silas keeps glancing up at me, his bright smile reaching his hazel eyes. Those are different.

"He left"—I hate telling my dad—"as usual."

That speaks volumes to Dad.

He cares for Redix. It hurt him too when he left years ago. And now, he's done it again, and he didn't even say hi to him.

"I see," Dad replies.

He was there that night. He knows pieces too. But the whole story?

Only Redix knows.

"What do y'all have new on those cases?"

Dad changes to a subject he knows doesn't destroy me. It only fires me up.

Jameson fills him on the details we know.

More like what we *don't* know.

We have no DNA. No fingerprints. There's evidence of assault but no trace of who's doing it. We're after a pro and Dad's always curious.

Once a cop, always a cop.

"What do you know about Senator Gentry Evans?" I ask Dad.

That cuts his eyes at me.

One fact we know about Gentry Evans *won't* be said aloud. Not with Jameson and this other hunk of a man, Silas, around.

The rest?

Dad purses his lips. "He and his family own half this island. Got their fingers in every profitable pie and every judge on their bankroll." He eyes me, warning, "They're not to be fucked with."

Dad doesn't believe that. Rules piss him off. And law? And power? He hates those too.

That's why he made a horrible cop, but a great vigilante. And why he's retired and divorced from Mama.

Yep, I'm a chip off his ol' block too.

"Gentry Evans brings his golf buddies around on his yacht." Silas tucks his long hair behind his ear and my heart jolts. That gesture. It's so familiar. "I ain't ever seen so many entitled assholes gathered onto one vessel before in my life."

"I believe it."

I'm afraid I'm staring because Silas is that stunning. *Just like him.* And he's not wearing a shirt. His hot body is Velcro and my eyes are stuck on it.

"When do they usually come around?"

"Why?" Jameson sounds more like my father than the real one next to me.

"Because maybe I should day-trip to Daufuskie."

I give zero fucks for making it obvious. I'm going after Gentry Evans like stink on shit.

Dad says nothing. I see logic firing behind his eyes, knowing exactly what I'm up to.

Am I worried? Maybe.

But it won't stop me.

"When's Gentry usually there?" I deliver my most disarming smile to Silas.

It works. His smile back warms me in places I thought only Redix could. "During high season, the second and fourth Saturdays. Like clockwork."

That gives me one month to find out more.

I have no evidence, but I know how evil Gentry Evans is. That's all the proof I need.

And I trust a group of rich men gathered for sport like I trust stepping on a stingray buried in the sand—they'll hurt you.

Jameson and I say our goodbyes. My stomach is growling for oysters.

Over lunch he keeps eyeing me, suspicious.

"If you go out to Daufuskie, Bryant." Finally, he says what's bothering him. "I'm your backup. Promise me. This is my case too."

"Copy," I say, seeing a text light up my phone screen on the table. I grin. It reads:

> Your dad gave me your number. This is mine. If you want that trip.
>
> Or anything else. I'm interested.
>
> Silas

Jameson's not pleased.

"Does that happen to you a lot?" He's smart, doesn't even need to read the text to read what just happened. "You meet a man and then he's coming after you?"

I stop smiling. "Yeah."

"What are you after?"

His sunglasses are off. I glance up and see it on his handsome face and it's a vulnerable ask. I know what he wants, what's he's after—me... in a gentle way.

"Revenge," I say with no apology.

Slurping down an oyster, my deal keeps falling into place.

CHAPTER FIFTEEN

REDIX

DEAR CANDY CADE,

I'm gotta write until my hand cramps. Until I can put in this journal what I want to say to you, but can't.

I'm back in LA.

This new series I'm doing is fun. You'd love it. I'm a rock star. I know. Not a stretch. The hair, makeup, and wardrobe are killer. All 90's grunge stuff.

I'm learning to play the guitar for the role too. It makes my days too short.

Because my nights are too long.

Because you're not here.

Because big shock; I fucked up again.

Do you know how many times I've almost called you? Or dicked out and texted you?

But what can I say except "I'm sorry."

And if that sounds pathetic and not good enough in my head, I know it will to your ears.

What I need to tell you is I'm keeping you from getting hurt. But your smart Detective mind will ask the follow-up questions so that won't work.

Remember all the times I protected you? I need you to. Then maybe you'd understand.

How protecting you made me feel like a badass with his gorgeous princess.

I know you hate shit like that, but it's true. I was my best when I was protecting you.

Even at thirteen.

We were at the bus stop with other kids. You were listening to my iPod and dancing around and then suddenly you grabbed my arm, freaking out.

You looked down at your white jeans and I saw it too. You started your period. Your first.

I felt so bad for you. It was obvious. I mean, not like a crime scene, but there was blood.

The bus was coming up the street so we couldn't leave without everyone knowing. So I took off my sweatshirt and tied it around your waist to hide it.

All the way to school, you rested your head on my shoulder. You didn't feel good. You said you wanted to throw up.

I was worried about you, but I whispered into your hair, "It's okay. I'll take care of you."

Fuck, you wouldn't let go of my hand that day and I loved it.

Then I got into trouble in second block, remember?

That asswipe, Mr. Johnson, he made my life hell because I sucked at... well... everything. He called me out for wearing a ~~wifebeater~~. (Whoops. Sorry. You hate that word. I get it.)

I had on a <u>tank</u> underneath my sweatshirt.

And Mr. Johnson said in front of the whole class, "Mr. Dean, are you aware that you are in violation of dress code today?"

Well, fuck him. I was protecting you and I'd go buck naked to do it, so I answered, "Mr. Johnson, are you aware that your wife <u>loves</u> my dress code?"

Yep, two days in suspension was worth it.

It's our tragedy, Cade. I'd do anything for you. No matter how it hurts me.

I already have.

And still when I get so close to you, I lose it.

I did that night I danced for you.

You looked so damn cute in your shorts and bra with your hair slicked back and no makeup on.

I love you like that.

<u>Like I really do</u>.

You're stunning. Natural. Confident. Seriously, Cade, no one has a face like you. They used to pay you thousands for it, but now it's all mine to worship.

I wanted to kiss you because I'm drawn to your lips like a goddamn magnet. So I cleaned your condo instead. Anything to keep me from taking you to your bed.

And when I make you laugh?

You make my heart avalanche. Joy. Love. All kinds of feelings tumble through me.

I'll dance until my feet fall off for you.

But we're playing with fire. We always do. You get that look in your eyes when you get turned on and it makes me so fucking hard. My body takes over watching you come.

Damn, I get lost in you and I never want to leave.

You own me, Candy Cade.

No matter how far I run. No matter where I go. No matter who's by my side.

You must know I'm yours. Even if my body can't be anymore.

And you're right. Angie's in love with me.

I didn't notice it but now that she's met you, she knows. I'm in love with you and she's doing crazy shit.

Eric, my assistant, he booked us dinner at Chateau Marmont. My manager wants me out with Angie for the paparazzi to "catch" us on a date.

It's all bullshit for press.

In the past, Angie was good for the show and didn't cross a line. And she has a real boyfriend now. He's a nice guy and cool with our deal.

But last night, she followed me into the men's room. She'd been drinking and was all over me. She tried to get me to drink. She tried going down on me. She didn't care if we got caught or that I'm fighting to stay sober.

I told her to stop. I was so fucking pissed off. She was breaking our deal and I didn't want her.

Then she got mad and stormed out saying, "Why? Can only your gorgeous model girlfriend have your body now?"

She has no clue.

No one does.

Not even you, Cade.

I wanted to drink that night. So bad. I ordered a beer from the bar and stood there in front of it for ten minutes before I walked away.

Because I feel so lonely.

Our secret is killing me and the only thing I wanted more than that beer... was you.

I know it now. I think I always did.

The only reason I want to stay sober?

The only reason I want to live?

It's you.

CHAPTER SIXTEEN

CADE

There are more people than grains of sand here.

It's Memorial Day and I swear Coligny Beach looks like Times Square on the Atlantic.

But not even the bad memories or crowd can piss me off. Because I have a date. Well, not a romantic one, but it's the first time in two months that I've felt excited.

Yep, two months and ten years and I need to change; anything to move on from Redix.

Maybe I'll take that Silas guy up on his offer. But I can't make it obvious. He's dad's friend.

I'll wait until July and go to Daufuskie and see what I can get on Gentry Evans.

Going with a shirtless Silas? That'll be a bonus to explore.

Or maybe my "no dating a guy I work with" rule is bullshit.

Maybe I should give Jameson a chance.

Shit, with the way he's smiling at me now while my flip-flops dodge towels on the sand headed his way? Some of our work crew is sprawled under beach tents and yep, exceptions can be made.

I've never dated a man.

Why not start with two? Silas and Jameson.

Come on. That'd be a fair try.

Scratch that. *Look at Jameson's happy trail.*

Make that a *hot* try.

I mean, Redix and I never dated. We were inevitable. There was no courtship, only pure combustion.

Shards of him are still lodged in my heart. But they don't hurt.

I'm such a liar.

"There she is, *finally*." Jameson holds out my favorite beer. He already opened it for me.

"Sorry, y'all." I yank off my tank and shorts and stuff them in my beach bag. "I had lunch with Mama. She got her lab results yesterday."

"She's okay?" Penny looks worried, sitting in her chair under the tent with Nina, her baby girl, asleep in her arms. "It's not bad news again?"

"No, thank God." I take the beer Jameson offers me and plop down beside him. "All's looking good."

"Speaking of looking good..." Jameson no longer annoys me. "Bryant, your body in that tiny, white bikini is a felony offense."

"*Annnnd....* here we go." Penny laughs. "Who's winning?"

"Me," I reply. "I have twenty-six. Deputy Horny has twenty-four and you're behind at only fourteen."

How many times we can turn law enforcement into sexual innuendo is our favorite drinking game.

I'm the champ.

"Oh yeah?" Penny kicks a little sand my way. "Breast milk would leak your intelligence too."

"That's fifteen now." I'm glad Penny's back. "Keep it coming."

"That's what he said," Penny sings back.

Yep, we're on a roll.

Jameson's hand, it lightly brushes over my thigh while he reaches for the cooler, and...

It flips my stomach.

What the fuck?

Our flirting—it's been a joke. Something to break the tension because I'm obsessed. Scanning through the files, searching databases, and online, I'll do anything for the break we need.

Flirting with Jameson, I'm not trying to find love.

I just want to find my smile again.

"You know, you two are obvious, right?" Penny teases me later.

Jameson and the other deputies are throwing a football. I was content holding my sleeping goddaughter. But that just made my happy stomach sour.

"What are you talking about?"

"You and Jameson." Penny pops a frozen grape in her mouth. "Y'all are obvious as hell. Watch, you'll fuck right here on the sand within the hour."

"Oh, shit. That ruins it then."

"Why? He's *not* coming back. And even if he does, I'll fucking strangle you if you give Redix Dean another chance. Give Jameson the chance."

"Not if the whole office knows. I'll never live it down."

"What if y'all work out? What if office romance turns into something serious that no one can give you shit for?"

I switch shoulders, resting Nina on my left one while I watch Jameson laughing in the waves.

"Cops fucking *can* happen. Cops living happily ever after together—that doesn't." I glance at Penny. "Just ask my parents."

The fact that my parents are opposites was a major factor in their divorce.

The other two reasons bother me.

How Dad retired early because he snapped one night. He got too rough with a man caught abusing his own daughter and Dad almost went to jail for what he did to him.

And then there was all the hell Dad caught from other cops because his wife became the Sheriff... and his boss.

When will all men be fucking adult enough to handle women in charge too?

Not soon enough for my parents' marriage. It ended when I was twelve.

"I just wanna see you happy. You've been miserable for weeks." Penny points to the dozen men feet away. "Any one of those guys would give their left nut to be with you. I think Jameson is worth a first try. He's hot as hell."

"Nope." That's all I need to know. I've been so blinded by heartbreak that I almost fucked up... and fucked Jameson. "I'm going back to my M.O. No sense in breaking my one-night streak now."

"Well, we did have some fun, didn't we?"

"Yep."

I pat Nina's tiny back. I'm not ready for this yet though holding a sleeping bundle in my arms soothes all my broken edges.

"I met a hot guy on Daufuskie," I tell her. "He wants a date. And every year, thousands of Marines train minutes away. When I wanna get laid, I go into any bar in Beaufort and it's like shooting sexy fish in a fucking barrel. Easy peasy, do me pleasy."

Penny howls back. "Do you remember that one Marine? The one before I met Hank?"

"The one who was hung to his kneecap and showed everyone at the bar?"

"I won more than a big bet that night. My God, I couldn't walk for days."

"I thought Redix was hung but I swear, you fucked a horse that night."

Penny sounds back with a believable *neighhhh* that has me rolling back in the beach chair. I have to set Nina down in her carrier.

"What's so funny?" Jameson approaches, curious about our loud giggles.

"Penny's gonna buy a horse."

"You like to ride?" His innocent ask only adds to the joke.

"Oh, I *love* to ride"—Penny's shameless—"yippy-ki-yay, motherfucker."

That does it.

I fall over laughing. God, I needed a day like this, back with my friends and not thinking about Redix Dean every damn hour.

I make it until five o'clock until it hurts again. Sipping

another beer beside Jameson, I watch a cute couple walking by.

They're teenagers, clearly in love. The smiles lighting up their faces brings it all back. Me and Redix. Particularly on this beach. Our beach.

The one that went from our haven to our hell.

"Hey, Bryant, where'd you go?" Jameson nudges me.

"What?" I can't take my eyes off the couple.

"I was telling you the good news. The one about the surveillance footage I found."

That gets my attention. "What is it?"

"You mentioned a man with a parrot on his T-shirt, right?"

"That's what Natalie remembers before she blacked out."

"Well, I got a guy in a parrot T-shirt. I found it on some liquor store surveillance recorded last month."

"Which store?" My pulse climbs, hope rushing my chest with this major break in the case.

"The one off Pope Avenue." Jameson tsks. "But you can't see his face. Just the shirt. It wasn't the right angle."

"Fuck." Hope leaves with my exhale. "Everyone goes to that liquor store. That's like finding a drunk needle in a glass bottle haystack."

"But it's a lead. The first one we've had, so you're welcome."

"Sorry. You're right." I clink my beer to his. "Good catch."

"Looks like we'll be spending time at the liquor store."

"Looks like we're hunting parrots."

I chew on this lead while I kiss Penny and Nina good-bye, and while me and the guys pack up our gear. Throwing sandy tents in the back of Jameson's Jeep, I notice dark clouds rolling in.

"Shit, the bottom is gonna fall out."

"Did you ride your bike over?"

"Yeah." I point to it locked up next to others.

"Throw it in. I'll take you home."

Thoughts of *should I* or *shouldn't I* date Jameson have me biting my lip all the way to my place.

What if he's the one?

What if I've been so blind to other men because Redix Dean has kept me in the dark for so long?

The one-night stands I have? I'll only let a man fuck me from behind so I can close my eyes and imagine Redix instead. He's the only man I feel safe with, the only one I really want. If I imagine him, I can come.

Yep, that toxic habit needs to stop.

I glance at Jameson.

"Something on your mind, Bryant?"

He knows my dilemma. The man is wicked smart.

I don't answer while he pulls into my parking lot and helps me with my bike. Not that I need it, I just want more time to consider my next move.

Jameson doesn't give me long.

After I lock up my bike, he steps me back, gently pressing me against the grill of his Jeep.

"What's got you thinking, Bryant?"

Damn, he can be sexy when he's not so serious at work.

"Us," I reply, my lips inches from his chiseled chin.

"Is there gonna be an 'us'?"

I can feel his hard cock pressing against my hip. Something about his green eyes, they make me question everything. I don't like all the answers I'm getting.

"There shouldn't be."

"Why not?" His lips draw close, *very close.*

"Because we work together and have cases to solve."

"And because she's still in love with me."

A voice fires from the shadows, shooting straight into my heart.

"What the fuck?" Jameson's head snaps around.

I wrench away from his touch, knowing exactly what I'll see the second I peer around him.

Redix.

He's leaning against the wall beside the elevator to my building.

Waiting on me.

CHAPTER SEVENTEEN

CADE

MIDDLE OF THE NIGHT by Elley Duhé

Nope. I made a thousand rules why this can't happen.

I pull away from Jameson, rage hitting me like a bullet.

"Leave, Redix." How dare he explode into my life again? "You had your chance. And left. As usual. We're done."

"I need to talk to you, Cade." He doesn't budge.

"She said you need to *leave*." Jameson's steps threaten a confrontation. "Do it or I'll make you."

"I'd like to see you fucking try." Redix's sneers can piss off the Pope. "Come on. Bring it, big boy."

Redix has two inches and lots of muscle on Jameson, but Jameson has skills like me, ones untrained muscles can't fight.

This can't happen. Not again.

"Both of you put your dicks back in your pants," I snap. "We're not playing whose is bigger because *mine* is and I'm not dealing with any shit tonight."

Jameson touches my arm. "I'll stay if you need me."

"She doesn't need you, dude." Redix keeps poking the bear. "And she *never* will."

That charges Jameson toward Redix, but I grab his arm and turn him around.

"Stop!" I gun my eyes up at his. "Don't be baited by him. Just go. I've got this."

Anger tenses his jaw. "You sure?"

"No one fucks with me." I offer him a smile to cool him off. "I'm fine."

"See, she's real fine with *me*." Redix taunts. "I'll take care of her *real* good."

"Shut the fuck up." I glare at Redix. "Ain't no one paying you for lines right now so be quiet and pretty like you know how."

That turns Redix's sneer my way. Exactly how I plan.

Anything to get these bulls back into their pens.

Jameson doesn't take his eyes off Redix while he backs away, climbing into his Jeep. He leaves without a word, and I feel bad.

All Jameson does is everything nice for me, even swallowing his pride.

Throwing my bag over my shoulder, the sky begins to pour while I stomp off toward the stairwell. Like hell I'm getting stuck in an elevator with that man.

"Cade, talk to me." His voice follows.

"Eat a bag of dicks, Redix."

"I'm ready to talk."

His steps don't retreat, following mine up the stairs.

"Too late because I'm ready to kill you."

"Fine, let's talk and *then* you can kill me."

Dammit, he's hot on my heels all the way to my front door. My keys are in my hand, but I know better.

Once I open it, he'll force himself into my heart again.

"I'm serious." I turn my scowl at him. "I'm done talking to you. Keep following me and I'll arrest you for stalking because that's what this is. Now leave."

"Cade, I want to drink again." The look in his eyes clings to mine for help. "I want to drink again, and I have a bottle in the car but if I can talk to you, I won't. I'll be okay. I'll make it another day."

"Don't you dare manipulate me like that!"

The fear of it, how he teeters on the edge of death with his addiction; it's hell.

"This is your demon to kill, not mine! Go downstairs, throw that bottle away and then leave like you always do.

"It's your choice, Redix. You're the one who's had control all this time, of you and of *me*... but not anymore."

"I'm sorry. I'm sorry I left. I'm sorry I'm back at your door like an asshole. Okay?" His steps get too close. "Just let me fucking talk to you. Let me explain and tell you why."

"After all this time and now you're ready because it's what *you* need?" I bring my nose inches from his. "Yes, finally tell me, Redix. Which was worse? Everything that happened to us? Or the nothing you did about it?"

"Nothing? Is that what you think I did?" The agony in his eyes knifes my soul. "I did nothing *but* protect you from them, Cade."

That truth bombs through me.

No matter how I hurt, or how mad I am, I shouldn't have said that.

I know that much.

It was all my fault.

They were after me and Redix tried to protect me from those boys.

The tragedy is that we both got hurt anyway.

The guilt of it. The burden of it. It breaks me.

Before his eyes I fall into a million pieces of pain that pour down my silent cheeks, imploding my heart, making breath impossible.

He pulls me into his arms and I collapse where I belong. Where everyone can attack us from the outside but if we hold each other like this, with my heart pressed to his, they can't take this from us.

They can't take our love. This love we'll protect.

Redix can run all he wants. He'll never leave my heart and he knows that, so I let him back in.

It finds us with no words, only tears in my place with the lights off and a spectacular lightning storm raging outside while we lie together on my sofa.

Redix wraps around me, pulling my back to his chest and holding my hands in his.

That's when I notice; *his big hands are shaking.*

They don't stop until I gently press my lips to them. Twisting his legs around mine, he buries his nose into the nape of my naked neck, the sound of his choppy breath, the feel of his chest breathing with mine; we don't need to talk.

All we've needed is each other; to lie in our pain together until some of it washes away.

It feels like an hour passes while the storm blows over and the night grows as quiet as we are.

"I've been sober for one year, two months, and thanks to

you, one more day, Cade." His voice is hushed over my ear. "And in that time, I've been so alone. I haven't told anyone. I haven't been with another woman. After you, after ten years ago, I've never had sex sober. I couldn't get hard sober, and I didn't want to.

"I don't remember a lot of what I did or with who. And I'm so damn lucky all my tests came back clear. That, God I hope I didn't hurt anyone. But all I remember in flashes over the years was no matter who I was with, I was missing you."

My throat burns to the pain he shares, to the truth he dares to tell me.

It's been the same for me.

All I think about is him.

"I had to leave that other night because I was embarrassed." He keeps confessing, "I don't know my body now because it feels everything sober. I want to feel that with you again, but I can't control it. I could come in ten seconds or rip you apart all night. That's how powerful it is. That's what I feel with you. And it scares me because I'd protect you all over again, even from my own pain."

"It's okay." I turn around in his arms. "It's okay. I understand." I cradle his head into my neck and hold him back. "We can just talk and that's okay."

"I want to do more than talk with you, Cade. I want to laugh with you. I want to play games like we used to. We never stopped being kids together and I loved that. If I want happiness, I have to find it with *you*."

It's my truth too.

I lift his chin and trace my fingertip along it. "What kind of games do you want to play?" I want to ease his pain, our pain.

"Uno."

"Uno?" I can't help it. I laugh through tears. "Are you for real?"

"Yes." His smile is instant. "I always beat you at that game. Everything else is bullshit because you're too smart for me and always win."

"Okay."

I trace down his nose next, ideal masculinity blesses every feature of his face. His dark eyebrows. His dark stubble. The contrast to the light streaks in his hair. The way his lips are in a constant soft pout over a hard jaw. The way his eyes are a sky you dream about.

"I'll play Uno with you," I grin, "and I'll let you win."

"Let me make you dinner first."

"Good luck with that." There's peace in his arms, making my heart beat happy. "My cupboard is bare."

"No, it's not." He sweeps my long bangs back, tucking them behind my ear. "I went grocery shopping."

The evidence is obvious.

"You kept the key to my place?" The one Mama gave him. Typical, Gloria Bryant. She set us up. "I'll let you break and enter, only this once."

"Don't be mad. I had to put the ice cream in the freezer." I don't need to ask. "I want another ice cream date with you, but I've been dodging fans with phones for the past twelve hours. We gotta stay here."

"The units in this building are sold out all summer with your fans looking for you."

"Sorry about that. Welcome to my hell."

I'm thrilled to be back in it.

And I know we can only talk about this in small doses, so I let it go.

I'd rather have him than the truth, at least for a night.

It turns out, Redix is a great cook. His first year sober he learned the skill and I reap the rewards of his love for Korean food.

"Here." He plops an onion down. "Chop this."

I stare at it with a blade in hand. "How?"

He laughs, nudging my shoulder. "How can you *not* know how to chop onions? You're twenty-eight and..."

"Don't you dare say 'and a woman.'"

"*And*... you have skills to kill a man with a knife, but you can't slay an onion?"

He's breathtaking when he smiles at me.

When I let him teach me.

Wrapping his big body around mine, he guides our hands and all I want to do is never let him go. The onion and truth make me tear up again.

"When I hold you like this"—his lips press to my ear—"it feels like we've been apart for ten minutes and not ten years. Is that weird?"

"No." Everything feels right. "That's called best friends."

It's the best meal I've ever eaten.

Later, I sit on the kitchen counter watching him clean up because he won't let me help with that.

"Tell me what it was like." So much I don't know about his life now. "Like how did you go from Hilton Head to Hollywood?"

"I got in my car that next day and drove to LA. You hear about actors who struggle for years but I lucked out. My modeling portfolio and connections had me an agent by the time I got there." He clicks the dishwasher shut. "I landed *Romeo Returns* within my first month and it's been a wild ride ever since."

"What's your relationship with Angie?"

I won't tell him how the thought of them together makes me sick. I'm jealous over no man but Redix.

He winces like he knows anyway. "She's tricky."

That hurts. "How?"

I have to know.

Never will I be the other woman, or other Uno player, or whatever we are.

"My manager introduced us and said she'd be good for me. Angie's got a show and wants publicity. We did the awards circuit together and she gave the interviews, repeating the stories my publicist told her. We're a PR stunt, not love.

"Then I went out one night to a club without her. I guess I was so lonely in the lie that I got so wasted I almost died. Eric, my assistant back in LA, he found me barely alive on my front steps. I didn't even make it inside. I went into rehab for six months and Angie stuck around for that and the year since."

"She's in love with you."

"I fucked her twice before rehab, not since. She knows the deal. We're business and friends. Having her on my arm keeps the focus on our fake relationship, not my real addictions."

"Nothing happens between us if you're with someone else, fake or real."

He can decide right now because my mind won't change.

Redix holds my stare while he reaches into his back pocket for his phone. Pressing a few buttons, he places a call.

"Hey, Ang." Silence. "Yeah, I'm fine. I'm back home." Silence. He talks to her with his eyes on me. "Yeah, I'm with her." My cheeks warm. "And I'm gonna kiss her tonight."

My heart jolts. "I'm gonna make this perfect with her again." My stomach flips. "So I wanted to tell you. To be honest. We cool?" Silence, while my mind dizzies. "Yep. You too. Bye."

It's just like that.

Do I feel bad for Angie or good for us? But that's Redix. At least he told her the truth.

He steps between my thighs spread open on the countertop.

Is this really happening? Ten years and we'll finally kiss again?

I'm floating above a reality I can't believe.

"I could do it right now, Cade." The satin of his lips slides over mine and the room spins. "But I mean it. I'm gonna make us perfect again."

Turning around, he opens the freezer.

The couple of minutes he takes to prepare a lemon sherbet ice cream cone finds my heart overwhelmed by how he remembers.

Urging his way back between my thighs, he presses his lips to the scoop. The heat of his mouth melts the cream. He holds the cone up to mine to do the same while he asks, "Magnolia Cade Bryant, can I kiss you again and all night?"

I smile with drips from my lips. "Don't call me that."

He grins with drips from his. "Well then shut my mouth up with yours."

With my sudden inhale, his lips are sliding sweet over mine. It's a rush of lust and tears pulling me back into him. The return of us, it's crushing me, and I love it.

It has his hand dropping the cone in the sink and pulling the nape of my neck into his grasp so we can have more. More of us. More of our love. Every gentle swipe.

Every light lick. Everything about our reunion fills the tiny kitchen with our moans.

He cradles my jaw in his massive hands and won't stop with his kiss, with his tongue.

I taste him and lemon and tears and oh my God, I've missed him. It surges from my lips, firing through my core and wetting my sex. It's sudden. It's powerful. It's every need I have demanding him again.

I wrap my legs around him and draw him in.

With a groan into my mouth, he grabs me tighter, his hips thrusting between my thighs.

My heart, my body, I burst because he's sober... and hard as hell for me. The steel of his shaft crazes my body for more, so much more, I'll never get enough of him.

He grabs my hips. "Candy Cade." His nose nuzzles against mine while we catch our breath. "Do you know why I *really* call you that?"

"Why?" I pull his hair knot free so I can lace my hands through his thick mane again.

"Because you're the sweetest thing in my life." Strands tumble over his shoulders while he drags his thumb over my bottom lip. "You're the only one this special to me."

That truth has us reaching for each other, our lips and tongues searching, again and again, finding the pieces of us we lost along the way.

He picks me up and I hold onto him while he walks us back to the sofa. I'm losing time with my body wrapped around his. Lying me down, he's on top of me and back in my arms.

We kiss for so long my lips swell and my muscles go liquid, weak with pent-up desire. I can feel his massive need too, urging into me.

It's a pain I can't bear any more.

"Redix, what can we do?" I huff through our kiss. "I don't care if you come in ten seconds or rip me apart." My tongue tangles with his and whose groan is deeper, I don't know but I rip my mouth away. "Just touch me again."

He lifts my tank top off and his eyes darken at my white bikini top underneath. The day on the beach, it's still warm on my body.

"Damn," he says, "you smell like suntan lotion." He gently bites my neck while he murmurs down my flesh, "This smell on you makes me horny as fuck."

My cotton shorts are next. He tugs them off and I hope he's going to mount me right here.

"This is what I mean." He stares down at my tiny bikini bottom taunting him. "I worry that I want you so bad I'll hurt you."

I take his hand, "then start at the beginning, like the first time you touched me," and place it between my thighs.

It was Redix who found my desire.

Taking his time with me, he slowly searched until he made my back arch, answering with "yes". I tried as a teen, touching myself. It felt good but I never got there, my frustration making it worse.

Lying next to me on the sofa, he thrills my body again, sending shocks through me as he pulls my bikini top off, cool air pebbling my nipples.

"Fuck, you look so goddamn beautiful," he growls, tugging my bottoms off next.

The exposure, the anticipation, he knows every move to take me there.

"Spread your legs for me, Cade. *That's* how you like it."

Yes, I do. Open only for him, the brush of his fingertips tickles over my folds. Redix knows my secrets.

"You like it slow." He whispers in my ear. "You like me to tease you, to take my time, to get you so damn wet."

His mouth is next, his tongue matching his light strokes, its wet caress indulges my nipples, lifting my hips for more of his touch inside.

"Redix, please." I need more.

"*Shhhh.* We got all night."

His fingertips, they're tickling up and down, his touch dancing over where I must have him but not touching me there.

"Let's enjoy this." He is with his middle finger circling, tracing sweet torture over where I'm open, slick, and needing him, but he doesn't enter. "We've waited so long for it."

I let him take me slow, through the tease like he knows how. He was the first one here and he's so good at it.

It has me spreading for him, craving more, and loving the lack of sensation; the lush caress of his touch over my sex until I feel it. It's here, thrashing inside me and wanting to reward us.

"You're ready." His mouth leaves my nipples dripping before he hums over my ear. "You're so wet and ready for me, aren't you?"

"Yes." I want to cry.

He kisses my ear. "Beg for me."

"Please, Redix." He's teased me to snap.

"Again."

I'm secure in his gaze, in his touch. I can do this. "Please make me come."

"Is that what you do? You come thinking about me?"

"Yes. Only you."

"*Now, Cade.*"

He spanks my pussy so hard, hitting my clit and

breaking me in half as my back, my neck, my shoulders, they bow off the sofa with a loud scream. The climax, the satisfaction, the ache; they hit at the same time because he's not inside me where I need him.

It's not enough.

It's been my pain and pleasure and he knows it, priming me for more.

"Again," he growls, staring at me, claiming me, and looking so fucking hot. He's not stopping with two of his fingers sliding in slow.

And I can't stop the yearning, my loud moan at his penetration, at feeling his flesh enter me again.

"Redix, please, you can be harder now." At seventeen, I needed him to be tender, to be slow. Now my mature body, my experienced sex, it demands his hard advance. "Harder." I cup my hand over his and shove his fingers deeper inside. "I want you so fucking hard."

"Like this, Cade?"

Devilish delight takes his eyes. It's scary and I want it. His hand starts to pound, his fingers taking me while his palm pummels my clit.

"You love it like this, don't you?" He has my body twisting for his touch, writhing and rolling to get every inch of him. "Come on. Show me how much you need me inside this sweet, wet pussy."

I spread even wider for his force while his mouth takes my nipple harder than he ever has before. It makes me cry out for him, so loud the world can hear how desire denied for so long sings from your lungs and you don't want to breathe. You only want more.

I only want him.

His lips hover over my nipple, his taunts and touch driving me mad. "You like it hard like this?" His hand jerks, his long fingers curving deep inside, all the way to my core. "You like it rough, Cade?" He's found where I'm so tender. "Because I can be so fucking rough with you." He's so intense, making my head lash, not in refusal. "I want you *that* bad. I always have. I want to fucking rip you apart until you come a million times for me."

My body begs with my words, "Yes, Redix, don't stop."

I'm shaking with tremors from a depth I've never felt. A surge of sensation, pain, and pleasure whirling inside my sex to the sensitive spot he's pounding, unrelenting to the place he's claiming as his.

"For me, Cade." His eyes lock on mine. "You're *all* for me."

He watches, how with no sound I fall apart for him, quaking over him, every muscle contracting while I feel the tide of it rush over his fingers. Stars fill my vision while I'm pulsing so hard over his touch that I can't move. His kiss takes my soft gasps until I find logic and breath again.

"Fuck, look," he says, "look at what I can do to you now." His hand drips with my clear arousal. I feel it pooling under me too. His fingers are in his mouth. He's sucking the new taste of me, the well he tapped before he swears, "God-damn." There's wonder in his eyes. It matches mine, surprised he made me come like that. "Fuck you're hot."

He dips in for another taste, making me moan. Licking his fingertips wet with my cum; he's watching me, he's hungry. The tent in his jeans looks agonizing and so does the strain in his eyes.

"Can I touch you too?" I want everything with him, but I don't want him to run away again. "However you want."

He sits up and rips his T-shirt over his head, throwing it on the floor before he unbuttons his jeans and lies back beside me.

I love how tall he is. How big everything is on him—hands, feet, cock. Everything about him makes me feel safe beside him.

"Like this." He picks up my hand and trails it down his sculpted torso. "Touch me like this, like it's really you again, like I've been imagining you for so long."

His skin is hard silk, and I remember how he likes it.

How he loves my lips on his chest, my tongue licking his nipples. It all comes back to me while I skim my fingertips from the base of his barely exposed cock up to his belly button. Back and forth, all night long I could treasure his flesh. And his smell. Vanilla and leather fill my nose while my mouth goes next, down his iron chest to his rock abs flinching softly to my kiss.

Damn, he's beautiful.

I linger over his hips covered by jeans. I know he's commando underneath. I know what's hidden in his jeans.

"Can I touch it?" Something is different for him, the way his ribs are panting.

He barely answers, "Yes."

I let him do it. He pulls his jeans open, revealing the tattoo on his right hip bone. It matches the one on my left.

Two small dorsal fins, dolphins, breaking the surface side-by-side.

I trace over the primitive black lines and the memory we share.

The first time he was inside me, the first time we made love at eighteen, two dolphins swam around the boat. We could hear them in the water. We peeked over the starboard side and laughed.

There they were, like we were busted... or blessed. We took it as a sign and got the tattoos the next week, permanent marks where our bodies met, where we joined and still are to this day.

I don't ask, it's impulse. Pressing my lips to his flesh, I kiss his tattoo, but he suddenly recoils. Like I touched him with a hot knife.

"Cade." He stops me. "Touch me instead." He pushes down his jeans, revealing his length resting heavy on his left side.

Good god, I'd forgotten how big and thick he is, how gorgeous he looks like this.

"Come up here and kiss me while you do it," he says. His hand guides mine over his thick shaft. It's warm velvet under my clutch.

Touching his hard cock again wets me even more while my lips skate over his. "It's okay if it's ten seconds," I murmur into his kiss. "We can do this again and all night."

And he lets me.

Three times I touch him like this.

Each one is like he's discovering something. Or remembering a pleasure long forgotten.

A few times I've been so drunk to the point of numb before. For nine years, he was. How it must feel for him after all this time, to be so awake again. It's like it's our first time without all the awkward. Only the trust and desire are here.

The first time is fast, my strokes making his body shake, his gaze in awe and prisoner to mine.

"God, Cade. Don't stop." He keeps my fist pumping while his lips tremble, while he's all mine and vulnerable in my tight grip. He doesn't gasp the first time. He just comes over my hand and with creamy ropes over his belly and sweet relief all over his face. It's beautiful.

He barely goes soft before he wants me like that again. Like he can't get enough.

The second time he trusts me more. He lets go of my hand and lets me indulge him. He lasts longer, writhing and moaning into my grasp, into my tight twist over his tip, and my long wrap pumping down to his base.

"Oh fuck, Cade." Getting him off gets me so wet. He's taking longer and fucking my fist like I need him to fuck me with those incredible hips, strong and hard and banging into my grip. His hand cups my breast, palming its weight while his gaze holds mine. "You're gonna make me come again. Shit, you feel so good."

His groan is so loud, his thighs shaking while he spills his cum over us.

The third time is an hour later. With my body pressed against his, feeling my ragged breath on his chest, my hand gripping him hard, he knows what I need too—his hand between my thighs.

And we do it.

At twenty-eight, at all that we've shared, we could do more, but don't need to. Not tonight.

It's our touch, our bodies finally together and we only need each other, to be safe and sighing the other's name.

By early morning, we're a sticky mess on my white leather sofa and don't care. The sun will be up soon and so will our second chance together.

"Should we shower?" He won't stop kissing me.

"Not yet." I don't ever want him to leave. Not one part.

"We're covered in my drying cum." He's not shy about that, grinning, "And yours. It's hot as hell."

"Yes, and I only want more of it."

He rolls on top of me, gazing down like he's finally home. "I only do it for you. I can only come with you."

I'm home too and suddenly, I believe him. How all those women and other times, it wasn't him. Just his shell. His body barely reacting on instinct.

But with us, it's always more. We couldn't be more alive together.

He kisses my forehead. "Can we sleep in your bed?"

Fear shoots through me. "No man has slept in my bed. I've never fallen asleep with another either."

He knows why.

"Makes me feel pretty special." He kisses my hair, softly. "It's like old times then. We'll fall asleep messy on the couch together."

I turn and pull a throw blanket over us before he hugs my back to his chest. We settle into each other, into our love still clinging to our skin, and I don't want to be anyplace else.

"Thank you, Candy Cade." His voice gets so deep when he's tired.

"For what?" And I get so soft in his arms.

"For saving my life too."

I squeeze my eyes shut to my tears, to his hands in mine again.

The weight of us is brutal and beautiful, and we hold on, sinking together.

CHAPTER EIGHTEEN

CADE

It's too dark.

I'm trying to find him, my feet stumbling over mounds of sand. Terror fills my lungs when I think I hear his groans of pain.

I'm hurting too.

"Redix!" I scream into the black wall of night. Only the ocean answers back with crash after crash.

"Redix!" It screeches from my soul, shredding my vocal cords.

I have to find him.

I have to save him.

It's all my fault.

A cracking noise startles me out of my nightmare. I shoot straight up on the sofa.

My police radio. It calls out across the dawn of my living room...

"We have a possible ten-ninety-five. Coligny Park. White female. Unresponsive. Medic is en route."

I jump up and grab the radio from its charger. "Bryant. One-forty. I'm en route."

It sounds next across the room. "Jameson. Two-twelve. I'm en route."

"What's going on?" Redix mumbles from the sofa while I dart down the hall to my bedroom. I grab a pair of khakis and a white polo with the Sheriff's emblem on it.

"Work," I call out over my shoulder throwing them on.

"Will he be there?" Suddenly, his voice is right behind me while I pull on my boots next.

Guess he heard Jameson's voice.

"Yes, he will. It's his work too."

I smooth my hair, tucking my bangs back before I clip on my duty belt. My gun is still secured in its holster.

"The real question is"—I turn to Redix leaning in the doorway—"will you leave again?"

He gently grabs my hand while I brush by him.

"I'll be here, with you, for the week. We can talk about the rest when you get home." He gives me a kiss before saying, "Be safe."

I screech to a halt.

I've never had someone worry about me.

Not even Mama. Or Dad. If they did, they didn't say it. Like it's taboo.

"Thanks." I peck his cheek before rushing out the door.

Fifteen minutes later and Jameson beats me to the scene. I swear he sleeps in his uniform.

Medic's already here. The victim is loaded in the back of the ambulance. Jameson's interviewing the man who found her. He's a local out for his morning run and not a suspect.

"She has no ID." Jameson steps to the side, debriefing me. "No phone. Nothing."

And I don't miss his terse voice, his eyes wanting to ask about Redix.

But we have a job to do.

"I'm going with her," is all I say.

"I'll meet you there."

The ride to the hospital lets me study the victim. Early twenties. Brunette. Yellow sundress. A red stain spilled down the front of it. White sandals. Blue toenails with a sand dollar painted on her big toes. It's a fresh pedicure. No sunscreen or sand damage.

I want to vomit.

Another victim in yellow.

Another victim who looks like me ten years ago.

The guilt is vicious.

After an hour in the emergency room, she's waking up. I want to hold her hand, but we haven't collected evidence yet.

"Hey there." I give her my softest smile. "I'm Cade. I'm a detective. You're in the hospital and you're safe. Can you tell me your name?"

The way the victim searches around, her eyes terrified while reality comes back to her—it breaks my heart.

"Kayla," she whispers.

"Hey, Kayla. I'm not leaving your side, okay. We're going to take care of you."

It takes three hours. In that time, Kayla consents to the rape kit. I pray for more evidence this time. It doesn't get answered. It's the same M.O. Proof of assault. No trace of who did it.

Kayla uses my phone to call her friends. She's renting a condo with them—a bridesmaids party here from Georgia for the week.

"When are you scheduled to check out?" I gently ask.

"Today."

"Do you know the company you rented through?"

"No, but Amber, the bride does."

"Okay." I jot notes on my steno pad. "I like your pedicure. Did you get it yesterday?"

"Yeah." Kayla's smile is weak. "We all got mani/pedis before we went out last night." She gives me the location of the place but can't remember the name. I recognize it. It's close to that same liquor store.

"I remember the bad storm last night," Kayla stares at the ceiling. "The Pelican was packed because everyone came in from the patio. I couldn't move. It was so hot. I was drinking to cool off. I'm not a big drinker. I get migraines from it. You have to believe me. I'm not that kind of woman."

"Kayla, I believe you." I stand beside her bed. "I believe you and every kind of woman, ones who never drink, ones who do, ones who get high or are just having fun. You have no reason to lie and every right to get justice."

"Will you help me? Will you find him? I don't want another woman hurt."

"Oh, I'll get him. So help me, God, it's a deal." She nods with relief. "Do you remember how that stain got on your yellow dress?"

Yellow?

My friend, Pamela Ryan, it hits me.

She wore a yellow dress when she disappeared. I had

borrowed that same dress from her and wore it that night—ten years ago. I didn't want to give it back, but she asked for it. It was her favorite.

And now it's my curse.

"We were in a group," Kayla answers. "We were dancing. Guys were around us." Kayla closes her eyes. "Someone knocked my arm. I remember because the drink was sticky down my chest."

"Do you remember who bumped you?"

"No." Kayla pauses. "Stripes. Navy and white stripes. I remember a guy's sleeves. They were long and I thought it was weird because it's like Memorial Day and so hot."

When Kayla's friends arrive, they confirm the same. "Do you remember anyone in a parrot T-shirt?"

The women exchange glances, shaking their heads no.

I ask Amber, Kayla's friend, who she rented their condo from.

"Sunset Rentals," she says, making my empty stomach twist.

That's five from that rental company—the one owned by Gentry Evans.

Out by the nurse's desk in the Emergency Room, I comb back through my notes.

Sunset Rentals.

Why target renters the day before they leave? One—they're relaxed, in trusting-vacation mode.

And two—I seethe. Police procedure.

If you target someone before they have to check out, it makes it hard for us to interview the victim, to collect all the evidence.

Sure, the victim can stay longer but by then, they want to escape from here.

Smart tactic.

Dumb assumption because I'm ready. I sleep with my radio.

"We found a lighter at the scene." Jameson startles me. I didn't see him come in. "We'll run the prints on it but can't be sure it's relevant."

"It's a lead, right?" He's not smiling back at me. "What did the cameras show?"

That park is under surveillance; any dumbass would know it.

"Nothing," Jameson replies. "We got her walking up from the dark beach and stumbling before she collapses by the bench."

"Shit."

He's not stupid enough to get caught on camera. It's like he knows where all the cameras are—more importantly—where they *aren't* on this island.

I check my phone. "It's almost eleven. I'm going to The Pelican. That's the third victim from there."

"You want backup or am I kicked out of this too?"

"I'll take the back-up." I ignore his jab. "You drive while I dig online."

We escort Kayla out of the hospital to her friend's waiting car. I give her my card. "Call me or email me if you remember anything or have questions. Either way, I promise I'll keep in touch."

Jameson drives and doesn't say much. He plays Bob Marley while I tap away on the laptop in his car, searching for the owner of the nail salon where Kayla and her friends went.

Because if there's anything Sheriff Gloria Bryant has taught me, if you want to find a criminal... start at the top.

That's where most of them are.

"Guess who owns that nail salon?" Fury strikes me at the find.

"The same man who owns half this island?"

"Yep. Senator Gentry Evans."

I text Penny. When she's on shift, she can go check that salon out.

While we continue our drive, Jameson finally cracks. "Did you let him stay?"

"It's complicated."

His lips press in a line of anger. "Broken hearts and Redix Dean aren't complicated. It's his M.O. It's clear as fucking day, Bryant."

I keep my stare out the front windshield, not sure how to answer.

He's not wrong.

"I'm sorry I got you in the middle of all this," is all I can say.

"I'll get in the middle of anything for you."

I'm about to thank him but he parks the car with a hard brake. We're at The Pelican and work is the priority.

"Let me handle this one." I see a woman, a server taking a smoke break by the back door.

I get out of the car and signal her my way, out of the range of the camera at the door while I ask her if the owner or manager are in.

"Not yet," she says. "They always run late."

"Typical." I keep my smile true and she grins back. "What's the manager's name?"

"Our Bar Manager, he's Derek Baucom and a new, giant pain in the ass."

"Really?" Yep, loose lips *and* pissed-off women can sink ships. "How so?"

"He brought in his man-crew from New York and won't

let us women tend bar anymore and make the good tips. It's bullshit."

"Sounds like it." And it sounds like the perfect cover for a crime. "Did he work last night?"

"Yep."

"When's he usually back in?"

"Late." She flicks her cigarette. "But he'll be here early Tuesday because like hell if I'm opening for him all week."

"Thanks." I shake her hand and step back toward Jameson's car, all that intel swimming in my skull.

In the minutes it takes for Jameson to get me back to my car at the crime scene, I search social media for Derek Baucom, and my starving stomach twists.

"Look at this." I show him my phone screen. "Derek Baucom, their new Bar Manager posted a month ago. Seems he owns a long-sleeved navy and white striped pullover."

Finally, smiles lift our faces.

"It's a lead," we say in unison.

Yep, this is why I won't mess things up with Jameson.

Too much is on the line.

CHAPTER NINETEEN

REDIX

Her Touch by SŸDE

Dear Candy Cade,

I'm sitting on your couch and damn! I'm happy. I don't need to be in your bed.

I just need you.

Besides, we used to sleep together on the couch all the time. Like that one afternoon we fell asleep watching *One Tree Hill*.

You loved that show.

I hated it. I only watched it to be next to you.

Holding you against me like that, I had the hottest

dream. Something about your tits and my cock and we woke up to my cum in my shorts and on the back of yours.

Yes, you were my first wet dream.

But we were seventeen then and it'd been a while since I had one of those.

But you didn't laugh at me.

You just rolled over and said you thought it was hot and started kissing me. Your hand went down my shorts and I got hard again and in a few more minutes—I swear with feeling your hand stroke my cock for the first time—I was coming again for you.

Shit, it's making me hard now and I'm twenty-eight.

God, my body is waking up to your touch.

Last night, I can't believe how much I felt with you. But it makes sense. I've dulled my senses for so long.

Now I'm wide awake... and sorry... and so fucking horny for you.

But it's more than wanting to fuck you again, Cade.

I want a life with you.

Mine's been so grey, like a silent film clicking on reels.

I swear I don't know how I survived like that.

But now I'm alive with you.

You're damn Technicolor.

I forgot how good this feels, me still smelling you on my skin and knowing I can have more soon. I haven't felt hope for so long.

Until now.

But then I remember our dark past and what you can't know.

How far back does our hell go?

More than ten years.

You told me about it. How when we were fifteen TJ and Gentry bullied you on the bus.

I'm so sorry I wasn't there that day to protect you.

But you told me how that senior—Charlie Ravenel from over on Daufuskie—punched TJ in the dick. They left you alone for a while because no one scared her. And she was hot, which intimidated the boys, including me.

And I watched it.

You changed after that. You started doing martial arts with your dad. It's like he wanted you to learn to fight back too.

But it didn't stop those two assholes.

TJ and Gentry.

I knew they were after you.

So that made them come after me too.

But that night.

It wasn't just TJ and Gentry.

I don't know who the third guy was, but he drove the car. You never saw him and I didn't recognize him either.

But I can't forget the tattoo on his forearm. His right one. It's the mudflap girl you see on trucks.

He was the worst one. Bigger and older. He's why I can't hear so good out of my right ear. He punched it so hard it bled and rang for weeks.

Fuck, my hand's shaking.

I gotta stop. I'm not doing this. I'm not remembering more.

I told you enough last night and now you're giving us a chance and I'm not ruining it.

We're going to be happy now.

I'm going to spoil you, Cade Bryant.

I know what to do, where to go, and everything so I can prove it.

How much I still love you.

CHAPTER TWENTY

CADE

An emptiness greets me when I get home. I hear nothing. My place is spotless.

"Hello?"

Silence.

It drops my nervous heart and my logic fears the worst.

He left again.

He got jealous about Jameson.

Last night, we were too intimate. It was too intense.

Me falling asleep in his arms? It reminded him of all we lost.

I'm fooling myself. Redix and I walk a fine line between

desire and disaster, and he'll always run. He'll always leave. He can't take it.

Can I?

Our love is a tightrope over hell. I teeter on it, walking down my hallway with a familiar ache threatening my chest.

My bedroom door is closed. Pushing it open, my heart leaps.

My Léger purple dress is on the bed; my Louboutin heels are placed on the floor in front of it. *He didn't leave.*

A magnolia flower sits beside my black clutch. Fuck him, I grin. *I hate magnolias.*

Glancing into my bathroom, a note is written in lipstick on the mirror. I walk in.

> *You're looking at the most*
> *beautiful woman alive.*
> *Be ready at 7. It's a date.*
> *With an Asshole*

Looking back at my bed, I'm shocked. How did he have time to buy those? A new pair of white lace panties and a matching bra are there too.

What's this sensation?

Hope. Romance. My first date with anyone.

With Redix.

I check my phone and have four hours to get ready and a text.

PENNY

Why do I feel like you're about to get your heart broken?

Again!

It takes her one ring to answer. "Please tell me it's not true."

"Let me guess; Jameson has a big mouth."

"Jameson has a broken heart."

"I never promised him anything and we never even kissed. And thank God," I say, "because we work together and have nine unsolved cases and—"

"And you have a hot, jealous, unstable, famous ex-fiancé who no man can compete with," Penny adds before I can keep explaining why this bad risk is a good idea.

"I love him, Penny." I watch my face in the mirror say it; never have I looked more certain. "We have a lot to work out, but I need to give us a chance."

Silence.

I hear Nina crying in the background.

"Is this his *only* chance?" Penny finally speaks. "Promise me this is the *last one*."

"I promise."

Do I really? Will I ever be over Redix?

I hear her pick Nina up. "Did you at least fuck him? Please tell me you did so some of this would be worth it."

"Not really."

I start rummaging through my makeup drawer.

"How do you *not really* fuck Redix Dean? One hundred and thirty million of his followers would."

"I guess we're going slow. His sobriety. My broken heart. Us being back together. It's a lot."

I've told Penny our history—every young-love detail up to that day.

When Penny asked why we broke up, I had to lie. I told

her that Redix wanted to go to Hollywood; that he didn't want to be tied down to me.

That story protects her because I can't get her involved, not in my deal.

No one can know.

Especially Redix.

"That sounds like a recipe for devastation." Penny doesn't sugar-coat. I love that about her. "Are you happy? I need to hear you say it with no bullshit."

I look up and consider my reflection.

A light is in my eyes. A real smile is there. I'm glowing, looking through the note Redix left me.

"Yes, I'm very happy."

"Okay. I'll holster my weapon for now. But he's dead if he hurts you again. And clean this up with Jameson. I got enough shitty diapers at home; I don't need it at work."

"Yes, ma'am." I smile. "Speaking of—work your magic at that nail salon this evening. Ask if someone was hanging around the same afternoon as Kayla and her friends."

"Copy," Penny replies. "What are you working on?"

"I got a Bar Manager to schmooze Tuesday."

"Please," Penny huffs, "just smile at him and he'd confess serial murders to your gorgeous face."

I take my time getting ready after our call ends.

Penny's just protective over me. I am a bit too but God, I'm so ready for this. Every part of my body, I prepare it for Redix, for whatever we'll do, I can handle it. Besides, it makes me happy and horny and time flies.

My doorbell rings promptly at seven. My hands shake opening the door and every reason why stands before me.

Fuck me now and always.

He takes my breath away.

No shoes on groomed feet. Perfectly tailored black

trousers. A matching dinner jacket. A tissue-thin white V-neck T-shirt showing off his smooth, carved chest. Hair tumbling down. One hand in his pocket and a "The Devil's Here for Your Soul, Ladies" smile on his face.

This is Redix Dean.

From behind his back, it stutters my breath, he hands me a pink tulip.

"Sorry." His grip was so tight, he broke its stem. "Guess I'm a little nervous."

My ankles go weak. If I cry I'll mess up my makeup. "I don't have a gift for you. Sorry."

"Yes, you do." His hand reaches for mine. "It's this."

"Wait." I tug at our tender grasp. "Is this a date?"

"Yes."

"Not until you ask me."

His grin back; it reaches between my thighs.

"Cade Bryant, will you please honor me with a date tonight?"

That only took nineteen years.

"Yes."

I float.

Held by his hand. Down the elevator. To the Mercedes he's renting. Over the familiar palm and pine-lined road he's driving down.

I don't care where we're going. More pink tulips are on the dash for me and I'm swimming in bliss.

There's a yellow orchid arrangement on the floorboard too, and still, I don't ask.

"Come on, Detective." He talks over our senior year playlist. "Don't you wanna know where we're going?"

"Nope." I uncross my legs, parting my thighs for his glance. "I like letting you be in control."

"Careful there, darlin'." His voice is lube sliding across my eager pussy. "That's dangerous permission."

"I'm prepared for danger."

He has no clue how much.

But right now? I'm prepared to ride him in this car.

God, this is going to be a long night.

After a bit, I realize where we're going first, and I fight back touched tears. He parks in front of Ms. Ryan's house.

Redix and Pamela were close too.

"I called her and asked if we could come by," he informs me while he carries the orchid to her front door.

Ms. Ryan is beside herself with our hugs and smiles. We spend an hour at her house. She gives Redix a tour though nothing has changed, not even Pamela's room. The three of us stand in front of Pamela's yellow bedspread and Ms. Ryan can't take her eyes off us.

We're holding hands. I can't believe it either.

"She'd be so happy to see you two together again." I've never seen Ms. Ryan so lucid, so alive. "She loved you both."

Redix squeezes my hand.

His is sweating. He's nervous and I didn't appreciate it until now—*this is his first time confronting that Pamela's gone.*

That something horrible happened to her and we may never know what or who.

Though I have a suspicion that haunts my soul.

"I just love watching you on the red carpet." Ms. Ryan feeds us salted lemon pound cake in her kitchen, her eyes sparkling for Redix. "My word you look so handsome. You make me so proud."

"Will you go with me next time?" He's chomping on cake, smiling through lips that want to pucker. "I have the

Golden Globes next January. Ms. Ryan, will you please be my date?"

"Don't you tease an old lady."

"I'm not teasing, ma'am." He reaches for her hand on the table. "You'd be the prettiest one there and I'd be the luckiest man alive."

I can't stop the hitch in my heart.

He just gave Ms. Ryan the other important thing missing from her life—hope, something real to look forward to.

I clench my teeth to keep from crying.

"Redix Dean." I hold his hand over the center console while we drive away. "Is it possible sobriety made you even sweeter?"

My hand feels safe in his and he doesn't say a word.

Deep down, I know how humble he really is. I'm glad to see it shine.

Minutes later, he's surprising me more by pulling up to the resort where we had our big fight.

"Come on," he says opening the car door for me, "we're righting every wrong tonight."

"You should know"—I take his hand, wanting to shove it under my dress—"that I want to be *very wrong* with you tonight."

The smirk on his face.

"Food before fucks, darlin'."

His beauty can guide me into hell... but it leads me to the restaurant instead.

The staff fall over themselves. Seating us at the best table. Getting a fast round of drinks, seltzer and lime for us both. Crab cakes are set down before we ask for them.

"Are you really a golf guy nowadays?" The eighteenth hole is right outside the window.

"I'm trying to pick up healthy habits." He sips his seltzer. "The owner here—Luca Mercier—he's a friend and we play. And this place is more secluded. I didn't want our date ruined by fans or tourists."

"So this really is a date?"

"Yep." He leans back in his chair. "You finally tamed me, Cade Bryant. You're my first date."

"You're mine too."

"No way." His eyes shock wide. "How'd you go so long looking that hot without a date?"

"It's a rule of mine. I don't date either."

"What *do* you do?"

Oh, here it is.

Do I tell him?

It's not fair really. I know a lot of his sins. Hell, the world does. I can only imagine what he's done that wasn't caught on camera.

"Tell you what." I'm addicted to deals. "I'll tell you two of my hottest stories, and you tell me two... of what you remember."

"Oh shit." He grins. "That'll make me jealous and horny and that's playing with fire."

"Same goes. I'll start."

A bite of crab cake gives me a second to think while the way Redix stares at me. The look in his eyes? I want to dive under this table and taste him instead.

"A Marine—"

"Great"—he rolls his eyes—"a *Marine*."

"Like a Marine can compete with you, Romeo. Hush, and let me finish my story."

I've suffered with jealousy over Redix and his women for so long, dishing it back out, in a fun way, it feels fair.

"He got us a hotel room. Then he asked if his friend could join us."

Redix's eyes narrow. "Man or woman?"

"Another man. Another Marine. They were both jacked as hell."

The heave of Redix's chest. I love it.

"I started with the first guy while his friend watched us. I made him go down on me and then I told him to fuck me slow like how we used to. I swear it was so damn hot."

"Did you suck any cock?"

"No."

Redix adjusts himself. "How did he fuck you?" It's turning him on. Me too.

"From behind"—I bite my lip, confessing—"it's the only way I'll fuck. And it let me watch the other guy jerking off to it. Of me getting fucked so slow."

"Did he fuck you too?"

Redix can never judge me. Nothing compares to his exploits.

And yeah, I've had my own. Because I can live with a broken heart *and* a pussy that needs to get fucked exactly how I want.

"Yes. I told him to go next. And I told him the same thing. To fuck me so slow I begged him not to stop. My pussy couldn't get enough dick that night."

His tongue licks his bottom lip. All I put in his head swirls in his eyes. Lust. Jealousy. XXX payback.

It's all true but so is the pain in the edge of his expression staring me down from across the table.

"With all the dick you can have looking like that, why can't your pussy get enough?"

I can tease Redix. I can torment him. I can take him on. Because we're equals.

But I'll never hurt him.

Even though I can.

"Because they're not you. I close my eyes and imagine you instead."

"Goddamn." His lids slide shut. "You're killing me."

"Your turn."

"Alright then." His eyes open and I brace myself. "Something hot I remember?"

"Yes."

"It involved a banana."

I gasp. I'm not prepared for that, and he's delighted by my shock.

"And the second hottest thing I remember?" He won't stop and I'm dying. The taboo. The image. I'm not jealous; I'm curious. "One of those jumbo candy canes."

"My god"—I sigh a moan he can hear—"you have a food fetish."

"You started me on eating lemon sherbet, Candy Cade, and I've been chasing your sweet taste ever since."

Why we stay for dinner, I don't know. But we do.

Every morsel on my plate has me ready to lie on this table and be his buffet.

"You owe me one more," he says. "I gave you two stories, you're next."

"It involves strip Uno."

His eyebrows pinch. He's really hurt by that. "With who?"

"You."

"We never did that."

"*Not yet.*"

He smiles with sin in his eyes.

When the server asks about dessert, Redix answers,

"No thank you. She'll be serving me hot cherry pie at home."

The server blushes. At Redix's sexy face. At his powerful fame. At his shameless reference.

I'm under his spell too.

He takes my hand and when I stand, the panties he bought me are slick with my arousal. I'm about to suggest a trip to the grocery store when the sight in front of us grabs my soul instead.

The couple standing in the doorway of the restaurant?

Senator Gentry Evans and his wife.

When Gentry's conservative smile aims our way, Redix's hand twitches in mine.

"Well, what a delight." Gentry's within choking distance. "Mr. Dean and Sergeant Bryant; bound together as usual." The urge to vomit at his voice slams me. "Mr. Dean, meet my wife, Stacey. She's a big fan."

The grip of Redix's hand over mine starts sweating again.

"Nice to meet you," is all Redix seethes back.

Stacey looks innocent. I feel sorry for her. She has no idea what evil she's married to.

I have to play this smart.

Despite how I want to sink my teeth into Gentry's neck and kill him right here, I won't. I have disastrous plans for him, and I need proof first.

"I can't believe it." Stacey gushes at Redix. "I'm your biggest fan. I loved *Romeo Returns*. And your movie—*The Tease*—it's my favorite. I watch it all the time."

This is justice enough right now.

Stacey doesn't care. So overcome by Redix Dean two feet from her, she's practically lying down, lifting her skirt, and spreading her thighs for him to fuck her right in front of her husband.

Most women would.

It twists Gentry's face. I chuckle. *This ass zit.* His evil can never best Redix's beauty.

I'm fucking loving this.

"Which was your favorite?" I ask her about Redix's iconic male-stripper films. "*The Tease* or *The Teaser*?"

Because he made two that had people coming in the aisles.

Yep, she's personally enjoyed those films.

More than once, I can tell by the flush under the pearls across her chest.

I squeeze Redix's hand back. He's gotta let me do this— for us—just one little dose of revenge for now.

"Oh Lord, don't make me pick." Stacey cuts her eyes at Redix. "I loved them both *so much.*"

Hell yes, she did. I can tell.

She loved those movies like me, moaning his name into a pillow.

"I'm glad they brought you so much pleasure." Redix joins in and...

Fuck you, Gentry Evans, because your wife would rather be fucking him.

And I assure you—she'll be imagining him every time you pathetically try.

Redix drops his voice. "I aim to please, Mrs. Evans."

"And you *always* do." I punch next.

"I'm a lucky woman"—I wink at Stacey before smirking at Gentry—"because most men can't hit what they aim for. Right, Mrs. Evans?"

I tug at Redix's hand.

He takes the signal, concluding, "I hope at least *dinner* satisfies you, Stacey."

We leave them standing in a pile of an awkward sex life from here forward.

I can't tell if Redix wants to laugh or lose his mind next, so I lead the way out to the valet's stand.

While we wait for Redix's car, I pull him into a hug.

"We're okay. Just breathe," I whisper into his chest. I can feel his heart pounding under my cheek. "Don't let him ruin us again."

Redix kisses the top of my head. "I'm really trying."

We don't say another word in the minutes it's taking the valet to fetch the car.

I just close my eyes and wrap my hands around his waist, squeezing him tight while he holds me back.

I wish the world would disappear but at least we have each other.

Click. Click.

My eyes snap open.

What the fuck?

A dumbass with a fancy Nikon is ten feet away, taking our picture.

"Hey!" I shout.

"Ignore him, Cade," Redix mutters.

The valet pulls the car up between us and the photographer who is still snapping pictures.

If there's a threat to Redix, yep, I snap too.

My long legs in these heels move fast. I can't be stopped.

Before he knows what's happening, I grab the photographer by the back of his neck and slam him down on the hood of the car. Snagging his free wrist, I wrench it behind him, bending back two strategic fingers that make him cry out while I snarl, "Say 'cheese', Motherfucker."

"Cade!" I hear Redix as fast as I feel his arms around my waist. "Cade! Stop!" He tries pulling me off him.

"Take another picture"—I force the photographer's fingers back more, making him scream—"and it'll be the last you take."

But Redix is too strong and my sanity returns.

I let the guy go, leaving him sprawled on the hood of the Mercedes.

"Damn, woman." Redix is laughing, lifting me off the ground and pulling me farther away. "Get in the car before you get arrested."

I don't give a shit. Like anyone on this island would arrest me.

The photographer scrambles away, caressing his camera like that's all he cares about, relieved I didn't break it instead.

The valets clap for my performance while I drop into the passenger seat.

I try calming my pulse while Redix keeps chuckling.

"You can't keep doing that, Candy Cade. Best control your cute temper. You're dating me and that's part of it."

Dating?

It makes me laugh too.

"So in three hours, we went from *a date* to *dating*?"

"Yeah." He aims the car toward my place. "Didn't you get the memo?"

"No." I cross my legs. That catches his eyes again. "You have to ask me first. Haven't you noticed? Telling me what to do will get your fingers broken."

CHAPTER TWENTY-ONE

CADE

Bad Together by Dua Lipa

I'm curious.

By the wrapped gift box Redix takes from his trunk.

By what he's revealed tonight.

I've always known under all his cocky swagger is a man who cares too much.

But I never knew he could be that kinky too.

I don't know what to think. Worried he has no boundaries when drunk. Or excited to see if he's the same sober.

But we need to go slow. He said sex is different for him

now and I understand. Like we have to be careful. Like if we join again, it could destroy us in the most beautiful way.

"What's in the box?" I tease him while unlocking my front door.

"When you win a round of strip Uno, I'll let you open it." He kisses my cheek.

But I don't win.

Sitting at my dining room table, I've lost two rounds along with my heels and dress.

I want to keep losing but what's in that box distracts me.

It's big and Tiffany blue with a white bow.

Redix sits across from me, fully clothed and fully amused.

The detective in me can't help it. "There's no Tiffany store in this state. How did you get that present for tonight?"

He grins, dealing our third round. "I've had it for a year and brought it with me this time."

I can't stand it.

Sitting in lingerie in front of him and now he's been planning this?

I don't pick up the cards. "I'm boycotting this game until I open that box."

"That's not the rules."

"I *never* follow the rules."

He tosses his head back. "Jesus, Candy Cade. You never had patience either."

"Yes, I do. I've had it for ten years."

That softens his face. "Okay. No more waiting." He slides the box my way. "For you."

The box is square. I pull the ribbon off and lift the lid to find three smaller boxes inside. They have gift tags on them.

It's his handwriting. I'd recognize it anywhere. He writes in all caps.

"Open them in order."

His voice is gentle, and so are his eyes watching me.

I open the one labeled "PAST". It's the biggest.

When I pull back the tissue, tears fall so fast I can't stop them.

It's the postcards I sent him when I traveled with Dad. He has them wrapped in a purple ribbon.

"You *kept* these?" I choke on air.

He stands up. Steps bring him to his hand reaching for my cheek.

"You kept my heart, and I kept our memories."

I stand up and his lips are on mine. A sob wants to escape my throat but when his tongue meets mine, it goes away. I sigh as it warms me, his gift, his kiss, his body pressing into mine.

"I'm still that same boy, Cade." His lips ghost mine. "The one who wakes up, excited just to see you every day."

"The one who spelled out 'Candy Cade' on Sweetheart candies," I remind him, "for Valentine's and I ate them for you, even though I feared the magic marker would kill me?"

"That one." Love swirls in his eyes. "Open your next gift."

I want him now, but I'm so touched by his gestures, I listen.

He stands behind me, wrapping his arms around me while I open the next box.

"PRESENT" it reads.

I know the shape. The size. The rattle. Yes, it's a box of Lemonheads.

"What's this for?"

His breath steams my ear. *"Tonight."*

A white-hot jolt of lust shoots through me. I hope I know how these will be enjoyed.

"Hurry," he says, "open the last one."

It reads "FUTURE" and it's a necklace box. I open it… and gulp.

It's a gold double-link pendant holding two chains together.

It's elegant in design, like the infinity symbol.

It's sexy in its message, like bondage links.

"Infinity, remember?" he asks making my belly flip as he takes the necklace from the box. "That's what I promised you."

Clasping it around my neck, I'm eighteen again.

We were waiting to buy wedding rings, so he gave me an infinity necklace as a promise.

He swore that's how long he'd love me.

Tragically, the necklace didn't fulfill its promise. It was taken from us that night.

Everything was but this, but us.

"This is my promise to try again with you," he says before kissing my neck with the chain around it.

It's strong and delicate in the same form, like us, and my heart slams in my chest.

He turns my chin. Gentle at first, he kisses me until it's not so tender, his tongue taking me with a fervor that makes me moan into his possession. He presses his forehead to mine.

"Cade Bryant, will you please date me?" He's putting my heart back together. "Again?"

"Yes."

And the pain ends with my exhale.

"You know what I feel for you." His voice strains. "You know what we've been through, and it will fucking overwhelm us if we talk about it, but not tonight. I want us to play. Can we?"

"Yes."

I want it too.

I could cry and hold him for hours at the brutal memories and sweet gifts he's kept wrapped up for so long... but not now.

I need this. *I need him.*

He unhooks the bra he bought me. It falls to the table. Kissing my shoulder blades, his hands graze the slope of my breasts, making my nipples peak.

I stagger into his touch.

"Climb up there now." His command is soft but his pinch of my nipples is hard, sending me into action.

I crawl on top of the table, on all fours, and hungry for this.

"Lie down." The sound of his voice, it's restrained and I'm desperate for what he's holding back. "And *be still.*"

With my breasts pressing against the cool wood, I let my body obey, lying flat on the table.

I trust him. Only him.

He won't hurt me; he'll only cherish me until I'm screaming for more.

But I don't know what to do with my hands until he takes control, lifting them above my head like they're in cuffs.

"Hold them there and don't move."

I turn my head to face him. "Kiss me after every command and then I'll listen."

That's my deal.

I'm not one to fully submit to any man.

He grins, bowing down while I lift my lips for his kiss.

It's gentle, negating his hard commands until he nips my bottom lip and his voice drops...

"This is our new game. Will you let me win?"

"Yes."

Eyeing me, he opens the box of Lemonheads.

I don't say a word, every nerve in my body anticipating this.

The slick surface of the candy barely touches my flesh. He rests it between my shoulder blades. I hold still so it won't roll off while he places a second lower, balanced on my spine. He touches the next against the small of my back and...

Will there be more?

God yes, I almost arch when he lifts the delicate band of my panties and tucks a candy under it, leaving it to savor at the top of my crevice.

I try not to move playing this game but I'm impatient, watching him step back to enjoy the sight of me.

"I told you"—he takes his jacket off—"you're my Candy Cade."

I'm not fighting him.

I just want him on me, in me, taking me, *please, anything*.

When he lifts his T-shirt up—his obliques, his abs—they all flex for my view and I stifle my sigh.

I might as well be cuffed because I dare not move or I'll lose.

He catches me adoring him and the smirk on his face warns he's going to do much more to me.

"I'll go slow with you. Slower than those Marines, and I'll make you feel *more* than enough."

"You know you're more to me."

I lift my chin carefully, asking for his kiss without moving the rest of my body. He lingers his lips over mine.

"Are you mine again, Cade? All mine to eat?"

"Yes," I whisper, and he doesn't tie his hair back.

His strands tickle over my arms to my shoulders as he takes his first treat. The wet heat, the tease of his tongue circling the candy; I'm melting. Gently, his lips lift the first candy from my flesh. The crunch, I can hear his bite while he licks and kisses his way down to the next one.

Thank God, he only played with four because I'm in chaos. And his silence, it's making it more intense. It's part of our game, his fetish and now it's mine too.

The second candy, the tip of his tongue won't stop his torment, his lips so soft, and my skin prickles to his kiss before he eats it. It takes him to the third candy.

I never knew this spot on me, with his lips brushing the small of my back, cascading thrill from my pussy to my toes, it's so sensitive. I almost cry out when he eats the third candy, electricity sparking down to my clit when he returns, kissing my back there again, and again.

I'm going to explode.

I know what's next and when he does it... I'll burst with lust I can't control.

It's soaking my panties. He's had them sopping all night with our first date. And they're useless with my arousal wetting through to my thighs.

I'm waiting, ready, breath held in my lungs... but he doesn't do it.

The candy tucked into my panties is still there, but his kiss isn't.

I gasp when it lands on the back of my thigh instead, his fingertips tickling the same trail up the inside my other leg, stopping just before where I'm screaming for him.

"Redix, *please.*"

It's insanity.

It's lust caged and shaking the bars of my body. "Now!"

I'm going to lose it. He has no idea what I'm capable of now. I can only play for so long before I *will* win.

"You want me, Cade?"

The heat of his mouth is right there, at the apex of every place he needs to be, some part of his body must be inside me, it must take my pussy now.

"Do it or the game is over."

He can hear it in my voice. I can't take anymore.

"Hang on, darlin'."

And he does it, and oh fuck, it's fast, and I cry out.

His tongue darts under my panties, scooping up the candy as he snatches the lace down over my cheeks before he yanks my hips up.

"On your knees," he demands, pulling me closer to him.

I'm open and on all fours with my feet hanging over the edge of the table while he leaves my soaked panties around my thighs.

"Spread for me, Cade, and show me my dessert."

I bow only for him, resting my cheek on the table while my ass is in the air, and damn, he does it.

I hear him pull the chair out to take a seat to dine on me, his fingertip swiping slow down my slit.

"So ready and glazed and puffy for me to eat."

The pleasure is sudden, so intense when his tongue flicks over my sensitive nub.

"Oh God," I gasp as he dives in, his tongue ringing my entrance before dipping in to taste me. It rolls my eyes back with a loud groan. Holy fuck, I'm drenched and I can hear how much with his slurp licking through my aching sex.

The caress of his tongue—its perfection—up and down,

his moaning pace doesn't stop devouring me. I want to cry but he's mastered my body.

No, *he's trained me*, taking me past shock right into a moaning, uninhibited lust.

"Oh my God"—I clench my fists still obeying like they're bound over me—"Redix you feel so fucking good."

The sensation, the strokes of his lips, of his tongue, and then his fingers across my pussy aching for him; it's shaking my legs.

"You're so fucking sweet, Cade."

His palms spread me wider, his tongue swiping over my clit first before plunging in, lapping up my deepest taste; this would be the most decadent death.

Then he does it. His tongue rings slowly over my ass and I bite back a roar while he murmurs, "*So* fucking sweet for me," into my depths.

I'm light-headed. I'm close. "Redix, I need more." I'm in a frenzy only he can help.

His fingers go next. "You need this, Cade?" Three of them pound hard inside and it's brutal and I love it. "You need me rough so you'll come for me?" *Pound.* "So." *Pound.* "Fucking." *Pound.* "Sweet." *Pound. Pound. Pound.* "For only me."

It growls through his voice because it's not a question. It's true as I cry out with his next fierce suck of my clit making me gulp for air and the words, "Oh fuck, yes," before I break.

My legs shake around his face. I clutch my hands and let my climax drop, all the fire in my veins rushing to that one spot he's claiming and cinching hard with his lips. I gulp and let go again, groaning with another spasm over his mouth. With my lips pressed to the table, "Redix," falls over them while I become weak and close my eyes.

"Come here," I hear.

I open them and he's standing by my head.

"Come up here," he says again.

I rise in a haze on shaking knees while he reaches for me, pulling me into a kiss that tastes like my cum and lemon dessert. I love the flavor. He kisses me until my sanity returns, until his lips dust over mine asking, "Where are your toys?"

"What?"

"It's been ten years. I know you have them. Where are they?"

"Second drawer in my nightstand." I'm not embarrassed watching him fetch them. Not after that. Not with what he wants next.

May our games never end.

I roll over on the table and take my panties off. I'm still dizzy but want to play too.

Scooting to the edge, I sit up and spread my legs wide. I can feel my pussy still dripping and glistening with light pulses for his return.

He walks back down the hall wearing only pants and desire.

When he sees me waiting open for him, his eyes drop with his jaw and the words, "Fuck, what I want to do to you."

I see what's in his hand and mine fall too. "Then do it."

He found my dildo.

"Is this what you've been playing with, Cade?" He holds it to my lips. I start licking it, wishing it was him. "You fuck this and think of me?"

"It's too small." I lick the shaft. "It's not as big as the real thing."

"It'll do for now." He takes a seat in front of me. I can

see the real massive thing under his black trousers.

"Show me how you do it," he commands.

I have no shame with him. Desire rules me and I want this.

I climb back up to my knees. I set the flat base of the dildo down on the table and hover, poised over its tip. "We share this, Redix." But I won't take it in. "We share this together or nothing at all."

"Alright." That sets him into motion. He unclasps his pants before lowering his zipper. "You like giving shows? You like watching too?" Reclining back in the chair, he takes his hard cock into his grasp. "Then let's fuck together."

I start my glide down and up, and I feel so dirty, so bad for him and I love it.

"Tell me," he demands, his fist matching my slow tempo. "Tell me what you do alone in your bedroom."

"I get up on my knees like this." I'm going faster now. My fingertips play with my tits. "I tease my nipples like this." I do it without thought because my body knows this private ritual. I'm not going to last. Not with how taboo this feels. Because doing this for him, with his eyes in awe, I'm the one on display but in complete control.

"I fuck this like I fucked you, wishing it was you again."

He stands up, his fist pumping faster over his perfect cock. And it is too long. Too thick. Perfect and too hard and leaking milky drops for me. He's going to lose it too.

"Do you remember how I feel?" He presses his forehead to mine. "How my hard cock drives in and out of your tight, wet pussy? How it tries to resist me? It can barely take all of me but I fuck you anyway and you love it." I'm stammering for breath at the memory, at the sight before me. "Because I do, Cade. I mean it—I jerk off every morning remembering you."

"Oh, God." It's a craze, a mania across my senses, imagining it then and seeing him now. His right hand is pumping over his swollen cock while his left takes my breast, his fingertips twirling over my nipples. "Oh fuck, Redix."

"Goddamn, Cade," he curses back with shaking lips. Mine tremble too.

He takes his hand from my breast and grabs the dildo. It's up to his mouth, his tongue licking the slick of my cum for him off it. The erotic display almost takes me, but he holds onto it and slides it back inside me.

"Ride it," he says, "and fuck it hard like it's me."

I do and I don't stop until I'm there, "Shit," and I'm shaking again. He's thrusting the toy into me, in tempo with the pound of his fist over his thick shaft and I'm done. With one deep groan, I'm swaying and letting the orgasm rip down through me holding onto his stare while he watches my safe destruction.

Redix.

I don't need to say his name aloud.

It's seared across my soul.

"Cade." His body stiffens, hard like a stone. "Only you."

He grabs the back of my neck and I want it too. I drop my mouth fast enough to take his salty spurts across my tongue with his gasps of "yes, yes," and "oh fuck, yes." He groans and more of it shoots across my lips. I love his taste, licking them clean as I lift back up.

"I always think of you," he swears as his hands grab my face, pulling me into our most intimate kiss.

It's our flavor, our truth and I don't know why he wants us like this.

Why he loves these games.

But my heart surrenders in his embrace because I'll never lose if I'm with him.

CHAPTER TWENTY-TWO

REDIX

Dear Candy Cade,

This sucks.

I miss you.

It's been two lonely weeks without you. And this heat-wave, LA in June, it's making it worse. It's like there's no place I can find peace without you.

I hated leaving you too.

We had a great week though.

I love sleeping with you on your couch. It makes you have to lie right beside me so I can hold you all night.

It meant a lot to me, the day we went back to Ms. Ryan's house. We finished replacing the boards on her dock because you've been so good to her, and I will too.

I meant it. I'm taking her to the Golden Globes with me. I'll have my stylist and team spoil her and give her the most incredible night.

Maybe you can come too?

Damn, that'd be incredible.

Like the thousands I spent to get the miniature golf course closed for only us. But it was worth it. Our second date. It was perfect.

Even when you were a smart-ass, giving me a blue golf ball to play with. "Like when we were seventeen," you said.

I know you wore that short dress with no panties on to drive me crazy. Bending over to putt the ball, I kept getting glimpses of your pussy. By the eighteenth hole, yours was so glossy for me.

And you beat me.

And I love it.

I'll lose everything just to see you smile like that.

Just to make you come like that.

When you let me go down on you in that pirate ship when we were done, it was nighttime and no one could see us, which sucks.

Because I can't get enough of your taste. It's like I've been starving and only you can feed me.

That's weird, right?

Then again, you loved it too. Fuck, when I make you come, Cade, you get so wet now, sometimes I can even make you drip. It drives me insane.

When I look up with my mouth on your pussy and see you watching me, I'm gazing at heaven. I see it in your violet eyes. How much pleasure I'm giving you. How I control your entire body with the tip of my tongue.

I know you want all of me.

I do too.

But we can't.

Not ever.

Our games keep you from finding out.

Have you caught on yet? That I won't take my pants off? That I won't fuck you?

I don't know how long I can keep this up because I want you so bad, I'm losing my mind.

But I'll never let anyone see all of me.

Especially you.

Not after what happened.

Like, I had to do a fucking sex scene today (literally) and I hate them.

On screen, a good editor makes it look hot for the audience but for the actors, those of us who aren't pervs, it's not.

I had twenty men standing around me while I had to act like I'm fucking a woman and enjoying it. And I felt sorry for the actor in the scene with me. Emma is super nice. The director wanted her topless with my face in her cleavage. Then he wanted my bare ass pumping into her for the shot.

Thank God we have Intimacy Coordinators now. She backed me up when I stood up for me and for Emma.

It wasn't in the script, and we can shoot that scene under a sheet without us being naked. I don't care if they stick a strapless thong on me.

The director started shouting at me.

"Suck it up, Redix. You'll do those damn BDSM BOUND perfume shots for millions, but not an innocent fuck scene? This is my episode, my vision and you'll do what I say."

I threatened to walk off set. Emma backed me up, so we got our way.

Those photos, Cade?

We'll never live them down, will we?

When people see BOUND perfume, they'll always see us.

And when I smell it, I remember you and that photoshoot.

Yeah, we were only eighteen but didn't look it. Mario Rossi, that man is a crazy designer, in a good way. He put us in black leather. Me in pants and no shirt, and you in a matching skirt and bustier. That's what it's called, right? I don't know, but fuck you looked like sex incarnate.

They slicked our hair back and our bodies down. And then Mario surprised everyone.

He put a collar on me and one on you with a gold chain connecting us.

It didn't look tacky. Or raunchy.

We made it look beautiful.

Because it was.

The photographer ate it up because everyone could tell —we were in love. We were bound together. We were still virgins but the tension was so hot between us, the lens caught it.

How we looked like animals about to mate for life.

We were.

It was only days later when we finally did.

Our parents didn't freak out about those photos but others did.

Remember how our principal threatened to kick us out of school for it? Like we cared. We were graduating in two months.

But Mama G raised holy hell, saying we were legally adults and doing our jobs and that they had no right to punish us.

I still see that picture of us in stores at Rossi counters, almost kissing and chained to each other.

It used to make me so proud and sad at the same time.

Because they gave you hell about that picture, spraying you with cologne in the hall at school.

Their cologne. Those guys. TJ and Gentry.

I've always wondered... if that photo of us is what finally set them off.

CHAPTER TWENTY-THREE

CADE

I TAKE a quiet moment to scope the salon.

The Beauty Hut is owned by Gentry Evans Properties, and I count eight hard-working women I bet he thinks he owns too.

They busy themselves with their clients, mostly tourists I can tell by their sunburns.

Locals know better. We shower in SPF.

When Penny came here the other week, she got nothing but closed lips. Her uniform made them nervous so we're back in plain clothes, getting pedicures while Jameson waits outside in his Jeep. He's still digging for the owners of that liquor store. It lists a holding company, but we want real names.

That's the dots we've connected so far.

The Pelican Bar. Sunset Rentals. The Beauty Hut.

Gentry Evans has ownership in each.

And wherever Gentry is, TJ lurks nearby.

Why they're so close, I've never understood. Maybe they bonded over their sick obsession with me.

"Cat got your tongue?" Penny asks from her chair next to mine.

"No. The Devil demands my attention."

"Which one? Redix Dean?"

"No."

She has every right to worry.

I do too.

I'm not used to having a "boyfriend", especially a hot celebrity one with a wild-boy past who lives thousands of miles away.

"Derek Baucom," I answer. "For a bar manager, he pours nothing but bullshit. I've been to The Pelican twice and he's knee-deep in it."

Both times I interviewed Derek about the victims from that bar, he squirmed. Behind his fake-ass smile and "I never saw those women before" refrain, I can see it.

He's lying.

There's something in his eyes that bothers me too.

Like he's delighted in my presence, like he has something on me but how? He doesn't know me.

His records confirm he just moved here from New York.

And yes, he owns a navy and white striped shirt. He wore it the second time I interviewed him.

Unfortunately, wearing long sleeves in June isn't a crime. Gentry Evans as co-owner of the bar that Derek

Baucom works for? It's not the evidence we need. TJ hanging out at that bar? It's not proof enough either.

I smile, thinking of my running joke with Jameson—they're all leads.

And it's *my deal*.

I'll lead those men into hell with me when I catch them.

"What about your other devil?" Penny asks. "Will he dare to return?"

"We're fine. He's working in LA and I'm working here. At least for a few weeks."

"You don't *sound* fine."

Shit, every time. She knows me too well.

"Yes, I miss him. I confess—Ice Queen Cade Bryant has finally melted for a man."

"You're not an Ice Queen. You're a big softie. And anyone would melt for him. Just don't be one of those women. Don't disappear for a man."

"Oh, I won't."

Because I have two other men I obsess over.

I don't tell her that.

"Excuse me, ma'am? Would you like a manicure too?"

The young woman beside my chair asks so softly I can't refuse. "Sure. Thank you." I offer her my hand.

She starts filing my nails and I notice it. Her hands are shaking. I glance up. Her eyes meet mine and she's not trying to hide it.

She's scared.

And she wants me to know.

"Can you show me where the restrooms are, please?" I ask knowing exactly where they are.

"Yes."

She steps back from the chair, letting me slide orange slippers on as she leads the way.

We turn the corner and walk down a hallway where the restrooms are at the end. She turns around and peeks around my shoulder.

It's clear. No one followed us.

"You're police, right?"

"Yes," I answer, "but we're not here for any of you. I'm here to help another woman."

I know a few of these women are undocumented. Their lives here are so precarious, like hell if I'd do anything *but* protect them.

"My sister." Tears well in her eyes. "She's missing."

"Does she work here?"

"No. She cleans for a rental company that has vacation condos."

"Which one?"

"Sunset Rentals."

That intel drops like a bomb.

It's a mad rush every weekend on this island to clean those rentals after guests leave and before the next group arrives. Those cleaning crews work crazy hard flipping dozens of units in a matter of hours.

I glance up. No cameras are on us, but I see the one by the back door.

"How long has she been missing?"

"Two days," she says. "It's not like her. She went to work and didn't come home. I went there yesterday morning to the office and asked for her. Her manager said she went out with some man after work. No, she didn't. She always comes home to me."

"But you didn't report it because..."

I stop and let her eyes answer me.

Yes, they're both undocumented and completely vulnerable to all kinds of abuse.

"Can you tell me your name?"

"Mai Le."

"And your sister's?"

"Cam Le."

"Do you have a picture of her on your phone?"

"The owner doesn't allow us to bring our phones to work."

Of course Gentry Evans doesn't. What a wicked way to control your staff.

"Tonight. Ten o'clock." I ask her, "Can you meet me at the QuickTrip just over the bridge?"

The security cameras at that gas station don't work. The owner, Ms. Dubois, she hasn't fixed them in years.

"If you can give me her picture," I promise, "I'll try to find her."

Penny, Jameson, all the other deputies, I know they'll help too. We don't give a shit about immigration status. We only want these women safe.

Someone's shuffling behind me in slippers. I whisper to her, "If you can't make it there, I'll be back here tomorrow morning. Okay?"

She nods quietly before darting back down the hall.

My logic fires while Penny and I check out. Before we leave, I quietly ask the staff if any man ever hangs around outside.

Each says no.

Penny glances at me.

We can tell something's up. Once we're back in Jameson's Jeep, I fill them in.

"This is new," I tell them. "Targeting locals isn't the M.O. It's been tourists, the young women visiting so far."

And they all looked like me. But Cam Le is Asian, the first woman who doesn't.

Frustration twists Jameson's face. "There's no way to confirm they're connected."

"They are," I insist. "I can sense it. And it all has to do with Gentry Evans."

"I agree," Penny chimes up from the back seat. "It's no coincidence."

"I'll back you up tonight." Jameson drives toward the office.

Penny has to go home but we'll keep her in the loop.

All day my brain is full, and my phone is empty. Redix doesn't call or text. I'm not worried.

I'm working and so is he.

By nine-thirty, I'm raging with impatience. Jameson and I are parked on the far end of the parking lot at the Quick-Trip, waiting for Mai Le from the salon to appear.

I'm staring at the lights illuminating the sliding glass doors of the convenience store, willing her to arrive.

Jameson's tapping on his phone and then I hear it, his tell—he clears his throat.

"What?" I ask.

"Nothing." He flips his phone over on his thigh.

"What? Get a hot sext?"

"Drop it, Bryant."

"Jesus, what's got you ill as a hornet?"

He turns his glare toward the driver's window. I can see anger dripping from his face in the reflection.

"You're scaring me, Jameson. What is it?"

"Fuck," he mutters, "I don't want to do this."

"Do *what*?"

I've never seen him this mad, not even at a crime scene.

"This." He turns his phone back over and taps the screen. "I'm sorry"—he shows me the image on it—"but he's an *asshole*."

My ears start ringing. My fingers go numb.

It's Redix and Angie on Instagram, holding hands over dinner on some outdoor LA restaurant patio.

My world flips. My eyes look away from the pain and can't find focus. *They're supposed to be over.* I heard Redix call Angie myself.

I can't think past it, past the deception.

It makes me want to scream.

"I'm sorry, Bryant." Jameson sounds a mile away. "It posted an hour ago. I'd rather it be me to show you than some random dick."

Everyone knows. That photo of Redix and me at the golf resort splashed all over the local papers and social media and press and fans went apeshit.

The famous BOUND perfume couple, our local star-crossed young lovers, they're back together.

I don't care. I'm so numb to that stuff, it doesn't faze me. The guys at work making dumbass jokes. My neighbors asking me where Redix is.

I've been too happy to care.

Now, I exhale happy and inhale horror.

He did it again.

Redix Dean lost my heart and all his chances.

"I'm fine."

I focus back on the front glass doors.

Mai Le is standing there by the corner of the building. I jump out and focus my anger on at least helping her.

Mai texts me the picture of her sister, Cam. I jot down all the notes. Where Cam was last seen. Where she likes to go. Eat. Shop. All of it. She shares what she knows of Cam's coworkers and the friend who usually gives her a ride to the island.

Once I'm done and say goodbye to Mai, I need something, anything, so I dash inside the store for my only relief.

Candy.

"Ms. Dubois"—I try to refocus, talking to the owner behind the counter—"you ever gonna fix your cameras?"

I'm glad tonight that she didn't. I didn't want Mai on camera. Nothing to expose her to even more risk.

"You and your mama." Ms. Dubois cracks a grin. "Y'all worry about me too much. I'm fine. I don't need no cameras when I got this." She pats the counter. Her shotgun is underneath it. *More power to her.* "You have a good night, sweetheart. And you send your mama my prayers, alright?"

"Yes, ma'am. I will."

Her kindness is a temporary relief from my shock, flashes of that picture of Redix and Angie firing across my mind.

Opening a bag of Skittles—because fuck Lemonheads now—I'm looking down as I walk out of the sliding doors and bump right into another force.

"Easy there, Sergeant."

That voice ruins my life more.

I have to rein it in, every ounce of strength I have to act like I'm not ready to murder someone in two seconds.

Because I am.

His hand on my hip makes it justifiable.

"TJ." The smile on my face is as fake as a beauty queen's tan. "Fancy seeing you here tonight."

"Just grabbing some smokes."

Fuck, he reeks of it and cologne. A gag grabs my throat while I glance past him.

Jameson's clocking our every move while TJ commands, "I'll grab a six pack and you'll join me."

This man is obsessed, powerless to stop himself. He's after me like my shadow, my dark hell.

"I'm on duty." I wink. "Some other time."

"You owe me a good time, remember?"

The yellow tobacco stains on his teeth; I gag again.

"Oh, I remember."

The pen in my back pocket? It'd look so good stabbed in his right eye. Or left. They're both on my tits.

His nose lifts.

"You don't smell like me tonight. Did you throw away my gift because you're back with *him*?"

Evil bends his eyes, his pupils carving over my cleavage.

God, he's twisted.

"I'm not back with anyone." That was about Redix and painfully true.

"You behave tonight," I say, really, I pray as I turn around and walk across the parking lot.

Normally, eyes on my body, I can feel them and don't care.

I've been eye-fucked and gawked at all my life.

But TJ's glare? It's more foul than the stench of the putrid dumpster in June I'm walking past.

"You know TJ?" Jameson asks when I plop into the passenger seat.

The entire Sheriff's office knows TJ.

He's a local, legal legend. Drugs being his most notorious offense. But somehow TJ keeps walking free out of every courtroom. Must be nice having Senator Gentry Evans as your best friend.

"Yeah. We went to high school together."

Jameson can't know more.

Or what happened.

Or what's next.

"His prints were on that lighter we found at the scene," Jameson says. "We got him on camera smoking there hours before Kayla was found."

"Believe me"—I pop a green apple Skittle in—"that may not be the evidence you need yet, but TJ is wicked like Gentry. One is just more high-class about it."

And TJ comes here at ten to buy smokes every night, I note.

While Jameson drives us back across the bridge, I fill him in on the details Mai Le shared. I text him and Penny the photo of her missing sister, and the other deputies on shift too.

If I can focus on helping these women, I don't think about the crush of my heart, the burn in my throat that wants to cry.

No.

This isn't about me.

CHAPTER TWENTY-FOUR

CADE

Hot Blooded by New Constellations

JAMESON and I search all night.

We take a break, a few hours to sleep and then meet before dawn and start searching again. We comb the island for every location Cam Le has been.

We can't find her.

Once Sunset Rentals opens, I take the lead.

Jameson interrogates like the Boston mafia. That doesn't work around here.

You use soft words and a sharp mind in the South.

I find Cam's crew mate, the one the office manager said cleaned the last condo with Cam.

When I ask what happened next, the woman's eyes shift, scared. "She went out with some man."

"Did you know him?"

"No. He picked her up from the unit."

"What did he look like?"

"I couldn't see him."

"What kind of car?"

"A white one. That's all I remember."

The woman looks terrified. I can't bring myself to scare her more. Besides, I know she won't tell me, too much is at risk for her.

"Those units down on Forest Beach Drive they were cleaning," I tell Jameson in the car, "see if they have surveillance of the parking lot. We need to find that white car."

Jameson nods. He's way too skilled at this by now. It's noon and we've burned through every location used by Cam Le with no leads but that white car.

There's nothing left to do until we get that footage.

We both hate it.

I'm in a swirl of thoughts when Jameson asks, "You okay, Bryant?"

I know what he's really asking about.

"Yeah. I'm fine. He says it's old. That the picture was taken two months ago."

Jameson huffs.

I don't know if I should believe Redix either.

It's like he's been caught red-handed and is blowing up my phone, guilty.

Thousands of miles away and Redix can fuck up and I'd never know.

Women or liquor or drugs. Or all three.

I hate this feeling. Vulnerable. Anxious. I'm walking on eggshells, waiting for him to crack and break us both.

Because yes, I love him, but I'm not dumb. Redix has proven what he's capable of.

He's texted and called all last night and this morning, leaving me messages. I checked them but I don't answer.

I don't think I should yet.

I don't know if I can trust him. Or me. I'm a live wire inside, ready to touch something and explode into flames so it's best men stay clear.

Except my dad.

I'm reluctant to keep my fishing date with him because I want to work this case, but Jameson reminds me we're in a holding pattern.

I don't even go home to change. I just leave my duty belt and gun locked in my trunk, needing a few hours on the water.

"Y'all two"—Dad casts his line an hour later—"you know I love you both, but I don't know if y'all can ever work this out."

We share the same doubts about me and Redix.

Usually, Dad and I don't talk much. We're happy quietly casting our lines for some cobia fish and drinking beer.

Today, I don't need to say a word either.

Dad knows Redix and I are trying to heal. And he knows the look on my face when it hurts.

"Well," I finally answer, "I know you can love someone but that doesn't mean you're meant to be with them."

Dad nods.

I'm talking about me and Redix... and my parents.

I know my parents still love each other.

I've caught Dad leaving Mama's several early mornings when he thought no one was watching. Especially lately with Mama not feeling well.

It's none of my business what's going on between them. I'm just relieved there is a 'them' to have.

"He does love you." Dad casts his fly again. "He fought like hell for you and that's why I love him too. That's why I forgave him for leaving."

"You're never going to tell me, are you?"

Dad knows more than me about that night. And though I begged for the first few years, he never cracked and told me.

"It ain't my place to tell anyone else's pain." His answer stays firm. "That's for y'all to work out. God love ya if you can."

"He doesn't want to talk about it. Then. Or now."

"He had to fix himself," Dad says. "You did too, and you can fight for yourself now."

That I know.

And when Dad flicks his eyes over to mine, it's like he knows just how much of a fight rages in my soul.

"Magnolia, you listen to me." That name. That tone. Jeff Bryant is not to be ignored. "What happened to you two. Y'all might not ever get justice, but you need to find some peace."

"I'd rather have the justice."

"Careful there." Dad's dark blue eyes, they hold a world of truth, of a pain he already knows. "'Justice for all' also means for the one who delivers it too."

Dad's words and last hug won't leave me. They wrap around me all the way home.

Everything else in me feels hollow. Snapping my duty

belt in the trunk back on, my stomach growls. My heart withers. Even my head rattles, empty.

I don't know what to think.

That's why it takes me a second to register the odd smell when I open my front door.

Pizza?

"Mama?" I call out.

But instinct has my hand on my holster, unsnapping my 9mm.

I always suspect. TJ. Gentry. Some sick fuck.

How long until one comes after me again?

They all know where I live.

And I'll never shake that memory, the one of TJ grabbing my wrist, of him taunting Redix, "Watch, pretty boy, while I make her suck my ice cream cone."

It shivers evil around my soul.

It has the ridges of my gun handle under my palm. I'm pulling it out, index finger finding the trigger.

I can do this, lightning fast...

"It's me." His huge silhouette steps out of the kitchen into my line of sight.

"Fuck!" My shoulders drop, so does my breath. "I almost shot you! What the fuck are you doing here?"

"I got on the first flight." Redix looks as shocked as me with his eyes on my gun. "You won't answer my calls or texts, so you left me no choice."

"No, it's *my* choice." I snap my gun back in. "If I want to talk to you, I'll answer the phone. Otherwise, this is stalking. Breaking and entering. Again. This isn't some romance story making it seem cute. This shit is scary. How'd you like it if you were pissed at me, and I showed up at *your* house, uninvited?"

"You're pissed at me?"

"Hell yes, I'm mad."

"Why?" His large body fills my small foyer. "I told you those pictures are old. They were taken of us at The Ivy in April. Paparazzi take them and use them later when they need the cash."

He steps closer, his eyes scanning my tense body.

I'm still on guard.

"You don't trust me yet, do you?"

"I trust the boy I rode bikes with. The boyfriend who held my hand on the bus. The one who used to dance with me on the beach. And then he left for ten years without a word.

"I don't know if I can trust the Redix Dean who came back. The celebrity who got so wasted he was caught at the Golden Globes with Jenna Anderson giving him a blowjob."

"I mean it, Cade." He's even closer, the smell of him overpowering the dinner he cooked for us. "We're back together and I'm not leaving you again."

"You're back in my life like a whirlwind and I just gotta hang on because I know it won't last. You always leave."

That shakes his head. "Yes, I have to go to work, for weeks to some bullshit location but I'm coming back to you, and I'll be faithful while I'm gone."

"Redix, how can I trust your words when your actions have shown me otherwise? Nine years of fucking up can't be erased by one year of getting it right. Not yet."

It hurts us for me to say it, but we're not kids anymore, or teens in naïve love.

It's the truth, as painful as it is.

And we've been through too much to deny it.

"You're right." His hands surrender. "I was fucked up for a long time and now I gotta earn your trust again. No more breaking and entering. No more stalking. It's your choice and I'll respect it."

He slowly searches my eyes saying, "Just please know, I never left you. I just had to find me again, but I couldn't for a long time because I found a bottle instead. But I swear, *I'm back now.*"

There's a depth to him few can see.

They can't get past his stunning facade to see his pain, but I always could.

It matches mine in the most hellish way.

"It's okay," I sigh.

"No, it wasn't okay. But I swear we will be now."

It happens too fast.

How I soften for his sheepish grin. How he always clowns for me. How he holds his wrists out for me to cuff them.

"Though I'd love for you to arrest me with those hand-cuffs. You look hot as hell."

I'm not hot. I'm relieved.

I touch the cuffs. "These aren't for play."

"You wanna bet?"

He's on me in two steps, his lips colliding with mine. His hand wraps around my neck pulling me in with no escape.

And I love his prison.

Tracing his tongue over my bottom lip, his moan is low, his grind into me hard. It forces mine while my tongue meets his.

Trust, joy, lust, every emotion wants to flood me when he walks me back against the wall, our bodies begging for the heat of the other. The force of his desire, of all his muscles, it traps me without restraint.

I grab the back of his neck and kiss him back, searching

for the soul I love inside him, stirring memories of every sensuous moment we shared and demanding many more.

"Jesus, Cade," he says into my mouth before he pulls back, dragging his thumb over the seam of my lips. "An airplane could crash land on your lips and all would survive. Goddamn, you're my rescue. Every. Fucking. Time."

Matching his awe, I rip open his short sleeve shirt. Buttons fall to the floor and he only grins. My lips are on his neck, my tongue wandering down to his hard pecs as they flex at my touch.

God, the flavor of him, it dominates like his seductive smell. I need more. He moans when I suck his nipple, telling me he does too.

"I want to taste you"—I start dropping to my knees, my hands on the button of his jeans—"every fucking drop of you."

I'm salivating for him. Yes, only he can fill this hunger...

"Cade, stop." He suddenly grabs my elbow, halting my descent.

It's quick. The frustration. The confusion. The hurt.

I rise back up. "Why can't I?"

He steps back. "I'm not—"

"Trust, Redix." I gently grab his hand. "We have to trust each other. That means *you* trust me too. And I want to. I want you so much and it's not fair. All those other women had you. And I let you have me like you wanted. When is it my turn?"

He does it, that gesture that sings the saddest song—tucking his long hair behind his ear.

"Cade, my God, I want you too. Believe me. Look." He grabs his cock. It's straining hard and ready under his jeans. "It's just..."

His eyes dart away.

"I'll never hurt you." I reach for his cheek. "And you'll never hurt me. Not if we do this together."

It hits me so hard; tears suddenly fall.

"We heal together. It's the only way."

He won't look at me. "I don't want to hurt you that way."

"You won't hurt me. I trust you with this. You're the only man I trust to touch me. The only one I can let go with."

He exhales, meeting my eyes. "It's gotta be my way."

"So far, I love your way." I smile, my body swearing it too. "There's whipped cream in the fridge for *your way*."

His smile back soothes my every edge while he insists, "Take the pizzas out of the oven while I shower first."

"You're ruining the romance."

"No." His next kiss is so right. "An oven fire ruins the romance."

He's only a few minutes while I set the pizzas out to cool. I hope they're frozen again by the time I'm done with Redix tonight. I only want to devour him.

Especially how he looks walking down my hallway. He's back in jeans while his hair hangs in long wet ropes I'd gladly hang my neck in.

"Let me take a shower too."

"Ok. I'll wait."

"No, you'll watch me."

Something in me fears he'll bolt the second I disappear into my room. Besides, it turns me on even more. Letting him lean against my bathroom vanity while he watches me through the shower glass enclosure.

When I turn the shower off, he's at the door, pulling it open and dropping to his knees.

"Let's make you dirty again," he insists, slinging my wet leg over his shoulder.

"You want to taste me tonight?" I lace my hands through his damp strands. "You want my candy, Redix?"

Need weighs his eyes down looking up at me.

"Yes."

"Only if I get to taste yours too."

He agrees, burying his face between my legs, his tongue slurping up shower water and my desire. Fuck, I've missed him. I roll my hips, sliding over his mouth, his nose diving in deep.

He groans when I clench his hair, controlling my glide over his face.

"Is it sweet?" Looking down, I marvel at his show. "Is my pussy sweet on your mouth?"

"Fuck yes," he murmurs back before his fingers thrust in hard. "Come on." He curls them deep inside. They're so fucking long like everything else on him that they're doing it again, that new insanity I crave, the one he floods my body with.

"Drip it down my hand, Cade."

I lean into his pressure, grabbing the back of his head for balance, for more of this thrill, and we both moan at his suffocation. I lose my mind to his touch, letting it shred the breath from my lungs when I scream out for him. Shaking, the lush frazzle of my orgasm comes over his face. I moan and drip again when I hear his bellow into my tender flesh.

Grabbing the glass door, I'm going to collapse. I need to lie down, to revel in this amazing demise while it leaves my body, but I won't.

I need his pleasure too, more than my own.

"Redix," I huff. "Please."

He stands up, wrapping his arm around me to replace

my depleted strength, but also to pull me into his favorite kiss. The one that tastes like me. I let him take my mouth next until I feel my legs again.

"It's your turn," I sigh, "however you want but we do this together."

Pressing his forehead to mine, a silence holds him. I'm scared he'll change his mind.

"On your bed," he finally says.

He's demanding my trust too.

But I'm ready.

Only he's allowed in my heart, in my bed. It's been my sanctuary all these years but now... he is.

The white bedspread barely sinks when I turn and sit on the edge of it.

Standing steps away, the wild look in his eyes, I know he wants this. Pressed underneath his jeans, his cock is hanging hard for it.

"Lay in the middle." He pauses. "On your back with your head on a pillow and spread your legs for me."

I obey.

Why I'm spreading my thighs I don't know until he opens my nightstand. He takes out my most indulgent purchase. It's purple, made to thrust inside while there's a dual flutter tongue on it. It was expensive but with forty-four settings? Nope, it's priceless.

He studies it for a second before pressing a button. It's obvious what he can do to me with it.

But not what I get to do to him.

I wait, refraining from any demands as he makes his, "We only do this if you're getting pleasure too."

I nod, watching him climb my way.

Redix back here with me, beside me on my soft bed, it's

almost too much. The tenderness of it. The vulnerability it creates.

He knows it, crawling to kneel beside my head, he can see it in my eyes so he asks again, "Are you sure?"

My mouth is watering. "Yes."

"No hands, okay? Let me be in charge."

"Okay." I've never felt so safe and so exposed at the same time.

The low hum of my toy fills the room. He tickles it, teasing it around my pussy and gauging my reaction.

My lips part at the pleasure—both pairs—opening with the need.

Watching his hand unbutton his jeans, I'm rapt by the sight. I swallow, ready for his full reveal. Pushing his jeans down his thighs, my heart stammers at his proud erection springing free, and at our tattoo, inches away from it.

Our tattoo.

I see his eyes take in mine too. Something flashes across them while I can't stop my hips from rolling for his gaze, for the toy he's teasing through my sex.

"Remember," he insists. "No hands."

I obey while he leans forward, and I turn my head for the fat crown of his cock inches from my lips. Watching my wonder, he thrusts the toy inside me and clicks it twice, making me groan and lift my hips off the bed.

"You want this, don't you, Cade?" God, the intensity in his eyes.

"Yes." I don't care if it's a beg. It is. "I want to suck your cock, Redix."

"Gimme that tongue and lick it first." The words drip from his mouth in that bourbon voice. He likes saying it as much as I crave hearing it. "Lick my cock, Cade," and I can't wait anymore.

My tongue darts out, meeting the seam under his sensitive tip for the first time in so long and we shake, our bodies shuddering at the reunion.

He stammers, "Damn, you feel good."

His taste, it's on the tip of my tongue, early drops of him within minutes of me licking and circling his tip, before dragging the point of my tongue down to his base and back.

My hips match the circling dance of my tongue, desperately seeking the satisfaction he's holding back with the tease of my toy.

"You want more, don't you?"

My eyes are open to his question, to his heft hovering over my mouth. This pillow cradles my head at the perfect place to worship him from below.

My God, he's divine. His cock is so hard while his face, it's laced with desire fighting care.

"Yes."

It's my favorite word to give him. I spread my thighs wider and open my mouth even more.

"Take more of me." Is that his permission or a command? "As much as you can."

I turn my head and body to the side, keeping my legs open for the toy, for his play through the lips of my soaking sex.

He lets me do it. Craning my neck, opening my mouth, I take all I can of his massive cock into my mouth.

"Oh fuck!" he groans, flinching back from my pursuit, from my throat taking him more. I want him so much, but he pulls back.

"Gimme a second." His breath is staggered. "Fuck, I'm so sensitive, I swear I'm gonna come in your mouth."

"I want you to come in my mouth." I challenge his eyes. "I want you to fuck my mouth so hard until I can taste my tears and your cum tingling down the back of my throat."

His eyes darken.

That look in them, I relish it.

He grabs the back of my head with his free hand, pulling me closer, positioning my mouth at the perfect angle.

With three more clicks of my toy, I cry out when he thrusts it into my pussy before holding it there tight, buried inside me while the flutter tongue on it indulges my clit with a maddening buzz. It's a frenzy over my nerves, inside and out, and pushing me to the edge.

"Say it again." His dripping tip is at my lips. "Say what you want, Cade."

I have no shame. No patience. No fear with him.

"Fuck my throat, Redix, as hard as you can until you come in it."

With a groan, he does it with abandon. I gasp for air and he's delicious. I can't stop moaning over his shaft, over the drips of my spit that he's dragging from my mouth over my lips and down my chin with his ceaseless pump. Controlling the back of my head, he's lost in the sight, in the pleasure of this. I'm watching him and he's watching me, making us crave even more.

"You're so beautiful, Cade." His hips thrust and I can't take his full length, but I relax my throat until we hear that *gluck*, that sweet suck of my lips, of my throat as full as I can be of him. "You're so fucking beautiful with my big cock in your mouth."

It's a tease, taunting me at my edge. It's also his truth. I can see it in his eyes, in his ask, "You love this, don't you? You love being a dirty girl for me." The doubling, the taste of him, the warm press of his hand holding the toy inside me like a damn circus of pleasure performing in my pussy; I'm going to come so hard.

"That's it." And he's watching it. "Dance that wet pussy over your toy while you make me come in your hot, tight throat."

I can see him. Taste him. I love him.

I can't take my eyes off him while gentle tears fall from their corners because I want this.

Because his thighs are shaking. His lush lips fall open. His sky eyes look into mine while they witness this—his fuck of my mouth until I feel the swell of him against my lips. He's going to take me with him.

"Come on, Cade." He sees it, demanding, "Let that sweet pussy come with my cock coming in your throat."

My scream, it's muffled by his mass and his loud growl. My eyes are open but it's blinding. "Yes!" He groans, his shaft pulsing over my lips while my orgasm, it bucks me against his hand and the toy. Quaking at the taste of him, warm and salty, "Fuck!" he shoots more down my throat, making me spasm again with our pleasure.

He's trembling on his knees before my face, and I don't know the sudden look on his. He pulls out of my mouth, pulling the toy out of me too.

"It's okay." I barely utter, "We're okay," as he yanks his jeans back on but doesn't button them.

He lies down beside me, searching my eyes, holding my cheek in his hand. "You're okay?"

"Yes."

Worry weighs his eyes. "You sure?"

"More than okay." I tilt my lips for his, reaching for his face too. "I'm hungry for more."

He takes me in a kiss with a chuckle, unafraid to swirl his tongue through his taste in my mouth. That only makes me desperate for another meal of him but the buzzing between my thighs stops us.

He lifts away and grins, grabbing the toy from the bed. "How do you turn this thing off? It has more buttons than the space shuttle."

He's almost not wrong.

I grab it, laughing and clicking the combo to turn it off. "Well, it does rocket me to the moon and back."

"How can my cock ever compete with tech like that?"

That stops my laugh, my eyes finding his gaze, assuring him, "Nothing compares to you, and no one ever will."

Devouring pizza minutes later, I'm still right.

He's more delicious.

CHAPTER TWENTY-FIVE

REDIX

Dear Candy Cade,

Sometimes when I see our future, I fear it.

Other times, I can't live without the hope of it.

Because for twenty-four hours I thought I lost you. I saw that damn post of Angie and me, and I knew it would hurt you.

I about lost my shit. You weren't answering my texts and calls, so I dropped everything to fix it. I told my manager I had a family emergency and I didn't show up to set. I've never done that before but fuck it.

You <u>are</u> my family, Cade.

Like I've always felt protective over my mom and little

sister too. I was the "man of the house" from a young age. Even my modeling money supported us.

But you're a different kind of family.

You're the one I chose.

You're the one more like me than anyone.

You've always been a gift my heart wraps around to protect.

Eric couldn't get me a charter flight home fast enough, so I had to fly commercial.

And coach.

No, my ass ain't too precious to fly coach.

It's too famous.

I had every passenger around me wanting selfies and snapping pics of me when I just wanted to close my eyes and pray you'd give me another chance.

I get it. I won't pop up in your life like that again. Hell, you almost shot me so that'll teach me.

But we worked it out. We always did because yeah, we've had our fights. You have a temper and I have no filter.

That's a hot mess right there.

Remember the fight we had over senior prom? I asked you to go with me. (That would've been our first real date.)

But you said no. That TJ and Gentry would ruin it for us.

At first, I was like, "Fuck 'em," and got mad at you for not going with me.

Those boys had been calling me names for years. From "pretty boy" to "model ass" to every gay slur in the book. By the time we were seniors, I was bigger than both of them.

I didn't worry about them.

I should've.

I think deep down you knew they were a threat.

You get that from your parents. You're a born detective. You can smell guilt a mile away.

But I was determined to have our prom.

So I rented a tux but didn't wear the shirt or shoes.

I showed up at your mom's with pink tulips. Some bloomed at the house where our bus stop was, and you used to say how you loved them so I cut a few from the yard. (Sorry, Ms. Parker).

I told you to put on a dress.

I didn't <u>ask you</u>, so by your rules, it wasn't a date.

But you finally stopped fighting me. You wore a white dress. I remember because you almost looked like my bride in it.

I hoped you would be.

I still do.

Our parents helped me. Our moms put lit candles in jars in a circle on the beach for us. They left a picnic basket too. And your dad hooked me up with some champagne and a speaker for my iPod.

I even got a wrist corsage for you. No magnolias, I told the florist. And it was small.

I know you think big shit is tacky.

When you saw the glowing candles in a circle like our own dance floor, it made you cry.

God, you're so beautiful like that.

When you're not pissed and trying to right some wrong, you give me your heart and it's like I'm holding a tiny bird in my hands. Delicate. Trusting.

You danced with me on that dark beach. We had it to ourselves and you kissed me, swearing it was better than any prom could be.

It was.

Our song played. I knew it would be the seventh on my playlist.

I got on one knee and proposed to you with "Chasing Cars" playing for us and fuck, you saw it… yeah, I had a few tears too.

People told us eighteen was too young.

Yeah, I agree for most.

But we were never like most, Cade.

The world shut us out from a young age, treating us like a beautiful circus sideshow to gawk at and we found each other in that loneliness. I always hated it. I never felt comfortable in it.

You're the only one who knows how it feels for me. When people want me, when they come after me.

Because they come after you too.

Everyone always took from us, but we only gave to each other, so much friendship and love.

I gave you that necklace, the infinity one that night.

And I will, Cade.

I will love you for infinity.

Because life is too small. It's too short to contain us. It never could.

You got to wear that necklace for a month. It was our happiest.

You think you lost it that night. You didn't.

I know who has it.

So <u>fuck him.</u>

I bought you a new one. I'm watching you sleep beside me and it's around your neck.

You look like an angel, you know?

Like when you're awake, your violet eyes are so intense, your beauty is too much.

What are those mythical women called? ~~Syrens?~~ No.

Sirens. Women who sound so beautiful they lure men to their death.

Yep, that's you.

But not with me.

You bring me to life.

I know how soft you really are. Like your heart. Like this bed. I'm honored to be here. I know why you don't trust men.

So when you sleep beside me like this, it's like you're an angel, only trusting me to protect you.

Because you know I will.

But when I look at you like this, after what we did tonight, I don't know what to do.

Or what can be next.

I love you, Cade.

But if we don't stop, that may be the most evil thing I ever do.

CHAPTER TWENTY-SIX

CADE

"You're going where?"

It's not like I report to Penny but we're a team and I owe her the update.

"I'm going to New York. I'm on a private jet Redix booked for me and they let you use your phone."

It takes Penny a second.

I don't blame her.

I've never taken a day off, except for family leave to help Mama. So I've banked over three months of vacation time and never planned on using it.

Plans change.

"Why New York? Why not LA where he lives?"

This'll knock her socks off. I can't believe it myself.

"Because I agreed to do a photoshoot with him and he's meeting me there."

Here it comes...

"A what? A fucking photoshoot? Are you a cop or a cover girl?"

There's no anger in her voice. Only shock.

"It's the ten-year anniversary of BOUND, the perfume ad we did. The designer, Marco Rossi, he's releasing its companion fragrance, FREE. He booked Redix for the new campaign—"

"And he talked you into doing it with him."

Now she sounds miffed.

"Sorta." The Atlantic sparkles outside my window. "He cut a deal with Marco and got him to pay us two hundred and fifty thousand each. Redix is donating his to his crisis centers and I'm gonna pay off all my mama's medical bills and donate the rest too."

"And the promise of a hot fuck in Manhattan has nothing to do with this?"

I wish.

Redix and I still haven't fucked, made love, whatever we want to call it.

He had to leave early the next morning after his surprise visit, leaving me hungry for much more and he's been gone for two weeks since.

"Look. It's the July Fourth holiday and I've worked every single one of them for six years. We're at a stalemate on our missing woman case and hitting our heads against a brick wall on the others. This is three days of me taking a break before I snap and heads roll."

"Okay, okay." Penny relents. "I get it. I'm losing my mind too at the progress we're *not* making."

"When I get back, next weekend, I'm babysitting. You've got enough milk stored and I want my goddaughter all weekend while you and Hank do God will only know what to each other. I'll even use this money and book y'all a suite somewhere. Deal?"

"Hell yes, that's a deal. I got no guilt over Redix Dean and his money spoiling me."

"It's *my* money."

"It was *his* deal." Penny's coming around quick. "What else is gonna be *his* by the end of this trip? Are you gonna come back Mrs. Dean?"

The mention of that? Of a future that far from now with Redix?

I can't see it.

I can't see past *my* deal.

The one I made with God. It's all I've focused on for years.

I gave up wedding plans for an event much more momentous.

But can I change?

With the way I'm feeling about Redix again? With every sweet thing he does, big and small?

I know he's feeling this too.

Nothing but a vast ocean is in my view... and ten victims... and one missing woman... and Pamela gone... and two broken souls if you count me and Redix.

No.

For their sake... I can't change.

"I'd like to come back laid for now," I answer Penny.

"New York and modeling? I'm not jealous about that," Penny says. "But if you finally get to fuck Redix Dean? Girl, I'd walk barefoot over hot pavement to New York City for that man. And my God when I got there—I'd ride him like the Kentucky Derby."

I snort the champagne I'm sipping. "I'll buy you the big hat."

"One with lots of feathers because, oh my, how I'd tickle his ass too."

His ass. His body. I'm dying for every naked inch of him.

I don't know why he's so shy, but I haven't seen or touched all of him yet. I'm in pain for one more time with him.

It makes me throw the rest of my champagne back.

"Feathers. Leather. Chains. I don't care." I lower my voice as the attendant comes by to refill me. "You have no idea how bad I need him."

"Yes, I do. You've tried hiding it all these years but you suck at it. You know I *caught* you one time."

"Caught me?"

I lift the full glass of bubbles to my lips.

"You were at your desk looking at your phone. The look on your face, I thought something was wrong with your mom. But when I came over to ask if you were okay, I saw what was on your screen. It was Redix and that video of him fucking that woman like a dog in a parking lot."

Another big sip of champagne cools the sudden burn in my throat.

All those videos of him, all the times he got caught fucking around. His fans and the press think it's funny. It's part of the sexy, rebel mystique of Redix Dean.

It's a myth.

That's not him.

I can see it in his eyes in those videos. That's what hurts

so damn much. It's not him in that body. He's lost in whatever drunk or high he's on.

"I know how much you love him, Cade." Penny's tone warms. "That's why I worry—you'd do anything for him."

"I'd kill for him," I mutter, trapped in that thought.

I didn't mean to say it aloud.

Penny laughs. "Just remember if he hurts you—"

"I know. I know. You'll kill him first."

By the time the plane lands in New York, I might have a slight buzz. I change and refresh on the plane. I'm woozy as a chauffeur drives me to dinner. Redix is meeting me there.

The maître d' at Le Coucou combs his eyes, from my heels, up to my black silk Gucci slip dress, to find my soft smile. It hides my sudden nerves.

Do I fit in? It's been ten years. For me and this dress. Isn't it vintage by now?

I shouldn't give a shit but I'm back in old territory of the discerning eyes of SoHo nightlife.

The maître d' winks. "I'm a big fan. BOUND is still my fragrance." I exhale... and want to hug him but just wink back. "Your *date* is waiting on you, ma'am. He wanted me to be *very sure* I called him that."

I can't help it; I'm laughing as I follow him to our table.

When Redix stands to greet me in his black sharkskin two-piece suit with no shirt underneath in front of the entire restaurant, I relish it.

Because under the warm glow of the huge candelabras above, his eyes soften with his lips and the gentle kiss he gives me.

Enough to be discreet.

Enough to declare it to the world.

We're together.

"Damn, darlin'." He pulls the chair out for me. "You're ready for the runway again looking like that."

No, I'm not. I don't want that life. But I want this. A romantic dinner with him.

Maybe... a new life too.

"I bet your parents are having a shit-fit that you're up here with me again."

He's delighted by that concept before sipping his seltzer.

"They love you, and you eat it up. Hell, I think my dad loves you more than me."

"That's impossible. But he *likes* me more than he does you."

"Shut up."

I toss a little piece of my baguette at him with a smile. It's probably true.

"You remember how he caught me stealing his expensive whiskey for us? I filled his bottles back up with tea like an idiot, like he wouldn't taste it. He never did whoop my ass for that."

"You got me there."

"I should've known I had a problem then."

"What? With whiskey?"

"No." His bad-boy smirk tingles my thighs. "... with doing anything for you."

I'm dazzled. Gazing back at him, I bite my lip and want to crawl across this table and kiss that adoring smirk off his face.

I don't get the chance because a woman appears by our table side instead.

"Redix! I want a selfie with you!"

Her lips keep moving after she barks. Yep, she's had too much wine.

"Excuse me, ma'am." Fury skyrockets through my veins. "We're trying to enjoy our dinner. *Alone.*"

"Don't be a bitch," she slurs. "I just want him."

A phone is in her hand. A fuck is in her eyes for Redix. And the dinner guests next to us are equally annoyed.

The napkin in my lap lands on the table with my toss.

"You'll get your selfie with him when you show me your invitation."

"*Cade?*" Redix watches. "*Darlinnn?*" He's amused.

"What invitation?" she asks, swaying inches below my rising tower.

"The one that invites me to kick your ass *after* you do."

She snaps her neck. "You don't own him!"

I step in front of Redix, blocking her. "Like a gun I do." It's a rush I can't stop to protect him, even from a drunk pain-in-the-ass holding a Coach bag.

"Alright, ladies."

Redix jumps up, wrapping his hand around my waist and pulling me into his embrace.

"Ma'am, if you want a picture of me then she's in it too."

She glares at us before storming off. The maître d', the sweet one, he's right behind her and sweeping her out the door.

"Sorry, folks." Redix politely waves his hand, announcing to the open room of dinner guests, "Dessert is on me." Then he whispers in my ear, "And you, because fuck, that turned me on."

He's on cloud nine, holding my hand while he shakes the hands of the other dinner guests who thank him as we leave. *These* folks he takes pictures with.

But I'm not thrilled.

I shouldn't have lost my temper. But it hits me so fast with him, I see red.

No, I see blood.

Blood from our past. And blood in the future if anyone threatens him.

He's always amused by my temper.

He has no idea.

It's more now.

It's a lethal deal.

We wait for the same chauffeur in the same Mercedes who dropped me off to pull up to the curb. Redix enjoys the time, giving me kisses and not caring about the paparazzi dickhead snapping pics feet away.

I ignore him too.

This is life with Redix, so I squelch my frustration about photos taken. His soft lips on mine make that a hard possibility until the Mercedes whisks us away.

When the chauffeur turns down Canal Street, Redix tells him, "Drive us up to Central Park and back, please. We want to enjoy the sights."

The grip of his hand holding mine over the backseat lets go. "I love it when you do that, Candy Cade."

He slides closer to me while covertly sliding his hand under my ass on the seat and my heart stutters.

"Why are you so protective over me now?"

His question reaches for my heart while the slick leather of the back seat lets him find his way to gathering up my short dress in his grasp until only my thong is in his way.

"Because you fought for me, so I'll fight for you too."

"Cade." It stalls his advance, his eyes saddening. "I don't want you getting hurt over me."

It's too late, and we both know it.

I lean toward his lips. "I'd do anything for you." That past, this present, the intensity of what we share, it makes my hips circle over his hand. "You don't even need to ask."

Desire shoots lightning across his eyes because he knows it.

"Anything?" he asks, his finger easing past my thin lace.

The chauffeur is watching the traffic while I turn and watch Redix.

"Anything." I'm sitting on his hand and a mountain of need for this. My thighs part, just slightly. Soft jazz plays loud enough to mask our conversation. My dress drapes long enough to hide his hand playing with my sex.

"You're so warm." His finger, one of them so thick and long, it slides inside me and I bite back a moan. "It feels so warm inside when you fight for me."

I love how he's watching me.

With his hair in a knot, only a few strands fall over his sexy face that won't stop staring at me; it's making me squirm.

He uses his other fingers, pulling the thin thong aside so I can do this. So I can rub my clit into the seat while his fingers fuck me from underneath.

"It's very moving when you protect me." His bottom lip, his teeth bite it before he says, "I feel it very deep inside."

Two of his big fingers slide in while 6th Avenue blurs by. I clench around his touch while the wet he's making me slicks the leather.

I sigh, "I feel you deep inside me too."

A saxophone wails through the speakers while I grind down on his fingers, craving more of him but this will do for now because I can't stop.

Redix Dean does this to me. Desire for him has me willing to risk all to satisfy it. I hang on to his gaze and let it happen.

"You like this feeling, don't you, Cade? Of being so bad for me. Of being my dirty little girl." He pumps them, sliding his slick fingers in and out. "Is there anything you won't do for me?"

He has no idea.

"I'll do anything."

The friction of my clit against this leather, it's rubbing that tiny spot that'll deliver tremendous pleasure.

"What will you finally do with *me*, Redix?"

A veil of lust drops over his eyes, of dark intent and I'm desperate for its arrival.

I need him so much it hurts.

It makes him slam three fingers and the words, "Whatever I fucking want, Cade," inside my tender opening. "You're fucking mine."

I muffle my gasp; the sear of pain comes before the fast rush of pleasure. It's glazing his fingers, smearing over the seat and *oh God*, he starts curling them hard, combing them down my walls deep inside.

I'm going to leave a shameless puddle behind.

"Redix." I can't say more.

My mouth, my body twists for him, demanding more but I have no sound, only the pressure he's raging inside me. It's so loud.

"Not tonight, Candy Cade." His lips near mine. "I want to eat my dessert. There are chocolate-covered strawberries melting for your nipples in our suite." He's jerking his hand. I'm grinding hard. His lips dust over mine, his free hand wrapping around my neck and holding me there. "There's a banana I'm gonna use on your hungry pussy too."

I burst. His mouth takes me in a kiss while I'm washed away in the current of his touch, his taste, his tease and kink of just how deep I want to go with him. To places dark. To places forbidden.

I let it wash over me, the permission and the pleasure as I gasp back into his breath.

I was wrong.

I am changing.

My whole world is crumbling wet over his hand.

CHAPTER TWENTY-SEVEN

CADE

THE MIRROR IS LYING.

This woman isn't me.

But I like her.

Marco Rossi sent over his glam squad along with our wardrobe. This fashion I'm wearing is as edgy as the night Marco has planned.

It's not just a photoshoot; it's an event. A huge party with a DJ and a dance floor in a chic SoHo studio. Our photoshoot will be open. Guests can snap their pics while the photographer does too.

Redix agreed that we'll do the arrival, the rope line into

the event, the photo shoot, and two hours after schmoozing the VIPs. After that, we're free to go.

But I don't think I'm ready to set the woman in the mirror free.

She's bound in leather, rejection, and pain.

Redix teased me to the point of a broken heart last night.

Yes, there was chocolate, strawberries, a banana, my writhing body, and his mouth devouring it all. It felt so good that I lost my mind, he had me crying out for him. Lying naked on top of the dining room table in the suite at The Crosby, I didn't understand why.

Why he stopped?

Why he won't make love to me?

Why does he pull away and get quiet?

I kept asking him and he tried kissing me into silence to soothe the sting of his rejection.

But I couldn't take it anymore.

I pushed his kiss away last night and cried alone in the shower. I slept alone too—in one of the bedrooms of this two-bedroom suite where I assume he slept in the other.

Because I need to know. Why? Why won't he tell me what's going on?

I've been understanding. I haven't pushed him. I love him and I'd never hurt him.

So why does he keep me at an agonizing distance? Why can't he understand that I need to know?

It's my story, my pain too.

I just can't remember it all.

Why won't he trust me if I'm trusting him again?

This denial between us.

It's as lonely as the past ten years without him. Maybe it's worse.

Because it's a taunt of my broken heart that deserves better. We both do.

We need the truth.

We need each other.

He tried apologizing by waking me up with a breakfast tray. My eyes were swollen from crying and they started again at the sight of him.

"I'm sorry, Cade," was all he would say.

He sat beside me on the bed, and I picked at my food in silence. I felt sick.

"Do you want me to cancel tonight?" He asked me around lunchtime.

"No." I stared out of the wall of paned windows to SoHo outside. "I gave Marco my word and I'll keep it."

I let Redix pull me into a silent hug while I tried to decide how much more of this I can take.

These past two months with him have glued pieces of my heart back together.

Like half of it's back; precarious slivers stacked upon another but he's holding his beautiful bare foot there, threatening to smash it again.

So this fierce woman looking back at me?

The one who's had enough?

She's a stranger I'm ready to meet.

The stylist strapped me into Louboutin Black Sleeping Beauty pumps. There's a red rose over my toes while their gold heels are adorned with thorns.

The many inches of my legs are glossed and bare up to the eight inches of this black leather miniskirt.

Even smaller is the wide black leather strap bound tight around my breasts, holding them up high and knotted in the back as my top.

My short hair is slicked back, and my lips match the

rose on the shoes. My lashes are done but they'll add more makeup I'm sure at the shoot.

But the real sight that captivates me in the mirror?

I'm wearing the same BOUND perfume collar from ten years ago. It's black. Simple. Elegant with its delicate gold hardware.

But the gold chain is missing this time.

I won't be bound to Redix tonight.

Like this new perfume.

Like ten years later.

I'm free of him.

If I choose to be.

I like this woman in the mirror... because I don't know what the fuck she's gonna do next.

MARCO WON'T STOP GUSHING over me.

And he won't stop with his hand around my hip, introducing me to every VIP in sight.

"My Goddess," he cries, "you must come back to me. Be my spokeswoman. A grown one now on every campaign with this body, this face with that short hair, Mio Dio, you are sex on two long legs."

It's all in good fun.

I'm not coming back and he knows it.

But he sure is trying.

And with me at twenty-eight and Marco a sexy forty-something, I know when a man wants to more than *work* with me.

I'm not his innocent virgin bound in leather anymore. I don't need fashion or collars to assert my sex and power. I have more than any restraint can harness.

Marco's coming onto me. The couple who owns *Oomph* magazine propositioned me too. Marco's hair stylist—she's acting very interested.

I feel like fresh meat and Redix is watching it all from across the room because the same is happening to him.

But no one gets a bite of me tonight.

I don't know what Redix will do with his savory body everyone's after too.

I never have.

"Where is your Romeo?" Marco sips a Negroni, searching the sea of chic people. "It's time for the show."

I point to Redix, but I haven't spoken to him.

He had no words either when he met me in the hotel lobby for our limo over here.

All he's wearing tonight is a pair of black leather pants, the matching black collar, and a cloak of tension.

Marco's PR team joined us in the limo along with Redix's assistant, Eric. On the ride over, they chatted about the night, the names we must know, the schedule we must keep...

All while Redix watched me with a storm in his eyes.

I looked back and saw no trace of the boy I knew, the young man I loved, or even the asshole who followed me into a parking lot.

Who is he now?

When we stood for the cameras at the rope line, blasts of lights, shouts of his name, a scurry of people told us where to stand, and he just held on to me, pressing his oiled flesh against mine.

We didn't smile.

We let the cameras take pictures while we tried to decide, with no words, if we could be saved.

Or if we're damned for infinity.

In a rush of assistants, I'm hurried across the room and plopped into a makeup chair for a retouch. Redix sits beside me for his.

After a whirl of people directing us, we stand in front of a white backdrop. Music pumps bass through the air. Lights on tripods make our almost naked bodies glow. Guests hold phones up. Marco talks with his team and the photographer.

This entire room, hundreds are in it, looking at us and I don't know who I'm looking at.

The points of my heels touch his bare toes and he's still inches taller than me.

The sky in his eyes stares down at me, taking in the landscape of my body, the terrain of the pain in my eyes too.

And I'm looking back at his.

Will this ever stop?

"Lightning!" Marco shouts. "I want it again. Give me your love! Your lightning in a bottle!"

Redix wraps his hand around the back of my neck, pulling me near.

The crowd cheers.

His grip squeezes, hard. The heat of his lips, it's inches from mine, and the restraint in his eyes, it won't let me go.

We don't kiss.

We don't move.

It's not part of the performance and it's not sure between us. Lights flash, cameras click, and we are bound to the question...

What will we do?

"Libera! Libera! Free!" Marco shouts, directing us. "Your fragrance. Your love. It's free now!"

"Can we be?" I whisper to Redix, reaching my hand for

his hard jaw, sliding it back into his silky strands. "Can we finally be free?"

I drag, hard through his hair, yanking it to pull his lips to touch mine.

The crowd cheers again.

And we hold for the shot.

For the camera.

For his answer.

It's seconds before he lifts his lips from mine.

"Is that what you want, Cade?" Agony rages in his eyes with the storm we barely survived. "You want me to leave, to be free of our love forever?"

I reach up, with no direction from Marco, no cameras, no world around us.

It's just us.

It's just Redix's storm and my battered shore and we must be unleashed.

"No," I answer him. With a snap, I drop his collar to the floor. "I want *us* to be free of this. Free of what happened."

The camera's clicking like mad, Marco whistles his approval, and the crowd does too but they're not here.

Only Redix's eyes staring back into mine.

"I don't care if it's ten seconds," I swear, "or if you rip me apart, at least we'll finally be free *together*, like you know we have to be."

I feel his lips, so suddenly they're on mine while his pull, it snaps off my collar too, and it falls to the floor.

My bare skin he's exposed underneath sighs at the freedom.

Our kiss, it's off-script and out of control and every sound around us loves it.

Redix's big hands cradle my jaw and he's sharing our love and our secret with his kiss.

I know they went *after him.*

I know they beat him.

And I know he saved me.

And now...

I'll save him.

I pull him in and kiss him back; able to hold his heart on fire—the scald of his pain—and not get burned.

It's my turn now.

I'll do it all for him.

The night is too long. The two hours we have to stay after; they separate us into the crowd of fans wanting selfies, of bodies touching mine, trying to claim it—it doesn't belong to them.

From across the room, I see where I belong. I see Redix suffering the same.

His assistant, Eric, is a true pro. Throwing his clout around, he gets Redix and me out on time. With a final kiss on Marco's cheek, and a dodge through a wall of paparazzi cameras outside, we find shelter alone in the limousine.

"Jesus, Cade." Redix lifts my chin so my eyes meet his. "With the way you look tonight, I mean it. You want us to be free together, but I'm afraid I'll hurt you when I do."

"No, you won't." I grab his thigh. "I'm stronger now. No man can hurt me."

"You tell me." His thumb traces over my bottom lip. "Just say 'stop'."

"No. *That's* how people get hurt." I graze up his thigh to his hard length bound by leather. "Earn my 'yes' and make me moan it."

His eyes slam shut with a slow shake of his head. "Fuck, I'm gonna lose it with you."

Lifting his eyelids, the tip of his finger traces over my

naked collarbone while he asks, "Are you still on birth control?"

"Yes. Ironclad. And my tests, they're all clear. Yours are too?"

"Yes. What about condoms? I have some."

"You're the only man I never used them with." I reach for his hand lingering up my thigh. "And I'd like to keep it that way."

I want nothing between us.

He can play his games tonight; I'll still get my way.

Redix is the only man allowed fully inside me: then, now, and always.

CADE

Savages by Kerli

THE HOTEL SUITE is dark when we open the door.

He doesn't turn the lights on. There's enough streaming in through the wall of windows while I stand under his nose, pressing my palms to his bare chest, his hands cupping my ass.

Every muscle on his frame is tense.

"You can change your mind," I offer. "But I won't change mine. I need this for us."

It's straining his face, all his desire and damage is ready to rage.

"I'm holding so much back with you," he says. "I don't know what I'm going to feel." His lush lips pull tight. "What if we remember? What'll it do to us?"

"I don't know." His heart thunders under my hands. It's as fragile as mine in this moment. "But I'll be there with you, I promise."

"I need to hear it again, Cade. Tell me what you want."

I'm not afraid.

I'm starving.

"You've shown me your tenderness, and gifts and games and five seconds." I pull his mouth to mine. "I've waited so long for you, Redix. Now I want you to rip me apart."

He pants against my lips. "There's so much I want to do with you." His hands reach around, untying my leather sash top. "I want to play dirty games tonight, but I need your hands tied."

He drags the leather strap over my breasts, tickling its buttery edge around my nipple until I stammer a sigh.

His eyelids drop. "Is that a yes?"

I never let a man do this.

Never do they have my trust. Or honestly, my time.

And though I want to feel Redix, I want to grab his back while he's buried deep inside me, I also want this.

He was my first at innocent sex.

I want him to be my first at bad love.

"Yes, you may tie my hands."

I submit them in front.

"No. Turn around."

I do it with a grin.

The bind he ties around my wrists, it's not that tight. Truth is I have the strength in my arms to stretch this soft leather enough to escape. That certainty lets me permit this because I'm beyond curious. I'm rapt by what he'll ask me to do next.

He guides my waist, leading us from the dining area of the suite to the sitting one. Two sofas and two chairs are centered around a fireplace. But in July, he shows no interest in that cozy space.

No, he guides me to the wall of windows.

Sixteen huge panels of glass paned by iron separate us from the buildings of SoHo. There are ones across from us while this building forms an L so other guests can see us too.

Illuminated windows of people doing their own deeds fill my vision. A curious eye could see through the night and watch what we're doing too.

"If we really want to be free." His hand reaches under my skirt, his fingers skimming my thrilled sex. "Then we let anyone watch just how much."

Oh my God, I've been on display all my life.

But like this?

Redix steps in front of me, between my body and the city outside, tickling his other fingertips down my cleavage, over my belly and back up to my nipples. His touch is welcome fire over my skin prickling in the cool air.

"Can I show the world how sweet your pussy is for me, Cade?"

"Yes. But only you can taste how much."

He's down on his knees, lifting the skirt to my waist and scooping his tongue into my lust with no pause. Lucky for us, I didn't wear panties tonight because nothing's getting in his way. His mouth, his nose, he's plunging in.

"Oh shit," I sigh at his aggression wobbling my knees.

I step them wider apart, I can't help it, he can eat more. He knows how. I've been his meal for months and he's a connoisseur for my desire with his fingers spreading me open, his tongue pummeling my clit into pure madness.

I'm gasping over his mouth, my naked breasts arched with my hands bound behind me, his tousled mane buried between my thighs, and my God, we're a sinful sight.

"Are you feeling free, Cade?" His fingers slide in while his glistening smile watches my reaction. "Are you letting them see how sweet you are?" They scissor, fluttering deep inside me before his mouth is on my clit again with the most exquisite suck. "What dirty little fucking girl you are for me."

"Oh fuck, Redix."

His free hand grabs my ass to keep my buckling knees standing. On these heels, it's not easy, but it makes my pussy the perfect height for his dessert. For the whip of his tongue across my sex. For his fingers mixing through me too.

My eyes drop heavy with the weight of an orgasm threatening to crash down through me.

"Be free, Cade." His dirty mouth hums against my pussy, his fingers fucking me fiercely while my eyes find focus out the window. "Show them how dirty you'll be for me. Drip that cum down my hand."

In my haze, I see a man's silhouette watching Redix eat my pussy and that's all it takes.

"Oh fuck!" I'm falling. My eyes. My body. My pleasure. It's rushing over him, wanting to pool on the floor but his hands grab my ass, holding me up to lick the last taste of my satisfied sex.

He stands up, his cock straining under his pants. "On your knees now." He cups my breasts, his fingers swirling over my nipples. "Will you moan yes for me?"

He pinches them.

"Yes." It tumbles from my throat, from my lungs still recovering.

His grab is kind, helping me lower to my knees that are still weak, but I feel the burn of desire to do this the second I'm before him.

This is new. My exposure. My submission.

It's wetting my mouth equal to my pussy while he drops his zipper.

Hell yes, we're free and it can't be fast enough, his grip pulling his length out from his pants, freeing it for my mouth to devour because I do. The moment his cock is before my lips, I take him with the speed my famine demands.

"*Daaammmn, Cade.*" He's hungry for it too. "Fuck yes, let me fuck that dirty mouth."

Not holding back, he cups his hands around my head and guides me down, holding me as far as my mouth can go, as far my lips can stretch until a slight gag hits my throat, and he pulls back fast. He lifts my face, making my watering eyes meet his. "Do you want it like that again?"

"Yes," I answer before darting my tongue out for his leaking cock. "Fuck my throat, Redix."

I want him to see this.

I want that man watching us to see this.

Everyone. Watch how Redix Dean submits to me while I'm on my knees.

I crane my neck, taking him in while he guides me too. His hard tempo. His sweet taste. I'm taking it all to get my reward.

"Goddamn, I'll never forget this." He fucks my mouth, watching my eyes. "Your red lips dripping over my cock. Your tits bouncing while I fuck your mouth. Your hands tied behind your back while you're on your knees. Your pussy's so wet because someone *is* watching us. They're watching me face-fuck you and you love it." I groan. I agree. I can imagine what we look like and I want it too. "Fuck, Cade, you're so bad for me it's beautiful."

The black leather of his pants. The BOUND cologne he's wearing. The feel of carpet under my naked knees. The tight wrap of his hands through my hair while I take him, yes, it's perfect.

His grip tightens. "They're gonna watch me come in your sweet mouth. Moan if you want my cum."

I moan so loud, the vibrations down his cock, I know he can feel them.

He staggers back, "Oh fuck," holding onto my head, his cock pulsing in my mouth before... yes... I get to taste him.

That flavor of his sober desire, his real desire, it's only for me and spilling down my throat and filling me with warmth. I drink every drop before I sit back on my knees, watching him gasp for sanity while he gazes down at me.

With a lick, I clean his last drop off the corner of my mouth before I ask, "What are we free to do next?"

He grins, dragging his hand through his strands before he helps me to stand.

I glance out of the windows.

There are enough shadows over our faces that you can't be sure it's us. But the lights outside, they hit the curves and carves of our flesh, the motion of us making any mature human sure of what we're doing.

"You're going to stay right here." He insists before his kiss sweeps through my mouth. I taste us, my tangy lust on his tongue mixing with his salty desire on mine. It's my favorite flavor as he chuckles through my moan. "Is that a yes?"

"Yes," I answer back before I nip his bottom lip. It's so sexy.

Steps take him to the dining room table. When he picks up an armless chair, every muscle on his gorgeous frame flexes and my eyes narrow.

That sight, that perfection of masculine flesh, more than any person has ever seen, it's headed my way and *all for me*.

He sets the chair down in front of me.

I'm confused. "What are we doing?"

"We'll play my game until I'm ready to fuck you." He sits down, grazing his palms over my naked hips. "With the way you look, it won't take me long."

"What do you want to play?"

I let his hands guide me, answering me and turning me around so he can unzip my skirt. It falls to the floor before I kick it away.

I'm exposed in front of the window, but he doesn't turn me back. His lips land on my ass cheek before he gives gentle bites and my shoulders drop with a soft moan.

It's so tempting.

I know he'd take his time with me but that's another thing I've never done—let any man have my ass. And I'm not starting tonight. Not with the way Redix is hung.

It's like he senses it across my flesh.

He knows my body so well; I'm not ready for that.

He turns me around and kisses my belly. I glance down. The sight, his adoration, it softens me, lust churning with love.

I know he does. It's in all he remembers, in the way he plays with my hair, in the way he laughs feeding candy to me. He hasn't said it yet, not again, but he shows me with the backs of his fingers cherishing softly down my body.

"I'm going to make you come again," he says with his

lips tickling over my belly button. "Watching you come will get me so hard again and then I'll be free to fuck you."

God, this man. I've never had a lover take his time to lavish me. Then again, I didn't let them. "How?"

Seduction pours from his eyes, from his mouth demanding, "Ride my thigh, grind your dripping pussy on it while I suck your tits and get you off and that man over there watches us." Grabbing my hips, he grins. "Is that a yes?"

I wet more right here. His wanton command. His body, a temple of sex. The leather of his pants like the leather of the Mercedes—the perfect mix of gloss with friction that my clit loves to ride.

It's a shameless one I'll give him and the city outside.

Straddling his left leg, I center my pussy over his strapping thigh and start. His hands grip my rolling hips with such strength in them, he's controlling my slide up and down. I'm so slick from before it's a slippery display within seconds.

"Look at you, Cade." He's staring down at the gloss I'm leaving behind. So am I. "Fuck, baby, that pussy gets so wet for me." His grip strengthens and I know I'll have bruises and I love it. "Look at how free you are with me. Look how you'll let me play anyway I want with you."

And I will.

What's unleashed in me? What has me doing this?

His tongue starts circling my nipple jutting out for him before he sucks it, hard, making me groan, because... *it's him.*

My body, my heart, my whole life is open to him again like it knows its origin. I'm right here with his desire asking me to do dark deeds with him and permission wails inside me, needing it too.

I'm more than seduced. I'm found again. Redix makes

me feel adored, safe, and so free to be bad it's beautiful to him.

Because only with him.

"Watch me." My demand lifts his gaze. His cock that never really went soft is getting hard again. "Watch me come for you, Redix."

I'm close. The spellbound look on his face, the glide of my slippery pussy grinding on his hard thigh, the heat of my clit ready to explode, the audience spying my naked ass giving this lewd show, I'm going.

"Watch me." My lips tremble and desire hoods his eyes as his cock firms to its fullest pride.

That's my poison and cure. That I do this to him. That I can get him so fucking hard by the sight of me, it shoves me over. The buck, the shake of my body, I almost fall at its power, but he grabs my arms, holding me while it flashes through my senses. My chin drops and I go limp with its release, but he won't let me disappear into it.

Cupping my cheek, he lifts my eyes.

"Are you ready, Cade? You've been begging for my fuck. Are you sure you're ready for me to rip you apart?"

My inhale, it's sudden. It's in control. "Yes." It snaps up my lungs and every part of me agrees. "Do it."

He grabs me like a doll in his arms but he's not being so gentle. Moving fast, he drops us from the chair to the floor. In a quick twist, he turns me around, on my knees while he kneels behind me.

"Bend over and spread that ass for me"—his hand gently pushes my shoulders down—"open that pussy up for me."

I hear him unsnap his pants as I touch my cheek to the carpet, my bound arms resting over the small of my back. Leather gives a soft squeak while he must be freeing himself for what I'm hoping for. His fuck, *yes please.*

But also that he'll remember, he has to ease in. With his size, I'll go blind with pain to the tips of my ears if he doesn't.

My groan, it comes from the deepest place when I feel him drag the velvety, wide tip of his cock up and down through my folds. *Yes, he remembers.*

"Fuck, Cade." He's right at my aching entrance. "Fuck, look at how your pussy opens so damn wet and swollen for me." Moving in a coaxing slow circle, he slowly presses in. "Say it again. Say I'm free to do this. That you want it like this."

"Yes." I jut my hips, pushing them back, greed growling through my command, "Fuck me, Redix. Please, God, finally fuck me again."

The stretch, the feel of him, inch by massive inch entering makes me moan while shivers shoot down my thighs, my walls giving slowly to take him and loving it. The burn of his penetration all the way inside; it becomes a searing heat melting away ten years and all the cold he left behind.

"*Yessss.*" I want to cry into the carpet. My cheek's pressed to it, my soul worshipping his return. "Yes, Redix."

I forgot. How this is where we belong. How our bodies fit. How when he's inside me, our love, our nightmare... it's all been worth it.

"Are we free, Cade?" His tempo picks up, pulling back out and leaving me so open, his void making me throb until he's pushing back in again. "Does my cock feel good filling up your tight puss—"

"Yes, Redix." I don't let him finish because I'm losing control with his fuck. "*Yessss.*"

There's an insanity to wanting someone so much. To missing them. To watching others enjoy them, taking them when you know they belong to you. It's not jealousy. It's our truth and our bodies know it.

We should never be apart, and we may never survive together.

"Is this how he did it, Cade?" It's hard, his grip on my hips, it's yanking me slowly down his length. "Is this how that Marine fucked you? And then the other one?"

I don't know the tone in his voice. But I know that's the part of our past he wants to focus on. The one where I let another man in, and then another, and it wasn't him. I can't see his face. I can only feel his fervor driving faster into my pussy. "Yes." And it feels so damn good. "Yes."

"Did you think of me?" It's a grunt, his question, and it sounds like it's killing him. "Did you think of me while you got fucked? While they fucked the pussy that belongs to me?"

"Yes." His hipbones start slamming, hitting hard into my backside and I brace for it, wanting even more. "I closed my eyes, and it was you, Redix. It's always you fucking me."

He grabs my wrists bound behind me and pulls against them, ramming into me hard, the slap of our bodies filling the room for minutes of this great grueling fuck. It's finally enough. He's more than enough.

"I'll fuck you so good I'll make you forget them all, Cade." My God, he *is*. He's free to fuck me as hard as humanly possible. "Did he make you come like this?" His breath's uneven. His cock's pummeling me, the force of him's hitting through to my clit. "Did you come?"

"Yes." It's that spot, the one only he can find. It's so deep inside, only he can reach it and grab my soul. "I said your name." It's pain. It's pleasure. Singing through my body, it makes me cry out at his punishing tempo and I need more. So much more. How do you get ten years back?

Both his hands grab my shoulders, lifting me up until my back's pressed against his sweaty chest. He holds me in the prison of his arms wrapped around my body and his cock *is not stopping.*

Those strong hips of his. They can dance in languid circles, and they can pile drive his mass inside you until you can't move.

And you don't want to.

"This is me, Cade"—his voice fills my soul—"ripping you apart like I need to. Is this what you want?"

He's in my core, thrashing my senses, hitting, stretching, and claiming every part inside.

"Yes, Redix." All the way to my heart swelling for him; I can barely speak. He's knocking the breath from me. "All of you." I gasp. "I want you."

"You have me. This is me fucking you so hard you can't breathe without me. This is me filling you with my cum and erasing every man from your body but mine." It's true. His hips hurt, hammering into the tender crease between my thighs and cheeks. "This is *my* cock, Cade, deep inside you, only you"— tears, they start falling from my eyes at his words pressed to my ear, carving into my soul—"where I belong."

I cry out.

It's too much and I love it.

What are we doing? We're a storm. We're a ruin and a wreck and we won't stop. The truth traps us as tight as his arms binding me, as tight as my pussy clenching around him, ready for the mind-splitting orgasm he'll give me no matter how much it hurts, and I need it like my next breath.

He's brutal. He's changed. He's mine and he's fucking me harder than I knew possible. "Redix, please." I can't take much more. He'll have all of me until there's nothing left and it's my bliss losing it all to him.

His fingers reach down and indulge my clit. "Every pussy. Every body. They were all you, Cade. It was always you." His words, they groan from a depth way back, from when our heaven became hell. "I did it all for you."

It's endless. The rapture he forces through me. My sex is pulsing and weeping for him and the memory that wants to take us too.

But we fuck ourselves into oblivion, into where it doesn't hurt us anymore. To where he's holding me so tight, the torment wants to beat us but bound together, our bodies fight back.

We can do this.

Our love wages a war, unleashing the lust raging inside us, letting it win all until pleasure screams from my lungs with him inside me. His loud cry follows mine, filling me and every desperate need we have, and nothing can fight this.

It's too savage.

It's too beautiful.

It's us.

CHAPTER TWENTY-NINE

REDIX

DEAR CANDY CADE,

There's a new freckle on your face.

It's between your perfect eyebrow and your sexy hair.

Damn, I can watch you sleep beside me and never want to close my eyes.

I want to reach out and treasure every inch of you again. I can't believe I'm here. That we're back together. I thought I'd die before I saw this day. I almost did. It's like you became a dream to me I couldn't have anymore.

But now I'm wide awake with you.

It makes me want to wake you to be sure it's real, but you look too peaceful beside me.

But I know what woke me. I hurt you and you won't admit it.

You groaned in your sleep when you moved in my arms and that stirred me. I feel guilty as hell. I was too rough with you. I can see the marks I left on your hips and on your arms holding you too tight because I never want to let you go again. I can't imagine how sore your pussy must be.

I didn't want to do it that way.

I've been dreaming about our first time back together for so long.

And it wasn't like that.

Because that was the most primal fuck of my life.

I lost my mind inside you, Cade, and I didn't want it back. I felt like an animal so desperate for you. Like I was trying to fuck away all our demons until only our heaven remained. To be so deep inside you, I wanted to find us again. I kept fucking you and searching and I went crazy with how good you felt, with all I can feel with you now.

Damn, our sex is volcanic.

Like destruction and creation at the same time.

I fear it.

And I need it.

That's why I stopped with you the other night. I had licked off all the chocolate trails I swirled across your body. I teased your pussy with a banana making you come twice. Then I licked you off until your hips came off the table and you were begging me to fuck you with tears in your eyes.

It killed me to break your heart.

I thought you were going to leave me. That my games of trying to satisfy us without fucking pushed you too far.

I couldn't talk through the panic, through the fear that we were over. But you stayed for the shoot. And when I saw you in that outfit, I started sweating at the sight of you. I had to fight back my dick getting hard. The jealousy I felt knowing everyone would see you like that too. Fuck, I watched you at the party and fought to stay sane.

Cade, you're gravity and no one can resist you.

I can't.

It's not a choice.

I <u>have</u> to be with you.

But you can't find out.

So I decided if I stay in control of our sex, if I can control your hands and what you see when we do, then you won't find out.

And to be back inside you?

For ten years I've been so lost without you. You're where I belong and it was worth the risk.

I knew it the first time I was inside you. There was a moment with you on top of me, with you looking down at me with so much love in your eyes that I came in seconds.

Yes, me being eighteen and desperate for years to fuck you had a lot to do with it. And you with that body and face, any man would lose control.

But it was much more.

We were on your dad's boat. We skipped school and you had it all planned for us. You even waited for the best weather.

I was so damn nervous. I jerked off twice that morning before I met you at the boat because I worried I'd only last a hot second.

That didn't work.

You set blankets out like a bed. It was a calm day on the water with no clouds, and it was still morning because we couldn't wait anymore.

I did everything I could to get you ready. I love that. How I still know your body better than my own. But like last night, I worried our first time that I'd hurt you. That's why you climbed on top and had control. And I got to watch the most amazing thing I've ever seen.

Us. Together.

I was barely inside you and your tight heat and that look in your eyes, it hit me so fast, so hard and deep that I came knowing... I'm yours.

I've known it for so long.

That's what I've been fighting all these years.

Because we belong together, Cade, and that's going to destroy us. Like we're going to burn it all down and see if anything grows back.

I don't trust it will.

I fear the truth will hurt you so much that there'll be nothing left of us.

Do you remember what happened after our first time?

We did it four more times that day. Each time I got deeper inside you and lasted longer. Because that's what my horny dick could do at eighteen.

Hell, it ain't too different now that I'm back with you ten years later. I can't believe how hard I get, and how hard I get again minutes later.

You're like my sexual fountain of youth.

But we didn't know better. Your body couldn't take five times. Yeah, it felt good to you at the time but then you got an infection.

Real romantic, wasn't it?

It scared me so much. That next day you stayed home from school legit that time because you were doubled over and crying on the sofa that it hurt every time you peed.

I thought I tore something inside you. That I'd permanently hurt you.

Mama G came home for lunch and found us there. It took her a second to know exactly what happened.

Remember what she said?

"If y'all are old enough for sex, you're old enough for its consequences." She wasn't mad. "Go on down to the store and get her some cranberry juice. And quit treating her body like a pretty pin cushion you gotta stick every ten minutes."

Damn, I love her.

She didn't shame us. She schooled us. Our parents were always cool like that.

But until the juice and the medicine Mama G got for you kicked in, the pain you were in, Cade, I felt so damn guilty. Like I had all the fun and you paid the price.

I remember telling you, "I'll go slam my dick in a door for you to make this fair."

That made you laugh while you pulled me down on the sofa with you and made me hold you while we watched *One Tree Hill...* again.

God, I wanna go back to those days.

When too much sex was our only problem. When you were thumbing through *Architectural Digest* and showing me what our house would look like one day. When I was booking modeling gigs and banking money so we could have that dream.

I'd do anything for that innocence again.

And you still are, Cade.

You're innocent to what happened, and I need to keep it that way. So much was taken from us.

I can't take that from you too.

CHAPTER THIRTY

CADE

Sunlight and sound—a shower—they wake me up.

That and the dull ache between my thighs. My pussy feels like I impaled it on a railroad timber.

I smile... because I loved every minute of it.

Glancing over, the bed is empty but there's a black leather journal lying where Redix was when I closed my eyes.

Since when does he keep a journal?

I'll never pry but I'm curious.

Wonder what he's writing? Did he give us five stars for last night?

I sure as hell do.

I've never fucked like that. So savage and beautiful at the same time. So intense it gives me a hurricane of butterflies just remembering it.

Redix held me for an hour after. I couldn't help my tears and I think I felt his too on my shoulder until it turned into gentle laughs that we finally did it. That we crossed over together and it didn't destroy us.

Quite the opposite.

"That was worth the wait," I sighed into his hands holding mine.

"Anything is worth us being back together," he said, turning me around and pulling me into his chest.

When he had time to pull his pants back up, I didn't know but I wanted him again. But he said he needed a shower and sleep.

He made up for it though. The back massage he gave instead had me asleep within minutes.

That gives me some ideas, checking my phone.

10:08 am glows back.

We have the whole day and we'll spend it right here, playing Uno and making love. As long as his body is next to mine, I don't care.

And no, it doesn't scare me. This need I have for him again. It feels right, destined.

So does a fuck in the shower with him.

Yes, that'll be steamy.

Throwing my legs over the edge of our sumptuous bed, the minute I stand up, I wince.

Okay cowgirl, make the next one a slow ride because your pony is sore.

Whatever. I just wanna wrap around him all wet.

The door to our bathroom suite is closed.

He's funny like that, so private lately.

Guess we're easing back into this whole "free" thing.

The sound from the triple shower heads drowns out the door unlatching. He doesn't hear me come in.

Steam clouds most of the view but my heart stops—he's so beautiful like that. Eyes closed. Head back. Shampoo suds rinsing from his long hair. The tattoo on his hip bone. Our tattoo. It's discernible through the haze.

I take a second, letting it sink in—*me and Redix. Together again.* Fully and finally fucking.

It's natural.

It's paradise.

I'm in love.

"Want some company?"

"FUCK!" His voice bombs the room, ricocheting off the tile and hitting me hard with shock. "Fuck, Cade!" And anger. He backs against the tile. "You scared the fuck out of me."

"I'm sorry."

I really am. I've been known to strike and ask questions later when I'm surprised too. "I just thought we could—"

"Can I have some privacy?" He jams the shower lever, shutting down the water and my hopes. "I'll be out in a second."

"Privacy?"

Something's off.

I get having time to yourself in the bathroom, but this is a shower. And after he fucked my brains out last night what is there to be private about?

"Why are you freaking out?" I step toward him. "It's me —you know—your best friend whose pussy you fucked last night."

"Yeah, well knock next time. Or better yet, respect a closed door."

"A closed door?" It's all wrong. Something. "Redix." I step to the shower threshold. "Why are you so mad? It's just a fucking shower."

"No." He reaches beside me, yanking the towel off the bar. "It's just fucking respect."

His tug, it's more like a rip so hard that he pulls the brass towel bar from the wall, clanking it to the floor.

"What the hell?" It lands by my foot.

He whips the towel around his waist. "Just leave, okay?"

His towel's secured fast enough for him to insult me more by pointing toward the door.

"No, it's not okay."

I won't move. My pulse, it's climbing with my anger. With more of his rejection. This makes no sense.

"Why are you acting like this? We go from the best sex of our lives to you not showering with me? What did I do wrong?"

"You didn't respect my privacy." He tries brushing by, but I block him. "Move please."

"No."

How did this happen?

From sleeping safely in his arms to waking up with the happiest smile to now a fight in the bathroom over a goddamn door knock?

"What are you hiding?"

It's something. Guilt drips from his face.

"You can't stop, can you?" That look in his eyes is back; it's cruel. "You always gotta know. You always gotta look too close." His grip tightens over the towel. His words seethe, "I'm not your goddamn case to solve, Detective."

"No. You're a mind fuck, so be a man and talk to me."

"I am a *fucking* man." He sneers, dripping inches above

me, his huge pecs swelling with anger. "A man who wants you *to leave*."

That hurt so much, spinning my world.

The powerful pull he takes me with and then the wrecking shove he slams into me next.

It feels constant. Brutal. Unfair.

It dizzies my head, bashing my heart with its madness.

"So you can bury your bare cock deep inside me and pound my pussy all night until you fill me with your cum, but we can't shower together?"

It's crude. It's harsh. It's the truth and it hurts like hell.

"Yes."

That's a punch so hard, I gasp. "What is it?" I reach for his towel. "Why is this between us?'"

"Stop!" He grabs my wrist, and it happens so fast...

It's a trigger, firing a memory buried deep, of TJ grabbing my wrist and starting my war.

My instincts fire. My mind doesn't work but my training does, so fast it shocks us both. My other hand, it grabs his wrist holding mine, twisting with force, torquing his arm around, his fingers sliding into my grasp where I bend them back, tension about to break his bones...

"Ow!" He shouts. "Fuck!"

I let go, not sure what I just did... but it hurt us both.

What just happened to me? To us?

"Sorry." I back away. From the shock. From the sudden shame. "I'm sorry."

I turn and run out of the bathroom. I can't see. Disbelief clouds my logic. A flood of tears blurs my vision while I grab my jeans still packed in my suitcase and get dressed without thinking.

I need to leave.

What I just did; it's bad.

I hurt him.

And that kills me.

"Cade? Where are you going?" Redix appears in the bathroom doorway. "It's okay."

"None of this"—I tug on a tank top—"none of this is okay."

My tears won't stop. Like there's a deep well of pain buried inside me and I just tapped into my darkest nightmare.

"I gotta go."

"Don't leave." Despair bends his face. "We'll be alright."

"No, we won't." I cram my things into my suitcase. "We won't be alright because you won't talk to me, and I can't take it anymore."

My toiletry bag is in the bathroom behind him. *Fuck it.* I don't need it.

I can't take another second of this. Shame. Guilt. Agony.

I'm suffocating.

"I'm so sorry I hurt you," I say, shoving on my flip-flops, darting next for my purse. "But that's how much this hurts me when you push me away like that and we have to stop. Because now, I'm hurting us both."

He steps my way. "I'm fine."

"No, you're *not* fine." My hard stare stops him. "You're better, but you're not fine. And neither am I." I sling my bag over my shoulder, my hand grabbing for the suitcase handle. "You don't trust me, not with everything like I do with you, and it hurts too much, Redix, because it's like they won. They broke us both and now we're breaking each other."

I don't know how I'll get home.

What flight, train, or bus will get me there, but I have to escape.

I can't look at him. Disgrace for hurting him so fast I didn't even blink, it fills me.

That's not me.

I'd never hurt him.

But I'm terrified... because I *can* hurt others... so fucking fast they won't know what hit them.

"Cade, wait. Lemme get dressed and we can talk."

"Are you going to tell me what happened?"

He's silent.

Not even his eyes answer me and I know he never will.

All my hopes, my happiness, gone.

I'm buried alive by his frozen beauty that holds our secret.

I turn toward the suite door but look back for one last moment with him, with my world.

He's a stunning smear before my crying eyes.

"Our love is so much. It always has been and, " I cry, "it's fucking killing me." My lips tremble. "And I just want you to know that whatever our truth was, whatever secret you're keeping from me—however bad it was—I would've still loved you, Redix. And I always will. And I know you love me. But you won't love *yourself* enough to give us another chance. And *that* just killed us."

CHAPTER THIRTY-ONE

CADE

A WEEK GOES by like slow hell.

The nights I'm working don't help either. This is the fourth one in a row where I'm sitting in an unmarked car parked outside The Pelican.

I'm watching Derek Baucom.

He's got an erratic schedule for a Bar Manager—a lot of coming and going from the place where you'd think he'd stay on shift.

But no, he leaves, drives to his condo in his black truck, stays there thirty minutes or so, and then goes back to work. Twice a night for four nights he's done it.

He's not going home for a dog. I never see him walk one.

It makes me sick, not liking my worst guess of what he's doing. But I don't have a warrant to find out.

I tried going through the garbage at his condo building but in that big dumpster, I can't tell what's his. I can't find any clues or proof.

My phone glows. I glance at it on the console.

And it's him again.

REDIX

I'm thinking about you

They're sweet thoughts

He's texted every day with something cute.

But I can't reply. It hurts too much, dragging out the pain. It weighs my chest down with a sob that won't come.

The first night I was home, I answered his call. It was awkward because I didn't know what to say.

"Cade, we can get through this." There was no asshole swagger in his voice, only desperation.

"Do you trust me?" I was watching the full moon glow over the ocean. "Are you going to tell me our truth?"

Closing my eyes, I held my breath for his answer.

There was none.

He didn't say a word.

Like his silence hurt less than a "no".

It didn't.

"I meant it." I felt so sick, all our dreams drowning. "We can't do this anymore. If you won't tell me then we have no future."

I ended the call.

Saying goodbye to him? Again? It would've wrecked me right there on my balcony.

It did anyway. Salty tears trickled into my mouth while the familiar ache kept me sitting there alone for hours.

Like I've done... for so many years without him.

Tonight, my phone glows again. I almost can't check it.

Doesn't he know how this kills me?

How I need to stop thinking about him? How maybe if I can make it a full day without remembering his lips on mine, his body holding me so tight, maybe I can wake up with a smile again?

Please.

I don't want to hurt anymore.

Relief hits me.

It's Penny. She knows I came home heartbroken, and she didn't rub it in. Not with this island buzzing about the pictures of me and Redix at the FREE perfume event. There's no place I can escape him.

PENNY

What's the difference between a pregnant woman and a lightbulb?

She's as bored as me. And trying to cheer me up. Sitting outside the liquor store, hunting for the elusive parrot T-shirt culprit, she's been pinging my phone with inappropriate jokes all night.

I love her.

I reply:

One's not very bright

I grin because she started this and it feels good and I need it. My ribs have cracked with all her dumb model jokes so it's payback.

PENNY

Oh! Burn! Good one.

No, bitch.

You can unscrew a lightbulb.

Dots appear. Jameson's diving in. He's undercover watching Coligny Park. He's been blasting us too.

JAMESON

How is life like a penis?

Oh, this is too fun. I've got five replies and a fingertip that can't tap fast enough.

It gets hard

It comes and goes

It's not good if it's short

...

I'm typing another when muffled voices lift my eyes.
Three guys, they're stumbling across the parking lot.
I glance at the back door of The Pelican. It's still closed.
My target hasn't moved.
Putting my eyes back down, the phone in my hand is a prop now while I pretend to be a distracted patron, not an undercover detective.
"Hey, pretty lady. You shouldn't be out here alone."
My periphery clocks pink shorts first. I lift my glare, only to find this dick weed growing on the other side of my window. A woven belt with sailboats on it. Blue polo shirt. Red drunk face.
Oh, what I want to say, but I can't blow my cover.

"Just waiting on my boyfriend. He'll be out any second."

"I'll keep you company until then." He reaches for my door handle.

This fucker.

It's locked.

And now... I'm pissed.

"You better leave," I snarl. "Now."

The guy behind him?

He leans across the hood of my car, peeping into the front windshield and jeering, "Nah. You *need* some company."

No, I need to press the gas pedal and turn you into roadkill.

The third guy, he's just laughing, like this is their thing —harassing women for sport.

It takes everything I have to put my nose back down. To ignore them while I text Penny for backup. Because one more move and these guys are gonna need a medic.

"Come on, gorgeous. We'll treat you nice. Better than that boyfriend."

The sick shit unzips his fly and pulls his limp boyhood from his pink pants and rubs it on my windshield. The other two laugh, staggering drunk, while this one taunts, "Come on. Roll down your window and suck on my anaconda."

It's barely a snail.

And I'm barely holding it back.

"Girl, you're too hot not to fuck with," he mocks and...

Red. Blood.

It drops a veil over my mind and I snap. My restraint, gone.

I grab the door handle, kicking it open so hard that it slams the guy in his pathetic dick, knocking him down.

"And you're too stupid not to beat the shit out of." I stand up over his sprawl on the ground.

The second guy, he steps over his drunk friend. "Stupid bitch!"

He takes a swing with his right, but I grab his wrist, pulling him toward me, my other hand striking the back of his neck and wrapping around it to shove his face into my kneecap. *Once. Twice. Three times.*

Fuck yes, it feels so good before I shove him down to the pavement too.

"You next?" I ask Chuckles, the third one who's barely standing with his eyes wide.

"What the fuck's your problem?" The first guy whines, scrambling up from the ground.

"Your useless, tiny dick."

I see over his shoulder. Penny's car is racing into the parking lot.

"You fucking bitch." The second guy crawls up. "You broke my nose."

"No. You took a swing at the wrong woman."

I keep my fists up, swaying in fighting stance because I want more.

The second guy wipes the blood from his nose with the bottom of his gingham shirt. "What are you? A fucking cop?"

Penny's car parks behind them. It's unmarked too.

"No." I drop my fists. "I'm payback for all the women you've harassed. Careful. Next one you bother might not be so nice."

Drops of lemon fall into her tea with a firm squeeze. Mama's eyeing me, contemplating just how much of an ass-chewing I'm gonna get.

"Well," she says, "my daughter finally made it to Paid Administrative Leave. Ain't I proud?"

Anyone else and I'd roll my eyes, but I'll never disrespect my mama.

"It's standard procedure, Mama. I was provoked."

"Uh-huh." She buys that like an extra car warranty. "You know the difference between your generation and mine?"

I'm not mad.

Mama looks too cute in her red beach caftan and matching hat.

I've got her laid out like the Queen of the Nile by the pool under an umbrella to get her some fresh air. *And* to let her chastise me for the trouble I got in for my bar brawl.

"Your generation didn't do anal?"

I can't help it. I gotta see her laugh.

It works. Ridiculously and so loud the whole pool can hear us cackling.

After we wipe the tears from our happy eyes, she says, "No. I would've taken a picture of him and his little dick. Flyers with his name on them would be tucked under every windshield at The Pelican for months."

"So you're saying you *didn't* do anal?"

"I did what every proper lady does."

"Which is...?"

"What in the Sam Hill I wanted to"—she toasts her tea to my beer—"and I did it with a smile."

This is the best day I've had in over a week.

Because this past one has been even worse.

Redix stopped texting me. It's what I wanted. And that

hurts even more. Like I ripped out ribs and it's hard to breathe.

Mama and I lounge for an hour.

I try focusing on other things but it's impossible because Redix's sister and her son are across the pool. They wave to us. We wave back and I just want to scream at the ache of missing him.

"You know I see it?" Mama adjusts her sunglasses. "How much you suffer over him. How you have for ten years. I leave you two alone because I respect y'all, but I know when my daughter is hurting."

"I'll be alright."

Mama can never know just how far I'm going to go to make it stop hurting us forever.

"I never stopped loving your dad, you know. Our divorce, I felt like I failed. I wanted to go back and make us right again." She turns my way. "But love can't go back, kiddo. You gotta move on and trust it will find you again."

Words won't come.

I can't speak with the grip that truth has over my heart.

I need to let Redix go.

I close my eyes, remembering when I should have let the dream of us die so we could find peace again.

It was ten years ago when Redix tucked his hair behind his ear and said, "Let me go, Cade."

His busted lip. His black eyes. His bloody ear. The bruises on his face, they matched the ones on my heart aching so bad I couldn't pull in a breath.

"Please," he said, "I don't want to hurt you. Go find someone else to love."

His blue t-shirt, his back in it turned on me and walked away.

My world, my heart, he left me standing there.

"Redix, please!" I had no pride, no answers, only an avalanche of pain begging, "Don't leave me."

But he never even looked back.

I don't remember the next minutes, the next hour. It was just him, driving away and Mama finding me still sobbing on my bed hours later, crying so hard my lungs burned.

"Let it out." I remember Mama whispering while I let every piece of me fall apart. I remember it now.

"Let him go," Mama said.

She was crying too.

"Well, here comes trouble with a capital T," she mutters now.

From behind my sunglasses, I open my wet eyes and...

Suck a dick, Fate.

TJ is on his usual prowl, stalking across my complex's pool deck on his way out to the beach.

"Well, this is quite the catch." His voice rasps and I retch. "Hilton Head's finest ladies by the pool."

That's TJ's danger; his delusion.

After what happened, it only took two years of me being home and smiling at him to convince him that I magically forgave him.

So desperate to believe his own sick truth, he denies the facts. It gives him the balls to walk up to our loungers like we're friends, like I want him.

It *is* what I want.

With Mama here; it's not.

Because nothing gets past her.

"We're just enjoying some family time." My tone is sweet. "Enjoy your day too."

Mama doesn't greet him though—not her typical tactic. Manners are her default setting.

But with TJ flames could freeze at the cold stare coming off her.

"Did you enjoy taking those pictures with Redix Dean?" The tone in TJ's voice? It's flat. It's creepy. "You lied to me. You said you two weren't together."

Damn, he's a gross fuck.

He thinks I belong to him.

He always has.

Swallowing my disgust, I have to make him believe it so I answer, "When someone pays you two hundred and fifty K for a picture, you can act like anyone's your center of attention."

"I see." He sneers. "Well, you'll *always* be mine."

With a smile toward my mama, he tips his sweaty visor. "Sheriff, you have a good day."

Shivers hit me as he slithers through the dunes toward the beach.

"Don't say a word." Mama's voice is ice. "I know what he is. And the less we speak about it, the better."

Is she telling me to move on from my past?

Or is she endorsing my future deal?

CHAPTER THIRTY-TWO

CADE

Paid leave or protocol; I don't like the days off.

It truly is a punishment because I'd rather be working.

I need to solve these cases but we've had nothing. No more attacks. I'm grateful for that. No more evidence. I'm losing my mind over it.

Even the surveillance video of the parking lot of the condo building where Cam Le went missing? It's infuriating.

"The cameras are angled toward the edge of the lot." I was baffled when Jameson came over and showed me on his laptop. I'm not allowed in the office. "It's like he doesn't want coverage of the exits and cars."

"It's like he's hiding something," Jameson added.

Gentry Evans owns most units in that building. It reeks of wrongdoing. Jameson got a warrant to search the unit Cam Le last cleaned. He said they found nothing, just a normal rental.

Penny interviewed Cam Le's colleague again. She agreed; the woman knows something but she's too scared to say it.

Jameson and Penny take turns watching her and other cleaning crews.

Secretly, I've been watching Derek and TJ. It's a wicked punishment because TJ only makes me think of Redix more.

It's been another week and he's left me alone.

It's what I want, right?

Then why does it feel so wrong?

I guess because we're really over.

I guess he'd rather keep his secret than me.

It leaves me untethered.

I used to be so tied to anger that he left. So attached to the hope that he'd come back, and we'd find each other again. But now I'm lost, adrift because I don't know who to blame. Me, for wanting the awful truth. Or him, for not wanting to say it.

My phone vibrates on the ottoman.

SILAS

Word is Gentry Evans will be here today at 12 with his crew

Wanna day-trip?

No. I know *exactly* who's to blame.

And exactly what I'm still attached to—revenge.

Sure

Pick me up? One hour.

Harbour Town

I can't break my promise to him; I text Jameson next with an invite. I know it's last minute, but hell can't stop me.

He replies:

JAMESON

Meet you there. Bringing a date

It doesn't bother me. I want him to be happy and he won't find that with me.

Good

It'll be perfect cover

Gentry Evans will never drop his guard around me on duty.

But if he sees me on what looks like a double date, day-tripping to Daufuskie Island, maybe he will.

The Saturday in late July is perfect weather. Meeting Jameson's date at the dock delights me too. She's gorgeous and super chill.

He introduces her first as an MMA fighter before even sharing her name.

"Cade Bryant"—Jameson's chest puffs up proud—"meet Scarlett Jones."

I shake her hand. She gives me a firm grip, and a gentle smile and I like her. Her company may turn this into a good day.

And when Silas pulls his boat into the slip and he's not wearing a shirt?

Maybe, finally, it'll be a great one.

Jameson drapes his arm over Scarlett's shoulder. "I told her she should come work with us."

We chat while Silas ties us off at our destination.

"I can't work for the police." Scarlett jumps onto the dock. "I have a record."

"Hell, yeah." Silas grins, wrapping a rope whip-fast around a cleat. "Y'all are my kinda company to keep."

I'm intrigued. By her. By this day.

We grab a picnic table by the edge of the water outside the crab shack. Positioning myself to watch the busy marina, I wait for a wicked man to arrive.

Not that anyone could miss Gentry's huge yacht. It's like a turd floating in a clear pool.

"What's the record for?" I ask Scarlett since she brought it up.

"Teenage stupidity." She has dimples when she smiles.

I toast her beer. "Guilty as charged."

"Who doesn't do stupid shit when they're young?" Silas's easy voice soothes my bruised heart... just a bit.

Around him, my mind wants to wander to Redix. He's his damn twin.

But I force myself to focus on Silas.

How his eyes are hazel and full of laughter, and not blue and swimming with pain.

"What did you do?" I ask him. "Since everyone's fessing up."

Silas tucks his long strands behind his ear, cinching my heart with *that* memory before he answers, "I fell in love with a woman I can't have."

"That's the worst offense," Jameson says, and I cough.

That was meant for me.

"Well, she's far away and finally happy." Silas gazes out

over the water like she's standing before him. "That's all that matters."

And all I can do is admire his sexy profile.

And wish the same was true for me and Redix. That he's far away and we're finally happy.

It isn't.

The hour passes. The beer is good. The fried shrimp are the best and I'm not taking my eyes off the marina while Silas fills my mind with fun conversation. Fishing. Boating. Then he asks me about my modeling, why I went from a glamorous job to a grueling one.

A white Pershing yacht glides into view.

Everyone knows who it belongs to.

"Because of men like that."

I point to the luxury vessel. Its loud music is almost as obnoxious as the party of men howling on it.

"We all hear that," Silas agrees before going to the bar for another round of beers and shrimp baskets.

I could turn and watch his sexy, shredded back of tan muscles. And that cute ass in navy board shorts.

But I don't.

I surveil from behind my shades.

The name of Gentry's yacht—*After Tail*.

It makes me wanna fire rounds into its hull and watch it sink... with all onboard.

"You know," Scarlett says, "it's doing shit like this that makes me want the job working security. I got a company, HGR Security, they cover high-profile clients: CEOs, celebrities, and such. They're after me hard to come work for them."

"You'd be great at it."

Jameson admires Scarlett while my stare won't leave the men on Gentry's yacht.

I count four so far, jumping onto the dock, bottles in hands and voices booming for all to hear.

"Maybe so," Scarlett says, "because I can tell you with one look at those men—they're big trouble in expensive leisurewear."

"Good instincts," I reply to her before swallowing down my gasp.

Holy shit. It's Derek Baucom, the bar manager from The Pelican.

He emerges from the lower deck.

"Well fuck me," I mutter. "He doesn't just *work* for Gentry. They're friends."

Jameson seethes at the intel while I start connecting dots, drawing a disturbing picture in my mind of how this is all coming together.

Senator Gentry Evans owns the perfect places to hunt for vulnerable victims—rental units, a nail salon, a beach bar.

Derek Baucom pours the drugged drinks for them, controlling his staff and the cameras not aimed at their crimes.

And I know it with no evidence...

TJ provides the drugs, the GHB so powerful they remember nothing while he reels in the victims from the floor.

But TJ's not on the boat today. This party he's not invited to because of his criminal record.

Not appropriate company for a conservative state Senator.

Still, behind closed doors, I know how far back Gentry and TJ go. You can't keep them apart.

I get it now.

These three are a vile triad with enough power, position, and poison to get exactly what they want... and not get caught.

Yet.

Minutes later and I'm at the bar, leaving my friends behind and knowing these jean shorts and yellow bikini top work like a lure.

More like a curse really.

"Sergeant Bryant"—Gentry's high-class drawl drags through my depths of disgust—"I see you're enjoying your time off."

He's standing too close to me.

His freckled arm brushes mine leaning on the bar.

"I'm making the most of it."

I sip my beer, clocking Derek behind him and sneering my way.

Derek's wearing short sleeves today and I fight the snarl of my lip at how it reveals a tacky tattoo.

A mudflap girl.

It's so sexist I want to chew it off his flesh.

Because, fuck, I hate the way he looks at me; all-knowing.

Of what?

How do I know him?

It's not from investigating him these past few months. It haunts me, like a splinter in my memory I can't dig out.

"What about you guys?" I arch my back, just enough, letting my thin bikini top serve a purpose. "What finds you mixing business with pleasure?"

Gentry can't help himself. He never could.

His stare goes right after what he craves, my body.

I swear if he lays a hand on me nowadays, he'll pull back a broken one.

"Taking care of my friends and family." Gentry's arm is

moist against mine and twisting my stomach. "Derek here is my cousin." *What the fuck?* Don't flinch. "He told me about the other night. About your trouble at The Pelican."

My glance flicks toward Derek.

Evil thoughts pool in his brown eyes sliming over me but I can take it.

I'm too familiar with this; might as well use it to my advantage.

"Careful what you believe." I bat my lashes... because *fuck these two.* I want to rip their balls off. "You know Hilton Head Island floats on liquor and lies."

"Make me believe otherwise then," Gentry taunts. "Your little dust-up with my customers? Why were you at my bar that night?"

Of course he wants to know. Careful.

"Just a ladies' night out ruined by drunk men. The usual."

Satisfaction glares from his eyes. "They weren't too rough on you, were they?"

"A fight's never too rough for me."

"Is that so?"

I want to puke at his lean toward my ear.

At his pussy-parching preppy clothes.

At his hair in a slick part.

At his traditional wedding band as he perverts my ear...

"I'd love to feel it again, Cade. Just how hard you fight back. How much will it cost me now?"

That memory flashes but I bite back the rage in my blood.

You didn't come this far to fuck up now.

I turn eye-to-eye with him, inches away from his thin, chapped lips... and smile like a priest.

"Your life."

Walk away before you do it. Right here. Breaking this beer bottle in half on the bar and stabbing the jagged edge into his jugular and twisting it with a laugh.

Because I want to, so much.

It hits me so hard that I have two choices—*move or murder.*

It has me in a blur, my steps aiming away from the crowd at the deck bar, toward the park across the sandy parking lot.

My pulse is in my ears. My heart wants to rip out of my chest and turn back, committing the bloody crime itself.

Because all I can see...

Is that night.

How Redix and I held hands by Coligny Park. I was wearing a yellow dress I borrowed from Pamela, wanting to be cute that night for him.

He goes back to buy us another ice cream cone because he wants more lemon kisses.

I do too.

I'm smiling, watching him from a distance, standing by the curb and waiting for the love of my life to return.

"Hey, gorgeous." A hand grabs my wrist.

Ten years ago, and I can still feel its cold clamp over my flesh, over my heart.

Turning around, I yank it away.

"TJ, leave me the fuck alone."

I was learning the skills then, how to break his hold, but Gentry was beside him. And his BMW, it idled at the curb behind them.

"Come on, Cade." Gentry's steps toward me weren't seeking fun. "It's almost graduation and you owe us a night."

They were after me.

You know it. You know when you're prey. When a wound, when a kill is next. When it's yours.

It washed over me then, turning my thighs to Jell-O and my blood to ice.

"Hey!" Redix shouted from the distance. "Get the fuck away from her!"

That's when our nightmare began.

And I can't wake up from it until I end this.

We'll never be free until I do.

That's the deal, God. I'm keeping my end. You keep yours.

I don't see the glassy water in front of me, the stunning Lowcountry glimmering on the horizon. I'm stuck in that hell, in that night, until I hear a deep voice.

"Cade?" It's Silas. "You okay?"

I don't answer him.

I don't turn around.

I only shake my head.

No, I'm not okay.

"You want me to drown an asshole for you?"

He's so sweet. It makes me huff with a small grin. "I wish I could go back." I talk to him and the water.

"Back to what?"

I feel his heat, how he's standing behind me, trying to protect me.

I turn to face him.

I turn to see a man so much like Redix before it happened.

The beauty of his face; Silas is a few years younger than me, but there's an intoxicating mix to him, an innocence with wisdom that seems so promising. Any woman could start over with a man like him.

"Back to feeling love again," I answer. "One that doesn't hurt."

The touch of his hand to mine; it's gentle.

"I don't think love is supposed to hurt."

"It does," I reply, "when you can't have the one you want."

That softens his face, like I shared his truth too.

He holds his arms open, and I take his embrace. I need it. I need it so much and he smells so fresh, like coconut and sex. His bare chest presses against mine and there's no history, no pain with him, only perfection.

Can I do this?

Do I really want this freedom?

To let go of Redix? Forever?

I close my eyes and I see Redix lying next to me on the sofa, tickling his fingertip over my bottom lip, "my Candy Cade," with his smile adoring me.

I can't hate him or blame him.

I know how much he loves me. *He proved it.*

I whisper into Silas's flesh. "Can you get me outta here, please?"

It hurts too much. I can't talk on the ride home. Or when Silas pulls his boat away. Or when Jameson and Scarlett hold hands up the dock ramp, waving goodbye.

I get a text before I jump into my car.

SILAS

I'm a boat ride away if you want to go forward

Not back

What's wrong with me?

Every amazing man I meet, I push them away.

If I were Penny, if I were my best friend, what would I tell myself to do?

Give Silas a chance.

No. Give myself a chance.

The thought is there while my elevator climbs to the third floor, and I hope the feeling reaches my heart too. I'm searching for it, grabbing the keys in my bag when the sight by my front door grabs me.

Three dozen pink tulips in three vases. Each with a note I read:

PAST

I know I've used up as many chances, at least three dozen. But please give us one more.

PRESENT

You're my truth. You're my every reason. You're why I'm still alive.

FUTURE

Please give me one perfect day and one perfect night with you. And then I'll tell you.

For infinity, your Asshole

CHAPTER THIRTY-THREE

REDIX

DEAR CANDY CADE,

My hand shakes writing this.

Your plane is landing and fuck me, I'm nervous.

No, I'm crazy.

Why did I agree to tell you?

These past few months. The days I got to spend with you. I never knew I could be that happy again.

It's like for ten years nothing excited me. I woke up and every day was a beige blur.

But back with you, my life is neon. It's bright again. Even sitting in traffic excites me because all I do is daydream about you and listen to our songs.

We've had the best laughs. The best talks on your sofa while I held you again. I don't have nightmares when I sleep with you.

And damn, our sex. It bombs me with pleasure I didn't know existed.

Then you left me in New York and that bombed us too.

(Me punching the wall after you left didn't help.)

I tried getting by without you. But no matter how hard I worked, or how many meetings I went to, or hours I spent bitching to my sponsor how I was right not to tell you, it didn't fucking matter.

He told me, "You never have to fear the truth."

Well... I fall asleep and wake up to my truth.

I love you.

And we're fucked.

Because the look on your face when you find out—it's going to hurt you so much, Cade.

It's what I do, right?

Hurt you every time.

Even when I'm not trying. Even when I'm trying to do the right thing.

Remember when you found out about Pamela?

We three were best friends. I swear we rode hundreds of miles on our bikes together.

As kids, we were perfect. I was the wild one. You were the smart one. Pamela was the sweet one.

That worked until we were fifteen. You went on a trip with your dad for the summer and Pamela and I hung out at first.

But I could tell she liked me.

She used to touch my arm and giggle.

Fuck, it weirded me out because I didn't like her like that. I liked you but she didn't know and you didn't either.

I felt like I was cheating on you, so I avoided Pamela that summer. That only made me feel like more of an asshole.

She chilled out until we were seniors. Then she started asking just me to come over and hang out because she didn't want to be alone after some dude broke her heart.

I got so worried about her one night so I went over. She hugged me and I let her. Then she tried to kiss me, and I freaked out and left.

I didn't tell you.

I didn't want to come between y'all. You two were so close. You'd talk the girly shit that bored me and that's how we three worked.

It's not like she was trying to fuck you over, Cade. We were all just so close.

And I'm a cocky fuck to say it but Pamela wasn't the first or last ~~girl~~ (sorry) woman to fall for me.

But then you read what she wrote in my yearbook. How she thanked me for always being there at night, for my hugs and stuff and she signed it, "Love you always."

Shit, the look on your face.

It was just the two of us sitting on the beach and I never saw such hurt in your eyes before.

I was worried you'd think I cheated on you. That I'd lose you for trying to be a good friend to her.

But you just got all quiet and stared at the waves.

"It's alright," you finally said. "She can't help that she loves you too."

You were always sweet like that.

You don't give up on people. You see their pain too.

"I like her like a friend. But I love you, Cade. Like you're-the-love-of-my-life love."

I'd never said that to you, not like that and you turned to me with tears in your eyes and gave me the biggest kiss.

God, I wanted to marry you right there on the sand.

That's why I never told you later about Pamela and TJ.

Yep, that's right. It made me fucking sick.

I knew it would you too and I didn't want to ruin your friendship or your memory of her later.

But she didn't know better. She got my new number from my sister and called me in LA. Pamela was in college and freaking out because she and TJ became a secret thing over her Christmas break, and she didn't know how to tell you.

I mean, she knew how much you hated TJ because he was always after you.

But she had no clue how much.

Or why.

I told her that TJ was a dangerous asshole and to stay away from him. Like I talked to her for weeks and begged her to drop his ass.

She said she would. She asked if she could come see me in LA after she did.

I know she dated him thinking it would make me jealous. She had no idea. It made me scared, so I agreed.

I'd do anything to protect her too. So she promised me when she went home for spring break that she'd end it with TJ.

And then... I didn't get any more calls from Pamela.

When my sister told me she went missing, I don't remember much of the months that followed.

I just drank until I didn't feel. Blame. Guilt. Grief.

It should've been me who disappeared, not her.

I wish I was stronger back then. I'd give anything if I could have saved her.

It only made me want to save you more. To never tell you or hurt you again.

You said if I want a future with you, I have to tell you the truth.

But the truth can't seem to stop fucking up our lives, Cade.

So I decided to try this...

I'm sitting here in the hangar in my car, waiting on the jet I sent for you, and I have it all planned.

One perfect day with you.

One perfect night together.

Something we'll always remember.

Because we'll need it.

Because after that, once I tell you the truth?

I pray that somewhere, Pamela's watching out for us.

She always loved you too.

CHAPTER THIRTY-FOUR

CADE

Sink In by Amy Shark

It MAKES me bite my lip; how Redix is waiting there with a pink tulip in his hand.

His big heart breaks me open.

The sight of him lighting up my shadows.

White linen pants. Black shirt open to his tan chest. Sun-streaked hair falling down. No shoes on, of course, while he leans against a blue Land Rover that's got to be vintage.

And he won't take his eyes off me.

Normally I'm so strong.

But my heart hammers. My knees shake.

I have to grab the metal railing, stepping down from the jet in the shade of the private plane hangar we pulled into.

I don't know what we'll do, or what he'll finally tell me, but with that look in his eyes, no matter what truth comes from his lips—we'll be okay.

He doesn't say anything.

Once I'm within his grasp, his hand cups my jaw and his lips are on mine.

The soar of my pounding heart, it takes my breath away along with his deep kiss claiming my mouth.

I've missed him so much, just the touch of him wakes my soul. His soft moan back, the heat of his skin against mine, it does the same to him.

"*Damn*, you're beautiful." His breath lingers over my lips, his fingertips twirling the infinity lock he gave me around my neck. "No questions, Detective, for one day. You'll let me spoil you. Deal?"

"Deal."

I'd agree to a forehead tattoo right now.

His sky eyes study mine and I can tell. "You're nervous?"

"You keep giving me chances"—his thumb tickles over my bottom lip—"and I keep fucking them up."

"But it's me, your best friend."

"Exactly." His gaze won't let go of mine. "*It's you*, my world, and I can't lose you again."

"You never lost me." My lips reach for his again. "And you never will."

He has to believe me.

It's our only chance.

I kiss him as passionately as I can, not giving a shit about the airport staff around us. He has to trust me, or we won't make it.

I may be his, always, but it doesn't mean we can live together.

Not without the truth.

"I've got one question," he asks, wrapping his hands around me in my mini sundress and pulling me near. My stomach flips feeling his cock happy to see me too. "Do you need a nap, or can I start spoiling you now?"

Jet lag ceases to exist in his arms. "I'm wide awake and ready."

He opens the car door for me, seeming far more at home here than he ever did in Hilton Head.

California suits him. He looks like their surfer king ambassador.

I've only been to LA a few times and that was forever ago, flying in and out as a teen for photoshoots with my dad as my chaperone.

I'm certainly not that teen anymore.

Not with the thrill between my thighs at the sight of him, at the silver rings on his tan fingers clicking against the steering wheel as we wind our way through traffic.

He points out the sights, telling me about his show, and I'm trying to listen, but I pinch my thigh not believing I'm here.

The sign we pass after a while reading "Malibu: 21 Miles of Scenic Beauty" isn't bluffing.

I kick off my sandals and put my feet on his dashboard.

"How long have you lived here?"

"I got this place when I went into rehab. It became my way to start over. My old house had too many fucked up memories."

"So you moved in once you got out?"

"Yeah, I worked with a designer to get it ready. I went right back to work too. I was fucking lucky I still had a job. But the showrunner is a friend of mine—Lorraine Morris. She's from Savannah actually, near us. We met out here when I was starting out and she said she'd write a show for me, and she did."

"That's *The Band,* right?"

I catch his eyes lingering up my legs, at how my white dress skims high up my bare thighs.

"Yeah. Lorraine held the production for me until I got my shit together. I'd do anything for her now."

"How much longer until you wrap this season?"

I hope it's not long. At this rate, I'll burn through all my vacation weeks trying to see him.

I already feel guilty as hell for taking days off again, but Mama told me to—playing the "you only live once" card. And from her, I had to honor the wisdom.

But I cheated a bit. I made Penny promise to keep me updated if anything changes. With Redix's pull, I can be home on a plane in hours.

"Just a couple more weeks." He grins my way and he's my home. "Then I have a film in Atlanta."

"Really?" That's hope. That's only a four-hour drive from Hilton Head. "For how long?"

"A few months if all goes as planned."

His lips purse. The veins in his neck tense too.

"What?"

"I might as well tell you now—Angie's cast in it too. It was planned over a year ago."

Dread fills me.

Why?

But I gotta give him a chance.

"Is she gonna be a problem for us?"

He reaches for my hand, "Not at all," squeezing it gently.

We let the tunes he's playing from our teens fill the minutes to wherever he's taking me. I don't care. I just let him rub his thumb over my hand and lead the way.

When we pull in front of a quaint shop off the Pacific Coast Highway, I read the sign above the door and melt.

"Ice cream for lunch?"

"They have a special flavor here."

The delight in his eyes when he takes my hand; I'll never stop loving him.

I hear the gasps. A few people recognize Redix when we walk across the stone patio into the tiny shop. But they don't approach him.

I hope that's a California perk.

"Dude!" The guy behind the counter points his chrome scoop at Redix. "You want the usual?" He glances at me. "Two cones?"

"Nah, man." Redix won't let go of my hand. "Just one, thanks."

I'm fascinated by the process as the guy whips up a blend on the cold marble slab before us. "What flavor is that?"

It doesn't look like our lemon sherbet.

His cocky eyes stop my heart. "Redix Road."

"How'd you swing that?"

He winks, "I kinda own this place now," reaching out for the waffle cone with his custom concoction in it.

Grabbing a few napkins first, he leads me back outside, pulling a chair out for me from under an umbrella-covered table.

"Tell me what you think." He offers me the first bite.

Vanilla cream. Lemon zest. Graham cracker. Something

herbal—basil—it zings across my palate, and I close my eyes... and moan.

"Damn, darlin'." He grins like a demon. "Ice cream on your lips and that sound in your throat? I'm trying to be a gentleman."

I can't help it.

It's so good that I go for two more delicious bites.

And I'm so ravenous, a drip lands on my chin.

He pauses and cocks his head and smiles so big I should take a picture. I've never seen him this happy.

Happy to take a napkin and gently dab the drop off my chin.

"I can't believe you're finally here with me," he says like it's a sacred ritual to him.

He takes the cone from my hand and gives a few licks with his eyes locked on mine.

That look, I know it; it changed my life.

Pressing his lips into the sweet cream, he melts it, and I can sense people watching with phones up.

He doesn't care.

"I promise—this is only with you, Cade."

He reaches around my neck and pulls my lips into his creamy kiss.

It starts off sweet, his lips sliding over mine until his tongue dances in my mouth and I explode. Memories firing with lust. My body tensing, wanting him, ready to straddle him in that metal patio chair.

It's killing me and I want this death. The romance. The passion.

He bought a fucking ice cream store.

I can't hold back, reaching around I grab his neck to take him now, and someone whistles across the patio.

He lifts his lips. "Now that'll go viral." His breath hovers over mine. "And this time... it's very true for me."

I kiss him again, not caring if we're on the screens of Times Square.

You give me Redix Dean, lemon, sugar, and our lips together, and I won't be stopped.

"Take me home," I insist, breaking his rules already.

"Hold your horse ride, darlin'." He's amused. And it looks so damn good on him. "I got hours to spoil you."

Giggles sound over my shoulder.

Redix peeks over it and smiles. "Do you mind?" he asks me.

"Make their day," I say.

He's so sweet about it. Four teen girls, young ones, are gawking at him. He buys them and their parents ice cream before wrapping his arms over their shoulders and giving them all the selfies their gushing hearts desire.

"Is that your girlfriend?" The girl with braces dares to ask him.

"She's more than that." He walks over and takes my hand as I stand. "She's the love of my life."

The group of girls "ahhh" and so does my heart.

I'm fourteen again too. I'm back in that innocence and that constant weight in my chest lightens.

Their parents corral them away while we clear our table to leave.

Then he wedges me against his car when we get to it, his husky whisper teasing me, "Do you wanna selfie with Redix Dean, little lady?"

Only he can wear arrogant and make it cute.

And I'm not fourteen. I'm horny as hell.

"Oh, you'll be taking pictures with me." I urge my hips

back into him. "But they won't be in a parking lot with my clothes on."

He's freeballing in linen pants like the sight of his arousal doesn't cause traffic accidents.

"Are you gonna spoil me too?" he asks.

I stroke his length quickly getting hard under soft fabric.

"Yes. It'll be a very dirty spoil."

He cups my hand, pressing it down hard. "That's called 'porn'."

My insides fire. Desire rushes my body at his thick cock in my grasp.

"That's called 'later'."

I stop my tease and grin at the proud chubby in his pants while he laughs and hops into the driver's seat.

Our adventure continues, winding down the shoreline before we stop in front of a funky cottage. Like time hasn't touched it. I don't ask. I just let him take my hand again as he knocks on a wooden gate.

A darling woman with gray hair pulled into a long braid opens it and greets him with a hug saying, "This must be her." Her eyes sparkle my way.

"Cade, this is Audre Locke." Peace fills his face. "She parties with me on the weekends and runs my favorite pottery studio."

Parties? Pottery? With a got-to-be-seventy-year-old woman?

Who is this serene soul and what did he do with the wild boy I knew?

Audre shows me around, proudly pointing to the bowls and plates Redix has been making for his new place.

I'm impressed by the white and blue glaze he's using on his designs. It reminds me of home.

"This is how you spend your weekends?"

"This and play guitar." He pulls me over to two stools sitting in front of tables. "If I keep my hands busy, a drink won't get in them."

"What else don't I know about you?"

I'm enthralled as he drops a ball of gray clay in front of me.

"Lots." He plops one down on the other table too. "This is the good stuff I *want* you to know."

Audre brings us lemonade with sugar cookies.

Someone gave her the memo on me.

She turns up the old stereo on the porch. Billie Holiday crones softly before Audre disappears inside, leaving me and Redix to our creations.

"No peeking." He insists as we sit back-to-back. "We'll surprise each other."

I start squishing the slick ball.

"What the hell do I make?"

I love this already.

"Whatever your hands dream up."

We're quiet at first, for a long time actually while we work, and I know what we're doing.

We're counting down the hours until he tells me, until this all changes.

But I swear I'll do this for him.

I'll make this day as perfect as I can too.

"Tell me." It's easier to ask with my back brushing his. "Why did you really come home this spring?"

"Well, Detective." He chuckles because he knows me too well; I can't help myself. "I owed my family a visit. And those teen centers mean a lot to me. I got my buddy, Luca—he owns that golf resort—I got him to support them too, so I owed him a donor party."

I'm quiet.

He doesn't mention me and tears bite my eyes, feeling forgotten by him.

That he moved on.

And I never did.

"I missed you too, Candy Cade." His voice is soft, and I gulp back my sob. "My mom told me about Mama G and all I kept thinking was how scared you must be, and I wanted to be there for you. For her too."

My lips won't open.

It's true.

I was terrified with my mama's diagnosis—pancreatic cancer. I still am.

I hear him turn in his chair before a supple kiss lands on the nape of my neck and my shoulders drop with a sigh.

"I had a perfect plan of getting sober and coming back for you," he confesses with his lips to my flesh. "But then I saw you again and I got all fucked up inside because damn, I missed my best friend and forgot how it feels when I see you."

His fingertips tickle down my arm. "It's like fireworks went off inside me seeing you in that purple dress again."

"Do you remember what we did in that dress?"

"Yes." Desire threads his voice making mine cascade down my body. "It was the first time I fucked you from behind. In front of the bathroom mirror. We went from clumsy virgins to racy adults that night."

I tilt my neck for more of his soft bites. "That was our first hotel room together too."

"What were our parents thinking?"

"That we were eighteen, had our own money, and there was no stopping us anyway."

And I need him to touch me again. *Now.*

But our hands are covered in clay and he tortures me,

instead. Straddling me from behind while his lips won't stop with their meal of my neck.

"I swear seeing you again." His lips singe my flesh and my panties soak. "Being with you again, kissing you, fucking you so damn hard. Each time I'm with you now, you have more of me. You've *got* to know I'm yours, Cade, no matter how much I change."

He nibbles my ear, melting my heart and I worry my pussy's gonna wet through my white dress.

"Take me home now or poor Ms. Audre is gonna see her own Redix Dean strip and fuck show right here on this table."

"Nope." I can feel his grin on my skin. "I gotta finish my gift for you."

The heat of his body leaves mine while he turns to pick it up, saying, "Once this is fired up, you'll think of me every time you use it."

I'm making him a lop-sided candy dish.

From him, I'm expecting a perfect plate, or maybe a breakfast bowl for my Froot Loops.

Instead, I turn around...

And he presents me with a clay dildo.

Almost to his perfect huge proportions and my snort is equally as big. "What the fuck?"

I start laughing and can't stop.

Because only Redix wouldn't give a hell.

Only he'd ask a poor old woman to fire up his massive clay dick in a kiln.

"You expect me to use this?"

"I expect to *watch* you." His clowning grin spins my world. "Why use soft silicone when this will be big and hard like me?"

I'm rolling, grabbing my sides and marveling at the balls he's perfectly molded too.

Damn, he's quite a ceramic artist.

"What color are you gonna paint it?"

"Blue"—he kisses my bare shoulder—"for all the years you left my balls that way."

"You're gonna offend Ms. Audre."

But I'm not offended.

I'm wetting more at the thought... and its size... and the show I can give him... and wondering how long it takes to fire that big boy up until it's ready.

"No, it won't." His grin won't stop. Neither will his kisses up to my ear. "She taught me how. She sells dildos on Etsy."

Stop it now.

I can't take it, grabbing my stomach, it hurts from laughing at the image—wild celebrity Redix Dean making ceramic dildos with Malibu's silver-haired potter.

Now that's a party.

"You're too much." I want his lips, his laughs, every-thing about him.

He gives them back, chuckling through our kiss.

"If you can take the real me, darlin', my blue monster dildo *ain't too much.*"

I don't remember laughing this much, not since we were last together.

And I don't know whether we're eighteen again or if we've found a new bliss, but I can't stop.

All afternoon he charms me. Spoiling me at a surf shop where he's already picked out a board for me and where he pops wood at the sight of me trying on a wet suit.

He gives me the giggles when we get pedicures together because he gets his toes to match mine—lavender.

His eyebrows won't stop dancing, joking about the foods he could find other uses for when we devour an early dinner.

By evening, my laughs are punctuated by yawns as the travel finally catches up to me. But when the black metal gates swing open to his oceanfront home, shock wakes me up.

"This looks like one of the homes I used to dream of."

It's a modern design of earthen rectangles stacked upon each other concealing what's got to be a breathtaking view of the Pacific on other side.

"When I saw this listing"—he pulls into the pristine garage—"I had to have it. I hope you like it."

Like it?

It's overwhelming.

My hand shakes in his while he ushers me inside. The entire back of the home is glass walls that are open to the oasis of palms and tall hedgerows offering privacy surrounding the pool and deck outside.

It's almost exactly like the homes I used to show him in magazines, pointing to pictures of white walls, white sofas, natural woods, and glass everywhere.

"Do you like it?" His hands gently turn me around. "I got this for you, Cade." A stillness washes over me. "I got it for *us*."

My world stops spinning.

My breath seizes.

I stop marveling at the view and focus on the sentiment. On what he just said.

All this time I thought he wanted to forget me. That he hated me. That he came here to get away from me because it was my fault.

But no.

He remembered me.

He was designing our dream home, building a sanctuary from our past hell.

More pieces of me heal as a happy sob escapes my heart.

Redix was never an asshole.

He was just a boy who became a man who wanted to share his big heart but didn't always know how.

This is how.

Cradling my wet jaw in his palms, he pulls my lips to his, saying, "I'll take that as a yes."

I give him a kiss from depths where only he belongs before insisting, "Now, Redix. I don't know what else you planned but fuck me right now. Right here on these wood floors, or on that white fur couch, or on those marble countertops. Anywhere... but fuck me now."

"Damn, woman." His nose nuzzles mine. "I spend millions but none of it can buy you patience."

"Because you gave me the perfect day."

I lift my dress off to only my drenched panties underneath and toss it on his smiling face.

"Now let's have the perfect fucking night."

CADE

Bad Love by Ry X

IN HIS BEDROOM UPSTAIRS, the view and aroma are all him.

Salt wafts with waves of vanilla and leather and I'm immersed in Redix.

"Your last surprise is out there." He points toward the balcony. "I wanted to wait until sunset to light those candles."

He put them in jars like our prom night on the beach. They surround the mattress he pulled off the bed. It's in front of the glass wall to the waves crashing beyond.

It's so romantic.

It's seduction laced with memories and it sews back together the ripped seams of my soul.

"You remember so much." I swear if he's not making me laugh, he's making me cry and all I feel is everything.

"This is how I imagined it." His touch lingers across my shoulder. "I used to lie in bed alone and dream that if I got you back one day, I'd bring you here for our first time together again."

I face him, worried.

"You didn't like our time in New York?"

"I loved it. I think I lost my mind fucking you again, but that's not how I wanted it to be. I know I hurt you too."

I'm the asshole. "I'll wait." I pushed him too far, to our savage night that left us raw.

But after all that time apart, it's what we needed.

To let desire rage from our bodies.

But we need this now.

To let it heal us too.

"However you imagined it," I say, "just tell me."

"The guest bedroom across the landing. You'll find all you need in there. A spa shower too. Take your time and meet me back here."

I like his plan and when I see a gift box wrapped in a purple ribbon on the guest bed, I love it even more.

In it, I find a white lace bra and panty set. It rushes my body. The panties are crotchless. The bra has no cups.

Under it?

My jean jacket.

The one he gave me for my sixteenth birthday. The one he wrote in purple Sharpie inside that's still there.

My Candy Cade,
This will keep you warm when I'm not
around. But I promise I'll be back for you.

I left it in his car that day... before that night.

And he kept it all this time.

And I keep shaking it off. The tears that want to take me, but desire keeps it at bay.

I know we have to swim through every emotion together, no matter how terrifying or terrific, if we want to crawl to shore together.

If we want to survive.

While I'm in the shower he taps on the door, telling me my luggage is out there if I need it.

Wearing his gifts, all I need is to slick my hair back, spritz on BOUND perfume, dab on some cherry lip balm, and grab one surprise in my hand.

Dusk colors the walls of his home as I find my way back to his bedroom. Lust pools between my thighs as I push all other thoughts away but him.

No matter what, I'll remember this night.

How I know he'll indulge me. How he'll make me beg and then deliver.

How our bodies always come together even if our lives can't.

With pillows stacked high atop the mattress outside, I don't see him at first.

Sunset smears over the ocean giving way to night above. Candles glow in a circle around the bed. There's a wooden tray beside it with his ceramic bowls. My steps travel over teak boards until I find him lying there and I gasp at the stunning sight.

He's nude, his hair spilling across the pillow while his tan, shredded body reclines across white sheets on the bed. With one arm relaxing above his head, from his biceps to his pecs to his dozen carved abs, it's all seducing my eyes to where he's very eager for me.

"May I?"

I'm brazen with my phone in hand. I never want to forget him like this.

"Be my dirty guest." His gaze follows me as I step onto the bed. "And stand right there."

He guides my legs to straddle his thighs, making my stance wide so the panties he bought me part along with my sex for his view.

"Damn, Cade." His palm starts stroking his cock. "You never stop being beautiful."

I take pictures without a word.

Every part of him; from his sinewed thighs up to his heavy cock and tan hand stroking it, to his trimmed patch up a thin trail to his belly button resting in the canyon of his abs; he's always been *beyond* beautiful to me.

I'm in wonder at my perfect match.

At the one who's never wrong about me.

At the only one who always feels right.

When my lens finds his eyes, they pierce right through to my heart with words that hang in the air.

I love you.

"My turn," he finally says.

I press RECORD for the video and hand him my phone. While he aims it up at me, I step wider and tower over his narrow waist.

"Should I leave my jacket on?"

"No." His next words wrap around my heart. "I'm back to keep you warm."

I take it off, tossing it out of our way.

He's spoiled me today, so I spoil him.

Tickling my fingertips across my breasts jutting high in this risqué bra, twirling over my exposed nipples, I tug at them for his delight.

He grins. "Yes, Cade, just like that."

I lick my fingertips and do it again.

His bourbon voice. "Yes, play with your pussy for me." It can seduce me happily into hell. "That's it. Rub your clit like I taught you. Get it so hard that you get so wet for me."

I am. I'm getting so wet, sliding my middle finger across the slit of lace before diving inside, my palm grinding over my clit; I make my body desperate for him.

"Show me," he demands and I move my hand, splaying my sex open for his view. "Fuck." He sees it. He sees everything, my pussy throbbing for his stare. "Fuck, I remember the first time I got your pussy like this. So full and pink for me."

I can't take my eyes off him, and my hand starts again and it won't take long. "You get so dirty and wet for me, now, don't you?" Not with him talking like that. Not with his cock like granite under me. Not with one hand tugging at my nipple while my other starts fucking myself like I need for him to, so soon, so hard. *God, I want him.*

"You're gonna come, aren't you?" It's in his eyes too. He knows my desire. "Do it, Cade. Be my dirty little girl and come like I'll make you come so hard tonight."

That promise. That need. It takes me, my legs teetering, quivers hitting my thighs while my shoulders collapse with the weight of release as my syrupy spasm makes me barely gasp, "Redix, please."

I drop to my knees with a shuddering surrender.

"Let me taste." He sets my phone down while I collapse beside him.

Taking my slick fingers into his mouth, the suction of his tongue is as strong as his groan. My cum is like the ice cream he loves to lick before he commands, "Strip naked and lie back and don't move."

I'm electric, desperate for his fuck, while I rip my panties off before my bra flings off too. He watches me while he dives his fingers into a bowl beside the bed.

When I see the crescent piece of ice he's holding, I know his game and object, "I need you to fuck me *now*."

"Oh. *I will* fuck what's mine." He pushes me down on the mattress. "But I'm gonna get you wetter than you've ever known for it first."

And he does.

Starting with a cold trickle, ice melts across my mouth before the heat of his tongue clings over my tender lips and I'm going to die and that's fine.

More than fine while he does the same, biting after the drips down my neck. Filling my clavicle with a puddle, he laps it up before circling my nipples with ice until they're freezing peaks. When his mouth finally takes them, one after the other into his hot, ruthless suck, my spine, it arches. Urgently, I cry out for him. But he does it. Again and again and again.

I'm huffing for breath while he murmurs, "God, I want you," down my belly that flutters for his journey of ice and fire across my skin. "Every fucking inch of you belongs to me."

I'm in awe, overwhelmed by the sensations of him, and please don't ever stop. "Close your eyes and just feel this." I hear his voice insist before he kneels between my thighs.

I close my eyes and open more than my legs to him.

He wedges them wider and leaves me like that, air caressing my tender skin screaming for him. The tease of it, he lets it linger before a cold touch greets me next.

"Your pussy's so hot for me, Cade." He circles ice over my clit and it's torture I love, making my legs jump while I hold back a scream.

"It's so hot, it fucking melts me." His voice, it slides warm inside me along with a frigid piece of ice. It frenzies my nerves to a sensation I can't take just before he sucks my folds, each one, over and over while he lets the ice melt. Then the lush lick of his hot tongue fires over my desperate, cold hood before the warm slurp of his mouth sucks on my pussy with a heat that lifts my hips for more as I hold back a roar.

Goddamnit, this ache hurts so fucking good.

"You're so wet now." It's him; it's my fierce need I can't control. "You're so ready for me." It's his fingertip, circling where I'm starving. "So pink and hungry." It's how he plays, drinking me for excruciating minutes and I'm in heaven. "Are you sure you're ready for my fuck?"

He barely touches my clit and I scream, "Redix, please!" I'm begging from my soul, from my greedy depths. "I need you."

"Climb on top." The mattress suddenly sinks to his flop beside me.

I open my eyes and find his fist holding his cock up, tall and full. "Take me, Cade. What you can of me, just like our first time."

I leap up and throw my leg over his. Madness possesses me, a craze for him no one can stop, no matter his size.

"I'll take all of you," I swear, replacing his hand with mine around his thick shaft. "All of you, Redix Dean. You fucking belong to me too." I sink down faster than either of us can handle and he bottoms out, hitting my soul.

"Oh, *fucckkkk!*" He groans so loud, his back bowing to my sudden descent. "Fuck, Cade." The shock, the lust, the vulnerable stance in his eyes watching me, it drives my hips rolling hard. "Goddamn." He grabs them like he can hold on, like he can control me. "Goddamn, you feel so good." But he can't.

It storms my body. His mass shoving out my breath. His stretch making me moan. The glide of his measure making me indulge. The frenzy in my clit, it's dominating my every move.

"Hell yes, ride me so slow." He starts guiding me while my thighs lift and lower, letting my pussy revel in his hard length, in how it loves resisting his tight invasion. "So fucking wet and tight."

Circling my hips, I lean forward, kissing his lips.

This is like our first day together, when we couldn't get enough of each other. When it was so new, we marveled at the power of our sex.

"Fuck, yes," he growls into our kiss, "this is how I remember us."

"We're so much more now." I exhale, "so much more," as his hands grab my ass, seizing me like I'm his lifeline. Like each long sink of my pussy down his cock is his favorite, and each lingering of my rise is his best reward.

Our eyes, noses, and lips hover over each other sharing our breath in perfect rhythm. By the hard clench of his hands, the urge in my body, all this time apart, and to be watching each other—we need more.

I sit up and lean back. Bracing my arms behind me on his thighs, I spread my pussy open to give him more of our show because this is my hunger for him, this is how we satisfy it. This is how he's more than enough.

"Damn, look at us." His jaw hangs. "Look at me inside you again. Look at you fucking my cock." His pecs tense while his eyes are mesmerized by what he's watching and what I can feel—the milky slick I'm painting up and down his shaft.

"I can see you, Cade. All of you." His eyes reflect our fuck while my hips roll, displaying my wild search, my arousal pooling at his wide base. "That's it. Spread your pussy." I need to find this with him. Show this to him. "Baby, you're so full taking my cock. Fuck yes, ride it."

I can. I will. All of him. This is mine. He's mine. His strong grip guides my hip. His other thumb strums my clit. His heart is grabbing for mine. His sexy eyes hold mine captive while my fingers take my nipple to the very point. "I'm gonna come, Redix." It's hitting me so fast. "I'm gonna come so hard on your cock."

"Yes." He's there and I'll take him with me, where he belongs. "Do it for me."

It's a thunder, it's a crash, it's a wet burst through our bodies while I don't know who is louder or who loses more control *but—we—do*.

It pours through our flesh, rushing ecstasy through every place we're joined, our eyes staring at each other while our storm rages through. It's only grown stronger in our years apart. The pulsing. The convulsions. The intensity. We share it until I collapse on top of him and his arms hold me while it leaves us both shaking.

"You were always with me, Cade." He cradles my head to his pounding chest. "And you always will be."

It pulls at my heart, moving my lips to his. The passion

in our kiss owns my senses until he pulls his lips away saying, "We're not done. I want more of us like this."

He lifts my ribs, "Come up here," pulling me up.

"What are you doing?" I'm still in a haze.

But the dare in his eyes; it rouses me fast. "I wanna taste our fuck dripping from your pussy." That does too. "I wanna taste my cum in your pussy where it belongs."

My legs shake with the taboo of this. With his hands guiding my pussy to mount over his face before his tongue scoops, dipping into where he left his pearly cum for me inside.

"Oh god," I gasp, looking down, watching as he devours me and I don't look away. Fuck, this is so erotic, so intimate. There's no limit to us and it's making me shudder, trembling at the erasure of anything between us.

He moans like he's been craving this. Diving his face, his nose, his tongue into my folds, his hand lifts mine, guiding it to his long hair, to grab a fistful of it.

And I know what he's telling me he wants. I do too.

"Do we taste good, Redix?" My hips move, sliding my glossy pussy over his face. "Does our fuck taste good in your mouth?"

He moans again, the grip of his strong fingers over my ass pulling me down to drink. Like he's been in a desert and can't get enough of my pussy, of our cum, of where I'm still open from his cock and our... fuck, this so is hot and he has no shame with me. His hunger only matches mine.

"Do you taste what you do to me?" I grip his strands tighter. I feel his tongue answering me. "How you get my pussy the wettest for you? How I can milk your delicious cum from your huge cock? How I'm suffocating your gorgeous face with my pussy. How this pussy belongs to you."

My dirty words are driving his mouth into a frenzy. His groans into my depths don't stop while my stride over his face won't either. The primal greed between us, the urge we can't fight. It makes me lift up and reach behind me, searching and I find it. His cock is hard again consuming our fuck and I can't contain my groan.

"Come here," he growls, yanking me back for his feast. With a fierce shake of his head between my thighs, he ravages me like a starved animal and I'm done, coming so hard over his mouth that I lose all sensation except the touch of him where I need him most.

It's a whirlwind, how fast he moves while I lose control. Flipping me on my back, he pins my wrists above my head while his knees wedge hard between my thighs, pushing them far apart and he's not stopping.

"Now, Cade." His arms brace above me, his lips glisten with our cum, his exquisite body tents over mine and I get this view. This delicious sight of him just before his magic hips start their ruthless dance into my depths.

"I can taste our fuck in my mouth." He drives in and I see stars. "I can see it dripping from your pussy." The fullness, the pressure, his fuck is brutal perfection. "I can feel you resisting me, wrapping so tight around my cock." In and out, he's thrusting. "I swear I'm gonna fuck you so hard again and you'll *love* the pain."

He does and the orgasm his merciless mouth gave to me doesn't disappear. Like a loud symphony it's still singing through my body lifting open for his.

"Yes, like this." It strains from his throat while his abs flex to his driving tempo and my hips rise to match it. His rhythm is perfect, glistening with sweat while his cock drums into me and I don't ever want him to stop. His eyes watch mine, then our sex, then back to wonder with me.

"Fuck, you feel so wet and tight. So swollen and hot. Fuck."

"Redix, do it harder." He worries he'll hurt me, but the only thing that will is if he stops. I'm desperate, pushing against his restraint. "I can take you."

"Grab my shoulders"—he insists, releasing my wrists—"and don't let go. Hang on to me."

Because we know it's going to wreck us. Like a tsunami, it'll wash away our years apart, the distance between us gone, and the pain... we can hope for that too. We can hang on to each other. We can do this so hard that it'll disappear in the torrent that's us together.

He lowers to his elbows, his knees pushing my thighs wider to where his mass bottoms out inside me and he starts moving in circles, driving into my core. "Don't let go of me, Cade." His forehead presses to mine, his stammering breath hovering inches from mine while I dig my nails into his shoulders. "Fuck yes, like that." He hisses so sweet at my possession. And yes, it's possible he can fuck me even harder as he claims every piece of me, pummeling my clit and I'm ready to scream in surrender.

My sex, my soul, they're soaked by his force everywhere inside and "Redix" is all I can barely say. But it's everything I feel barely hanging on to his flesh, on to my edge while I'm staring into his eyes. My demand, my vulnerability, my deal; it's all for him.

"With me." His breath shallows while the muscles in his back seize under my hard grip. "Do it."

His last thrust is merciless. It thrashes through me, snatching him too and dragging us down to our favorite depths where we gasp for breath, where every part of me floods for him, where he gives me every piece of him too. Another groan escapes my soul as I feel him pulsing inside, sharing more with his grunts, over and over, as we both wash ashore.

"I love you." He finally says it. It's welling in his eyes, gazing down at me. "I love you so much, Cade, and I never stopped."

"I love you too." Tears trail from my eyes, wetting my hair. My body sags with my gentle cry. "I love you, Redix, and I won't ever stop."

We were never meant to be apart.

But were we meant to stay together?

CHAPTER THIRTY-SIX

CADE

Clouds trail across the sky before a gentle breeze blows them away, revealing a twinkling brilliance above us.

It's been a perfect day.

Then a perfect night.

And we held each other in silence for minutes after it.

My head lies on his chest. His arms wrap around me, so do his legs but we're not saying a word and we know why.

We're afraid.

Do I really want to know?

Can't I just live in this innocence?

It's tempting. In his arms, I can forget all and only remember that I love him.

But it's not fair. It's too much to let him carry alone. He has for ten years and it almost killed him.

"I can't sleep." I kiss his chest. "Can you?"

"No." He squeezes me tighter. "I don't want this to change."

"But we have to." I lift my head and turn his chin my way. "We have to change. This secret. It's destroying us."

"I'm afraid the truth will too."

"Then let's be afraid together." I rest my head on the pillow we share. My eyes bore into his and I swear, "I'm in this with you." I reach for his hand. "Please tell me what happened."

"When I tell you"—his eyes glass with fear—"promise me we won't lose this. Not after everything we've been through to get here."

"I promise." I do from my soul. "I won't leave you."

I see the lump in his throat as he swallows down the pain. It keeps him quiet before he asks, "What do you remember about that night?"

"We were getting ice cream. You went back for our second scoop, and I was standing by the curb, waiting for you. Then suddenly TJ grabbed my wrist. I turned around and Gentry was behind me too, standing by his car idling at the curb. I knew it from the look in their eyes—they were going to hurt me. Then you ran over and the three of y'all started fighting. I tried fighting too but it was a tornado of fists and I got knocked to the ground."

"Do you remember who grabbed your necklace when you did?"

"No."

"It was Gentry. That's what set me off so bad."

"I thought I lost it because it happened so fast. Then TJ went after me while I was on the ground. He said, 'Watch, pretty boy, while I make her suck my ice cream cone,' and started unzipping his pants and grabbing my neck like he was going to make me suck his dick, but you started wailing on him, right?"

His nostrils flare. "Yeah."

"But as you got TJ off me, Gentry said, 'Fine, pretty boy. We'll take you instead,' and both guys had you, dragging you back into the car..."

Tears wet the pillow under me but I won't stop. "You screamed for me to run. Like it was either you or me and you let them take you."

The sacrifice in Redix's eyes at that moment, it's branded on my soul forever.

"And I'm sorry," I cry. "But I couldn't stop them. They shoved you in the car and jumped in too and it took off. I don't even know who was driving, but I chased after the car but it didn't matter. They sped away and I couldn't breathe. They had you. And it should've been me."

I fight back the sob confessing, "That's all I think about, every single day, that it should've been me. They were after me, not you, and I'm so sorry."

His thumb wipes away my tears. "I'd do it all again for you."

I kiss his palm, biting back the guilt. "What happened next?" I barely whisper, "Please tell me."

"You got your dad, didn't you?" He doesn't answer me. "Why didn't you get your mom too?"

"Because you had weed in your pocket, and I was dumb and eighteen. I worried you'd get busted with it. So I called my dad for help. If I called Mama, or the police, I worried you'd get in trouble and lose your career or something. I didn't know better."

"It's okay." He brushes back my bangs. "You did the smart thing. Your dad saved my life."

"How?"

He's quiet.

His hand starts shaking, brushing over my hair like it soothes him.

"I don't remember much, Cade, that's the truth. It was a shitshow of punches in their back seat. And then something stung my arm like a hornet, but I kept fighting. I clocked TJ's jaw real good and then my world spun into black."

"So you don't remember anything?" They drugged him. I try not to ask like a detective, but it's obvious and their M.O. "It's okay if you don't."

"I remember waking up some and being dragged. I could hear the ocean. I felt sand under my feet. I kept coming in and out and…"

His teeth grab his bottom lip in a hard bite.

I don't press.

I don't say anything.

"I remember TJ and the smell of cigarettes." His voice strains. "I remember Gentry smelling like fucking Abercrombie. And some other guy. The driver I guess. He was wearing your necklace by then and punching my face and ears. I tried to rip it off his neck but I couldn't move."

I give him the time he needs, my molars crunching to not let my reaction steal this from him.

This is his story, not just mine.

He anchors to my eyes before he continues.

"Cade, all I remember next is pain and then your dad. He had a fucking gun on them. He told them they'd better run like hell before he killed them, and I worried he'd do it for me so I groaned something like 'help'."

That sounds like my dad. He didn't kill them.

But I will.

I can't tell Redix that.

"Those assholes ran and your dad took care of me. He didn't even ask. It's like he knew why I was there with them and not you."

"I was looking for you too. Dad told me to hide at the park, but I didn't. I came out onto the beach calling for you. It was so dark and I couldn't see anything. I just felt sick because I had to find you."

"I heard you. That's when your dad called out for you."

"But when I found y'all, Dad told me to leave. Like he didn't want me to see you."

"You should've seen the look on your face when you did. I could barely see through my swollen eyes but that I'll never forget."

Redix's beautiful face; they beat it black and blue. Red drips fell from his ear, streaking his hair. His shirt was gone. His jeans were barely on and drenched in blood. It was soaking him everywhere.

"I'm sorry. I fainted." I remember up to that point. "You were covered in blood, and I couldn't take seeing you like that."

"Your dad took care of us until your mom showed up."

"My Mama? I don't remember that."

"She said you were in shock and took you home while your dad took me to his boat."

That night, hours of it are lost to me. I just remember waking up the next morning to the hell of knowing something horrible had happened.

"Why did he take you to his boat? Why not the hospital?"

"I wouldn't let him. While he patched me up, I begged

him just to let it go. That it would only make it worse for you."

"We could've thrown them in jail for what they did."

"TJ would've gone, but not Gentry, not with his family's power and that's why I worried. I didn't know who the other guy was and if he'd come after you too."

Questions swirl in my brain.

Like I should start an investigation, but I won't.

Not with the trembling in Redix's hand I'm holding.

Tonight, this isn't about my revenge.

This is about his peace.

But there are a couple of questions that have haunted my soul for years. That have left me aching inside for so long.

"Why did you leave me? You came over the next day and told me we were over, to find someone else to love and then you left. For ten years. And you took my broken heart with you."

It trembles my lips asking him.

His do the same, bravely answering while his eyes threaten tears too. "Because I didn't know how I'd hide from you what they did to me."

"What do you mean? Did they ra—"

"I don't know." He answers me fast. "I don't remember. When I woke up, I was in so much pain, there was so much blood, I don't know."

The detective in me knows, "That's evidence of it."

"You don't understand. That's not where I was bleeding."

"What?" I can't separate being the woman who loves him, who hurts for him, from being the detective who keeps asking. "What do you mean?"

"It's not your fault, Cade." His hand squeezes mine tight. "Promise me you'll know that."

I'm confused, "I promise," spinning in a haze of unknown while Redix slowly rolls onto his stomach and pulls the sheet away hiding his body.

It takes me tragic moments to see, to let it sink in.

My fingertips reach out to make sure it's real...

Oh my God, it is...

And sobs escape.

Tracing over his skin, I touch the horrific, jagged scar on his buttock—two dorsal fins.

It's our tattoo carved deep into his flesh.

They *did* this to him.

They hurt him like this.

Mocking our love, they branded his flesh because they were after me... but Redix protected me.

So they went *after him.*

There's no breath. No sight through my tears. No sound but my cries. My hands shake while all I can do is kiss his wound and let every piece of pain, of guilt flow from me.

Saline meets my lips pressing gently against his mutilated flesh and with his slight flinch, I only sob more. My tears fall over his scarred skin while he just lets me touch him there, finally understanding why.

Why he ran.

Why he hid.

Why he needed years.

Why he could never escape their torture because he'll be wearing it for the rest of his life.

"It should've been me." It's all I can think. *"It should've been me."* It's all I can say. *"It's my fault they hurt you."*

I'll never let it go; my deal.

"No." He rolls back over, lifting my wet jaw in his

hands. "No, Cade. I was there for a reason and I'd do it again for you. If they had taken *you*, it would've been a lot worse. What they could've done to you; that would've hurt us more and you know it."

I'm grabbing for breath. For logic through his words.

"I'm so sorry." I can hardly speak. I'm tethered to his eyes and barely hanging on. "I'm so sorry I got mad. I'm so sorry I fought you and left. I understand now." I need this from him. "Please forgive me."

"I never blamed you." His lips are on mine, gently tasting the tears we share. "I loved you then and I love you now and I never wanted to see this look on your face. This is *why I didn't tell you.*

"Why I was afraid to make love to you or to take my pants off. I've never let anyone see me naked until now. Except your dad. He cleaned me up and promised he'd never tell."

"He never did, I swear."

"I know. I trust him with my life. Like I do you and your mom."

"I'm gonna kill those men."

Because I can.

Because now I know their first victim was Redix and I'll be damned if they haven't hurt their last one because I'll do more than scar them.

I'll slit their throats.

"No, you won't." He hooks his finger under my chin, lifting me out of my silent vendetta. "Don't let them ruin us anymore. We're finally back together. You finally know and this is what I meant."

He bites down, tensing the muscles across his square jaw before he insists, "I'm not a victim, Cade. I'm not a sad story that needs special care. Or a case you need to solve. I don't need justice. I need peace. I lost nine years of my life trying to get my shit together and I did. And now..."

His gaze fills with love, looking down at our naked bodies, skating his fingertips across my belly.

"I want to be the man able to touch you, to let you touch me, to fuck you, to make love to you, to have fun again like we did today and they're not taking another *goddamn minute* away from us. Promise me."

"I promise."

Part of me does.

The other part?

It's going to take time... if ever.

The deepest sigh escapes his lungs before he draws another asking, "Can we stop with the questions now? This is our truth and it's time we move on. You're here like I always dreamed. We had a perfect day and I want three more together with you before you leave. Okay?"

"Okay."

I'm still reeling with what I learned but the scar on his flesh?

I only love him more.

For minutes he holds me and I'm even more determined —*I'll fight for him.*

"Okay," I say. "We get three more days of perfect together."

"And nights."

His grin is soft, trying to shift the mood to something lighter.

I help him. "Do we have to stick to nights?"

I can never make up for what he did for me, but I *will* die trying.

He rolls on top of me, smiling.

"You mean I can stick you every hour?"

"Remember what happened the last time you turned me into a pin cushion?"

He always does this. "That's why there's cranberry juice in the fridge." Smiling down at me, he'll do anything to make me laugh. "I'm gonna poke you for days."

"Can you poke me in the shower?"

"Yes." His lips cling down my neck. "If you let me do dirty things to you with soap."

For three days, God, I'll make Redix Dean so happy.

If you promise to keep our deal.

CHAPTER THIRTY-SEVEN

REDIX

DEAR CANDY CADE,

Your bottom lip pouts when you focus. It's so sexy I want to bite it.

In a sweet way.

And then your face, it's like an innocent doll.

But then you've got those violet cat eyes with those thick eyebrows that intimidate the shit out of people.

Sorry.

I'm staring.

You look so damn cute cooking in my kitchen. That sarong you've got wrapped around you? I'm gonna rip it off in about ten minutes.

So for now I'll just enjoy this, sitting on my sofa and watching you across the room.

Fuck, I'm happy.

I find myself writing that a lot lately.

We had a second perfect day.

You let me take you surfing. You're a good sport because these waves ain't like the ones at home. But you've always been a badass. You have no fear.

You paddled out with me and popped up like a champ and owned them until one wiped you out. I got scared when you didn't come up. I panicked and swam over, but then you did, coughing with a smile.

Moments like that...

Man, I fall in love with you all over again.

But are we kidding ourselves?

I've watched it cross your eyes today.

Yes, we can forget and have fun. I can make you laugh or make love to you in the shower.

I didn't know what my body would do, letting your hands slide down over my ass while I had you against the wall. But I was too deep inside you and wanting you so much that I fought it off.

How it hits me like a sudden punch when I feel you touch my scar.

It's like fighting back a wildfire that's going to explode.

And I catch them.

The quick glimpses you give my body now that I let you see it.

I'm trying. I'm walking around naked to make us both get used to it.

But I don't know if it's working.

I've always known that look in your eyes. When you

care so much for me, or someone else, that you forget yourself.

Remember how you used to let me and Renie stay with you?

My mom would have some dickhead boyfriend over and I didn't trust a strange man around my little sister.

Most of them didn't like me either. I remember one kept calling me "Brad Pitt" like he hated me and I just felt it. I had to protect my sister and get her out of there.

You let us spend the night with you. You gave Renie your bed and your stuffed animals.

We were sixteen and I loved that about you.

That you still had yours.

That you'd do that for her.

But Renie was scared to be by herself, and you only had a twin bed, so you slept on the floor beside her and I slept beside you. The look in your eyes. All I felt was guilt and love that we made you worry.

So you told your mom, didn't you?

I never asked you, but the next day my mom called and said that man was gone and that we could come home.

I think Mama G had something to do with it.

She's like that. Like a shadow, silent but watching. Reminds me of you.

Well, the watching part.

Not the silent one because damn, you have a mouth when you wanna use it.

Pun intended.

Hell yes, you used it on me this morning.

You went to your knees while I was brushing my teeth and I saw stars to you sucking my cock so deep. Now that I'm not hiding. Now that I can really let go, I did. I let you grab my ass while I grabbed your head and I thought you'd choke on me, but you kept moaning like you loved it.

Damn, you always make me come so hard.

Even with a fucking toothbrush in my mouth.

And our perfect night?

I'll never forget it.

All those other women I barely remember fucking. They're a blur but not you, Cade.

I see you, touch you, and God when I make you moan; it's locked in my memory forever.

I disappear in you. In your taste. Our taste. Fuck that turns me on. I've never done that before and now I won't stop. It's us together and so damn real. Like I'm finally alive again and I need to live every day with you.

But is it enough, Cade?

Our love?

Yeah, we can laugh. We always could. We can hang out without a word, or fuss over stupid shit like the right way to hang toilet paper. (OVER, BTW).

And like hell if we can't fuck ourselves into bliss.

But then I see it in your eyes.

How you're blaming yourself about me.

Your guilt?

That's what I feared.

That's what I tried protecting you from for ten years because it's tearing you up inside.

I fought like hell to get better and I love you so much, I don't want it to destroy you now.

Because it's not your fault.

I don't blame you.

But I know you blame yourself so I can't tell you how sometimes I remember things I don't want to.

So now, you fight your guilt while I fight my addiction and you don't know how strong it can be.

I worry it'll sneak up on us.

Like a rogue wave.

The only thing that's stronger... is my love for you.

And I promise, Cade, I'll hang on to you as long as I can.

CHAPTER THIRTY-EIGHT

CADE

I DON'T KNOW why they're putting makeup on him.

Redix perpetually glows.

And he keeps a sexy shadow of a beard that I love the tickle of down my belly.

But our perfect day three is on hold.

He got called to the studio for reshoots. Something about the producers changing the script for a love scene. They re-wrote it into a break-up since the actor playing his girlfriend won't renew her contract.

"Emma should be paid more so fuck them if they won't," Redix said, pulling us into the studio lot.

"Why don't you threaten to walk out to help her?"

It was an ungodly hour as he parked outside a row of trailers.

"I tried." When we got out of his car, he put his hand out for mine to hold. I loved it. "They'll only replace Emma's character with another groupie girlfriend. We're all dispensable at some point."

I don't see how.

Not him. Not with how Redix seduces any lens.

He *is* the perfect rockstar. Or Romeo. Or surfer. Or CEO.

The man can make the role of filing taxes wet your panties.

"I'm glad you're finally here," Eric, his assistant side-whispers while we watch from our chairs as the crew hustles around set. "I worried New York was a fluke. It's nice seeing your face with him in LA too since I've seen your name on so many papers."

"Papers?" I like Eric. He took care of us at the photoshoot.

"He didn't tell you yet?"

"Tell me what?"

When it comes to Redix, surprises aren't always good.

"He's supposed to so that you know."

"Know what?"

My nerves twitch. The three cups of coffee I've sucked down don't help.

"His house. He's supposed to tell you that he left it to you. He put you in charge of his estate too should some-thing happen to him."

The confusion. The worry. It's written across my face and Eric reads it fast.

"We made him do it," he explains. "Me. His manager. His agent. After his last stint in rehab, we made him get his affairs in order. It was decided his mom and sister would be too upset, so he said if anyone could, you'd take care of his things."

What shocks me more?

Redix's trust in me.

His dance with death.

Or his plans in case he does it again.

"How bad was he?"

If Redix trusts Eric, so do I. And for all the good Redix shares with me now, I know he's hiding bad too.

"If he starts drinking or using again? If you really love him? Don't enable him. Leave... and don't look back."

I've seen too much as a cop. Too many lives and people wasted. The scary picture is clear.

"That's why it's good you're here." Eric sips his tea. "And Angie's not."

"I thought Angie's history, an act."

A knot, it twists in my stomach.

"She is. Was. She was business to him, but he was more to her. And she never respected his sobriety. Like tempting him was a game."

"It's one she'll fucking lose if she tries that shit around me."

"I see what Redix means." Eric chuckles. "How you fight for him. It's good. He needs someone who cares about him and not his fame. I've never seen him this healthy and happy. I can finally relax."

I turn back, watching Redix in his cast chair.

He's grinning my way. He does look happy... and the picture of sexy health.

Munching on donuts from craft services, I watch for three hours how he shoots a sex scene with Emma.

How he gets into character, lying in bed with her on set,

shooting a hot scene that's so believable I feel weird—jealous, horny, and proud—an odd mix.

The Intimacy Coordinator negotiates how Redix will kiss from Emma's neck, licking down between her naked cleavage to her belly. He has underwear on while Emma only wears a flesh thong.

They reset for another angle meant to look like Redix is going down on her.

I twist in my chair and tingle between my thighs, knowing the act for real. While they reset again for a closeup of his face disappearing between her thighs, my pulse doubles.

Just before they call "Action" he glances at me and when they start rolling, his moan—*it's for me.*

A wet desire slides down my body.

Why did I wear a miniskirt today with no panties?

Oh, because we've been fucking every chance we can, but now that's a mistake because I'm so turned on.

Then they run the new scene.

It's where his character, the rockstar, leaves when his groupie-turned-girlfriend asks him in the middle of their sex to commit.

"Stay with me," she sighs, her eyes begging his.

"I never stay," Redix replies. "I leave. That's what I do."

My throat tightens. There's truth in his tone. You can see he loves her but it's not stopping him.

This is for the camera, right?

The heartbreaking drama unfolds as he pulls away and yanks on his clothes in a blur, leaving her sobbing on the bed.

"You're really good, you know." An hour later, I'm sitting on the table in his trailer watching him hang his wardrobe in his closet. He's done for the day. "Watching you act gave me all kinds of feels."

"Oh yeah?" The black t-shirt peels off him, his muscles flexing for my view. "Thanks, Candy Cade." His smile flexes too. "Seriously. That means a lot. That you like my work."

"*Were* you acting?"

His jeans fall to the floor. My jaw follows. Wardrobe put him in grey boxer briefs and his package hangs impressive from below his belt of obliques. *Fuck me.*

I stammer, "Or is that the *real* you?"

He steps out of his pants, eyes reading me.

"You jealous again?"

It's three steps across the small space and he's between my legs dangling over the table.

"Did you like watching my mouth on another woman, or did it make you wanna fuss 'n' fight like you do because, fuck, both turn me on?"

"I asked the first question."

He chuckles, "Yes, Detective," his lush lips near mine, strands of his hair framing his approach.

"I'm acting because I'm not a rock god or with another woman." His lips kiss mine through his words, "When I close my eyes, I'm the man who loves Cade Bryant, and only her."

Part of that I believe.

"How do you not get hard then?"

"Because thirty crew are standing around me and I know I can jerk off when I get back here."

"That's what you do in here?"

"At least once a day." The look in his eyes confirms it. "*I think about you all the damn time.*"

He pours that last line like honey while his thumb

grazes my nipple under my thin tank, and I want my own with him.

Sex. Action. Now.

"Do you trust me now?"

But he's focused on that need too; that this is more than lust. That we're together in ways no one can take from us again.

"Do you trust you're the only one for me?" he asks.

It's been like this since he told me. An intensity fueling our passion to depths I didn't know possible. Love and pain and truth and it makes us so real.

"Yes, I trust you," I swear to him, my heart warms with it too. "More than anything."

He rewards me with a kiss that thumps blood to my sex before I demand, "Show me what you do when you come in here thinking about me."

He pulls my hand down the narrow corridor to the small bedroom in the back of his trailer. Opening the nightstand, he takes out a bottle of lube before pushing his underwear to his ankles.

It doesn't escape me.

How he doesn't hide his scar before he turns around and sits down on the bed.

"I do it like this," he says.

The openness, the desire he shares with me as he pumps lube into his palm before he starts pumping his thickening cock.

God, he's gorgeous looking up at me and it's more than trust.

I love him.

I believe in him.

I believe in us and I strip down and step between his open thighs with my naked body awake to his hungry stare.

"Damn, Cade, this is much better with you *actually* here."

His kiss lands in my cleavage and we start our own scene. His right fist jerks his cock while his left hand teases my nipple. His mouth sucks my other one, making me weave my hand through his hair and pull him in for more.

The intimacy, the lust, the trust I feel watching him, I want it all again with him.

Another first we can share.

"Redix," I sigh as his lips leave my thrilled nipple dripping. "Have all of me. Right now."

He stares up at me and I can't tell if it's exactly what he wants... or what he fears.

The hand on his cock stops while both grab my hips and his lips skim my belly, muttering, "I don't want to hurt you."

I lift his chin.

"You won't hurt me. I want you to. You've given me everything and I'll give you all of me too."

His cock surges, leaking, and is that his answer? "Is it what you want?"

"To fuck your ass?" His middle finger glides between my slick folds. "Hell yes, I want to." His fingers spread my lips open to the cool puff of air he blows over my clit. "*If* I'm the only one who ever will. Promise me, Cade." His warm tongue flicks my sensitive hood after he demands it.

"*Oh fuucckkk,*" I reply to his tease.

And when the lapping of his tongue starts drinking me like I'm a bowl of water and he's a thirsty dog, slurping up my pussy and shaking my knees, the words tumble out, "Yes, Redix, I promise."

"Lie down." He makes room beside him.

I crawl onto the bed and flip over to see him going to his knees at the edge of it.

"I'll get you so wet and ready"—pulling my legs, he brings my ass to the edge—"*then* you can tell me where you want my fuck."

God, the look on his face, he does want me, all of me as he pushes my knees open. "Hold them wide like that and let me in."

Hooking my arms around my knees, I hold my thighs open to him. My sex, my body, my heart, they're splayed open for him and I want this. I'm so exposed, so ready for him to have all of me.

And he does.

His mouth dives back into my pussy with a hunger that lifts my shoulder blades off the bed. "Goddamn, Redix," I swear. Where does he get his appetite for me? I don't care.

I'll be his goddamn meal for life he feels so good.

"You're so fucking sweet for me, aren't you, Cade?" He sinks two fingers into my syrupy walls. "Just like this." Sucking my clit, he thrusts and curls his digits inside and pleasure floods my flesh, my lungs huffing for more.

"Yes." He's going to make me come like this, so many times until I'm begging for him. "Redix, please!"

And he does please me. Twice I come with his mouth devoted to my clit, to my pleasure while his finger teases, then breaches my ass harder for more. It doesn't end with him. There's no time, no way I want him to stop. "Redix, I'm ready."

"Ready for what?" His finger probes my ass deeper while his eyes lock on mine and a devilish smile is in them while he flicks his tongue across my clit and I'm on goddamn fire before he asks, "What do you want, Cade?"

Five hundred of him to fuck me now and forever, but I'll take this.

"Fuck my ass." Even the command frees me.

"You sure?" He presses two fingers inside to prep me while I groan because he loves hearing me say it again.

"Please, Redix."

Still watching me. Still grinning. Still ramming his fingers in my ass, he sucks my clit again before he taunts again, "Are you sure you want me to fuck this tight little virgin hole too?"

I couldn't be more bold, more desperate. "Fuck my ass *now*, Redix."

"I'll go slow." He stands up at the edge of the bed. "Just tell me if you want me to stop, or if you want more."

Everything he's done for me, I'll always want more of him.

I grab his thick cock after he covers it in lube. "Let me guide you."

"Take your time," he says while his fingertips tease my pussy, keeping my urge for him so my body will permit this.

Gazing up at him, I ease in his tip. The way he's looking down, watching us, I want it too. "More," I demand the feeling. I want him and he pushes in. "More." The pressure, I exhale, trying to soften, to relax, slowly taking him in. "More."

He's stretching me, his fingertips thrilling my pussy like he knows how while the hard mass of him slowly drives in. Teasing my clit, he mixes the pain with sweet pleasure.

"Is it all for me, Cade?" His eyelids hang heavy, watching what he's claiming. "Am I the only one who'll fuck your ass?"

"Yes," I sigh. He's the only one... in every way. "More."

Suddenly, it shoots to the tips of my ears, scorching across my lungs, the burn of him, the ring he's blazing through inside while he's found the very tip of my clit, his wet finger dancing across it. I crave his fire until it ends.

Until he's filling me, body and heart. Gently, he slides two fingers into my pussy too and there's no reality but him and I go crazy, keening at the pleasure.

This isn't an act. This is real and we've always been this way. We always get lost in this paradise together, just us, never wanting to leave. We can survive together here, forever.

His fingers, his hard cock, every part of him cleaves to my walls and I'm blissed out. "Are you all mine now?" He draws back giving me relief, but I don't want it.

"Yes." I can't stand it. "Again, Redix. Please." It's thrashing, the need, the demand in my body while he drives in again. The euphoria in my clit that he's pinching while he does it, "Oh my God", I'm losing my mind.

I open my eyes to find it and he's looming over me. "Who makes you come, Cade?"

"You." I'm possessed, loving his control, his plunging cock in my ass and fingers claiming my pussy. And I don't want this pleasure without him.

"Who kissed you first, who touched you first, who fucked you first?" It's taking him too, his thrusts quickening. I don't know how much I can take. "Who makes your pussy come? Who's fucking your ass for the first time?"

"You." But he feels so good. He always has. "Always you."

"I'm yours too." Breath, he can't find it. Me neither. Pleasure, it's the only thing we feel and I'm going to break for him. Only him.

How is it possible two people can love each other this much? Want each other this much? Survive so much and keep coming back for more?

There are no answers but our truth.

It's the look in his eyes when he swears, "I'm the only

one who'll fuck your sweet, tight ass and I swear I'm gonna come so hard when you do." It's going to break him too, the tremors across his flesh matching mine. "Come on, Cade." It's fracturing through me, his massive cock urging into my ass, his tender fingers teasing my pussy, his heart held in my hand, his thighs shaking with mine. He smacks my clit. "Make us come with my big cock in your virgin ass."

It's blinding. The pleasure that takes my body, the release of my spasms, I scream out for him. The whole studio can hear me, and I want them to know I'm his while my body seizes and he falls over the top of me, groaning deep in my ear.

All our love, all our lust, it's right here, pulsing through us and no one can take it away.

He buries his face next to mine while I wrap my fingers through his strands. Kissing my cheek, he chuckles into my flesh. "Goddamn woman, you make my legs weak."

"I can't *feel* my legs." I pull his chin up for my kiss. "I only feel you."

His nose nuzzles mine. "I don't want you to leave."

I dread it too. "I have to."

"I'm coming home next weekend."

"You have to work."

"I have to see you so I'll *make* it work."

"Redix." I search his eyes. "We're okay now. We love each other and we'll make this work."

He nods, seeking my kiss again for reassurance.

I want to promise infinity with him again. That everything is fixed and we're healed.

But I hear it—a distinct ring from the phone in my purse on his table and I know...

That's Penny.

That's not good news.

CHAPTER THIRTY-NINE

CADE

"He's doing what?"

This is crazy.

I'm talking to Penny on my phone, throwing clothes in my suitcase, and trying to rush back home because she says Jameson's about to go rogue to bust these cases open.

"He found out the liquor store is owned by Gentry Evans too." Penny sounds equally pissed. "The store where the Parrot T-shirt dude was spotted. So now he's gonna surveil Gentry's yacht." She also sounds worried. Me too. "That's The Pelican, the rental company, the nail salon, and the liquor store. It's all a trail to Gentry, and Jameson's gonna blaze a path to catch him on it."

"Yeah, well with the way he goes in like a blowtorch in a tissue factory, he's gonna burn these cases to ash—all eleven of them."

"Eleven? Girl, you've been California-dick-dreaming with Redix Dean. We're up to ten now unless you forgot."

No, I didn't forget.

It's eleven cases if you count Redix.

Because I do.

Glancing over at him, he's sitting on the foot of his bed, texting on his phone to get my charter flight home moved to as-soon-as-fucking-possible.

"You gotta talk some sense into him," Penny insists. "He'll listen to you."

"Why me?"

"You know why. Jameson's in love with you."

"He's not in love with me. He's with Scarlett."

That flicks Redix's eyes up lightning fast and I wince.

Fuck, my mouth.

It has no patience.

"He's just frustrated." I keep talking to Penny. "We all are. We've been at a stalemate with these cases for over a month and it's making us all crazy."

"Well crazy is going after Gentry Evans without back-up. I'll cover his ass by day but I'm not chasing that rich, sick motherfucker across the dark Atlantic. I have a baby to go home to."

"Alright, alright."

See, this is what happens when I take time off and dare to be happy—fucking man-shit hits the fan and ruins it.

Story of every woman's life.

"I'll call him."

I wrap up that call to Penny and stop to zip up my suitcase.

"I got you leaving in two hours." Redix looks hurt. "You'll be home before two a.m."

"Thank you. I'm so sorry I gotta leave like this."

I step to the edge of the bed and hug his head to my cleavage. He kisses that spot and then the necklace he gave me.

"This is my job. You get reshoots and I get real shit."

"Call him." He doesn't look at me. "I know you need to."

I know Redix isn't thrilled about Jameson.

But if I can watch him pseudo fuck another woman, he can deal with my partner who's lost all patience.

I tap the phone still in my hand, holding Redix with the other. It's two rings and Jameson picks up.

"Hey." My tone is flat.

"Hey."

So is Jameson's. He knows where I am, and he's pissed about it.

"It's *our* case. I waited for you. Remember? Daufuskie? You gonna wait for me too?"

The seconds he takes to answer find me pulling away from Redix and walking to stare at the ocean, imagining I'm at Jameson's desk instead and trying to talk some sense into him.

"I overheard Gentry at The Pelican," Jameson finally answers. "I was there with Scarlett and I heard him bragging about how he's been partying on his yacht. I'm getting your friend Silas to take me out to follow him."

"So you went behind my back and called Silas too?"

My blood, it's starting to boil.

"If I avoided every man in love with you, Bryant, there'd be none of us left to work."

"Goddamnit, Jameson."

"What, Bryant?"

"Do I gotta call you off like an attack dog? You go after Gentry without me, with just you and a civilian, and you're gonna shit this up. I know that water. You're from Boston. You don't. I grew up with that man. You didn't. I've dealt with him before. You haven't."

"Well, you're not here, doing *your* job. I am."

That hurt. Spinning my head. Bruising my heart.

"Don't you dare." I can barely speak.

Because he has no idea.

This is more than my job.

This is my deal. My past. My pain. The love of my life, Redix, and my revenge.

Something touches my shoulder. It's Redix standing behind me, but I can't face him as tears drop down my cheeks.

How did I get here?

Where two men like me. One man loves me. And two others I want to kill. All because I don't want anyone else hurt because of me.

"I'm sorry, Bryant," Jameson speaks through my stunned silence. "You're the best fucking detective and I'm sorry. I'm just frustrated."

"I care about my job." It's all I can exhale. "Too much."

"I know you do." Jameson tries soothing more. "I'll wait until tomorrow night and we'll go out then."

"Copy."

I end the call.

"That's a lot of passion for just a colleague."

Redix's tone isn't mad.

It's right.

It's worried.

"There's a lot of unsolved cases."

"Cases that involve Gentry and TJ?"

"I can't prove it yet." I turn around and bury my head in his chest, wiping my tears on his T-shirt. "But I'll die trying to."

"Don't." His hug is too tight and I need it. "They're not worth it."

"No, they're not. But their victims are. They're worth the whole fight."

And I don't say it. But I know the truth now.

All of it...

After what they did to Redix? To those women?

They're worth more than a fight.

They're worth murder.

CHAPTER FORTY

CADE

She Was out in the Water by One Little Plane

THIS SHOULDN'T BE awkward as hell... but it is.

It's midnight and I'm on a boat in the middle of the Calibogue Sound with two men.

One who's so mad at me that I never gave him a chance; you can take a chainsaw to the tension between us.

The other is so sweet to me, hoping that I'll give him one; he's as tempting as dessert on a diet.

But I love Redix.

That truth hangs heavy in the humid air.

An hour before, Jameson met me at Harbour Towne with a Po' Boy sandwich, trying to make up for his insult and it worked.

I don't want to be mad at him. We need to click to work.

Silas was kind too.

He packed a cooler with two gallons of Arnold Palmers—sweet tea and lemonade.

"I'm no cop," he said, pouring me a cup before we headed out, "but I know we gotta stay sober and caffeinated for this."

The August night on the water is calm. The quarter moon gives us some cover while Silas's marine radar lights up with all the boats anchored along the sound on a summer weekend.

"Where do we start?" Silas asks.

"Let's head out to open water." Jameson stands portside, looking through night vision binoculars.

"That's not Gentry's style." I sit beside Silas who's kicked back in his captain's chair. "He likes his Lowcountry too much. I know his favorite spot."

"Was that intel you planned on keeping to yourself?" Jameson's still pulling his jealous boxers out of a wad.

"No," I answer calmly. "I'm sharing it now."

"Where to, Sergeant?" Silas smiles my way.

And I like him.

It's like his gorgeous feathers can't be ruffled.

"Savage Island, down Bull Creek. That used to be one of his favorite spots."

Silas eases the throttle down. "Dare I ask how you know?" He keeps smiling at me while we go slow enough to talk quietly and not draw attention.

"Because he never stopped asking me to go there with him when we were teens."

The island's name is befitting.

It's now private but it used to be a plantation. Gentry used to go on about how his family was gonna buy it and say to me, "Come with me and let's go savage, Cade."

His sick joke used to roll my eyes.

They never did buy it and I never went.

Silas swishes us through the water with no lights on. Jameson was smart to call on his help. Only my dad knows these creeks off the sound that lead to the ocean better. But I've scoped them myself, noting secret spots where no watercraft glide by.

We slow as we make another hairpin turn through the marsh grass.

"They're gonna see our boat on the radar if they're looking," Silas quietly warns. "Just like I can see theirs. That's gotta be it."

He points to a red blip on the radar. It's not moving and anchored up the creek offshore of the island.

"They don't know you or this boat." I crouch down low. "That's our advantage."

Silas maneuvers us into a spot down the creek from the yacht. He kills the engine and drops anchor. Grabbing his rod, he keeps the ruse going like he's night fishing while Jameson and I stay low, scoping through our night vision binoculars.

We can see in clear green Gentry on the deck of his yacht. He's with a woman who's not his wife. It's the Office Manager from his rental company. I'd recognize her blonde hair bun and huge rack anywhere.

"Well, Mr. Family Values sure likes his wine and other women," I mutter watching them sip glasses. "Typical."

"I see movement in the galley," Jameson reports. "Looks like one, maybe two others onboard."

I'm praying for a miracle—like Cam Le, the missing woman—to emerge and seal this guilty case shut.

"It's TJ," I report, knowing his white visor from a football field away. "And look… motherfucker is wearing a parrot T-shirt."

"I'm getting the video now." Jameson's using his pair of binoculars to record while I roam my scope across the vessel, checking for more movement.

Nothing.

I move back to our suspects and grin. "Looks like it's a party for three now."

Gentry's office manager has a great pair of tits she's pulling out of her bikini top for both men to enjoy. TJ's sucking on one while Gentry's on the other and Jameson clears his throat.

"Enjoying the show?" I need to crack the ice between us.

"What's the show?" Silas asks, keeping his voice low and casting his line.

"We got two men sharing tit duty," I answer. This would almost be fun if it weren't these two sick fucks. "And oh, wait… she's going *down*."

The woman drops to her knees before them while they drop their zippers. I want to gag but she's got that job right now.

"They *are* close friends," Jameson mutters. "They're sharing her."

"It looks consensual," I say. "Why, I don't know because I'd rather suck a sewer line than those two cocks."

Silas snorts, Jameson chuckles, and *"Hooolllyyy shhhittt,"* I huff.

I can't believe my eyes.

"What?" Silas is desperate to be in the know.

"Gentry's going down too... on TJ. Holy fucking shit, I never knew this about them."

The sight is blowing my mind while I'm watching Gentry and this woman blow TJ.

"Didn't they go to high school together?" Jameson asks, scoping the sight too.

"Yes." Pieces move, changing the picture I've had in my mind for so long. "I knew they were close. Now I know why."

"You think TJ's been blackmailing Gentry over this?"

They're moving.

Gentry's standing up and kissing TJ while he drops his shorts. They're madras, I can't see it, but I know it.

I'm in shock. "Gay, bisexual, I'm totally cool with it. But this?" TJ bends Gentry over the captain's chair and starts fucking him while his lady friend offers her tits to his mouth. "I can't tell if this is sex or love, but they've been doing this for a while, that's for sure."

I drop my binoculars, letting the logic seep in.

"I always thought Gentry was in charge, like he kept TJ loyal with money and got him to do his bidding."

"It's looking like TJ's *very* in charge to me." Jameson's still watching them.

"That don't mean anything," Silas says. "Top or bottom in sex doesn't translate into life, business... or crime."

"That's true." I don't ask how Silas knows that, but he's right. "All this time, I thought Gentry controlled TJ with his power and money. But now they're secretly a couple? And TJ's wearing that parrot T-shirt too?"

"You think TJ's the ringleader?" Jameson asks. "And he's using Gentry for access to victims?"

My mind draws their evil design.

How Gentry uses his rental company and that woman, the Office Manager, to find the tourists, the young women renting his condos. Then he tracks their movements across every business he owns on the island, using cameras to find the targets.

Inevitably, some end up at The Pelican where Derek Baucom, the bar manager, steps in. Using the drugs, the GHB in liquid form that TJ supplies, they pour it into the drink of the victim and TJ works the floor, scooping up the victim off camera.

Where is Gentry this whole time?

Waiting outside in one of a dozen cars he owns.

Where do they go?

Any one of the hundreds of condos Gentry owns.

And the wicked dicks know me and how our small island runs; if they wait until the night before check-out, it makes our job hard. We don't get the time we need with the victim to form a rock-solid case.

The worst part?

The victims—they all look like me at eighteen. Like that night when I wore Pamela's yellow dress and they couldn't get me, so they went after Redix instead.

"I don't give a fuck who the ringleader is." I twirl the infinity necklace Redix gave me. "They're both guilty and going down."

A sudden pang—it nails my heart thinking about Redix.

How he told me to drop it.

Yes, he'd want me to get justice for the victims. But revenge? That would betray Redix and the peace he wants now.

But what about the victims? The ones who look like me.

What if there are more? What if the law can't catch these men?

And what about me?

What do I want?

If I can't have justice, do I want love or revenge?

CHAPTER FORTY-ONE

REDIX

Here Comes The Night by DJ Snake, Mr Hudson

Dear Candy Cade,

I still smell you on my sheets.

You left Lemonheads on my kitchen island. I finished them with a smile, thinking of you but I left the box there like a Candy Cade centerpiece.

You forgot your hairbrush in my bathroom. It smells like lavender.

I found your "Woman Up" T-shirt and smiley-face panties in my dryer.

Ok, Detective. I confess. I might've humped the pillow

you slept on while holding your panties in my hand.

Yep, I'm guilty as hell, and please, cuff me. (We're doing that next time I see you, I swear).

Because I can't stop thinking about you.

Because I miss you.

Because I love you.

You've been gone two weeks and I couldn't fly home and it sucks.

I've been stuck here. I'm having great days thinking about you and horrible nightmares with you gone.

It's like telling you unleashed something in me.

It was good for us because you wanted to know and now we're together.

But for me?

It's haunting me even more.

It's that tattoo.

The one of that mudflap girl.

It keeps flashing by the side of my face. It's covered in sand. And then I scream out. The pain, my body remembers it. It's a razor flame ripping my skin open. That's when they cut me, I think.

Tattoo guy was holding me down and laughing. I remember that now. And your necklace, it was swinging from his neck.

Then I wake up and I'm covered in sweat, but I reach over and hug your pillow and I can survive another night.

I swear, Cade.

Only you make it okay.

You're the only reason I believe in love.

Like I love my mom and sister. And my nephew, I love him so much. My favorite is building LEGOs with him.

BTW. Don't freak out.

But I want to marry you and have a mess of kids

together. You're a softie around babies. And to have one with you?

Wow. My heart just jumped.

We've got a ways to go but it's all I want.

It's the only thing I'm living for.

But for now, I gotta go to Atlanta.

Warning - this psycho-thriller film is gonna be a shitshow.

The cast did table reads this week before we shoot on location and Angie was in rare form. She's playing a house-wife obsessed with me, her sister's boyfriend, and I swear she's gonna win the fucking Oscar.

Because Angie is obsessed with me.

I can't tell you because I know you'd snatch her bald if you knew.

She's throwing a hissy fit over our ice cream video.

That shit went viral, and Angie went ballistic. "I guess you're Instagram official now," she said all jealous like.

Fuck, it's pathetic.

I don't need a fucking post to tell the world I love you. That I always have.

And I know you hate that shallow shit too.

But now I gotta spend three months with Angie wanting to tan my hide.

No, fuck my hide, more accurately but I can ignore her.

Because I'm gonna see you as much as I can. I've got a week in Atlanta next with pre-production bullshit... and then I'm coming home.

Luca, my friend who owns the golf resort, remember? He's putting on a charity golf tournament. We're going to build another Teen Crisis Center.

I want one in Charleston next.

Luca cares about kids because he's a dad. He's got the

cutest little girl and he's a widower now and raising her by himself.

And now you know why I do those centers.

If I'd had a safe place I could've gone ten years ago. Like where counselors talked to me, maybe I wouldn't have left you to find a fucking bottle in my hand for the next nine years.

But I'm okay.

You're my safe place now. You always have been. When I hold you, I don't hurt. You're my world and all I want.

It makes me wonder what you're doing now. It's two here, five there.

Are you home from work? Did you get my gift yet? I sent it special delivery. It should be waiting by your door.

I want to see you open it and smile.

I'll video you now.

CHAPTER FORTY-TWO

CADE

My phone vibrates on the cocktail table. I glance down. It's Redix trying to video call.

"Romeo is ringing." Penny sees it too. "Millions of women would answer that call."

I text him.

> Still at work
>
> Gimme a couple hours?

His reply is fast.

REDIX

Any time for you, Candy Cade

"Girl, you got him wrapped." Penny sucks down her Sprite before declaring, "That video of your ice cream kiss is all the evidence required. It's so hot and I gotta say, sweet as fuck."

Our ice cream kiss went viral and people glance at me now. It's why I can't go undercover. Between being five foot ten and the woman Redix Dean loves bound in leather or covered in ice cream, I'm as obvious as an airhorn blasting through a funeral service.

Fuck it. Our love is worth it.

This is worth it too—watching Derek Baucom who knows we're watching him work.

I wanna see what he'll do. Because guilty men always crack. You just gotta step on their nerves hard enough until they do.

"Yes, and everyone can know," I answer Penny, "we're back together and yes, it's for good."

"What exactly will that look like?" she asks. "A sergeant dating a celebrity? The hottest one in fact with a wild past?"

"He had his reasons." Flashes of that scar on his buttock hit my mind like ice water, shooting guilt through my veins. "And he's not wild anymore."

"If you say so." Penny's eyes go back to Derek behind the bar. "If Redix Dean has changed and makes you happy, then I'm his biggest fan."

Suddenly, Derek glances up at me and grins, then he goes back to grabbing bottles from the well and pouring concoctions at lightning speed.

"What's his deal?" Penny sees it too. How every spare glance from that man is on me. "Do you know him?"

"No." Fuck, do I? I don't break my stare. "But I know his sick cousin, Gentry, and their putrid pal, TJ."

The thought of those three men working together; I'm obsessed.

"We got traces of GHB on Kayla's yellow dress." Penny lowers her voice. "We got TJ spotted in the parrot T-shirt Natalie remembers. And we got Derek on Instagram in a striped shirt also seen by a victim." Penny throws her tattered straw on the table. "And none of that is the evidence we need. It's all circumstantial dots on a map with no connection."

"Give it time." I think of those evil men. Of ten years ago. Of Redix. "It'll surprise you what it can do."

An hour later, Derek looks like he's clocking off before the dinner shift.

Penny pays our tab while I go out to a car I've rented this week. From the passenger seat, I put on a white T-shirt and a baseball hat with long blonde hair extensions sewn in. Sunglasses too. I've got three disguises, and this is my favorite.

Keeping my nose down on my phone, I text Penny I'll do the tail of Derek home. Tomorrow, we watch TJ again.

Minutes later, Derek's truck roars to life in the parking lot. I let him turn onto the highway before pulling out behind him. I stay far back, expecting him to take his usual route home through the busy traffic circle, but he doesn't.

Surprising me, he turns right, and I have to react on a dime, switching lanes to follow. Winding through residential side streets, he parks in front of a group of townhomes. They're off a golf course and often rented for tournaments.

This is new.

I stop a block away and watch him amble up to the front door, press in a code, and enter.

Then nothing. For two hours.

He's in for the night but why this new place? I'll be back tomorrow while he's at work to check through the dumpster and snoop around.

Until then, I drive by, using my periphery to note the unit number when I grin, spotting what's on the door of the condo next door to the one he entered.

A doorbell camera.

Thank you, technology and paranoid people. Many criminals forget about those little gadgets.

I don't.

I memorize the condo number with the camera and call Jameson, hands-free.

"Hey." He sounds bummed.

"Hey, did I interrupt a hot date?"

"Nope. She moved to Atlanta. Took the job there with that security company so I'm nursing a beer alone."

Scarlett took that job with HGR Security? I don't blame her. They were stroking a huge check to recruit her. Women in private security are rare and highly valued.

Sometimes I'm tempted to do it too.

"I need you to run a search on Palmetto Bluff, unit number 1803. Find the owner." If I give Jameson a lead, he'll perk up. "They have a doorbell camera and I want the footage. Derek Baucom just went inside, next door to it."

"On it."

"Penny and I are on TJ tomorrow. You?"

"I got Gentry at the golf course. That man might as well hold office there and not at the capital."

"They all do—putters, pricks, and politics—this country runs on it."

I end our call and work my way home. Shaking the day off with a deep exhale, I focus on calling Redix when I get there. Throwing myself into work helps for hours but when I get home, there's a hollow silence that matches the one in my heart.

I miss him.

A box sitting by my front door lifts my lips when I see it's from him. I wait until I change and sit on my balcony lounger with it on my lap to start our video call.

"You stalking me again?"

His handsome face fills the screen with his pool behind him.

"How the hell am I supposed to date you long distance and not be able to send gifts?" He swigs a seltzer. "Packages aren't stalking are they?"

"Legally?" I start opening it. "No."

"Well, damn darlin', I wanted to break the law for you."

"That's my job." *I'm not joking.*

"How was your day, Detective?"

"Not as exciting as yours."

"Come on. Thrill me with your boring details."

I tell him how we're watching a bartender, but I don't bring up TJ or Gentry. They've stolen so much from us; they aren't taking these simple joys too.

Redix won't stop smiling through my mundane story. "Do I ever tell you how proud I am of you?"

"Every day." One of the many things I love about him. He trusts that I'm good at this. Too damn good actually. "I'm proud of you too."

"You're gonna be real proud when you open your gift. Set your phone down so I can watch."

I prop my phone up against a candle on the table beside the lounger. "You gonna give me a hint?"

"It doesn't require one."

I glance at my phone; guilt drips from his grin. The

bubble-wrapped bundle inside has me certain. Yep, I open it and laugh at the blue ceramic dildo.

"It's huge."

"We miss you." Lust hums in his voice. "Do you miss us?"

"Yes." Kissing my phone isn't desperate, right? "Don't let it go to your pretty head."

"Too late." Lying back on his lounger, he holds his phone like I'm on top of him. At that angle, I can't resist his request, "Will you show me how much you miss me?"

"Right here on my balcony?"

It's dusk, but yards away the summer beach below is still full of people.

"Even better." He moves his phone to track his other hand. It rips open the Velcro of his board shorts, revealing the real, hard thing and it's torture, seeing what you need to survive like water... but it's only a screen. "Let them see how much you miss me."

"It's not fair." I lift my sundress. "Anyone looking up here can see me, but you have full privacy there."

It thumps through my blood. The risk up here. A warm breeze across my bare thighs. My arousal puddling for him. How he's watching me...

The size of this thing.

"Press record on this call to make it even," he says. "This can leak, or you can sell it. I don't care. I'm proud of how much I want you."

Pushing his trunks down, he kicks them off as his nudity fills my screen, surging my body with heat. He's a goddamn painting, a Renaissance of porn waiting to perform.

I press record because I *will* repeat this ritual many times.

He grins. "You need to get it wet first."

"If I put this in my mouth, teeth will crack."

I lick it instead and he groans at the sight. "Fuck, I miss you." His palm skims up and down his shaft lying heavy on his abs and it's so fucking hot I don't need much spit.

This vision of him wets me, making me bold because I need something. And if it's not his real cock pounding me into bliss, I'll try this one.

Pulling my panties off, I do the same to my dress before pulling the lace cups down on my bra, exposing my breasts for our pleasure.

"Goddamn," he sighs, "play with them like I do. Lick your fingertips and pull at your nipples."

This is how we'll do this; thousands of miles away and he can direct my body and I won't fight it because I can't.

He tells me how to play with myself, directing my fingers to thrill my flesh. "Tickle your clit like I do. Lightly with your fingers. That's right. Now use your middle finger..."

The sound of his voice, the ocean waves and beachgoers fill my ears and I'm so fucking turned on.

"Are you wet for me?"

"Yes." I can't take my eyes off him.

"Finger your pussy. Is it ready for me?"

It's soaked and aching. "Yes." It almost hurts without him.

"Then show me." The pump of his fist over his cock is rhythmic, pacing himself for my show. "Fuck my dildo for me."

I turn on my lounger. It has no arms so I can spread open for my phone propped up on the table and he can watch it all. Leaning back and grabbing the chair behind me, I use my free hand to start wedging the fat tip inside. It's cool, hard, and slick and teasing me; I want him so much.

"Like this?" I ask, easing it in. It's his proportions, stretching me, thrilling me. "Is this what you want, Redix? You want to watch me fuck this for you?"

"Yes." His eyes fill with hunger. Pre-cum drips from his tip as he spits into his palm before stroking his gorgeous shaft and lifting his hips into his tight grip. "Fuck yourself until you come on it, Cade. Do it so fucking loud and moaning my name."

Oh, I will.

It's a new sensation. It doesn't bend or buzz like my toys and it doesn't fill me, not like the manic response my pussy gives to Redix's real cock inside.

But this is so hard, rigid, and big... and this is so hot.

With my bare feet on my balcony, I lift my hips, spreading wide and opening myself up to this pounding display for him, for my phone.

"Can anyone see you?" He's enthralled, his horny eyes are glued to his screen and my sinful show. "Is anyone watching how dirty you get for me?"

I glance over the edge of my balcony and sigh. There's a man—a jogger with no shirt on, sweaty and standing alone. He's hot and the bulge in his shorts is obvious as he's watching me, knowing what I'm doing though he can't see the whole show.

That's only for Redix.

"Yes. A man can see me." I feel it from the peaks of my nipples to my clit shrieking with pleasure. "He's hard and watching me fuck for you."

"Let me see how wet it's making you. Show me my toy."

I pull it out and lift it up to the screen, close enough for him and the man below to see. The giant phallus glistens with my arousal on it.

"Now, Cade. Fuck it now and come because I'm going

to." He is. I can tell by the pump of his hips into his fist, his cock swelling to bigger than his replica. "Fuck it so hard for me."

The video is recording him, jerking off for me, his eyes captivated by the sight of me as I go for it. As hard and fast as I can, I wish it was him, the real him touching my flesh, taking my body, and sharing my life. Fuck, I want him so much and this force inside me isn't enough. It's getting so slick and slippery with need.

"Yes, Cade." He's matching my tempo, dancing on his edge too.

"Oh God, Redix, I..."

Drop the dildo on the concrete balcony. Blue ceramic breaks in half with a loud crash between my feet.

His eyes go wide. "Did you just break my dick?"

I can't answer. It happens too fast.

I go from almost coming to laughing my ass off and he joins me.

"Damn, woman." He's rolling on his lounger, tears wetting the corner of his eyes. "Leave it to you to fuck me so hard you *break—my—dick*."

"Here's a fat tip." I pick up the half that was his dildo's head. "Put a handle on it next time."

That starts another round of laughter and I swear my stomach hurts and I love it. Glancing over, my audience of one is gone and I lie back on the lounger to recover. Redix is so cute, how he hides his laughing face behind his arm.

"I miss you." It's a sigh, a painful one because it speaks from every part of me.

He rolls to his side, holding his phone like we're sharing a pillow in bed. "I miss you too."

"Can you give up Hollywood and we'll run an ice cream shop together?"

"Yes." Something in his eyes; he's only half kidding.

I ask about his day, and he tells me about table reads and how he spent the afternoon finishing his last pottery plate.

"Can I send them to you?"

"All the pretty bowls and plates you made? They're for your house."

"I'd rather you think of me every time you eat frozen pizza."

"I think of you all the time." And the feeling returns. The one where I need him but he's not here. I let my fingers wander down to finish what we started. I let him watch me too. "Redix, get here."

"I will. I promise." He's starting again too, the urge in his eyes matches mine. "Real soon."

It doesn't take me long. Not while I'm watching him. I'm right back to where I was in minutes, gasping and crying out for what I can't feel right now.

For what I've wanted for so long, and now I have it... but he's not here.

"Redix, please," I beg from my cliff, falling for this man, every time. It isn't about pride when there's this much love. "I need you." I'm so close, and so is he, the muscles in his abs, his bicep, they're tensing up to my climax. "I need you..."

And it bursts. I show him, my love, my lust, how it flows from me. It's all for him.

"Fuck, Cade."

He can see it, watching my little river over the chair before he's coming too, his own creamy ropes spilling across his tan abs, while his back arches into his grasp, but his eyes, they never leave mine.

With him gone, it's a new void I can't stand. "When will I see you?" It hurts.

He pulls the phone down to his face like he's pulling me near.

"Next weekend. I've got us a suite at the golf resort. I'm gonna spoil you again. Every fucking chance I can, okay?"

"Okay."

It scares me. How much I feel for him again. I didn't realize how numb I'd become to it before this.

Redix talks about how alcohol and drugs numbed his pain all these years of missing me.

Me too. My heart, it froze. All I cared about was revenge. Was training for a fight. Was planning a perfect cover.

I didn't feel the pain.

I do now. With one ice cream kiss, he melted me again.

"Hey, Magnolia Cade?"

I hate that name. "Yes?" Still, I answer him.

"I love you." The screen stays over his face. He's not acting. I can see it in his eyes. "I'll always come back for you, I promise."

"I love you too. No matter where you are, I always will."

But our love. It wasn't enough these past ten years to beat our pain.

It is now?

CHAPTER FORTY-THREE

CADE

IF THIS IS SPOILING, then let me die rotten.

The bed linens under me are the softest I've ever felt. Our resort's personal butler delivered the best ice cream sundae to our suite's door and this time *I* devoured Redix like a treat.

There's the shower we took in the luxury spa bathroom after. It was almost as indulgent as the in-room couples' massage he scheduled next.

There's the Marchesa dress bag hanging in the closet where Redix is hiding my surprise outfit for dinner tonight.

Then there's the small gift box on the desk in our suite. And... *there's him.*

He's staring into my eyes from the pillow beside me.

I know what he's doing.

He's giving me every gesture, big and small, to make up for what we suffered apart. It's working. Not because of his gifts. It's because I feel whole again. Because he's my present, past, and future.

"Do you have to bring that thing with you everywhere?"

He plays with my hair, asking about my police radio charging by our hotel bed.

"I'm on-call." I play with his hair too, twirling his strands around my index finger. "I'm yours as long as hell doesn't break loose."

"Will you take it to dinner too? I got a special one planned. Me and you. Luca and his daughter. It's her fourth birthday and we want to spoil our ladies."

"It stays in my bag, I promise." My fingertip lingers down his nose. "And you don't have to spoil me anymore today."

"Alright then." His grin almost works. "Get up and iron my shirt, woman."

"Uh-huh. I'll get right on that." Did I mention lying beside him? It's luxury too. "How's Atlanta?"

"I'd be an asshole to complain about the Presidential Suite at the Waldorf."

"Swanky."

"It is. I put a guest fob in your purse. Come see me anytime." His eyebrows dance. "It has lots of windows and a dining room table just waiting for us."

I linger my fingertips down his abs next, "that's a tempting invitation," seeking what's below.

"Save that." Gently, he stops my hand. "I got more plans tonight."

"Speaking of plans." It's been on my mind for weeks.

"Eric told me about yours, for your house and estate. Why didn't *you* tell me?"

"I was going to, but I didn't want to ruin our perfect days with the worst part of my life"—his thumb tickles my hand—"and I'm ready for something new with you."

I'm finally brave enough to ask. "How bad was it? Your drinking?"

"Well, I had beer and eggs for breakfast. Beer and steak for lunch. That kept me steady for work until it was time to clock off and then I'd ride a river of vodka or whiskey into hours I don't remember. That's where Eric came in. I've tried to, but I can't pay that man enough for keeping me alive."

"How'd you stay so fit?"

"Genetics and hours in a gym can hide a lot of pain. All my dad gave me before he bailed on us was the high-functioning alcoholic gene."

"Do you worry you'll lapse again?"

"It ain't sobriety if you ain't humble. I decide every day, sometimes every hour, not to drink."

"It's my fault. Your drinking. It started after—"

"Hey." His finger lifts my chin, his eyes swearing it to mine. "It is NOT your fault. I was drinking and getting high long before that night. You know that. I wasn't comfortable in this skin. Too many people looking at me all the time. Fucking King of Coligny Beach or Hollywood's Romeo. I hate that shit. People always after me. It's taken me years to learn to live with it."

"I know the feeling."

It's a horrible one. People always want something from you when you're cursed with DNA many deem attractive. Yes, there are many far worse things to suffer. But no one is immune. Even the pretty pay.

"That's why you're my one gift," he says. "You see the real me."

"I see the boy who made me playlists, and laugh, and Kraft macaroni and cheese. What do you see in me?"

That makes him grin. "I see the girl who put Hello Kitty Band-Aids on my scabs." I laugh. I forgot about that. "I see a woman who holds my hands and they don't shake." That hits my heart. "You always took away my pain, Candy Cade."

"You always protected me from it."

We don't say it. Our eyes speak the memory.

"I still want to protect you." The way he lingers his fingertips across my cheek. "I'll give you everything I have."

"I don't need *everything*." The bow of his lip beckons me to trace it. "Just my favorite parts."

"Oh, you'll get that too." It's sudden, his roll, landing on top so he can gaze down at me. "You get my house, my millions, you'll take care of my family... and every part of me." He starts nudging in, hard.

I spread my thighs. "I thought we were saving this."

"With you"—it's my favorite slow sigh as he enters—"I'll give you all right now."

THE SPOILING CONTINUES TO DINNER. I look like Redix's Oscar date in the gown he bought me. The nude fabric with red silk rose embellishments clings from my right shoulder and sweeps to the floor.

He even dresses up. That means he wears a shirt under his tux. And shoes. It's only appropriate as our four-year-old guest of honor steals the show.

"Gia," her dad softly instructs, "what do you say for your birthday present?"

Gia's dad, Luca Mercier, has got to be the sexiest CEO on the planet. Like literally he is because Redix told me earlier how paparazzi are after him now that he's the most eligible billionaire.

It's not a hunch. It's a fact—hot, single dads with billions are global catnip.

Luca's daughter jumps down from his lap, her brown curls springing with her fearless bounce. It's like she owns this resort—well, she sorta does as she strides over to Redix, puckering her lips up for his cheek.

"Thank you for my shark, Red."

It's cute how she shortens his name to suit her.

Redix bought her a yellow stuffed shark. Apparently, they're all the rage for kids.

"You're welcome, princess." He takes her peck on his cheek.

"Redix and I got close," Luca explains, "when we met on the golf course recovering from our darkest days. He'd come to stay with us and let my little angel brighten them." His eyes light up talking about his daughter. "Looks like you brighten his now."

When Luca smiles my way, there's warmth in his eyes. I'd wish the same for him, to have love again, but maybe it's too soon.

Redix told me how Luca's wife passed away two years ago.

And I can see how Gia makes Redix smile. I've never seen him so tender, maybe with his nephew, but this bursts my ovaries.

Maybe one day, we will...

"Thank you." Gia turns to me. I can tell she forgot my name but that's okay.

"You're welcome."

"You look like a princess." Her small hands play with the roses on my dress.

"I tell you what, you be the princess and I'll be your friend, okay?"

Without hesitation, the little girl climbs into my lap and every thread of me unravels to her embrace.

"She, uh..." Luca stammers to explain. "She misses her..." and he stops when I smile.

I understand. Gia misses her mom so I let her sit in my lap and play with the roses on my dress because I can only imagine how I'd miss my mama too.

The feelings, the wishes I start making as Redix holds my hand later while we walk back to our suite—I never dreamed this far ahead.

I lost them to a nightmare and I never thought I'd get them back.

"I know what you're thinking, Candy Cade."

He beeps open our door but won't let go of my hand. I don't answer while we let it close behind us.

It's gentle, his light grip of my neck, pulling my lips towards his saying, "I wish it too."

His kiss claims my lips while he unzips my gown, and my resistance falls to the floor with it.

I didn't know this was possible again.

The butterflies in my belly, the flutter of my heart, the tears he brings to my eyes making love to me so slow, so perfect. We can't capture it in our hands, though we try holding on to the love between us. My hand caresses his scar while he's deep inside me because I can.

I will love away our pain. I will stand in our fire and

burn it down to find what's new; what we can build with nothing but this love, our promise—infinity.

"Cade." He clasps my hands in his over my head. "I want it." He's holding my gaze, holding every part of me—heart, body, and future. "I want all of it with you."

The race of our hearts, the way his body takes mine into the softest moans, he has me.

"I am." I promise to his breath lingering over mine. "I *am* with you."

It's the happiest I've been, closing my eyes in his arms minutes later.

"You didn't open your last present," he whispers in my ear.

In the moonlight through the curtains, I see the small gift on the desk. It's not a ring box. "This is my gift." I kiss his hands in mine.

"So is the car I bought you."

"What?" I roll over to find him grinning. "I don't need a new car."

"Yes, you do. It's a fresh start for us. Your car goes back too far."

He's right. My car makes me think of that year. The last one we were together.

"Redix, I don't need you buying me things. I've loved you since you were riding an old, red Schwinn bike."

"That's why those are keys to a new, blue Land Rover."

It doesn't stop.

He's overwhelming me with everything perfect. Perfect days in Malibu. Perfect nights here. Perfect gifts. Perfect sex with the most perfect man.

All this love. "I don't know what to say." All this hope.

"Well, damn darlin'... that only took twenty years." I can

see his grin, his kiss searching for mine in the moonlight. "I finally got that sexy mouth of yours to shut up."

Only he can say that in the cutest way.

Especially when his lips are on mine, and then his body, and then finally, an hour later, he's sleeping beside me.

CHAPTER FORTY-FOUR

CADE

It splinters through the peaceful dawn; through the dream I was having about a tiny hand in mine.

"Possible ten-ninety-five. Heritage Hotel. White female. Unresponsive. Medic en route."

It's instant. Dropping my feet to the floor, I answer my radio, "Bryant. One-forty. I'm en route."

In a whirling snatch, I throw my uniform on from my suitcase. That hotel is around the harbor from this resort. I'm minutes out.

"You gotta go?" Redix isn't mad. He's barely waking up.

"Yep." I rake my hair back.

"When will you be back?"

"No telling." I snap on my duty belt and grab my back-pack. "I'll keep you posted."

"Hey." His voice, it can summon me anywhere.

"Hey." I walk to the edge of the bed, grabbing the hand he's holding out to pull me down to his kiss. "Go get those motherfuckers."

My lips caress his before it charges through me, confessing, "That's the deal."

"I love you." What it means to have him say that to me every day.

"I love you too." I let go of his hand and turn towards the door. "Have fun at golf. Raise some millions."

"Oh, I will, *Candy Cade.*"

He annoys me... and that makes me smile while the door slams shut behind me.

The quiet morning street whizzes by while I race my unmarked car to the other hotel. I see her standing out in front, the hotel manager waiting for me as I park by the entrance. For the first time, I beat Jameson here as the ambulance wails into the parking lot behind me.

Showing my badge, the manager informs me while we cover ground fast, "I found her in the hallway outside her room. She won't wake up." She leads the way, running up a flight of stairs to the second floor.

"What's her name?"

"She's checked in under 'Sarah Matthews'."

I see her on the floor. Rushing toward her, I don't see any trauma. But I see the M.O. Brunette. Yellow shorts. Young. Pretty.

Bile burns up my throat.

"Sarah?" I can't touch her, not without the latex gloves I snap on from the pocket of my cargo pants. "Sarah, can you wake up for me? You're safe."

I squat, checking her pulse. It's there but low. The elevator dings. That's the medics coming up.

"Who checked in with her?" I rise, asking the manager and reaching for my gun while I take the keycard she's offering.

"No one. But I can check our cameras, the tapes from last night."

I nod but I'm focused on the now.

Who's in this room?

I don't have backup yet but I'm sick of waiting. With a beep, I slam the handle and kick the door open, gun raised and ready to fire.

It hits me fast—the stench of cigarette smoke.

I glance left to the bathroom. The door is open and in the mirror above the vanity, the curtain is pulled back from the shower.

It's clear.

Aiming my weapon, I step through the foyer. It's a fatal funnel, anyone could fire on me here, but I don't care.

Someone was in here minutes ago.

The room opens to a king bed, unmade, in the center. Gun up, sight ready, I check the other side of the bed. No one. No cigarette butts. Just an empty room, Sarah's luggage on the dresser and a window, its curtains open to the morning light.

I kick the burgundy bedspread draped over the floor aside and hope rushes in—two vials peek out from under the bed, like they rolled there, unseen and forgotten.

Minutes later, while I'm with the medics in the hallway loading Sarah up onto the gurney, Jameson comes running down the hall.

"What do we got?" His eyes scan the scene.

I don't need to explain except I tell him the good news.

"We got this." I lead him into the room and point to the floor. We're waiting for forensics to take pictures, but I'm elated to show him the evidence left behind.

One vial on the floor.

He nods, encouraged.

I grin back.

The other vial? It's in my pocket. And part of my deal.

It's after two o'clock before Sarah wakes at the hospital. Whatever he drugged her with, it was potent. In that time, I learn she's from Miami. She's here with her boss for Redix's golf tournament.

I texted Redix earlier to keep him posted. He texted back once with a quick:

REDIX

I love it when you kick ass, Candy Cade

I don't hear from him the rest of the afternoon. I understand. We're busy.

When her boss storms into the Emergency Room, his face is red with anger and sunburn from the golf course.

"Is she okay?" He glances at Sarah resting behind the curtain. "Shit, she's like a daughter to me."

I can tell, he really does care.

"She will be. Was she with you last night?"

"Yeah. We were with a tournament group at The Deck Bar. It got late. She told me she was tired and going back to her room. That's the last I saw her."

"What time?"

"Between midnight and one."

We'll check the hotel tapes for that hour. That's all her boss can offer while he waits for Sarah to be released into his care. The rest is the usual. There's evidence of assault but not who did it. But now we have that vial. Jameson rushed it to the lab for analysis.

The other one is still in my pocket, calling to me like a siren's song demanding revenge.

That cigarette smoke? That was TJ.

I don't need proof to know his smell. If he was dumb enough to leave vials behind, he's getting sloppy and maybe... we finally have his prints.

It's five o'clock by the time I open the door to my and Redix's hotel suite at the golf resort. I already checked the hotel bar where a party is raging after the tournament.

"Where's Redix?" I asked Luca, returning his quick pecks on my cheeks. He's so European, so sexy that way.

"He left a long time ago," he answered. "He went up to your room, I guess."

But he's not here as I'm scanning it now.

This hotel room? I have the same unease as I did in the one this morning.

Like TJ was here. But that's impossible.

The service cleaned the room. My luggage is still on the chair. The dress Redix got me still hangs in the open closet. The gift box too, it's sitting on the desk... but the car key is gone.

And so is Redix.

I call him.

And three more times that night. It keeps going to voice-mail. Finally, at two a.m. I leave him a message:

"Hey. Are you okay? Call me please." I pause, staring at the rolling black ocean. "I love you."

CHAPTER FORTY-FIVE

REDIX

Dear Candy Cade,

I'm so sorry.

This fucking journal. It's not working.

This swanky suite. I don't want to be alone in it.

I had to get out of there. I had to take the car I gave you and drive so damn fast off that island and to Atlanta because I'm never going back there again.

What the fuck was I thinking?

I had my shit together. I had you. I had everything I've dreamed of for us, for so damn long.

And then it happened.

I was shaking hands, thanking the foursomes lined up in

golf carts for their support. The tournament was going great. I even dressed for it. I wore a damn navy polo with white shorts to look the preppy part, to look like a man you could donate your thousands to.

I'd do anything for those crisis centers.

Then a hand grabbed mine. I glanced at his eyes before I looked down at his choking grip. It was trying to hurt me. And I saw it.

The tattoo.

The mudflap girl.

Our grasp strangled while I looked back up at him but I didn't recognize his face.

But fuck me, Cade. He had your necklace on.

It was him. The guy who drove. The guy who held me down.

I jerked my fist away about to punch him with it.

Then I realized Gentry sat beside him. And TJ, looking like shit warmed over, sat behind them on the cart.

All three of them stared me down and I was back on the beach with them, memories flashing like lethal grenades in my mind.

"We always enjoy your hospitality, Mr. Dean." Gentry always sounds evil.

"How's your wife?" I asked him. "I can tell she *wants* my hospitality."

Fuck them. I didn't let them see it, Cade. I glared back, ready to rip them apart. I swear I can now.

Tattoo dude thought that was funny. Gentry didn't. Neither did TJ.

"How's your girlfriend?" TJ asked. "She always did have a thing for ice cream." Fuck, his teeth are so brown. "I think it's time she got a real mark, a real treat." I clenched my fist to punch him first before wailing on the others while

TJ laughed, "I bet she'll moan like you did when we give it to her."

I pounced, but arms were around me so fucking fast I didn't know where they came from.

"Gentlemen." It was your dad. I invited him to play with me and Luca. "Make another illegal scene here, Senator"—he took on Gentry first—"and I'll make sure this whole damn state knows about it."

He held me back. Damn, Cade. Your dad's been more of a father to me than my own. He keeps appearing like an angel in my life just in time.

Luca came over too. "We got a problem?"

Luca is a wall of muscle and intimidating as shit. The three of us could've taken them easily and I wanted to.

"Not at all." Gentry knew it. "Y'all enjoy your round. And Mr. Dean"— he tipped his fucking visor at me—"I'll be very generous with you... as usual."

He pulled their cart away and I was going to chase after them and bash their heads in with a nine iron.

"Hey, man. What was that about?" Luca could tell shit was up. "You okay?"

"He'll be fine. He's strong." Your dad answered for me. He wouldn't let go of my arm to keep me from doing something stupid. "This goes way back. Just give him time."

I don't remember the next hours on the course with your dad and Luca and his buddy.

That night kept flashing and I felt sick. Since I couldn't kill them, I had to do something.

We got back to the resort, and I'm sorry Cade. I ran.

I didn't have a choice. It's a craze in my veins, hijacking my mind and the only way to be free of it is to run.

And not look back.

Not even for you and my God, I'm so damn sorry.

I've tried so hard, but I can't turn this around. This nightmare in my mind. It won't stop.

I try closing my eyes and thinking of you. And I can. I see every beautiful moment with you but then I see that night.

That look on your face when TJ grabbed you.

Fuck. I love you so much, Cade.

When they grabbed you, they took my soul.

And they won't let me go.

How can I ever be free of them? Even just to breathe because I can't.

I can't stop the memories.

There's only one thing that works. I'm just gonna have one beer. There's some in the minibar.

Just one beer, I promise, then I'll feel better and then I'll call you and I'll be okay.

CHAPTER FORTY-SIX

CADE

Wild Horses by The Sundays

Forty-eight hours is all I can suffer.

He's not answering his phone or texts. Eric, his assistant, won't answer me either.

"Go." Penny grabs my hand shaking on my desk at work. "There's nothing to do here. Go get him."

For all her jokes and bitching, she loves me and knows I'm dying inside.

"The prints though?"

How can I do this?

I'm forced to decide between some justice for these victims and going after the man I love.

"We got one of them—Derek Baucom." Penny keeps me focused. "He must've realized he left that vial behind and knows we're after him. He's in the breeze but we'll catch him."

The prints from that vial scored the evidence we need.

That's one down—two more to go.

Because TJ was in that room with Sarah too, I know it without evidence. He and Gentry get away with it... but not for long.

"Check every single rental Gentry owns." I'm desperate to catch them. "Derek's truck hasn't been seen crossing the bridge. He's on this island somewhere."

"Jameson's on it. Gentry's fighting the search warrants but he doesn't own every judge. We got this." Penny squeezes my hand. "Now get the fuck out of here."

Jameson glances up from his desk. He hasn't said much but knows what's going on.

I let Redix Dean in my life again. I believed in our love. I had such hope...

And he left me.

Again.

But "I told you so" isn't on Jameson's face. No, he hates this for me.

Something's wrong and everyone can read my anguish.

My mama and dad too.

It's like they did an intervention on me last night, shocking the shit out of me by knocking on my door together.

"Sometimes you walk away," Dad said, "because that's what's best if you really love someone."

He had me wrapped in his arms, standing in my kitchen

and I felt twelve again, crying like when he and Mama divorced, and he tried explaining to me why.

"And sometimes you fight for love," Mama said. "Sometimes it never dies." She took my hand and Dad's. "Like maybe we should have. So many precious years we've lost apart."

Their legacy is mine—a decision I have to make.

Fight for love or let Redix go?

A memory slams my heart. At his place in Malibu, we were making pizzas from scratch... and a huge mess.

Redix swiped pizza sauce down my nose. "That's for later."

I flicked flour at him. "That's gonna start a food fight."

"That's what I'm bettin' on." He pressed me against the kitchen countertop, beaming at me with that devilish smile that lights up my world. "I love it when you fight."

I rested my hand on his thudding heartbeat. "Why?"

He pressed his hand over mine. "Because you look so beautiful when you do." His lips drew nearer to mine. "And because you always win. I'm counting on it."

That kiss turned into a pizza burning and him buried inside me. My legs wrapped around his waist while my hands grabbed his back with tears in my eyes because I couldn't hold him close enough.

I'll never let him go.

"I love you." I peck Penny's cheek and jump up from my desk, duty belt still on before grabbing my bag from my chair. "Hold the fort down." And I'm out the door.

Atlanta is four hours away and those miles between us?

Nothing will stand in my way.

"Hello?"

Speeding down the interstate, I answer my phone hands-free.

"Cade? It's Scarlett. I called Jameson for your number."

"Hey."

I can't really talk. I'm focused on the crowded road to Atlanta and on what I'll find when I get there.

"Hey. Look." Scarlett pauses. "I hate doing this, but I'll always help another woman."

"Yeah?" My stomach twists. Scarlett's in Atlanta. That much I know, afraid of what I'll learn next.

"I'm training with HGR Security. I'm shadowing this guy, Wade, and we're cast security for this film down here."

"And?"

"The film is Redix Dean's. You know him, right? Y'all are sorta together?"

"Yeah."

My foot presses the gas pedal down to switch lanes in lightning zigzags.

"I think you should get down here. He's not good. That's all I can say. I'm not really supposed to tell you, but I know trouble when I see it."

"I'm an hour out."

"Okay. Good." She's quiet. "You need help?"

Tears threaten. Every time I've been in the shit, another woman has been there to get my back. From high school on the bus with that Charlie girl, to Mama, to Penny, to Scarlett.

"Can you meet me at the Waldorf?"

"I'll be there."

GPS and my fear, they race me there, cursing through Atlanta's traffic until I drop my keys in the valet's hand at the front of the posh hotel.

Grabbing my bag from the passenger seat, I see Scarlett leaning in the breezeway and waiting for me.

Her eyes flick down to my duty belt. "You come straight from the office?"

"Yeah." I search for the key fob Redix left me. It's buried at the bottom of my bag while we storm through the lobby. "Thanks for this."

"Anytime."

We don't say anything in the elevator. I know she'll get my back. I just don't know who'll protect my heart.

Swiping the fob in front of the opulent door with brass handles, I shove it wide open.

"Cade!" Eric jumps up from the sofa in the suite's living room. "What are you doing here?" He looks like hell collided with crap.

"Where is he?"

His eyes dart left toward a door. That's the bedroom.

"How long has he been in there?"

How long can I stand here until I'm ready to confront this? I don't know if I can. Because it's in my throat about to strangle all breath away.

What did he do?

Eric shifts. "Since last night."

I charge toward the bedroom door.

"Cade, don't!" Eric can't stop me.

No one can.

The door opens to my kick, and so does my heart, the one Redix's ice cream kiss and gifts and home and love had glued back together. It explodes again into a million pieces.

My breath, my hope, our dream, dead.

Three naked bodies; they're on the bed. Redix. Angie. And a woman I don't know.

"What the fuck?" Angie pops up. The other woman giggles, quickly hiding her phone behind her back.

That's a mistake.

Redix doesn't wake up.

I seethe at Angie, "Get out." A silk thread, pulled tautly, it's holding back my rage.

"Fuck you, crazy bitch." Angie's true colors show along with her huge tits. "You don't own him. I do again so *YOU* get out."

It happens so fast. My gun. It's drawn from behind my back and aimed at her.

"Damn fucking right I'm a crazy bitch for him." She's in my sights. "Now get the fuck up and out of here. Right now."

Giggle girl screams, jumping out of the bed.

"And give me your phones," I snarl.

She's been taking videos of him passed out. Guilt hangs as obvious as her blonde hair extensions.

Redix still isn't moving.

"You're fucking crazy!" Angie scrambles out of the bed behind the other woman.

Scarlett stands in the doorway, hand out, waiting for their phones.

Redix STILL isn't moving.

But I am. To his side. His color. It's pale. His breath? The wild life that screams from his beautiful lungs?

I can't see it.

"Redix?" It's training. Instinct. I check his pulse, trying to find it while tears start falling because...

I can't.

"What did he take?" I aim my gun back at Angie, my vision smearing with agony.

"Nothing." Angie's eyes are suddenly wide and scared.

"Bullshit!" My aim is perfect, my fury uncontrolled. "I will fill you with fucking lead, you pill-poppin' bitch. Now tell me!"

Her feet shuffle, bloodshot eyes flicking to her Prada bag on the floor while her hand shakes in front of her shorn pussy.

"What did you give him!" Pressure, it's building. On me. On the trigger. *I will pull it for him.* A million times, I will. "Now! Where's the bottle you gave him?"

Eric appears behind Scarlett, his face frozen with shock.

"Call nine-one-one," Scarlett urges him. "Now!"

Scarlett blocks the doorway, sneering at Angie and her accomplice. "Hand me the fucking bottle," she says, "and your phones if you want to walk out of here still looking pretty."

Angie scrambles for her bag but I can't focus on her. On anything else.

I drop my gun on the bed. "Redix." I shake him. "Wake up!" His shoulders, his cool flesh in my hands. His life is my home...

And it's slipping through my fingers.

"Wake up!" I rub the valley I live in, his heart, my most cherished place.

He's naked and too still, too void of breath.

"Wake up!" My fingers go back to his neck, searching, hope dropping from my grasp. "Please." I can't find his pulse. "No. No. No. No."

I can't think. I can't do this without him.

"Don't leave me." My lips press to his. No matter how long. No matter how far. He always came back to me. "Don't leave me." He said he'd come back for me.

I'll wait, breathing every breath for him until he does. "Don't leave me again."

From the moment we met…

His smiling lips crushed the candy cane I gave him. "What kind of name is Cade?"

"My first name is stupid, so I make my mama use my middle name—Cade."

"Your name is 'Stupid Cade'?"

"Funny." I hit his arm. I liked him. "No, it's 'Magnolia' and I hate that name."

"I like magnolias." He hit my arm back. He liked me too. "They're fun to climb."

He sat beside me and didn't leave my side. That's when we became best friends. "Thanks for the candy."

"You're welcome." He made me happy. "I got plenty to share." I opened my Hello Kitty purse and gave him my heart and he's held it since. It beats for him.

My best friend, his caring eyes, his big hands holding mine, he can't leave. "You promised me. Candy. Bikes. Ice cream. Candles. Pizza. Love." Tears, they stream over my lips brushing his. "You promised me infinity."

He always took care of me…

"I don't feel good." I started my period. "I wanna throw up." My head rested on his shoulder, and I wanted to stay with him forever.

His sweatshirt wrapped around my waist; his lips whispered in my hair. "I'll take care of you, Candy Cade." He held my hand and didn't let go. He protected me. He sacrificed everything for me. Even himself. "It's okay."

And I held onto him. I cherished him.

I always will.

God, I'll give up heaven for him. I will live in hell. Just for him to open his eyes.

"Please don't do this." His skin is sticky. With sweat.

With sick. With everything killing him inside. "Please don't leave me."

But his eyes won't open. His lips won't smile. His mouth won't say one more asshole joke. Or kiss me. Or call me "Candy Cade." Or swear that he loves me. "Don't leave me." I can't feel anything else. "Redix, please, I love you."

A slow thud—his artery—it beats under my fingertips. My tears, they fall from my chin, dripping onto his. "It's okay. I'm not mad. It's okay. Come on. Wake up for me."

There's nothing he can do. No woman he can fuck or mistake he can make or years he makes me wait. Pride dies when you hold death in your arms. When you realize love is all we live for, all we'll die for.

I pull his limp body into my embrace, rubbing his back while he slumps over me. He's so heavy, the weight of this threat, I'll fight it for him.

"Please. I'm here. I'm not mad. Wake up for me. I love you. Please."

He has to hear me. He has to know I'm here. I always will be.

Time, it's a blur. All I can do is rub his back, willing my breath into his lungs, my life back into his.

Or he can take me with him.

I'll let him. I want him to...

until...

hands are pulling him from my grasp.

"We got him, ma'am." It's an EMT. Two more are standing behind him. "What did he take?"

"This." I hear Scarlett. "And alcohol." Eric's standing beside her while the room descends into every effort to save him.

The sight of his limp body thrown onto the gurney. His

hand flopping almost lifeless by his side. The oxygen mask they smother over his face, forcing air into his lungs.

I throw up on the bed.

"Cade." Scarlett's there in my storm, holding onto me while I can't tear my eyes away from my worst nightmare.

My world leaves with his body rushed out of the room. Reality goes too. I'm in a car. Scarlett's. I'm in an Emergency Room. I know them too well. I'm in a haze, a hell for hours until Eric appears in the waiting room.

"He's stable."

The sobs, the relief, I don't care who witnesses it. Scarlett won't let me go until I can breathe again. "I have to see him."

"That's not his wish." Eric stands there, drained but determined.

"What?"

"He left instructions, Cade. If this ever happened again. No visitors. He's going straight to rehab."

I jump to my feet. "But it's me."

"*Especially* you," Eric says. "He never wanted you to see him like this."

"But I'm in charge of his estate, you said."

"That's if he doesn't make it. Until then, his orders are in writing. He doesn't want to see you."

My shoulders draw up. "Good fucking luck getting me to go." My fists clench. "I'll never leave him."

Everything urges me toward him. Scarlett stands up beside me.

"Don't make me do it." Eric's face, it's full of remorse. "Please leave with dignity or I'll have to call security."

My gun's still on my belt. My logic can't accept this. My heart can't stop bleeding every drop of love, of any pride I have left. I'll lose it for him.

"Don't do this." I'm about to do something crazy through tears, my vision blurring with them. "Please. I have to see him." I can feel it taking over.

"I'm sorry." Eric won't move.

"Come on." Scarlett stops me, wrapping her arm over my twitching shoulder wanting to reach for my gun, my only way to get to Redix.

"Give him time," she says. "He'll come around."

The disbelief, the defeat, I walk with it out of the Emergency Room.

"Take me back to his room," I tell Scarlett when we crawl into her sports car.

I still have the key fob and I want to know what the hell happened.

It doesn't make sense.

How did we go from the most incredible night, where he swore his love to me and dreams for our future, to two days later and he relapsed? And he fucked Angie? And some random woman?

What forced him to the edge of death again?

I comb his hotel suite. Empty bottles, of beer, of Absolut, of Johnny Walker, fuck, it's a mess. But I know him. This isn't him anymore. It feels so wrong.

Scanning the room while Scarlett checks the bathroom, my eyes fall on the nightstand.

The nightstand.

When we were teens, he always kept candy in his nightstand for me. Lemonheads. Like he knew I belonged in his bed.

I pull the brass ring on the drawer and there it is. His black leather journal. The one he's been writing in for months.

Sliding down the edge of the bed, I have to read it. His darkest thoughts. His pain. His secrets. They'll be no more.

What fills my eyes over the next hour reading it?

I barely can through my tears. They're falling over the pages, over all his capital writing, over all his love. Over all the answers I need.

Gentry with his taunts.

Derek Baucom was the driver, the third guy.

TJ targeted Pamela before she disappeared.

How Redix tried. How he fought until he could take no more.

There's one last journal entry. It's barely legible. Like he wrote it drunk.

Hey Candy Cade,

Remember how I used to carry you into the ocean? It made you laugh. I wanna go back to those waves with you. I wanna drown there, loving you for infinity.

Hey, God.
He I'm the beginning.
I'm the end too.

CHAPTER FORTY-SEVEN

CADE

Gravedigger by MXMS

PAMELA RYAN WORE a yellow sundress the night she went missing.

It was the same one I borrowed the night they went after me and took Redix instead.

Pamela was always sunshine.

Redix was the wild one who made us laugh. I was the moody giraffe, the one picked on, and Pamela was light and smiles, loving me despite my scowl.

And now I know...

How much she loved Redix too. I understand.

And that she dated TJ before she went missing. I don't need to know more.

There's glass in my throat thinking about her. My heart hurts too, rejected by Redix and scared for him. It's been three days and I've heard nothing from him.

Deep down, I fear it. Like he's gone for good. So I'm not waiting anymore.

Too much pain, too many people hurt, laws that don't work, fuck it, I know what I need to do.

Checking my makeup in the mirror, I have it all planned.

Flat sandals so I won't be too tall. Bare legs lotioned up to a sheen. Jean shorts, their hem kissing my ass cheeks. Hair swept softly back with sparkling butterfly clips. Eyes done to doe-eyed perfection. Lips glossed, asking to be kissed.

And yellow.

A yellow sweater tank secured around my neck by one thin strap, it barely conceals my braless breasts.

I look harmless. Ready for a date. A drink. A night of fun.

A murder.

"Wanna come over?" Penny calls me for the fourth time today, worried. "I got pizza, beer, and Lemonheads."

"No, thank you." I love her, so she can't know. "I just need time."

"Tomorrow then?"

"Yeah." But she can be one of my alibis. "I'll get coffee and donuts."

"The breakfast of cops?" She snorts. "I'll take a dozen powdered ones."

"You got it." I end that call to Jameson calling too.

"Hey." I try to sound calm, not ready for blood. "What's up?"

"Going out for beer. Wanna come?"

"Where you going?" Because I gotta avoid him.

"The Deck Bar. I can pick you up in fifteen." He's checking on me. He's also scoping Gentry. "You need to get out of the house."

"I need to stop crying."

That isn't a lie. Because all I feel is tears dripping with rage.

"For all the shit I gave you, Bryant, he loved you. It was obvious. You just can't fight anyone's demons but your own."

Fight my demons?

No. I'm going to kill them.

"Thanks." Someday, Jameson's going to make a lucky woman very happy. Not me. My heart is lost on another man... who's gone. "I'll finish my pity party tonight. Wanna fish with me and Silas tomorrow?"

Because I like my life complicated and my alibis simple.

"Sure. It's a date."

And that's as good as it gets for covering my ass.

No one else is guilty. This is my deal...

Me and you, God. You promised. Redix will be free.

We all will be when I do this.

No ONE on the island knows about the Land Rover Redix gave me. Scarlett had it delivered back here from Atlanta. It smells like a new car and breaks my heart. I park it a block away from the QuickTrip and walk to the gas station.

Hiding in the woods on the edge of the parking lot, I know he'll show up for his nightly run for smokes.

Ten o'clock. A few minutes late and he jumps out of his beat-up Mustang for his legal drug.

I walk across the lot, pacing my entrance to time with his exit.

It's perfect. Like it's written in the stars.

"Well damn, Sergeant." TJ's too thrilled to see me. Like he loses all logic around me. "Got a date?"

"I did." I don't smile. "Until she stood me up."

The cameras at the corner of the building? They don't work. And Ms. Dubois working inside? She'd never rat me out. She's loyal to my mama.

"Be *my* date then."

His golf shirt reeks of his cologne and evil. Both he's put on me for years. And his eyes? They never stop ripping my clothes off. This yellow top? He's drawn to it like a target.

"I ain't got an ice cream cone," he sneers, "but I got shots."

"I'm too old for ice cream." That feels true. "And bars and people only piss me off."

He likes my salty mouth. It draws him in like honey as he asks, "Let's go burn one then where you won't get busted."

Burn one? What doesn't this man smoke?

"You know what?" My tone, it stays low and slow, not too eager. "Yeah. It's been a shitty week."

The score in his eyes, that I finally said yes, he can't see through his blazed mind to question why. His stained teeth grin. "Well alright then."

"Meet me on my boat."

"Harbour Towne?"

"No. Too many cameras there." He thinks so I won't get

busted. That's true. But not for smoking weed. "Ms. Ryan's dock. You remember where it is?"

Since he went after Pamela, he knows.

"Yeah, it's been a minute, but I remember."

"Gimme an hour. I gotta gas up and I'll meet you there." I gotta keep him motivated. "I'll bring some wine."

The way he leans toward me, I fight the urge to punch his dick. "It sounds like I'm *your* man now."

Fuck, he's delusional. That's why he's so dangerous. He doesn't dance with the same logic as most.

In his mind, everyone wants him. "No" isn't a word. When he hears it screamed or slurred, he believes deep down... *you really want him.*

And I do.

Dead.

I try to make myself blush, asking, "Red or white?"

"White and sweet," he says, "like I like my women."

A gag, it hits me and it stops my eyes from rolling. "See you there." I move to step inside the store.

"Where you going?" He barks like he owns me.

I turn, tasting sweet thrill. "To get candy, of course."

It doesn't take much time. Why would it? I've been planning this for years.

The dock where I'm picking TJ up, I pull the throttle back, slowing my approach to it over an hour later. I've replaced all the deck boards on Ms. Ryan's dock so it'll be ready for this.

And if Ms. Ryan witnesses this crime, she'll never tell.

They say women have big mouths. Maybe some do. Our hearts are bigger though, able to keep a guilty secret for any woman who needs protection.

They gently clank, the wine bottles I brought on board.

Usually, it's a rookie mistake to have glass on a vessel.

But glass bottles have corks, ones you can punch a tiny needle through, filling the bottle with something extra.

That's what I've been waiting for. Well, one thing. The right poison. Using what TJ has against his victims, I love the poetic justice.

And the other thing I've been waiting for?

I wasn't prepared for it.

How much I'd fall back in love with Redix—not that I ever stopped. How his laughs filled my heart. How his smile soared my soul. How when his lips were on mine, the world stopped. And when his body joined with mine, I didn't need anything else.

My love lives with him.

What is he doing now? Detoxing with shakes so bad they're torture? Beating himself up for relapsing? Feeling guilty that he cheated on me? Wanting to be free of this? How has this burdened him for so long?

For ten years, he fought to survive it.

This is what I've been waiting for; it's my turn to fight for him.

He'll be free.

And the victims? They'll get justice. And they'll be no more after tonight.

Once we catch Derek. Once we get that last shred of evidence we need on Gentry. Once I do this, giving TJ everything he wants, I'll get it too.

Answers. Proof. Revenge.

Standing on Ms. Ryan's dock with the full moon behind him, even TJ's silhouette is wicked.

"I thought you were standing me up."

He's annoyed I made him wait fifteen minutes... because impatience reveals the truth.

"It's a no-wake zone. I had to go slow." I don't kill the

engine. Reversing back, I edge the boat up to the dock, close enough for him to jump aboard. "And we have all night."

He likes that answer as he lands on the deck and steps my way. "Where we off to?"

Cupping his hand, he blazes up a blunt without asking.

"I got a spot I like."

I've scoped it for years. Noting how vessels rarely go by. How even as the tides change, I have enough depth not to run aground. How the hungry gators like it too. They've been good company over the years.

TJ uses the time to scope me. Standing beside my captain's chair, he marks every spot down my body; plans he's been making since I was fifteen.

"Your boyfriend know you're out here with me?"

"No one knows where I am." That's true. "And he's not my boyfriend." That hurts.

"You two. Two of the prettiest people together?" Smoke slurred with envy escapes his lips. "You never belonged with him. You belonged with us."

He offers me a toke. I have to take it, to make him believe. His spit on the paper touching my lips twists my gut. I clench my teeth, saying with my generous exhale, "I belong with no one."

He laughs. "You're always feisty and hot as hell. That's why we can't resist you."

The bow of my boat, I snake it to my spot, pulling back to neutral feet from the shore. It's the perfect depth here.

"Grab the anchor." I ignore his comment... for now.

TJ blindly follows my command. While the anchor splashes down and he secures its rope, I open the cooler. With his back to me, I pull the cork on some cheap muscadine and fill a glass.

I offer it to him with a smile. "I'm a red girl."

Who's drinking a safe bottle of Merlot.

We clink full glasses. Taking his first sip, I watch his eyes plan his crime after he gets me drunk.

My plan? Keep him standing right here, between the two chairs, under the hardtop of my boat where there's more privacy.

And surprises waiting.

"Why do you always say 'we'?" I bite my lip. "When you talk about Gentry? Why is it always 'we,' the two of you?"

"We're close." The sips he's taking delight me. "No one comes between us."

"What about *me*?"

"You bond us." He steps toward me. "He'll hear about tonight." His stench fills my nostrils. "He loves the graphic details."

Everything I am holds back as my stomach turns, my throat gags, but I let him do it and it's so foul.

His kiss. His thin lips soiling mine, his teeth clashing into mine while his tongue trashes my mouth. My fists clench when his hands grab my ass, groping his moist fingers under the denim to get his first attempt at my body.

It'll be his last.

I shift my weight, letting his touch mangle my flesh and heart; *I don't want this.*

But I want revenge.

And it starts. The move I've practiced, the way I know how. I moan into his ashtray mouth. Seizing his hand on my ass cheek, I lift it to my breast for his grope... all while my other hand finds the zip tie handcuff I tucked in the seat of my captain's chair.

He pants, grabbing both my breasts and I moan back, driving his body into a frenzy. While I grind against his cock, over and over, he's slobbering over my lips while I loop the cuff around his wrist, grabbing his other one and binding them so fast, he's too horny to know what just happened.

"What the hell?" He stumbles, staring at his bind. The drug is kicking in, making him sweat. He slurs, "Is this a game?"

"Yes." I squat before him, my mouth inches from his hard-on under madras shorts. "I like it kinky."

He gazes down at me like his dream is coming true. *Mine is.* My hand skims up his skinny thigh under his shorts while my other reaches for the metal cuff tucked under my chair. It's attached to a nylon rope that's attached to a cinder block on the other end, hiding the whole time.

My lips near his zipper and he reeks. His words are as repulsive. "Yes, bitch. Do it. Suck my ice cream cone now." I smile. *Click, click, click, click.* The cuff locks on his ankle before he can resist.

"Bitch." He kicks his foot, not able to budge it. "What is this?"

I surge up. The yellow bandana I tucked in my back pocket? It's shoved in his mouth before he can ask more. The piece of duct tape I stuck to the side of my chair? I rip it off and smack it over his mouth before I spit in his face.

"This is revenge."

With knife strikes of my hand, I hit pressure points, his nerves wincing as he cries out to my blows every time he tries shoving past me.

The drug, his favorite one, he's getting clumsy. Stumbling back, he falls into the chair behind him.

The euphoria in his eyes, the side-effect has him unafraid.

"You have minutes to live," I tell him, "and answers I'm gonna get in them."

The heave of his chest slows. He won't resist me. He won't even scream.

I yank the tape off, pulling the bandana from his mouth. "Where is Pamela Ryan?"

I need to find her, to give this peace to Ms. Ryan so she can finally say goodbye. It's a fate I need too.

For Pamela. For Redix. To finally let them go.

A grin rises, revealing his stained teeth and soul. His eyelids start dropping. "You'll never find her."

I've suffered him too long not to know him. "She's still alive?" It's shock. It's hope. "Where is she?"

"She's his."

"Who?"

Gentry or Derek?

The bob of his chin, he threatens to pass out on me so I slap my hand across his face, loving the sting in my palm while his eyes shoot wide open. "Who has her?"

"She's his and you're mine." It's a hallucination in his eyes, of the truth. "You were always mine."

I know where his sick logic goes. To me. To Redix. "You cut him, didn't you? It was you?" My grip squeezes his chin; I hope I break his weak jaw. "You were always jealous of him."

With delight in his eyes, he gazes up at the stars. I can see that vile night in his eyes.

"The tattoo y'all share." He slurs. "It should've been mine." He sighs. "So his pain was mine instead. It was *all* mine. The way he screamed and moaned while I tore into his flesh; it was *all* for you, Cade."

It's lightning, the power through my veins into my right

hook crashing into his cheekbone; I don't care if I break my hand.

"The next scream of pain?" I hook with a left and do it again. "It's all yours." I punch down next, smashing his pathetic dick with my fist. "And this is *all for him*." I uppercut his balls.

That doubles him over in pain.

I hope he pukes.

My hand, it grabs his neck, squeezing hard and forcing his sight to mine.

"I was never yours. I'll always be his. I'll always love Redix Dean no matter what you did to him, to us. You're a sick, pathetic fuck. No one wants you, TJ. Everyone wants Redix Dean and so do I." I spit in his eye. "I'll love him until the day I die."

That hits him, somewhere deep in his drugged psyche, that was a knife to his demented ego. I see it shake his core.

"All those women you hurt?" I snarl. "Who looked like me? You had to drug them because no fucking way did they want your nasty hands on them. Men like you and your pitiful dicks; you need to be killed off."

His artery under my fingers, I feel his sluggish pulse, and I press down, trying to stop it. "Where is Cam Le? The maid for Gentry's condos?"

The focus in his eyes, he can't find it, slurring, "She's his."

"Where?"

She's still alive. So is Pamela. I will find them.

"Where we like to play." His mind is there, not here. "Where I'm gonna play with you."

He's deranged.

"No." I shake my grip, rattling his skull. "I'm the one playing now, Motherfucker."

His neck squeezed in my grasp, my bicep tenses for this, it's trained for this. It's a matter of minutes and my call when.

"See how much fun this is, TJ? You thought pretty girls were only for fun, didn't you?" My teeth, they clench with every fucking time men like him hurt someone. "We're also for murder. We'll kill you all." The power in my grip, in my rage, it's blinding. "This is real fucking fun, isn't it?"

Lucidity, in one fast flash it takes his eyes while he sneers, "None were as fun as him."

It's gone. My logic. My restraint. All I see is Redix while I let it possess me, while I let my deal, my revenge take the life from the man who hurt him. Who hurt all those women.

And this doesn't hurt me.

Not at all.

I don't care what happens to me. If my soul is damned, I squeeze harder, choking with both hands now. If I lose my mind too, it can go.

As long as those women have justice, as long as Redix doesn't hurt anymore.

TJ and all my pain, all my tears, Redix's scar, his battered face, his strong heart, his love and fight that never gave up for me, I'm doing this. For every woman TJ hurt. For Redix...we'll finally be free.

I don't even hear it.

The engine of the boat trolling up behind me.

"Magnolia Cade, stop."

That name. That voice. It could summon me out of hell.

And it does.

I glance up... and it's Mama.

"He's mine." Mama's standing on Dad's boat. Dad's

steering, sloshing beside this boat while her eyes lock on mine. "He's *always* been mine."

My hands drop, my jaw too.

What are they doing here? How did they know?

TJ slumps over in the seat. He's still alive, barely, but he doesn't deserve to be. If life makes it back into his lungs, he'll only hurt more people.

We know it.

And now I know it too.

What brought my parents back together? Me and Redix and justice.

My dad kills his engine and drops his anchor. He jumps onto my boat, his old one.

"I had Silas put GPS on this boat when I had to use it last. That's how I found you." He grabs my arms while I search for my reasoning.

"Listen to me," he says, "this is for us to finish, not you."

"But I need to—"

"No, you don't." Mama's voice is calm. It always is, just like the iron in her eyes when her mind is made. "I needed to do this years ago, just didn't get the chance, not wearing a badge."

"You can't—"

"Yes, I will." You can't argue with her. "This is my justice. Those boys? Those men now? They're hurting other women. They hurt you, my baby, first. Then they hurt, Redix, my boy too. I love him like my son, and this is my job to finish."

I'm stunned. I don't know why. Dad was the vigilante, not Mama. But facing down death has changed her.

I should've known.

She's been watching me this whole time. And Dad's been tracking his old boat.

He flops TJ's body onto his new one, letting it hit the deck with a thud.

"Clever," he says of the handcuff around TJ's ankle that's secured to a rope attached to a cement block Dad has tucked under his arm while he crawls back onto his boat.

"What are y'all gonna do?"

"What I should've done that night," Dad answers, pulling his anchor back up next.

"Don't speak another word about it." Mama's drawl warns before she looks back my way. "What did you find out?"

Of course I interrogated him first. She's raised me too well.

"Pamela is still alive. So is that other missing woman."

"Oh, thank God." Mama grabs her chest. "Then you go find them and catch their ass."

This leaves Gentry left to deal with. And Derek.

The engine on Dad's boat sputters back on while silence takes us all.

My parents saved me from committing the worst sin for the best reasons. And somehow, I don't worry about what this act, what this secret, will do to them.

Someone hurt their kids. Someone hurt innocent people.

There is no guilt, no sin.

TJ sentenced his soul the minute he put a knife into Redix's flesh.

Yes, God. This was the deal.

CHAPTER FORTY-EIGHT

CADE

Over a year later…

I wedge my toes underneath a pile of sand, keeping my bare feet warm in the October breeze.

Some days this month, it's warm, like summer doesn't end. Other days, they're like me. Cool. Muddled. Not sure if they'll let the lonely darkness take them.

My friends have left for the day but I'm still here letting my ass get numb watching the Sunday beachgoers. Despite it being off-season, this beach, Coligny Beach, it's rarely empty.

Except at night.

I know this too well.

Penny with her pregnant-again belly had me laughing today.

"I thought you were too tired to fuck," I joked with her.

"Please"—she chewed on her favorite frozen grapes—"all I had to do was lie back and let Hank do the work. It's only fair. He works for ten minutes, gets us both off, and then the next nine months are on me."

"More like *in* you." I try hiding the pang of what I'm missing inside.

I would've liked a baby. Or three.

"I don't know if I'll ever want kids." Scarlett sat on my other side, swigging cider. "But the ones I'm working for sure are cute."

Scarlett's working a job on Daufuskie Island. Her coming around to hang out too; it's made life bearable.

"Any babies of Daniel Pierce and Charlie Ravenel have got to be cute," I said.

That's the famous couple she's working for. Everyone knows now that they live on Daufuskie. It exploded over social media, and I feel sorry for them. Between his fame and her job, that's a security nightmare.

Luckily, they have Scarlett on their HGR Security team. I'm sure glad she was on mine.

"Daniel Pierce *is* a hot man." Scarlett grins. "Who only has eyes for his hot wife."

"Is Charlie still a badass? She was when we were in high school."

"More than you can imagine," is all Scarlett can say about her job. I respect that. I respect secrets.

I have my own.

My girlfriends left an hour ago, but I still can't move. I

don't want to go home to an empty condo, to my empty heart.

I can always go bug my parents. They're back together until Mama has enough of Dad and sends him to his boat for a few days.

"If I want a man under my feet all the time," she says, "I'll wear him like high heels."

They're cute though. Like they're honeymooning again.

But we never speak about it. Not once.

We know better.

Jameson wouldn't keep quiet about it for the longest time. Too many questions filled that man's mind and mouth when TJ stopped popping up places.

"What happened to him?" Jameson wouldn't let it go. "You think he's shacked up somewhere with Derek Baucom?"

We haven't found Derek. We found his abandoned truck at The Pelican, but he got off this island unseen. We know how with no proof. Gentry and his "After Tail" yacht, he helped Derek disappear.

Gentry in the meantime is doing evil business as usual, appealing search warrants of his condos, throwing his political sway around.

So fuck him, I searched through dumpsters outside them. Don't need warrants for that.

It filled me with rare hope. I found used sanitary pads in a white garbage bag dumped outside the condo I last saw Derek disappear into. The one by the doorbell camera. Though the camera only showed Derek entering from the front, I know a woman was there. She could've been brought in through the back.

By the time we got the warrant, that condo was clean.

But I know Derek had a woman hidden in there. I suspect it was Cam Le.

They're my next deal—Gentry and Derek.

"Maybe it was drugs." I swirled a French fry in ketchup, unable to look Jameson in the face about TJ's disappearance.

Until I did. I worried he'd see my guilt.

But Jameson only gave me that other look.

The one that wanted me.

I got so close again. I made myself try. Almost a year without Redix, with no word from him; I was broken. I closed my eyes and let Jameson kiss me in the parking lot of The Deck Bar.

It slammed my lonely body, hard. Because Jameson was... hard. Planes of shredded muscle. A hot mouth tasting of mint, moaning and hungry for mine with his rigid cock pressing into me leaning against my Land Rover.

He inched my skirt up and parts of me responded, needing something. But the part of me that matters, my heart. It couldn't. Not with him.

It belongs to someone else.

"We have to stop." I gently grabbed his hand about to reach between my thighs. He would've found me wet, but that's not enough anymore.

Something in me shut down. To every man.

"We can't do this. It won't work."

"Bryant"—his lips lifted from mine, huffing with lust and frustration— "this is the last time. I won't lose any more pride over you. You know if we try, we'd be so good."

"I know if we try." I dropped his hand. "I'd break your heart."

Two weeks later, Jameson put in his resignation.

Yep, I send every man off this island somehow.

Scarlett got Jameson a job working for HGR Security. They're just friends now. "Not meant to happen" as she put it.

Lately, when I talk to Jameson, he sounds good. Flying in a private jet to exotic places, he's the private detail to a rare bird—a woman billionaire.

Last time he called, he sounded happy. Too happy. *Uh-huh*—I grin—I know the sound in his voice.

Jameson's in love.

So is that couple. Those teenagers playing in the waves. They're cute.

She's got her arms wrapped around his neck, protesting as he carries her and wades in thigh deep. He's laughing and gazing back at her because she's loving it.

I used to.

Redix did the same with me, picking me up and wading into the surf while I giggled into his shoulder. Until one time, it wasn't so funny.

He plunged us under, and a rip of a wave took my bikini top with it.

I dropped my shoulders under the water while we tried to find it.

We couldn't though. "This is what you get for dragging me out here." I wasn't amused.

"Damn, right." He was thrilled. "I'd drown to see your gorgeous tits."

"Redix! I'm serious!"

He tossed his long wet, strands back and laughed. "I am too!" Putting his back to the shore, he shielded me from eyes aimed my way. "Come on. Let me see them."

I couldn't resist him then or ever. I stood up; cool water and the breeze teasing my flesh.

"Goddamn, darlin'." He couldn't take his eyes off my

nipples rising for his stare. "Can I have them for my birthday?"

"Maybe." I ducked back under, suddenly shy by a wave of lust. "Get me out of this damn ocean first."

"I'll take care of you, Candy Cade."

He confused me at first, reaching to untie his swim trunks and yanking them off underwater.

"What are you doing?" I tried peeking. Even then I wanted him so much.

"I'm gonna save you." Picking me up, he wrapped my legs around his waist and we paused, that position making my pussy tingle while he kissed me promising, "They'll all look at me now and not you."

Hell yes, they looked at him.

Squeals, oohs, and nervous laughs took the beach while Redix Dean strode out naked from the waves. I buried my blushed face in his neck while he carried me and his swim trunks in his hands.

"How y'all doin'?" he asked their wide eyes while he walked toward our towels yards up the beach.

The saltwater dripping from his nude warm skin; I was safe. My body held in his strong arms; I was home.

He glanced down at three women on the beach, holding full wine glasses and smiling. "Enjoyin' the big show, ladies?"

Because he was then and still is now.

The most beautiful, big, and wild heart. My most beautiful best friend.

I still miss him.

And the tears still come.

There's a painful ache you get when you miss someone. It hurts, like a bruise on your soul and time presses down on it. You don't want to breathe. You don't want to move. You don't want to do anything but feel the pain because it's all you have left.

And powerful memories.

I heard he's out of rehab. And he emerged looking healthy... and peaceful.

Without me.

Without our past haunting him.

God made good on her deal.

He's free now.

I'm not and that's what I wanted—to swap our places like I wanted to that night.

I'm the one with a dark secret now.

Paparazzi were there after Redix left rehab. Tough to say if that was planned by his team, but they got cute videos of him later on the patio of his ice cream shop in Malibu. He treated dozens of families to free ice cream. The smile on his face, sitting on a bench beside a swarm of kids, he was licking a cone and the light was back in his eyes.

Happy for him, it made mine water then.

Like they do now.

I drop my shades over my eyes.

Like hell if anyone can see me cry.

CHAPTER FORTY-NINE

REDIX

DEAR CANDY CADE,

The nape of your neck, how your dark hair comes to a perfect point showing me the exact soft spot to kiss?

It pulls me to you, Cade.

Hell, who am I bullshitting?

Everything pulls me to you.

Like this journal. It's tan. It's new. Kinda like me.

I guess you found my old one. I guess that's good. You know everything now.

How I never wanted to hurt you. I just wanted to protect you. That's why I never told you those things. Because it kills me when you cry.

Because I'll still take all the pain for you.

Remember when we were twelve and too big to be at that playground but of course, we didn't listen?

You started a game, a stupid one of "let's see what we can jump off of." Me, like the idiot I always am for you, thought it was the best idea ever.

And it was.

Until you jumped off the top of a sliding board. Damn woman, you forget you have bones that can break.

But it broke my heart because I heard the thud when you landed, and I knew it hurt. You curled in a ball and bit your lip until it bled to keep from crying in front of me.

"It's okay." I climbed up the sliding board ladder. "I'll do it too."

"Don't" was all you could barely say watching me.

"Hey, Candy Cade!" I'd do anything for you. "Watch this!"

That's what everyone says, right? Just before their next trip to the Emergency Room.

I jumped and landed beside you. My ankle broke and the ground smacked me so hard for being so damn dumb.

Because that hurt like a motherfucker.

"Are you crazy?" You reached for me, worried I was hurt. I was.

"I am for you," I said before I puked in the grass from the pain.

But then I got a badass cast with crutches for two months. And I got you carrying my backpack and spoiling me.

Fuck, if that got me more time with you? I was ready to jump off buildings next.

Instead, Cade, I jumped off the edge of sanity into my hell.

Because that's what happens to me when I drink or pop pills.

I popped a beer open that afternoon and after four more beers in minutes, reality disappeared. I don't remember much.

My memory's kind that way.

But I had lots of dreams about you. I wanted to stay in them with you. I had you and no pain and that's all I wanted. In my dreams, you kept holding me and telling me it'll be okay. That you weren't mad. That you loved me.

And I held on for you. For those dreams with you. I didn't let go to whatever was pulling me under because I wanted a life with you more.

But when I woke up, I couldn't face it. How I hurt you. And me. And everyone I loved. How I fucked up again.

I can't tell you the shame of it. How it feels bigger than me and like I'll never win.

But I tried.

I swear—my life, my addiction—it feels like I'm trying to turn the Titanic around... on a motherfucking dime.

And I did it this time.

No more secrets. I told my sponsor, my group, my new counselor, and every damn person who'd listen, I told them all what happened, all my scars and pain. And after a while, it worked.

I was free.

My sobriety feels different this time. Like I crossed over. I guess I shouldn't say I'm a new man. I'm a better one.

I'm a man who's staring at who saved him. Who he loves.

She's sitting right in front of me on the beach.

Our beach.

CHAPTER FIFTY

CADE

My back pocket vibrates, waking me from my stare contemplating the line where the ocean kisses the sky.

SILAS

Wanna go fishing?

Wanna grab some beer?

Me? I just wanna see you

He's a temptation. One I've resisted for over a year. We hang out. We laugh. But something holds him back. Me too.

Is it the way he looks so much like Redix? It's a bitter-sweet marvel and I don't know.

Maybe I should let go. Maybe if I do, I'll drift safely toward Silas, toward a new shore, and not get sucked under in this ache.

Because I can't stay in this pain forever.

I make myself reply. It feels strange. Does that mean it's wrong? Making my fingertip text him back, I'm tired of hurting.

I just want

...

It stops me.

I don't know what at first until I really hear it. Above the waves sloshing to shore and the wind blowing over my ears, there's a song playing behind me.

"Chasing Cars."

My chin starts trembling, shaking with my lips quivering; I didn't think I could cry any more. The sky blurs and my shoulders, I try to keep them from shaking into sobs, but they do because...

this can't be happening.

This isn't chance. This isn't coincidence. I close my eyes; *it's him.* And I can sense him, hearing his call. He's sitting right behind me.

"Is this stalking, Detective?"

That bourbon voice, I huff a laugh, joy filling my lungs with the air I need.

"Yes"—I turn my wet chin so he can hear over my shoulder—"it is."

"Does that mean I'll get cuffs and your hands on me too?"

"It means I'll beat the shit out of you."

"I'd rather"—his voice draws closer—"you beat the fuck out of me."

His heat, it rises over my back, warming through my long sleeve shirt.

"Beat the fuck out of me, Candy Cade." His lips find my ear, reaching for my heart again. "I deserve it for what I did."

Remembering his limp body, his eyes that wouldn't open, I can't speak. What emotions tumble through me, smashed like broken shells in the surf, I don't know but I can't move.

He does. His tan legs appear in my side vision. "Is this seat taken?"

"Yes."

"Who are you saving it for?"

My sunglasses, I push them atop my head, pushing all pride aside too. I look up at him, not afraid to answer, "For the love of my life. For the one who promised me infinity."

Wearing only board shorts, he sits down beside me on the towel, my breath burning as he faces me.

"I'm so sorry, Cade." He swallows hard before he barely says, "I don't know what else to say."

"Yes, you do."

It's in the sky of his eyes staring at me. "And I love you."

"Say it again."

"I'm so sorry I hurt you, Magnolia Cade Bryant, and I love you. Like the love-of-my-life love and for infinity."

Tears burn my eyes like the fire in my chest at his body, at his face so close to mine. I turn away, the horizon giving me breath. Giving me a moment.

"Say more." Because it's not enough.

"I'll never be able to say it enough." He can read my soul. "But I can tell you what I've kinda figured out."

Silence protects my heart.

"Last time." His toes wedge in the sand beside mine. "I got sober for everyone else. That's been my life. It's been for everyone else. From my drunk dad who made me the man of the house at eight. To my mom who I smiled at every camera for. To my little sister I had to protect."

He's quiet, his next words strained. "To the best friend I fell in love with. To the guy others assaulted. I don't regret it, but who else was I? I didn't know. I got sober for everyone else I loved but I didn't love myself yet."

I chew my lip, hearing every truth I've known about him all this time. It's not too different than my own.

"But this time, I got sober for myself." His foot wedges closer to mine. "Last time, I didn't want to die. This time, I want to live. I want to live for me, for the man it's taken me a year to know and love."

He mirrors me, wrapping his arms around his knees bent in front of him, and turning his gaze my way.

"And that man is very fucking humbled and sorry that he hurt you. And I know you saved my life. And you don't owe me anything else but please just let me thank you for that."

It's in his voice. *He has changed.*

He was never one for words, not ones that talked about himself, about how he felt. He was always too focused on me, on everyone else, on being what we all needed.

Only in tender moments between us, when no one else was around, when his body was touching mine did he say what he felt.

When we were kids, it was how happy he felt. When we were teens, it was the desire we felt. As adults, he's finally saying what I've seen in his eyes all along.

He sounds like his journal, like he knows his truth and he's not afraid to share it. In fact, he's made peace with it.

I can feel it in his body relaxed next to mine. Like the connection we've always had, I feel it fill mine too.

I level my eyes at him. "Tell me about this man you've learned to love."

His smile, it melts my frozen edges. "He likes playing guitar and surfing. He likes writing in his journal and helping kids in crisis, like he was." It warms my soul. "He likes playing Uno and burning pizzas. He likes making ceramic dildos." A chuckle lightens my heart. "And he's really in love this woman who likes candy but loves him even more. And he's so fucking sorry and he really misses her."

I do it first. My hand slides across his scruffy cheek, seizing his silky strands and pulling his lips to mine.

He matches me. He always has. Perfectly. His big hand cups my wet cheek, his kiss seeking mine and...

It's not in me, with his lips taking mine, so soft, so sexy— I can't find it.

I have no anger. No jealousy. No betrayal. We've been through too much.

He protected me. He almost died for me. He swapped my pain for his, and I held him in my arms with his life barely hanging on.

Only a fool would stay angry when life is this precious; when love is this great.

"I forgive you." I slide my lips over his, not wanting to lose his touch. "I was never mad at you."

His nose nuzzles mine. "You should be."

"Since when do I do what I should?"

"I mean it. What I said."

"Which part?"

"All of it." His eyes anchor to mine. "From the depths of my soul, Cade, I swear it. I'm so sorry."

"Never say it again; the sorry part. But the love part? Prove it to me, Redix Dean."

A giggle breaks the air. I glance over his shoulder. A group of teens is turned our way. Their phones too.

You can ignore Redix Dean like a tide of elephants.

"Take me home," I insist... in every way.

His hand reaches for mine, "I know just the one," and pulls us both up.

I thought we were going to my place. I thought I would be alone forever. I thought this day would suck like all my others. I thought I was being punished for what I almost did; though I'd do it again for him.

He won't let go of my hand, guiding me through the crowd, smiling and pushing through to protect me; I don't need it.

I just need him. Because I thought wrong.

Because *this* is right.

Us. Together.

CHAPTER FIFTY-ONE

CADE

LOVE ME HARD by Elley Duhé

MY EYES, I can't take them off his profile. Even though I don't know where he's driving us. Even while he's filling me in on all the good news.

The bad stuff?

I don't want to talk about it anymore. It's stolen enough from us.

"I've been filming in Savannah," he says. "You remember my friend, Lorraine Morris?"

"Yeah."

He's holding my hand on the center console.

"She's doing another series and she asked me to do a guest role, a few episodes and I said yes. She's covered my ass so many times."

"How long are you here?"

"Another month or so."

"And then what?"

He takes his eyes off the road, the one draped by palms and Spanish Moss, and glances my way. "That depends."

"On?"

"On if I can stay and ride bikes with you."

I laugh. I can't help it. There are so many memories between us. That's one of the happiest ones. I don't answer him. I'm too distracted by the driveway he turns in to.

It's a huge home but understated, blending into the trees around it.

"Where are we?"

I know this island. This is beachfront, the most prized part of it. Whose place is this? Is it one of Luca Mercier's houses?

Getting out of the car, it's his turn not to answer. His hand reaches out to mine, leading me to the front door. When he holds it open for me—an empty living area, windows, a pool, dunes, and seagrass—they greet me before the Atlantic does.

The shock. The wrap of his arms around my waist. The way he vows, "I'm not running anymore. This is my new home here." It takes my heart while his voice softens. "And if you'll let me try to win back your trust and love, I hope it will be *our* home here."

Standing in his empty living room, I turn to him. "You don't have to *win* me back."

"Cade, I relapsed and I cheated on you. I slept with two women. I don't remember it, but I did."

I'm so tired of this. Of guilt. Of pain.

"Yes, and you saved me from three men. We're more than even."

His jaw clenches, his eyes not believing me.

"Redix, I thought I lost you. And all I cared about was that you lived. That even if you never came back to me, at least you were okay. This was never about years apart. Or about other women. Anyone who gives a shit about that hasn't held the person they love in their arms, thinking they're gone. My love for you is too big to ever feel betrayed."

"But I fucked up. And you kept taking me back. Then I *really* fucked up and I should have to fight for you now."

The pause. It's long while the memory moves like a shadow across our eyes.

"You *did* fight for me. And I'm not anyone's pushover, or trophy to win back, or stubborn hard-to-get-game. And anyone who judges me otherwise can go fuck themselves and the tomorrow they assume they're guaranteed. I know my worth. I know my heart. And I know that I want to be with you."

He throws his chin up, fighting back tears. "I don't deserve you."

"Yeah, *you do*. Because I've always loved that man you love now too. And I want to surf with him, and help other kids with him, and play Uno with him. You can forget guitar because I have no fucking patience. But I'm all about burning pizzas, ceramic dildos, and letting him call me 'Candy Cade'."

His hands, they cradle my face. "So I get my best friend back? You'll give me another chance?"

"I'll give you more than a chance. I'll give you infinity."

"Careful, darlin'." He presses his forehead to mine. "That's a long time to spend with an asshole."

"Not when it's as cute as yours."

His grin lights up my heart. "When have you seen my asshole?"

"Tonight."

He gives me kisses through laughter and tears before a tour of the house. Its white marble floors and white walls with natural wood-trimmed windows are empty of furniture. But full of our love as he saves the owner's suite for last.

It's massive. White carpet meets glass doors to the pool deck and ocean beyond. The only thing in the room is a Bali-style king bed with two pillows, sheets, and a blanket.

"How long have you been here?"

"Too long without you."

I hear it in his voice. Worry. "What's wrong?"

"What will it look like? Us trying again?"

"What do you want it to look like?"

"Well…"

His left hand, the one with a silver ring on his index finger, it tucks his hair back and my heart leaps because he doesn't turn away and leave me this time.

"I've only had two years to dream about it." Instead, he faces me to say, "I want ice cream kisses and to fuss about toilet paper and what we watch at night because no more *One Tree Hill*. I want to ride bikes with you, red ones like when we were kids. I want to vacuum and water our plants. I want to nap on the sofa with you. I want"—all of it, every wish I've had with him, it won't stop flowing from his mouth —"years from now, if we're ready, to make a beautiful baby with my best friend."

Have I ever felt this happy? Have I ever felt this ready to live again?

This is everything I've ever wanted and it's right here—a future with Redix.

I close the last distance between us. "Can we start trying now?"

It's sudden. It's been waiting.

The grip of his hand around my neck pulls me into his kiss—our kiss—the one that flows heat through my veins, the one that lightens my heart.

His tongue dances with mine while our soft moans find their familiar rhythm.

His hard body urges against mine and it's been over a year and arousal explodes through my every nerve.

I need air. I need to yank my top off. I do because there's a fire in my sex we need to quell while I stand before him in my bikini top, my ribs huffing for breath.

"Fuck," he sighs looking at me. "I missed you."

I drop my jean shorts to the floor. "Take ten seconds or rip me apart again, I don't care because I missed you too."

"Oh, I'll do both," he replies, reaching to tickle his fingertips under the edge of my bikini bottoms. Lust weighs his eyes down, but he thinks it through.

"Cade, I've been sober and celibate ever since. And I'm clear."

Fuck, that turns me on and soothes my heart that he's waited that long again.

"What about you?" he dares to ask.

"There was someone else."

Pain flashes across his eyes. "It's okay. I didn't expect you to wait on me, or to even forgive me."

"We did wait on you." I grin. "Me and Mr. Blue."

"I thought you broke him." We stand so close.

"Only in two pieces. I glued it back."

He chuckles. "You fixed my dick?"

"Yep." I strip off my bikini.

His eyes watch mine as they drop along with his board shorts to the floor. "Look." His real one springs to large life. "You've fixed my dick in many ways."

I barely touch it. "What about you?" Pushing it down to the vice of my thighs, I tease his tip with the wet that's starting to coat my crevice. "What kept you satisfied?"

"I've destroyed six pillows and have carpal tunnel from moaning your name."

His hips thrust gently into my gap while my nipples graze inches below his. He stopped waxing his chest. It's so sexy, the hair dusting his sculpted pecs. And his arm, he has new tattoos.

But nothing captures my gaze more, falling down his shredded body, than the matching tattoos we have.

We stare at them, his fingertips lingering over mine, our past, our connection—two dorsal fins paired for life.

His light touch over our story, it makes me tremble.

"I stopped my birth control," I confess that too. "It made me more depressed and I didn't need it."

"We don't need it," he says, "at least, I'm ready. But I have condoms."

"Redix, I'm ready too, but what if..."

The sight of him, of life slipping from his breath, I can't shake it. It'll haunt me forever.

"Life is nothing but 'ifs'." His hands lift my jaw. "And if I get to spend the rest of my life with you, Cade, it'll be the happiest one."

Our kiss, it affirms everything, his tongue sweeping gently through my mouth, all my hesitation, gone. "No condoms. I've waited too long for this. For our dream together."

His arms sweep me up before he tosses me giggling onto the plush new bed.

"Lie there," he demands, smiling, "on our bed where you belong."

I spread my thighs. "Then climb up here with that big cock where you belong too."

He picks up my foot instead, kissing my ankle and muttering, "You need more patience."

"You *need* to fuck me."

He kisses a trail up my calf while his knees crawl onto the edge of the bed. "I need to make you beg for my fuck."

I'll be screaming for it because his hungry mouth is leaving wet trails up the inside of my thighs.

He's right, I have no patience with his gorgeous body climbing over mine. With his tongue next, circling warm around my nipple, then the other.

"Beg for me, Cade." He nips at my nipple, his hard shaft urging against my thigh.

Has someone got a megaphone?

"Please fuck me, Redix." I'll shout it for all to hear while I grab his strands, trying to lift him up to where our bodies align. "Please."

But he pulls away. "I need you louder and wetter."

Turning his body around then grabbing mine, he uses his strength to flip me over.

"I've never done this before," I sigh, lying on top of him with my pussy in his face and his beautiful cock in mine.

"I don't think I have either." He goes back to kissing up my thighs, the pull of his hands, he spreads me open, confessing, "Damn, Cade. You have a model pussy too. So glistening and pink for me."

His praise makes my thighs shake and he hasn't even started.

I'm staring at his cock, hard and flexing up, seeking me too. I kiss his tattoo, our tattoo, every part of him to the deep ridge of his Adonis belt, following its path.

I moan as my tongue finally licks from his base, up his thick vein while his tongue thrills me, from flicking my clit lightly, to long flat licks. The sensation rolls my eyes back before he's dipping into my entrance and tasting my nectar for him.

Oh fuck, this is so good. I wrap my hand around his base and hold his tip up, swirling my tongue around his crown while his deep moans vibrate through my pussy.

I want him, as much as I can. Wrapping my lips and hollowing my cheeks, I slide my mouth so tight down his shaft.

There's no way I can take all of him, but his hard taste is taking me to the edge of where I end and he begins. It's getting smeared and lost in our reunion. Those strong hips, he lifts them, trying to fuck my throat while his tongue starts pummeling my clit, the sound of him lapping through my desire taking me along with my glucking sucks of his.

It's a storm of sensations. His aroma seeps from his sexy flesh—vanilla and leather. The saline taste of him in my mouth, his hard velvet dragging over my lips, the strong wrap of his hands around my ass cheeks as he pulls me open for his feast. His firm nose, his stubbled chin, it makes my most sensitive skin scream with lust at his soft mouth diving into my depths.

"Cade, I'm gonna come." His voice fills my ears along with his cock in my mouth, swelling with the same certainty. "Fuck you taste so good, I'm gonna come in your mouth."

I'm ravenous, my hard grip slapping his tip against the flat of my tongue before I insist. "Do it." I take him as deep as I can again, letting us both enjoy my soft gag. "I want to taste you in my throat, Redix," I swear it before I take him again.

"*Fuuucckkk.*" His groan is muffled in my drenched lips, sucking on each one while his grip, it's so hard and probably bruising my flesh.

I love it, moaning over his cock while he shakes his head with his mouth buried in my pussy. He's ravaging me like his last meal while the arch of his back, it comes with his loud groan and suddenly I taste him.

His hot, salty spurts make me lose it, the firecracker of my clit exploding at the double satisfaction of his mouth and mine, his sex and mine, both of us drinking the other in.

I need to catch my breath. I need us to never end.

My head, my body, they rest on top of his, the heave of his chest matching mine until we both calm.

"Come here." He gently rolls me over, resting me on my back while he turns again, his kiss finding mine, his long strands tickling over my face.

I love how he does this, how he craves our taste. I do too. Craning my neck for his mouth, I need more of him, and he knows it, muttering through our flavor, "I'm never done with you."

I lose all time. All the minutes gone to every part of me that hurts, he heals with his fingers, the back of them, or their tips, he uses everything to cherish every part of my flesh with his touch for so long.

"We can't lose this again, Cade."

He's skimming over my heart; it knows it's him. It's beating for his touch.

"I know." I linger my touch down between his pecs to

where I count his abs and all the time we spent apart. "People will die before I let you go so easily again."

"My hot-tempered woman." His eyes laugh. He thinks I'm joking. "You know it turns me on when you fight for me."

"How quickly can you get turned on again?"

I leap up, faster than I've ever shown him I can, grabbing his wrist and pinning it above his head. When he laughs, trying to grab my other hand, my grip clamps down like a snake, pinning that one down too.

"Fuck!" His smile soars. "Keep being rough with me like this and I'll be hard in a second."

I grind on his cock. "Oh yeah?" Thrilled at how it firms for me. "You wanna be rough?"

"Fuck yes." He pushes back. I let him. Flipping me back over, I flop onto my back, loving this. "You want it rough, Cade?" He climbs off the edge of the bed. "You sure?"

My hips, he yanks them down, perching my ass on the edge of the bed while he stands at the perfect height between my thighs.

"Yes." I lift my legs in the air, letting him grab my ankles and spread them wide apart. "I can be *so bad* for you, Redix."

"Show me then." His grip on my ankles is tight. The muscles across his shoulders rip down his arms tensing with urge. "Play with your pussy for me and show me how bad you are."

I dip two fingers in and fuck, I'm soaked from his mouth and my release. He looks down, rapt by my show, at my pumping inside where I ache for him.

"I'll be such a dirty girl for you, Redix Dean. I'll let you fuck my pussy. Fuck my ass. Fuck my throat. You can even fuck me in front of a room full of people. I want them to see how bad you make me."

Lifting my fingers to my tongue, I suck the taste off before I do it, again and again, until his cock swells ready again.

"I'll fuck you like that and more, Cade." His fat tip, he nudges it against my fingers. "Do you want this? Rough?"

"Yes." I'm pulsing for him. Reaching for his length, I wedge him into my pussy. "I'd kill for you to fuck me, Redix. And only you."

He doesn't hesitate. Flexing those hips, he thrusts inside me, and it throws my head back, my body crying out at the small pain groaning into my strongest urge satisfied.

'You want me like this? You want it hard like this?" His grip on my ankles squeezes hard, like the pound of his mass driving inside me and smacking through the air.

"Yes, I do." I'm at his mercy, bending my knees and curving my hips under, tilting so I can take even more of his possession. "All of you."

He leans over, letting go of my ankles, the beautiful weight of him pressing my knees to my chest. I'm so open, so ready, and so willing to take everything he gives me.

"Fuck, Cade." And there's no stopping him. I can see it in his eyes staring back at mine. "Fuck, I missed you." His hips, the way he curves them into hard plunges to my core. "So much."

"Redix," I sigh, calling his lips to mine.

He hears me, from across a million miles he can, pressing his mouth to mine and our truth is here. Time disappears to our deep kiss, to our tongues caressing before he lifts his mouth from mine to watch us, to watch his stunning plunge into my everything wide open for him to take; this can't end. Over and over, we kiss, we cling, we crave the sight of us joined, till the pleasure builds and it's innate to our sex.

He starts thrusting faster and I start climbing to my favorite brink.

"Watch us together." His breath shallows. We're trembling and can't tear our eyes away. "How we belong. Me inside you."

How can he do this? His gaze holding mine captive. His body mastering mine. He's fucking me deeper, harder than I can wish for, discovering new places, new aches inside me and I missed him so much too. The pain of it slipping away as he dives back in where he belongs, inside all the cracks of my heart. It's whole again.

"Redix." I don't know where he's hitting, what perfect deep spot he found, my heart, my soul, but it's his. A lightning frenzy of my nerves, it's balling up fast and getting ready. "Redix, please." I don't know what's happening to me, but it's him. It's us and I gasp before it detonates. "Don't stop."

Crying out, I can't control it. It owns me, gushing from my core, streams in pulses dripping over my flesh and coating his.

"Oh fuck." He marvels at it too. What he just did to me. "Fuck."

And I can't stop because his ruthless hips don't. With all his strength, his thrusts take me again, my thighs shaking feeling the little rivers he's releasing between my cheeks. "Fuck, Cade, yes. Keep squirting for my cock."

He's gazing down while I can see it, the seize of his every perfect muscle, a deep groan clutching his ribs. "Cade." He can't stop it either, what happens between us; his grunts while he comes, and my moans feeling him pulsing inside.

I reach for him, pulling him down and wrapping my legs around him. He rolls us over, wrapping around me too and we don't need words. We just need this.

My tears at his return. His kiss of them away. All the pain, all the waiting, we let it go to have this again.

"Now that's how you make a baby." I can't resist the joke.

"I failed Sex-Ed, remember?" He tickles his fingertip across my bottom lip. "Because *you* were my Sex-Ed. Besides"—he's going to kiss me again and I'm going to love him forever—"we have infinity to keep trying."

CHAPTER FIFTY-TWO

CADE

Fine Line by Harry Styles

Iᴛ's the best week of my life.

He goes to set, and I go to work. When he gets a day off, I take one too and we spend it furniture shopping in Savannah.

Since Redix doesn't give a shit about that stuff, I get to pick out items and he just smiles, loving that I love this.

He's more focused on this Saturday. It's Halloween and my favorite holiday because of, duh, the candy.

"I'm in charge of the costumes," he informs me while he

preps our dinner, his chef's knife going to town on some radishes.

"Oh, really?" I'm still struggling with this whole onion-chopping-crying-torture. "Where are we going in said costumes?"

"That's my secret, Detective."

A lock of his hair falls from its knot. It's kissing his lips where I want mine.

"Don't I get a hint?" I can't see through the burning tears.

"Yes. It's circus themed." He pops a radish slice into his grinning mouth. "I'm the elephant of course."

I try to laugh but I can't see shit.

"Jesus, Candy Cade." He grabs a paper napkin and starts blotting my tears. "Let me do this before you lose a finger."

"Onions will not beat me."

I'm blind, it's official.

He keeps dabbing and I keep crying until he shoves the cutting board out from under my nose.

"Tell you what." I can tell he's smiling by his tone declaring, "New house rule: You cook desserts and I do dinners. Deal?"

"You had me at sugar."

"Second rule: Toilet paper goes over."

"Uh-huh. I'll flip it back right every time I pee."

I'm pulled into a hug where I wipe my tears on his T-shirt. "Will you at least let me win at Uno?" He murmurs into my hair.

"Now we're talking."

Days later, he makes the perfect pirate and I'm his wench as we take his nephew, Nicolas, trick-or-treating around our new neighborhood.

All the kids running around, all the candy rustling in bags, it's pure bliss. Especially when Redix takes my hand while we stand on the sidewalk, watching Nicolas sing out "trick or treat" to a couple who opens their front door.

It's two men, both in full puppy-face makeup while one is holding the cutest baby dressed like a cat.

"That's gonna be us one day," he whispers into my ear.

"Then you better take my bounty tonight."

He grabs my ass. "Can I take your booty too?"

This feels so right. "Yes, you may."

It makes me want to rush home, but we revel in this for another hour until his nephew is exhausted and his sister, Renie, is in our driveway picking him up.

"Good night!" I wave to her from the front porch as she closes her car door.

The night has quieted. The sidewalks have cleared of the holiday revelers. The light of the full Hunter's Moon filters through the tree branches, their leaves fluttering in the breeze.

I'm stilled by the moment.

Redix is inside, getting ready for our own celebration while I draw a deep breath, so happy until...

The low rumble of an engine pulls me back, drawing my attention to a black sedan, a BMW. It slowly drives by our new house.

I stare at the tinted windows and can't see who's driving but...

Something feels off.

I go back inside, locking the front door and hitting the alarm code. My service gun, it's in a safe under the new nightstand by our bed with my police radio charging on top.

We're safe.

I let it go, the odd feeling, for the rest of the night. It's not hard with a distraction like Redix Dean wanting to play dirty pirate and I'm his wanton wench. Hell, we don't even need the costumes.

"Four eighty." My radio splits the night air hours later. "We have a wellness check requested for a 'Charlie Ravenel'. White female. Thirty-four. Daufuskie Island. Last seen at four p.m."

The grab for my radio with that name; it's instant.

"Bryant. One forty. I'll take it." It's not classified as a priority call but it is to me.

Redix grumbles from his pillow. "Did they just say 'Charlie Ravenel'?"

"Yeah."

"I'm working with her. She's detail for Riley Chase." He rolls on his back, awake as I am now. "Is she okay?"

"I don't know." It's five hours until daylight. I can't go on the water, not on duty and not without backup. And the office is slammed tonight. It's Saturday and Halloween, other calls take priority.

But I want this one.

Charlie Ravenel saved me years ago. And like hell if I won't return the favor.

I try to sleep a few hours in Redix's arms, but it won't work. At least it soothes my nerves, feeling grateful for this life with him now, but I'm worried about another woman.

Is Charlie okay?

I'm dressed before dawn. Grabbing my puffy jacket from the walk-in closet, it stills me—my clothes hang on one side, Redix's on the other.

Wow. How life can change on a dime.

And sometimes, thankfully, for the better.

"Tell her I said 'hey'," Redix calls out from our bed

while I clip my belt on. "Tell her I still owe her a day fishing."

I hope that's the case. That it's something harmless, but I know the hell that Charlie Ravenel and Daniel Pierce have been through this past year. They've faced down lethal threats.

"Will do." I lean over, kissing Redix goodbye. "I'll be back later."

"I'll be waiting." He grabs my pillow and hugs it to him with a grin.

I don't make him wait long. Three hours later, I'm back home and find him in the kitchen whipping up omelets.

"Everything okay?" He returns my kiss. "Is Charlie okay?"

"She is now."

I don't like it.

Now I have to keep two deadly secrets from Redix.

What Charlie Ravenel did to keep her family safe.

And what I did, what my family did, so that we can be free and others on this island can be safe.

One isn't my secret to tell—I'll go to my grave backing up a woman like Charlie Ravenel.

The other, it terrifies me if Redix ever finds out. He said he wanted peace and my deal delivered. Just not how he'd approve of it.

But now the secret scratches at my soul like a rat in a cage.

I know I did the right thing, the only thing left to do since courts were built by men and laws weren't written for women.

Still, death is the greatest burden. No matter the reason.

Redix is so strong now. I've never seen him shine this

bright. I've never heard him talk this much or square his broad shoulders even taller.

I'll carry the secret now. We have too much hope, our future together is too bright.

"Glad she's okay." His lips peck mine. "Now eat up. I've made breakfast and plans."

His plans involve a surprise in the garage because he's spent the last two days in there, forbidding me to enter. When I'm finally allowed in, he takes his hands off my eyes to my surprise, and I gasp before I laugh.

"Two red bikes!" They're perfect. "You got us two red Schwinns?"

"I painted them to match. I'm going down the list of all the things we want together." His lips nuzzle my neck and I'll never stop falling for him. "Tonight, we burn pizzas again."

But this afternoon, we're riding. Everywhere. The November first day is mild, perfect for exploring the wide sidewalks we used to roam as kids.

Redix tells me to lead the way. "So I can watch your ass," he informed me before pinching it.

For a moment, winding down the black paved sidewalks, I think of Pamela. How she's somewhere out there. I've been looking for her. The trail to her is cold but I won't let up. I'll never stop searching for her or for Cam Le.

The other victims, they're safe. I couldn't give them details or a day in court, but when I called them, I tried to let it sound true from my voice—no one is after them anymore.

"Hey, Candy Cade." Redix pulls up alongside me at the crosswalk. "Let's get some ice cream."

The joy on his face, it's like we're ten again. Like fun and friendship are all we know.

But then I glance down at his bare sculpted chest and abs under the white linen shirt he's left unbuttoned... and we share much more together.

He is *very* much a man—the only man I'll love.

I lead the way to our spot, the one where we had our first kiss and where our nightmare began.

That's all in the past.

I can feel it as his lemon sherbet-coated lips slide over mine now, kissing me through his murmurs, "I love you, Candy Cade."

We don't care about tourists feet away with their phones up. Nothing comes between our love anymore.

"I love you too, Redix Dean."

He pulls his lips away and nuzzles his nose to mine, asking, "If I get on one knee again for you, what will you say?"

"*If?*"

"*When.*" His smile, it shines through my soul. "*When* I get on one knee, what will you say?"

"Do you want an answer now?" His sky eyes, I can fly in them. "Or should I wait?"

"We've waited long enough." His hand cups my cheek. "I want to know—"

"Where is he!" The sudden shout makes me jump. "Where is he!"

Redix snaps his neck around. I glance past his shoulder.

Gentry Evans is charging our way with a black BMW with tinted windows idling at the curb.

That curb.

The same one he, TJ, and Derek attacked us from.

"I know you did something, you crazy bitch." Spittle drips from Gentry's thin lips along with his fury. "Where is TJ?"

I charge past Redix, protecting him and aiming right into Gentry's wrath. My forearm snaps up to Gentry's neck. "You better back the fuck down, Senator." Out of my right side-eye, the crowd that gathered for me and Redix is witnessing this too.

Who should fear this more?

Me or Gentry?

"I know it was you." From the look in Gentry's eyes, he's barely hanging on to sanity. "I know you did something to TJ."

"Back off her"—Redix seethes while he reaches around me and shoves Gentry's shoulder— "or I swear I'll fucking kill you this time."

"She did the killing." Gentry drops that truth bomb, and it explodes my world apart. "Did she tell you that, pretty boy? What she did for you?"

"Get out of here," I snarl. "You're fucking crazy. And you're making a career-ending scene."

The only thing more powerful than Gentry's fury is his ego, his need for a clean reputation. He's filthy as fuck, but only Redix and I know just how much.

Gentry glances at the crowd, at phone screens in the air. He yanks at his golf shirt, smoothing its wrinkles before looking back our way.

"This isn't over." He lowers his voice. "I know what you did to TJ, and I'll destroy you for it."

I step to him, nose to nose.

"And I'll take you down with me, Motherfucker—to the gates of hell we go. I don't know what happened to TJ, but I know you have Pamela. And I know you have Cam Le. And I know you're hiding Derek. And I will rip your fucking world apart to find them."

The eerie peace that floods Gentry's eyes; it shakes my core. But I won't show it.

"Leave," Redix growls at him, "or I'll rip you apart myself."

"Don't get too comfortable here, pretty boy." Gentry steps back. "Y'all play house all you want. Just know"—his sneer, it takes me back ten years and I want to scream at its return—"you're playing house with a murderer now."

He turns and slithers back to his car.

My soul weeps. I know what just happened and I can't face it.

"Cade." But his grip turns me around and I make myself look Redix in the eyes.

What stares back at me; he's never looked at me this way.

All I've ever seen in his eyes is love, laughter, passion... or pain.

All for me.

What's there now? It's this one question, it's after him now. *"What did you do, Cade?"*

NOT THE END

Keep reading for a sneak peek of **WITH HIM**

Please, my amazing reader, take a moment and leave your honest review of

AFTER HIM

It means everything to me. Thanks, and hugs!

With Him: A FMM Why Choose Suspenseful Romance

All For You Duet, Book Two

Available for free in Kindle Unlimited

WITH HIM: A FMM Why Choose Suspenseful Romance

When you're torn...
Why should you decide?

I'm caught between a man who hates me and one who wants me.

And yes, it's possible to choose—I love them both.

Redix is the only man I've ever told I love. We're connected in ways that brand my soul.

Silas is a man of new temptation. He only wants to free me from my dark past.

But what do I want? What do I need?

All I've known is a love I'd kill for.

All I feel is that I want to save them both...

__With Him__ is a steamy, fast-paced second of a duet featuring a menage between a tragic hero, a free spirit, and a love that heals. It has a HEA with hot scenes and dark themes that may be sensitive for some readers.

They say behind every good woman... are three men ready to tempt her. This is the story of Stacey Evans, the wife of the evil senator. This is what happens when she helps Cade get revenge.
Get **TEMPT HER** now.

What dark secret hides between Luca and Scarlett? Join my monthly newsletter for a free sneak peek chapter of **MAKE HIM**—coming Fall of 2023.

How did Silas seduce Cade and Redix into a love that breaks the rules? Why did their love leave Silas only wanting more?
Read **WITH HIM** for free in KindleUnlimited.
Book Two in the All For You Duet

Meet Charlie & Daniel in the **COME FOR ME** series—a deliciously twisted, steamy series about sacrifice, love, and second chances.
PIERCE HER, HUNT HER & CHASE HER
Now available in a box set for you to enjoy.

What happens on the secret vacations Stacey knows about?
What kind of holiday fun do Silas & Eily, Cade & Redix,
and Charlie & Daniel enjoy together?
Ho, Ho, Hang on for this one!
The surprise title, cover, and book will heat up your Winter.
Be the first to know; get my newsletter today.

Love Is a Bitch by Two Feet

CADE

I'm going to hell anyway, so I might as well commit this sin.

Because this one feels like heaven. Like pure bliss sliding through my veins, desire erasing every reason why I can't fight this anymore.

Because I want this.

And they need this.

Redix kisses the nape of my neck while he slowly unzips my dress. The teeth of the zipper open and so do I. Air rushes my exposed back where his fingertips linger down my spine and then trace back up to the straps of my crimson dress.

Before he drops it to the floor, his body presses against my back, every part of him hard while his husky whisper asks, "Will you choose us, Cade?"

For the man in front of me, I have chosen him in so many ways.

Silas's kiss is different. Tickling his lips over mine, his tongue plays like he's going to spend forever in this moment and I don't want it to end either, not with where this is going.

"Yes," I answer through Silas's lips indulging my mouth, his hands skimming my hips while Redix gently bites down my neck making me moan at him dropping my dress to the floor.

I'm exposed in every way.

My darkest desires. My torn heart. My haunting secret.

I can't decide what I want except for this right now. Standing in a black lace bra and matching panties, I love two men and I won't choose.

Why should I?

I'm not the only force binding them together.

Redix slides my bra strap down, kissing my shoulder, sending tingles to the tips of my fingers.

There's as much passion and question in his kiss as I'm holding in my heart. His long strands tickle across my back while we share something taboo, something that may mend us, and with everything we've already shared, we need to do this.

We need to decide.

Do we hate each other for what I did?

Or do we love each other so much for it?

I don't know what to feel except his lips across my flesh, his steel body pressing into mine, his warmth and smell are so familiar that I'm safe taking this risk.

Yes, I can let go for now and not know. I can choose us for two nights.

Because Silas is skimming the lace of my bra, the see-through fabric pulled taut over my pebbled nipples. He's touching my breasts like a sacred relic to treasure.

There are questions between us too.

Silas traces his fingertip over my nipple, the attraction between us slashing arousal to my belly down to a lush ooze between my thighs. Pinching his fingertips lightly over my sensitive nub, he twirls his touch knowing how to tease me because that's what we did for so long. Teasing each other to the point of such trust. To the point where the attraction between us isn't the question.

It's the love.

What does love look like between people when you don't see it the same way?

I try letting go of my questions, letting go of my need for answers, and I can... for now.

With Redix tugging down the lace cup of my bra, exposing my flesh for Silas, and saying, "Taste her," I lose my grip. With him palming my full breast, lifting my nipple to Silas's waiting mouth lowering to devour me; I'll keep falling. With the sudden heat that cascades down my body while one man sucks my nipple and another holds it for his taste while he gently pinches the other.

I'm going to drown in this pleasure with these two men and if I don't ever breathe again, maybe I shouldn't. Maybe this should be my end because I don't know my next day or answers.

Nothing in my life makes sense. Everything's out of control.

And that's what I always need; control.

But I lost that the minute I almost killed an evil man. A man who hurt Redix, who assaulted him because of me. A man who deserved it for hurting other women too, so hell yes, I had to do it.

But every day since has been a hell of the loneliest days, then the most passionate nights, followed by months of emotional chaos raging through my heart.

Redix hates me for what I did for him. And the reason I did it is why he'll never stop loving me either.

All while Silas anchored me in this storm and I didn't know another man could be my best friend, but he is now.

We've shared so much, the longest talks, the biggest laughs, the forbidden nights. I brought Silas's world back to him and he's been my accomplice while I wreak havoc on the world of evil men.

So that's my life now.

I go from a cover girl to a cop to a criminal to a cunt dripping for two perfect men.

The heartbreak and the healing of these two men lavishing my flesh for what will surely be a night of them fucking me into my last shred of a self is that they share so much.

More than me.

It's beautiful to me that they have each other too. That they found comfort in the other. But in a world like ours, with cameras hunting Redix for his fame, expectations burdening Silas because of his name, and laws restraining me in my job, can it last?

It's an assault on my senses, embarrassing if it didn't feel like fate that they look so much alike with the same long hair, square jaws, lush lips, and eyes that claim your soul. And their bodies? Redix is taller but Silas still has a few inches on my five-foot-ten frame. Muscles shred down both men's tan bodies and their hands hold expert talent at thrilling my flesh.

I'm so lucky... and I'm so *fucked*... in every sense of the word.

I'm standing between two beautiful mountains of masculine perfection and this valley is a paradise for most.

I just fear it'll be my hell too.

As Redix travels his hand down my belly, making it flutter as his fingers sink under my panties while Silas won't stop sucking my nipples, my God what are we doing?

"Damn, you're so wet for us, Cade." Redix's voice; it's imprinted on my soul. I'd know it in a cacophony of a million because I've always and only wanted him.

Until he didn't want me.

Until he couldn't even look at me.

Through shouts and tears and excruciating silences, we destroyed each other and we've been trying to recover ever since. Can we?

He needed peace and I needed space and what if that's how we'll work?

Silas swept into my days and thrilled my nights and I could be another woman. Someone new. Someone free.

Then I'd see Redix again and I could never change. I could never stop loving him or wanting to sob at the ache of missing him and no matter how he smiled for others, I could see the question burdening his eyes.

Can he forgive me?

Because no matter how we fill each other with fury or hurt, the love is there and the passion is all-consuming.

"You're so fucking beautiful," Silas murmurs, sinking to his knees before me while Redix's fingers tease through my soaking folds.

I look down into Silas's hazel eyes that have brought me nothing but peace, the perfect man to start over with. He's been my joy even though my life has been a raging hell.

But we're so different.

I've never met anyone like Silas. Rules don't govern him; he won't let them. Freedom is all he demands and he wants it for me too.

But love comes with obligations. It makes us sacrifice. It makes us cry. It isn't always about what we want. Love has seasons; hot summers, and sometimes cold hell.

At least, that's all I've known of love.

"Can I, Cade?" Silas's lips are so close to mine, the ones needing these men to fuck me so much it's insanity in my body and who is he asking?

Me or Redix?

Redix sinks his fingers inside my hungry pussy, the one he was the first to have, and I groan at the depths only he can touch. It's art, it's poetry, it's exactly how to touch me because he discovered my desire first.

But mine is *not* his to give away.

I gaze into Silas's eyes and he's asking *me*.

Because in our months together Silas has taught me so much. About sex, about love, about how big a heart can be, cherishing so many and breaking for a few.

This is what he's been teaching me: that I belong to no one.

That I can let go of one idea of love, and trust another will grow back.

"Yes."

It's my answer, it's my permission to give as Redix sinks his fingers in deeper and Silas drags my panties down my thighs.

They planned this. They orchestrated this night. They need this too, answering their questions. Surprises I've learned about Redix. Secrets I know about Silas.

The three of us need to do this together.

Redix spreads my folds for Silas's tender kiss and I'm chained to this wall for them to share me and I know…

This is the only way.

My world spreads open to them and this is how I've been torn for so long. Because this is about more than these two men.

This is about two others who are still out there.

Two evil men who've hurt so many they deserve to die too. They tried to hurt me first, but Redix protected me. He took their violence for me and our storm has raged since. Waves of revenge and justice for my plans for both and I won't give up. I will find the women they took. I will get back the dreams they stole from me.

The question is…

Who will I share those dreams with?

Redix and I wanted that life together. We fought for those dreams. Are they gone? Is Silas the one I'm supposed to share them with? Because I could. I can see those dreams with either man.

The real question. The real secret I haven't shared is that maybe I don't want either.

Maybe I want a life with both of them.

Or maybe I want a new life alone.

Redix turns my chin for his kiss, the one that reaches in and cradles my soul. I whimper at our truth, tears springing up to feel his love swirling with hate. But we can still do this. The love is stronger.

Silas kisses my lips, his tongue greeting my tender clit and I groan into Redix's mouth at Silas's lavish attention. He's everything good and I cherish him.

The two men start claiming me, for just two nights, and it overwhelms my heart, my sex weeping to know...

How did we get here?

ACKNOWLEDGMENTS

My husband and best friend: I wake up to coffee and your sweet notes encouraging me to write. Your love and support make this possible. I'm lucky I found you, Green Eyes.

My family: You hush about the house when I'm writing. You always knock and encourage me. And for the ones who read my steamy stuff, well, I warned you. And I love you all.

My friends: More like partners-in-crime because y'all are the best bad influences who make me laugh and keep me very real and sane. I just wish I could see you more, but when I do, damn, I'm blessed.

The KLS Team: I'd say more a "family". Thank you Kat at Kat's Literary Services for your edits and cheers. And Deborah, you are a Proofreading Goddess. Thanks to this amazing group who helps bring my pages to life.

My Cover Crew: Hats off to Caroline Johnson for the gorgeous covers she designs for me. I love seeing them on my bookshelf. Big hugs to my cover model, David Bodas. You are a beautiful soul who helped me turn my story into a dream. Big thanks too for Rafa G and his gorgeous photos. I'm so proud.

My Beta Team: Deborah, Jennifer, and Marsha. Thank you for helping me shape this story so close to my heart into something many will (hopefully) love. Your comments, edits, and texts are gold to me.

My Review & Street Team: You always have my back (more like my covers) and I'm so damn thankful. I cherish your posts, reviews, and support. Big shout out to the Banana Book Club. Our monthly smut laughs warm my soul. I truly can't do it without you all.

#Bookstagram & #BookTok Followers: It's true. There *is* a community and a world of friends online. I'm overwhelmed by the amazing people I've met and now adore. Every day you make me smile. Thanks for your comments and support. And keep 'em coming.

Author Friends & Mentors: You inspire me. You school me. You help me and keep me going when it ain't easy. Thanks for the Zooms, emails, and coffee chats. You keep me strong.

Best for last - READERS: Thank you for taking a chance on my story, for giving your time to share this with me. You take my story into your heart for a short time and I'm humbled. When I get your messages, posts, and emails, they are the greatest gifts. And I promise to keep giving you more. Huge hugs.

AFTERWORD

This story became much more than I ever thought. At first, it was a story about a badass, beautiful vigilante. I wanted to flip the script on a man "avenging a woman's honor." But when it came to who that man was, this character, Redix, rose from my heart, parts of which come from my past.

I know and love people who have survived violence, and people who have proudly earned their sobriety. And I know a few that didn't survive. They live on in my heart.

If violence has affected your life, please know you are not alone. You are strong and others are there for you too.

Please consider visiting www.thehotline.org for the support you deserve.

If addiction has affected your health, there is help. There is hope and there are many who understand.

Free and confidential support is available to you at 1-800-662-HELP/4357 - the national helpline of SAMHSA (Substance Abuse and Mental Health Services Administration).

ABOUT THE AUTHOR

Kelly Finley hates writing bios but appreciates that you made it this far. So here you go...

She lives in the Carolinas with her sexy husband and cherished family. A rebel with many causes, she fancies black leather, dirty jokes, big hearts, and smart mouths.

Dedicated to writing books featuring characters with proud love, shameless heat, brave hearts, and whip-smart minds—she's most likely at her keyboard putting the next spicy story on the page for you right now.

She likes to call it **#shamelessfiction.**

Want to connect with Kelly and her readers, aka. **The Lemonheads** (when you read AFTER HIM... you'll get it)? Follow her on Facebook or connect using the Discord App.

Use this invite link for Discord = https://discord.gg/H47nZKhWQN

tiktok.com/@kellyfinleybooks

instagram.com/kellyfinleyauthor

facebook.com/KellyFinleyBooks

goodreads.com/goodreads_kelly_finley

bookbub.com/authors/kelly-finley

amazon.com/author/kellyfinley

After Him

Kelly Finley

© 2022 Kelly Finley Publishing, LLC

Visit the author's website at www.kellyfinley.com

ISBN: 978-1-7374516-8-6 (eBook)

ISBN: 979-8-9866222-0-0 (paperback)

Edited by Kat Wyeth (Kat's Literary Services)

Proofread by Deborah Richmond (Kat's Literary Services)

Cover design by Caroline Johnson

Cover photography by Rafa G

Cover model - David Bodas Ventas

 Created with Vellum